101 REYKJAVIK

A Novel

Hallgrímur Helgason

Translated by Brian FitzGibbon

SCRIBNER

New York London Toronto Sydney Singapore

SCRIBNER
1230 Avenue of the Americas
New York, NY 10020

SCRIBNER and design are trademarks of Macmillan Library Reference USA, Inc.,
used under license by Simon & Schuster, the publisher of this work.

For information about special discounts for bulk purchases,
please contact Simon & Schuster Special Sales:
1-800-456-6798 or business@simonandschuster.com

DESIGNED BY ERICH HOBBING

Text set in Bodoni Book

Manufactured in the United States of America

1   3   5   7   9   10   8   6   4   2

Library of Congress Cataloging-in-Publication Data
Hallgrímur Helgason, 1959–
[101 Reykjavík. English]
101 Reykjavík : a novel / Hallgrímur Helgason ; translated by Brian FitzGibbon.
p.   cm.
I. Title: One hundred and one Reykjavík. II. Title.
PT7511.H297 A61513 2003
839'.6934—dc21   2002029434

ISBN 0-7432-2514-7

To Hlynur

"U can't B dead all the time."
—Cary Leibowitz

CHARACTERS

LOLLA: an AA counselor
HLYNUR BJÖRN: Berglind's son
PÁLL NÍELSSON: a dentist
THRÖSTUR: a friend of Hlynur's
LERTI: Páll's son
ROSY AND GUILDY: a gay couple
PRIEST
MARRI, REYNIR, AND TIMER: bartenders
SIGURLAUG: Páll's wife
KATARINA: a Hungarian princess
BERGLIND: Hlynur's mother
HÓLMFRÍDUR (aka HOFY): Páll's daughter
HAFSTEINN: Hlynur's father

Family members, cabdrivers, organ-delivery boys, barflies, guys, extras, girls, whores, clerks, anchormen, etc.

Most of the action takes place within the 101 Reykjavík postal area.

1

THE ONLY THING
I KNOW I AM

Anyway. I normally try to wake up before dusk. To get some light into my day, check in, punch my card. The sun is a time clock. Even if you're not working. For the sun or anyone else. Hey. Solar system, welfare system.

Waking up never gets easier. It's like you've been buried for four hundred years and have to claw your way through six feet of mud. Every day. The light filters through the curtains. All of a sudden it's as if the numbers on my radio alarm were years. 1601. Woke up too early, not due to be born for another four hundred years. Ah well. I reach out for the Coke supply, have myself a flat one. One stale morning kiss. You should never kiss a girl the morning after, there's always that putrid smell, like she's started to rot, like she's died. Usually she's died. One shouldn't sleep around. Sleep is death. Resurrection every morning. Resurrection of the flesh. My man, always the first one up. I find the remote under my foot, haven't quite mastered switching the TV on with my toes yet.

Channel 52: interview with a German bar owner. He's pulling three steins. I want a beer. Take another sip of Coke. Channel 53: British gardening. Channel 54: recording studio in Madrid. Channel 36: an Indian singer (20,000). Channel 37: weather forecast for Southeast Asia. Looks like they're in for a sunny weekend in Burma.

I surf around. No pussy. How come there's no porn shows in the morning? Have these people never heard of a morning glory? At least there'd be something to wake up for. Breakfast porn. My lit-

3

tle man, always the first one up. Maybe that's how they're programmed. Cos it's easier to get the rest of me out of bed once he's up. That little giant. That throatless muscle-pumping Cyclops. Has a head but no brain, or maybe he's used it all up, coughed up all his little gray cells. I refuse to get up until he gets up. I grab him by the throat and wrestle with him, but he doesn't give up until we're in the john. I milk him into the palm of my hand. Why don't fortune-tellers read wet palms instead of peering into coffee cups? There's my life mapped out for you, sprayed into my hand. Trickling down the undulating streams of my lifeline.

Cigarette. A day is like a cigarette. A white cigarette tracked by the sun as its smoldering embers vanish behind the clouds of smoke and die in the yellow filter of the night. The sun and cigarettes. Both equally hazardous to your health. It's getting dark. Hardly worth opening the curtains. I fasten my watch, chain myself to time, the rotations of the planet, the sun, the whole system: 16:16. I go into the kitchen. Cheerios. Already waiting for me in the bowl. What's going on? Is she trying to mom me up again? A bit too much. She's put too much into the bowl. The right portion is 365 rings. I shovel them down with some milk. Radio. The first song always sets the tone for the day. "Passion," by Rod Stewart. Not so sure about that.

I look Woody Allen in the eye. When is he going to enlighten me? It's bound to happen someday. That's what posters are for. I turn on the Mac. The Mac greets me. She should be home by now. 1637. Yeah. I can read the years on my wrist. Each day is a history of mankind. Christ is born at midnight, the Roman Empire passes out in a wild all-night party, and then the Vikings meet at the crack of dawn, already gang-banging by nine. The lunchtime news is read from the Sagas—"A huge fire erupted at Njal's place last night"— and then a nap after lunch, slumber, the plague, Dark Ages, until we wake up to the blast of that Michelangelo guy's chisel in 1504. The Renaissance. Shakespeare scribbling furiously to meet a 1616 deadline. The history of mankind is a long day. The Thirty Minutes War. The Six Seconds War. A long working day. It's almost seven by the time Edison sees the lightbulb. 1900: supper and news. The history of humanity has finally reached the dining table, or we've just eaten, all of us full, zonked out for another endless night in front of the box. Everyone waiting for the clock to hit 2000. I mouse on to the Net. Check my e-mail. Nothing from her. I type:

Hi, Kati.
Reykjavík calling. Hope you had a good day. We're getting late up here, running out of days. You know. Wintertime in Iceland. The Kingdom of Darkness. And everything Johnny Rotten. Went to the bar last night and then to some after-party. There was a girl there who'd been to Budapest and she told me about a bar called Roxy or Rosy. Do you know it?

Bi.—Hlynur.

I'm half dressed when the phone rings.

"Hlynur," says Thröstur.

"Thröstur," says I.

"How's it going?"

"Yeah, OK. You didn't turn up yesterday."

"No. Did I miss anything?"

"Nah. We went back to Jökull's afterwards."

"And what? How was it?"

"Yeah, OK."

"Any action?"

"Yeah. Lóa was there and Sóley, and two lanky model types."

"Tasty?"

"Yeah. One of them was a real *Cosmo* type, but the other one was more *House and Garden.*"

"And what? Are they there with you now?"

"No, that's just the TV. What are you up to?"

"Hey, I saw your dad. We went to the Castle, myself and Marri, and there he was, he was great."

"You're bullshitting me."

"No, he was great, man, bought us a round and then invited us back to his place afterwards."

"Did you go?"

"No. He gave us conflicting addresses."

"Are you sure it was him?"

"Hey, Hlynur, I know old graybeard when I see him."

"How did he look?"

"Yeah, fine. Kind of third-dayish."

"Out of his skull?"

"Yeah. He was pretty sozzled, all right, but he was in great form. I mean he was fun and so on."

"Yeah."

"Yeah. He spoke about your mother a hell of a lot . . . and you. You should look him up, you know."

"Hmm."

"So what d'you say? How about tonight?"

"Don't know. What you have in mind?"

"Just the usual, the K-bar or just the Castle, maybe; it's a wicked place, I'm sure you'll bump into your old man there."

"What time were you there at?"

"Kind of one-ish."

"I don't know."

"OK, I'll give you a buzz."

"Yeah."

"Hlynur."

"Thröstur."

Mom works at the Imports Office. Mom *is* the Imports Office. Mom's name is Berglind Saemundsdóttir. Mom drives a red Subaru. Mom comes home from work between five and six. Sometimes she brings Lolla with her and she eats with us. Lolla's actual name is Ólöf, can't remember the second name. Haralds- or Hardarsdóttir. Lolla is a lesbian. Been one for ages. She celebrated her fifteenth lesbian anniversary this autumn. She's heading for a golden watch from the Icelandic Lesbian Association. Mom is the Imports Office. Mom always brings something home for me. T-shirts, Coke, a belt, a tape, popcorn, cookies. Today she comes home in the year of 1735. I hear the rustle of plastic bags, and then she knocks three times before walking in.

"Hi, darling. Wasn't sure whether you'd want these or not. Got them in Bonus's."

She throws three pairs of white underpants wrapped in noisy plastic onto the bed, as I swivel around from the computer. Then she walks to the bed, takes the underpants, puts them on the bedside table, and starts tidying up.

"How did it go today? It's a bit stuffy in here, Hlynur dear. Wouldn't you like to open the window a bit?"

"Huh?"

"It's been a while since I washed these sheets, hasn't it? Shall I take them now? No, can't do them until tomorrow anyway. Is that a Coke bottle in your bed? I bought some more if you'd like. Lolla's coming for dinner later. How's it going, darling?"

"What?"

"Didn't you say you were doing some job for Reynir?"

"There's a delay. I'm waiting for him to give me the SyQuest disk."

I turn back to the computer.

"Well, then. Think you can use these undies? Hope they fit. Only had large. Shall I bring you a Coke?"

"Mom."

She comes over and puts a hand on my shoulder. I can feel her breasts on the back of my neck.

"All right, darling. I won't disturb you. What, are you writing in English?"

"Mom."

"Oh, I'm sorry. Curiosity box."

She kisses the crown of my head and leaves, saying, "I bought some sirloin steaks and Lolla's bringing some red wine. We're going to be posh tonight."

Sirloin is my favorite. She's definitely trying to mom me up. Something's up.

I'm on the remote until they call me. A quiz show on Channel 29: What's on TV? Question: What's on Eurosport between 10 and 11 A.M.? Must get up earlier.

They're talking about Heidar, the beautician, when I walk in.

Lolla says she likes him. I like Lolla. She's got serious breasts and she's funny. The laughing type. She might take the piss out of me sometimes, but she often comes with something to smoke and she brings nice vibes to the place. Mom's more fun when she's around. Especially if she smokes with us. It kind of moms her down a bit. They're good together even though they're different. Mom is fifty-six, Lolla thirty-seven. They met in the Faroes. Or Mom was there for some kind of committee meeting or something. Mom is kind of National Channelish, but Lolla is more cable-channel 2: I don't know her that well, I haven't watched her enough, there's more to descramble. She's an AA counselor. An AA counselor. She's full of good alco stories, especially when she's pissed. Drunken stories never sound as good when they're told sober. We live on Berg-thórugata and eat in the kitchen.

Mom: "Didn't the underpants fit? I bought him some underpants today, in Bonus's."

Lolla: "Bonus undies? She'll be a happy girl who gets her hands on them. Do they have the logo of the little pink piggy on them?"

Me: "Don't know."

Mom: "Haven't you tried them on yet?"

Me: "Mom. Any cabbage left?"

Lolla: "Pricks always remind me of pink piggies."

Me: "Oh yeah?"

Lolla: "Yeah, so cute . . . and tasty . . ."

She laughs. Mom grins. I smile a JR smile.

Me: "I thought you didn't eat pork. Aren't you a lesbian?"

Mom: "Ice cream anybody?"

Lolla: "Less b than bi. But no, I was thinking more of you, Hlynur, my dear. . . . You have that kind of piggy bank look. . . ."

Me: "How d'you mean?"

Lolla: "Well, you know. You're always saving yourself up, aren't you? You're not exactly splashing it around. Aren't you always saving up for the one and only?"

Me: "What's this all about?"

Lolla grins at Mom, who has stood up.

Mom: "Enough of that. Shouldn't we have some ice cream and talk about something else?"

Me: "Hey, Mom, have you been blabbing to her? Whatever happened to privacy?"

Mom: "She's only teasing you, Hlynur dear. Lolla dear, are you sure you wouldn't like some more?"

Lolla: "No thanks, I'm full . . ."

Me: ". . . full of crap. Where's the paper? Maybe I should check it to see if there are any flats to let."

Lolla: "You're not thinking of moving out, are you?"

Me: "Mom, did you buy the paper?"

Lolla: "I mean, you're too old for that now, aren't you? Thirty-three years old . . ."

I have a sudden longing for a secluded cell where people don't knock on the door but have to ring a bell. Just me and me alone, the two of us, with our computer, TV, a sixteen-tape weekend, the entire Woody collection, away from all lesbians. There's something about these brazen women, women who are just as smart as men, pussies with their tongues in the right place. I can't take them. You never know how to talk back to them. You're paralyzed. Especially if they've got breasts as well. Then it's just like there's some kind of swindle going on. I mean. Women look a hell of a lot better than we do, I'll say that. But we were supposed to get the brains instead. And now they've taken them as well. What's left? They've got it all now. Brains and looks. And we just lie there speechless with that brainless beast in our hands, squeezing out his last few cells.

Mom belongs to another generation, before brain surgery became the standard thing. Mom presses her side up against me.

"Now, now, Lolla dear. My little Hlynsey can stay here as long as he wants."

We smoke a joint after the ice cream. Lolla rolls. Two joints. I get one of them (sulking with her has its perks sometimes). We move into the living room. The news is slightly less boring through the haze of a spliff. Normally I can't stand Icelandic TV. Talking about fish all the fucking time, and the sea this and the sea that. What smartass had the bright idea of going down to the bottom of the sea to grab a bite? Those snowbanks look quite appetizing on grass, like ice cream. Vanilla in the West. Nougat on the North

Fjords. They're both out of it now and start rambling on about the underpants again. Oh no.

Mom: "But didn't you tell me you needed underpants? He always needs underpants, I don't know what he does with all those underpants, I feel I'm always buying underpants for him. Ha ha."

Lolla: "He probably leaves them around town like a visiting card when he's . . . It's quite common among single guys who want to avoid commitment. They deliberately leave their briefs behind, all . . . ha ha . . . pissy yellow and smelly. That way there's less of a risk of the girls ever wanting to see them again. . . ."

Me: "Well, some girls are really into golden showers, aren't they, Lolla? And even golden flowers, too. . . ."

Lolla: "What?"

Me: "I keep on telling you, Mom, you're the one who's always losing them."

Lolla: "Aaaah . . . Beeerglind . . . ha ha ha . . ."

Mom: "Ha ha. What? What do you mean?"

Me: "In the wash."

They're really getting into this underpants thing now and dare me to try them on. I don't know, maybe I'm just too stoned to stay in my clothes. Suddenly I'm standing in the living room again in nothing but my Bonus briefs. I strike some poses. They gasp and wow like two women at Chippendales. Women don't watch stripteases the way we men do. They just let loose and go straight into top gear. Men freeze into their shells and slip into low drive, become so deadly serious, swallow their Adam's apples. Lolla asks me to come closer, pulls on the elastic and snaps it, says they fit perfectly, and then adds: "In his current state, that is." And they fall about on the sofa with shrieks of laughter. The one-eyed idiot is on eye level with her and I get the feeling—even though Mom is there—that he wants to stick his head out to look her in the eye. Time to get out of there.

It's 2315 when Thröstur rings. We're well into the future by the time I turn off the TV and the Mac. Midnight approaches as I mosey on down Laugavegur. Icy darkness and snow that can't decide whether it's coming or going. Something primeval lurking in the air, from time immemorial. Certainly primitive to have to walk all this distance, my ears white and stiff in the wind, frozen, fragile porcelain ears. And when I walk into the place we're back to square one. The year 0000.

The Castle at midnight. Not exactly wicked. Despite the name, it's just a cellar. "The Dungeon" might have been more apt. You step down into the past. A dire, bluesy little piss hole: a murky cave, phony brickwork on the walls, complete with (fake?) swords and armor. Prehistoric rock music spurting through the speakers, a tinny sound, like the records have just been dug up in some archaeological find: Black Sabbath, Deep Purple, Led Zeppelin. "Eye of the Tiger," as it happens, when we walk in, myself, Thröstur, and Marri. A trip down mythology lane. Feel like I'm in one of those *Quantum Leap* episodes. Ancient Greece, except everyone's wearing jackets. Bacchus behind the bar cracking his whip, the old master torturer, fat and furious, thrashing the mob—eternal slaves to alcohol with blistering wounds on their backs—impressively equipped: the beer taps like levers on the torture rack, the thumbscrews tightening each time they're pulled. He can afford to laugh with the arsenal he's got behind him: Hot-Shots on the shelves, Black Death. Juggling his bottles like guns, he levels them at his victims, metallic spirit measures screwed to the nozzles like silencers. Uncapping the beer bottles with his teeth, he hurls them into the room like grenades, shakes Molotov cocktails. Pours boiling acids into poisoned goblets, and the customers sign their credit card slips as if they were signing their own death warrants. A highly combustible situation. Alcos tanked up to the hilt and sloshed women staggering about with boobs full of gas. One of them (3,500) comes over to ask me for a light, as pissed as a newt. I feel like I'm about to set her ablaze as I lift the flame. Her face ignites and she thanks me with a kiss, a 43-percent-proof kiss. I slither away but can't seem to wipe off the taste of cod liver oil left from her lipstick.

It's an oblongish place, with a bar about the length of a small-town swimming pool. The really sozzled ones are at the deep end, clinging to the ledge. Opposite the bar there are some sofas made out of some unknown material that seems to suck in light. People vanish into them like black holes. The only lighting here seems to come from the bottles on the glass shelves behind the bar—a whiskey yellow glow: like a faint dawn beyond the mountains of Kamchatka—and three pairs of earrings in the armchairs. And some teeth here and there glistening in a smile.

"I can't take this."

"Sure you can, we're just taking a look, you know. You're always so fussy, Hlynur."

Thröstur and Marri seem to have a third eye for this kind of stuff. Maybe I can't take it because I know Dad could be here. Going out "gallivanting," as Mom sometimes calls it. Maybe because in the olden days there used to be galley slaves. Yeah, that's exactly what these are. Slaves drooped over their salt-beaten benches, chained to the bar, rowing over oceans of beer, braving the whiskey main, each man clinging to his years, the years of yore, the years of oars, holding their wretched lives in their hands. It could actually make you feel seasick, this place, with all these people rolling about.

At the bar we find three free stools, those who sat on them before us obviously dead drunk by now. Executed by alcohol. We take our places on death row. Thröstur is tall, with arms and a chin. He's slightly taller than me. I'm six feet. He has this dodgy goatee beard, kind of patchy and shabby. Like he's got a few loose nerve ends dangling from his chin. He's a bit of a nervy type. Thröstur, the thrush, always fluttering about. Marri is shorter than we are. Marri's real name is Marel. Something to do with the sea. He's a bit like a fish out of water. With those bulging eyes and sudden twitches. One's a fish, the other's a bird. I'm neither fish nor fowl.

We order three beers. Thröstur starts talking about the difference between bungee jumping and parachute jumping. He says it's like the difference between sex with love and sex without it. I don't quite get it. I make out a silhouette of a man at the far end, just his back, looks like he's pissing. The man beside us is wearing a baseball cap and a hippopotamus-hide jacket so thick it takes him a while to turn around to us. He's got eyelashes on his upper lip and thick lips around his eyes. He's young, if one can use that word. Question:

"So how are you, guys? Did you just get out?"

"Huh? No, we just got in."

An ancient Peter Frampton number blasts through the speakers. "Show Me the Way." Feel like I'm at the Icelandic Natural Science Museum, which has been closed down for the past twenty years. Stuffed animals covered in dust. Except that most of the dust in this place has been snorted up through people's noses. A substance that gives fairly stable highs. Those cold glazed eyes and desiccated, mummified faces. Thröstur says this place was once used to store spare parts for American cars. Spare parts. Nothing's changed. Die here and you'll wake up on a kitchen table in a house on the back of Smidjuvegur with a kidney missing and a tattooed wound.

Marri nudges me, signals me to turn. Dad sails past. That's him, all right. That face. That expression he put into my mother's womb. He sails past. Like a ghost. Like a specter out of some old Idnó Theatre drama. Slowly sails across the stage, somewhere in the depths of the scenery, elbowing his way through the curtains, causing ripples and waves. He doesn't see us. His clothes look OK, his beard and hair, too, and his cigarette is still in one piece, but his glass looks unpaid for. Twelve hundred krónur's worth of whiskey. Somehow you can just tell it's been rung up on plastic money. Another one of those and he'll sink the ship. He takes a swig, I watch it all float away: rugs, carpets, parquet, his entire apartment, company, car.

"You've got to talk to him."

"No. I can't take him right now."

Suddenly I get that smell. That's no Pierre Cardin. No, that's Dad. Hafsteinn Magnússon. That good old Old Spice. Not a bad choice for a ghost, though. He rests his glass on my shoulder and I turn. The smile that made me. The smile that bedazzled my ma. That was many teeth ago. Completely false now. Still, though, he looks pretty good. Those red cheeks actually suit that gray beard, if one can talk of color in the darkness of this rock-'n'-rolling cave. In fact he looks too good for this place. What's he doing here? This ain't his scene.

"Hi."

13

He says that like he's referring to himself. His state of mind. A high hi.

"Hi."

"Just the man I needed to talk to."

Don't like the sound of that.

"Oh yeah?"

"Yeah, I just need to have a chat with you, what'll you have? I'll buy you a drink and we'll sit down here, just you and I, and have a powwow together, man to man."

Pissed man to man. He treats me to a beer on his card, and I leave the guys at the bar with their four eyes and follow Dad through the rain forest to the corner. We sink into our separate holes, under some kind of spear contraption on the wall. A twenty-three-year-old guitar solo erupts and he has to speak up, comes too close. I can only listen to him with one ear. He starts off with a long intro. The bottom line of which is that I'm his son and he's my dad.

"It's about your mother. I know we're divorced and all that, and you know that too. That. I know it's none of my business what she does now, us being divorced and that. But I'm also. I'm mainly thinking about . . . er, you, it's about that friend of hers there, what's her name again?"

"Lolla?"

"That her name? Yeah, the little dark-haired one. With the beauty spot."

Lolla has a fairly noticeable beauty spot on her right cheek. A bulging freckle with hair. I picture it now, see nothing else: a beauty spot about the size of a fingernail hovering in the air before my eyes, furry. Like a homosexual fly. I nod.

"Yes, you know what I'm talking about. Anyway, she's a lesbian."

"Yeah?"

"Yeah, you know that, and they spend a lot of time together, don't they? Don't they spend a lot of time together?"

"Yeah, she comes over and eats with us sometimes."

"Yes, exactly, yes, and. They're together a lot. I hope you don't mind me asking, but does she ever stay with you?"

I study his face. We're not very alike. My face is like his face whittled down to look like Mom's. I take after my mom as much as my father will allow me to. He has a pretty big nose. Mine is small and the glasses make it even smaller.

I look into his eyes. These are eyes that look back. Eyes that can no longer look ahead. Are there no glasses for people who can't look life in the eye? Maybe he should just wear shades.

"No."

"Are you sure? Are you sure she doesn't sleep over sometimes?"

"Yeah, she sleeps with me sometimes."

"What!?"

"Joke."

"What I'm trying to say here, Hlynur, is that I think your mother is a lesbian."

The song ends right before he says that last word and it comes out far too loud. I look at him again and glance around. Some fat old dipso queen of tarts (7,000) deep on the sofa with a linocut face looks at us, and smiles at me. I see her lipstick moving. It seems to be saying: but I'm not. I'm not a lesbian. I check out her breasts a moment before looking back at the old man. No centerfold. Even though he's drunk Dad somehow manages to strike a sober Hafsteinn air. There's a slight pause before the next song begins—"Highway to Hell," it got to number 17 on the American charts in '79, the summer of my driving test, he lent me his car or, more to the point, made me drive him everywhere, symbolic or what?—and we can talk again now.

"So what do you say to that?"

"I don't know. Why do you say so?"

"I just think so. A friend. A friend of Sara's saw them together in that gay bar. The one down Klapparstígur."

"So?"

"So they were obviously there for each other."

I can feel the tip of his nose in my ear. Feels like his prick, penetrating my auricle. Dad's the crazy Scotch king who pisses in every ear and drinks from every beer. "Thou art begotten of a king" . . . Yeah. I smoke Prince.

"You don't say anything?"

An AC/DC silence.

"You don't say anything, maybe it's all the same to you, maybe you think it's OK? Imagine, she's almost sixty, and all of a sudden she's a lesbian! Just like that."

"Better late than never."

We're in a queue in front of the K-bar. There's a new bouncer who obviously hasn't done his homework. Doesn't know us. I've never seen him before, apart from the tattoo on his neck. A little bit more originality, please. The time is almost 200 and we're stuck out here in some kind of ice age. This is what's called going out. I'm in black jeans with my pockets full of fingers, a white polo neck and leather jacket. Difficult to make out what shoes I'm wearing—in the crush—but I think it's those black ones. A girl (30,000) in front of us in the queue says hi. I just nod. She works at the video rental store on Skólavördustígur and I've rented some porn from her. Marri passes me a cigarette and we try to heat up on it, feel a slight warmth in our lungs. Like the heat off a Primus stove in the North Pole. The Amundsen brothers. Takes us at least twelve years to get in.

We scan the place. I wipe the mist off my glasses. The K-bar is nothing more than a 35-square-meter room. It's packed. Like twenty cigarettes in one packet. I take one, free some space, on the way to the bar, through the dancing crowd. Girls on film, girls on film. Duran Duran. I sense a breast rubbing up against my elbow, and say two dull hi's, before I spin and get sucked up to the bar, like a lottery ball that unexpectedly turns out to be one of the lucky numbers of the evening. And the next number is Lóa (15,000).

Hassle number one:

"Hey hi! Great night last night."

"Oh, you were there too?"

"That's right, pretend you don't remember anything, oh no you don't."

That's just one of the sixteen lines that's being spoken in this place right now. Lóa is like Channel 68. You have to zap sixty-eight times before she'll come on. And you've normally found something more interesting by then. Keisi is behind the bar tonight. Keisi, the Creamboy. I order three beers from him. Lóa's still there:

"Do you drink? I thought you didn't drink, I've never seen you pissed. I thought you were one of those sober-drunk types."

Oops, here we go again.

"That's right, I'm sober, been dry since birth. I was conceived during a piss-up, but I haven't tasted a drop since. Maybe it's because Dad is an alkie and Mom is a lesbian, but I came out of the closet tonight and decided to celebrate, you know, go the whole way, and fit into the family mold."

"Wow."

I manage to hand the guys their beers without spilling them on anyone, and there's a free table. Or some free chairs at least. Two chicks are dancing on the tabletop. We sit down and just sit. I look up at some orange stockings as I exhale my smoke. Thröstur and Marri grin at me, and Thröstur whispers into my ear in English:

"How much?"

It really gets on my wick when people speak English. Sounds so bloody corny. What Thröstur actually means is: How much would I be prepared to pay for a night with that one in the orange stockings. It's this thing we've got, a tagging system for rating women. I check her out again. Her blond hair takes over where her stockings leave off. Long light hair. Long light-years away. As is her brain. Can't quite see the canyon between those dancing legs, despite the mini. Neat breasts, mind you, canned pears that don't obscure her face, which has obviously been cut straight out of a Versló College album. Nothing else to report. This is what we call a pony.

"About twenty-five."

"No, more than that."

"No. Thirty with a receipt, minus five if it's under the counter."

"Brain-y!"

Another phrase Thröstur has recently bought from me. It used to always be "Yessir!" or "All right!" I look around. Know 30 percent. The rest a bunch of social security numbers. Some crowd with new and better social security numbers. Eygló Manfreds (kr 75,000) is there. She's a newscaster on TV. Ey-Gló Day-Gló. Thröstur once said he'd give his left arm for her. Thröstur is left-handed. Not sure Eygló Manfreds would be into a one-armed man. Probably makes it easier to "cuddle," though. Sigrún always wanted "cuddles." Haven't cuddled since. I've never actually spoken to Eygló Manfreds, but she gave me her chewing gum once. Dóra (25,000) is there too, and Magga Saem (30,000). And Timer at his table in the corner, the fat master with his ZZ Top beard.

I like the K-bar because it's so crammed and the music is so loud. You don't have to dance or talk. We sit. "Scream." Michael Jackson. And Janet (3,500,000). I scan the room again. There's Hertha Berlin (kr 150; i.e., the price of a bus ticket; i.e., the price of a one-way bus ticket). She wants to sit with us. No way. Don't bug me! She clambers onto the table, ungraciously nudging orange stockings out of the way. The ponies almost collapse onto Þröstur, but manage to steady themselves against the wall. They're too ponyish to kick Hertha off, and climb onto another table. One of their heels spikes a candle floating in wax. Hertha Berlin plonks herself down beside us. Her thighs begin to spread out. Fortunately she's wearing Levi's. They hold. She gives me a broad smile. What does she want? Me to count her teeth? Marri beanbagged her once, sometime toward the end of the last decade. Everybody's got a hungry heart.

"Hi, Hlynur. I just heard you came out of the closet. I've always suspected as much. Or have you been engaged all along?"

"No, I just took the phone off the hook."

Time for the john. Hólmfrídur is in the passageway, she says hi, I say i. I piss into the bowl and look at the yellow wall, picturing the graffiti: "My ma's a dyke." Could it be true? And is it a problem? Lolla.

First, second, and third hassle:

Hólmfrídur blocks my path as I return. I don't know what I'm supposed to say. She says, "So what have you got to say for yourself?" I say, "Me? I say er." She says, "What happened to you? You just walked out!" But what I hear is: "What happened to you? You look wiped out!" so I say, "Why do you say that?"—"Huh? Say what? It's a fact! You just walked out."—"Yeah, I've been wiped out. Work and stuff."—"Work, are you working?"—"Yeah, just a

small job. A computer thing."—"Right, just at home, then?"—
"Yeah."—"I've tried calling you, you never answer, don't you listen to your machine?"—"Yeah, but it's been sounding a bit . . .
croaky lately."—"Oh yeah? Some kind of flu or something, is
it?"—"Yeah, something wrong with the heads."—"Nothing too
serious, I hope; not Alzheimer's or anything."

We're talking like a freshly divorced, six-year-old couple, which
is weird because we've only slept together two or three times,
and the last time was two or three weeks ago. Not that we ever
actually slept together. More of a hit-and-run job.

Hólmfríður lives in the Hlidar neighborhood. Alone in three
rooms. Dreams of filling the other two. She's in her third year at
teacher training college. Her dad's a dentist. She's got two teddy
bears and a poster by Monet or Manet or Menuet up on her wall.
And that's about it. I'll spare you the frilly details. She exudes
nothing but street cred and toughness here in the K-bar, with
those red streaks in her hair, that stud in her nose, and those
baggy dungarees, but back at her place it's a daddy's little won-
derland, a dainty Laura Ashley fairground reeking of tastefully
good taste; even the cigarettes you smoke taste of autumn leaves.
A haven where no color would ever dream of offending another,
and the spectrum never strays from the straight and narrow of
beige; a place where even the window shades smell of soap. We all
have our dark side. And this is hers. Everything so spic and span
and feminine, as if her dad had been over the place with his suc-
tion pipe, and scraped the tooth yellow walls with his minuscule
burrs (to give it that rustic look), and pumped the cushions with
anesthetic, everything so antiseptic and sterile. Like stepping
into a pair of gums, those gums they use to teach up at the university.

"Some nice drill work you've done here," I said to her, glancing
at the walls on my first visit, after almost putting my feet up on the
table beside a ceramic bowl full of wooden apples—and this
before I even knew her dad was a mouth doctor—but she didn't get
it, not even when I added, "all you need now is a good screw."

"You always come out with these sentences," she said, "you
and your sentences."

My life in sentences. Life sentences.

Hofy is a square with a stud in her nose. It's a glistening plaque on a foundation stone that belies the rest of the building. Her soul is like a movie in slow motion, every time she opens her mouth you yawn.

The lights come on, the time is 300, and an atmosphere of impending execution weighs in the air. Like the filming's over, and everyone stands around in a daze, like extras interrupted in the middle of a frantic fistfight scene on the tabletops. All of a sudden everyone looks so ordinary. I still had half a glass of beer left, but now it's nothing but a puddle on the table. Hofy has that effect on people. Dampens everything in her path. Thröstur and Marri are talking to some buff:

"Hey, Hlynur, you saw *Naked Lunch*, he's saying John Torture wasn't in it."

"John Turturro," I correct him.

"Turturro, then."

"No, we're mixing it up with *Arizona Dream*, no, *Raising Arizona*, no, hang on, what's that movie called? The one with the writer in that hotel and the wallpaper and that?" says the buff.

"Yeah, just a sec. The Coen brothers," I say and run the data through my brain.

"Yeah. What was it fucking called?"

"*Farting Blink*," I say.

"That's the one, yeah."

"No, *Barton Fink*," I say.

"*Farting Blink* . . . ho ho . . ."

"So who's in *Naked Lunch*, then?"

"Can't remember his name, but it was the same guy who played Robocop," I say.

Barton Fink. Where did I see that? Yeah, in London. With Dóri. Dóri Leifs. John Goodman in flames. We could do with John Goodman in flames right now, to heat us up out here in front of the K-bar in the freezing dark ages. Like fifty demonstrators standing outside the gates of the Mongolian embassy at midnight. Hey. If all Mongoloids were to live in one country and form a state of their own, it could be really scary if they ever got their hands on nuclear weapons. Reynir saunters over. With some wicked-looking bird (kr 60,000), despite the makeup behind her ears. He's talking about the video he's just completed. For some artsy-fartsy rock band called Blöxill. Sounds like another seven videos you might have seen. His cell phone rings somewhere inside him. He answers, and says he's on his way, with a crowd. Meanwhile I'm forced to talk to his bird. I choose the first snowflake that springs to mind.

"Are you Kevin Costner's daughter?"

"No, why do you ask?"

"Just. It was about time."

"About time? What do you mean?"

"About time somebody said that."

Words are snowflakes. They fall. At this moment there are 12,674,523 snowflakes falling over Reykjavík. Every head that now lies sleeping at the National Hospital is crammed with sentences. All over town, in computers, on pillows, in sofas, on the phone, on bookshelves: there's an entire galaxy of sentences being sprinkled in the air, words that fall into lines that somebody somewhere will have to speak. "Are you Kevin Costner's daughter?" Someone had to take that one on. Not my fault. Sorry.

Reynir knows of a party. Hofy tags along, plus friends. Her friends are a few noticeable notches below her on the beauty scale. Stand there on either side of her on the podium, in second and third place, looking up at her with reverent eyes. Girlfriends. Always one edible one and two inedibles. Have you ever seen two equally beautiful girlfriends? Hofy clocks the address. She seems to be talking to everyone and no one, the snow and the cold, but is actually talking to me. I exhale some smoke and ponder the difference between cigarette smoke and the smoke of my frozen breath. There isn't any, actually. Although tobacco smoke has more of a matte finish to it, somehow, a slight tinge of color. It's more human. Pollution is human. John Goodman in flames. Yeah, there's a warming thought. What we need here is a cab. A hot one with a fat driver. On our way down Skólavördustígur I find my remote inside my jacket pocket. I take it out, point it at a car approaching some traffic lights, and press stop. The car stops. Old trick. Part of my repartee. They laugh.

We three-car it down to 9 Stangarholt. The master of the household is a guy called Haukur Hauksson, a Talking Heads fan. This apartment is far too plush for an after-party. A Salem atmosphere. The glass tabletop is as sacred as the vinyl of *Speaking in Tongues*. David Byrne CDs on display in a glass cabinet, like the porcelain at Granny's.

We end up in the wrong place at first, follow some noise up to the floor above. Crazy scrap metal blaring out (Metallica: "Seek and Destroy"), but then some loner pushing forty comes to the door, a thin-haired anorak. He invites us in, but I instantly smell a rat. The place is suspiciously empty, and we don't fall for that old lonely guy ploy: there's a party in the building so let's make everyone believe it's at my place. A lonely soul locked in a body full of longings. I sit down for a bit anyway, and take a moment to remember the bass player in Metallica. Jeff or Cliff Burton. Wiped off the map after some heavy gig in the Swedish countryside. In '86, I seem to remember. Slap-shot into eternity on Swedish ice. The girls flutter around the anorak, puffing cigarettes. I stand up and check out the bedroom. He should just stay in here. This is the kind of guy who should never be allowed to leave his room. Looks like a cordoned-off archaeological site. A grave. Some pagan tomb. The crumpled bedclothes reveal the mold of his bulky body, a perfectly preserved fossilized stratum, even though the bones have been removed. I've got some women's perfume in my pocket (Trésor, stole it from a party at Lilja Waage's [80,000]) and spray some on the pillow. That'll earth him. That'll make sure he never leaves again. He does, however, want to follow us to the party downstairs, but I soon put an end to that. Spurt him with perfume and call him a wimp!

"What a creepy pervert," says Hofy friend number one (kr 1,490), as we step into the corridor. "Did you see the socks he was in?"—"No," says friend number two (kr 1,690)—"I mean, they were pink, he was wearing pink socks. You tell me."

I pull a crumpled scented sock out of my pocket and dangle it in front of them. Same color.

"Hey, where did you get that? Did you nick his socks? What's wrong with you, Hlynur? You're just not normal, are you?"

"Not anymore. I came out of the closet tonight, haven't you heard?"

Hólmfrídur has reached the landing and looks up:

"What?"

"Nothing. Hlynur Björn was just coming out of the closet." She looks at me, all wide-eyed, and I make mine wider to stop her from swallowing them. Still have some iris left. She smiles and turns to her friend, the one going for 1,490.

"Oh, that's just another one of his sentences."

This party at Haukur Hauksson's, the Talking Heads fan, turns out to be a total Dullsville. No dope, just dopes. "Burning Down the House" blurts from the speakers, and I couldn't agree more, even though I could kill those talking nonsense heads for that bullshit between the choruses. Some overpriced act of violence in a frame on the wall above the sofa, which is currently occupied by some well-oiled Gibb brothers exchanging reminiscences about their good old scouting days. Give us a break. Some butch girl in the kitchen shrieks with laughter, as if she were trying to convince us of her right to live. I check her out (10,000). A real fag hag. I've no choice but to slip into a soft chair beside some harpsichord player, opposite the new Spielberg in town who's pitching this totally brilliant idea for a film script. Aliens from outer space who sneak into the country hidden in containers.

". . . but what we don't know is that in the meantime they've come back in the car and they chase them, right? And this is where the punch comes: it was a spaceship all along. A spaceship, right? Ha ha. You know, a ship from space. Spaceship. And they sail away, right? They just sail away! This is good! This is fucking brilliant!"

The harpsichord player says "right," but suddenly gets beamed up by some girl. Uh-oh. Spielberg is now turning to me. The whiz kid wants to talk about the "budgetary aspects" of this great movie of his. Christ. I can't stand talking to people. Not this one-to-one stuff. Not this eye-to-eye lark. And he's looking into my eyes. Don't look into my eyes. He might just as well stick a needle into them. Time to call in the rescue team.

"Hey, Hofy!"

Her face snaps to life, like cornflakes under milk, and crackles as she walks over. I ask her for a cigarette even though I have some. Evacuation procedure. She hovers over the arm of the chair. My rescue chopper from the coast guard. That's settled, then. It's straight to her emergency room.

We walk up Langahlíd. The time is 600. Still five hundred years till dawn. Will Háteig's Church have been turned into a tourist attraction by then? Yanks in their Bermuda shorts, thanks to global warming, looking through their guidebooks and looking up in awe—"That's really amazing"—and Japs with video cameras? I seem to be walking Hólmfríður home. Yet another picnic in her forest of falling leaves. Back to the cozy nest, the kingdom of matching colors. Looks like I'm going to be sleeping with her. She takes my arm. No. I can't stand that. Some car might drive past, with some freshly woken eyes inside thinking: "Oooh, Hlynur Björn with her . . ." Professional detachment, that's what we need. Just two separate individuals setting off to work. Two mechanics on their way to the garage. But, oh no, there's always all this arm-in-arm, arm-over-shoulder stuff first. And those meaningful glances. Like a patient on an operating table trying to establish eye contact with his surgeon. It's only an operation, after all. In fact condoms should come packed with more items: a smock, rubber gloves, a hairnet, a mouth mask. Everyone should be equipped with their own medical bags, night kits. And a white sheet over the woman, with a hole. A clinical operation. No feelings, apart from the inevitable physical ones. Women.

"Did you really steal those socks from him?"

"Yeah. Just one. He was such a loner."

"You can be so hard sometimes."

"Yeah. It would cost you a groaning to take off my edge."

"What d'you mean?"

She wants me to take my shoes off. Ah well. Why don't I take off my glasses too while I'm at it? I tiptoe like some faggot on the parquet. She can't go into the living room without going into (a) the bathroom, (b) the bedroom, (c) the kitchen. She calls out, asking

me if I want some tea. I say yes so as not to say no, and point my
remote at the TV. Three test cards. What kind of a society do we
live in anyway? I turn it off. She strolls back in her home-team outfit: comfy flannel trousers made of some kind of bath-mat wool and
a pajama top. What a turnoff. The hamburger in the ad versus what
actually comes out of the packet. Ah well. She puts the tray (a tray,
typical her) with the teapot and two cups down on the table, lights
the candle, dims the lights and cuddles up to me, and says:

"Better let it brew for a while, it's so hot."

"Yeah, too right. Don't want to burn our lips now, do we?"

What the hell am I saying? I'm no longer me. I didn't even say
it as a joke. I could have made it sound like a joke.

"Have you seen my new teapot? Mom and Dad gave it to me."

"No. Er. Where did they buy it? Abroad?"

"Yes, they just got back from Mexico."

"Right."

"Ever been to Mexico?"

"No."

I suppose I should add "And you?" but can't be bothered. No
need to, as it turns out:

"I went with them last year. It's quite a special place to go to.
Everything's so . . ."

I'll spare you the rest. Hofy in the hotel. Hofy on the beach.
Hofy with sunstroke. Hofy with excess luggage. Hofy in the duty-
free. I try to show some interest in this stuff. Ask her if they
caught any food poisoning. Bingo, her mother got diarrhea. I try to
hold the conversation on her mother's diarrhea for a moment, and
smile with secret relish (I can feel myself slipping into the warm
mud bath of her mother's soft turds), but see that it's not going
down too well. Hofy is too straight to laugh about her mother's diarrhea. Halldór Kiljan! What am I doing here?

"Have you never wanted to go to Mexico?"

"No."

I am in Mexico. I wanna go home.

I stretch out for the pot and pour into my cup. Tea's better than
talk. She pours into hers and I look at the candle, and then at her,
and she at me, and we're ready to go. Pressing our lips, we push

out into a sea of tea and breast the waves, leaving a trail of white-winged thoughts in our wake. The dark, gloomy, tea-golden ocean sprays laughter into our lungs and warm grins into our stomachs. The eye of a storm is beginning to droop like the sun on the horizon under the sky of China teacups, swelling and simmering with inter-Twining waves of foam prickling on my tongue.

English breakfast by the sea. You love me and I love tea.

Yeah, it's not bad.

H ó l m f r í d u r P á l s d ó t t i r. My tongue comes in there somewhere between those letters. In her first name. Between the *m* and the *f* (best to steer clear of her father's name). *M* and *f*. That's how she kisses. Mildly and faultlessly. We rub our faces together. I'd like to remind you she's got a stud in her nose. "Does it hurt?"—"No, no . . ." She smiles. We smile. I'm caught between a rock and a soft place. Jagger at home at Christmas with Jerry Hall (200,000), and hot coffee on the stove, but still thinking about his Christmas Eve Herzkulova (240,000). I'm hot. As horny as a priest in my white polo neck and leather jacket. Defrock myself. Got my hand under her pajama top, groping her right breast. I want to spend my old age groping breasts. Like that old geezer of ninety-four who married Anna Nicole Smith (2,900,000). Start on the breast, end on the breast. She doesn't want to undress here. Maybe she's afraid of soiling some memories connected with this sofa, maybe she and Papa chose it together in Ikea. She leads me in. We undress separately. I prefer it that way. People ought to be able to take care of themselves. We're already naked by the time I remember my johnnies are in my leather jacket. Tiptoe on the parquet like a bespectacled centaur. The trees are dancing techno in the windows. My favorite pastime: walking through strangers' apartments with a hard-on. If I were a burglar that's all I'd ever do. The evening paper: "Naked Burglar in Barmahlíd." During my journey through the living room and back to the bedroom my little friend droops from 90 to 45 degrees. This is that big an apartment.

The opposite sex. I've barely entered the room when he's already sprung back to attention again: 45 degrees in two seconds flat. Those females, all they have to do is come up to you and he's up on his hind paws like a flash and drooling, just like at the party tonight. Any bumboat will do the trick—anything down to kr 500. The second she enters his territorial waters, the radar activates and a lighthouse rises in my pants. This brainless creature asks no questions about price or value. At least dogs have a sniff first.

Women want foreplay, a warm-up band. Stiff Little Fingers before Sting. I feel Hólmfrídur as she kisses me. She's got soft white skin, which I'm into, and looks quite good here in the shimmering glow from the lampposts outside, stiffly shaking in the wind. Women might have different faces, different bodies, different breasts, but as for the pussy . . . I don't know, but to me it's always just the same old bacon sandwich, same old wound. Although you have to break through the crust sometimes. But not now, it's gaping. Hofy. Yeah. I manage to pull a condom out in mid-kiss, bite the wrapping, and rise. She watches me put it on. I'm an air hostess standing in the aisles, demonstrating the use of a life jacket. This is the johnny Nanna Baldurs (45,000) gave me at her party, as a joke. It's light red. All of a sudden I feel like I'm pulling her lips around my dick. Nanna. That little narrow pink mouth of hers, all the way back to her tonsils. Right, then, Hólmfrídur dear. Are you ready? OK. Let's get down to it.

After a few thrusts she says: "Don't you want to take your glasses off?"

She takes them off for me. Oh no. She might as well be removing my nose. The tinted glasses removed. The filter between me and the rest of the world.

From now on it's just a question of rounding this thing off. I plug away. Two thousand attempts to ejaculate. But the concentration is gone. Lost that vital distance, nothing between us now.

I'm back behind my glasses. Glance at my watch: 08:37. Take a picture of me now. I'm Stan in Laurel and Hardy. My head propped up against the pillow, a tuft of hair sprouting in midair, and that pathetic hangdog expression on my face. I don't sleep. I don't sleep with people. Hólmfrídur sleeps her Laura Ashley sleep. Lying on her stomach. Her left arm lies across my chest, 600 kilos heavy. A bench press. Obviously some kind of couple posture. I manage to slide from under her arm and slip into my Bonus briefs without waking her. Slither into a trouser leg and sleeve, leaving nothing behind but the shriveled condom, the snake's shed skin. She stirs as I'm tying my laces in the hall. I feign not to hear when she says, "Hlynur?" and make my Elvis-has-left-the-building exit. Flee like a thief. Hoof away from Hofy.

Out on the street, I'm me again.

My name is Hlynur Björn Hafsteinsson. I was born on 18.02.62. Today is 15.12.95. I lie between those numbers. I was born on a Saturday. Today is a Saturday. Life is a week. Every weekend I pass away. One week. A history of mankind precedes it, and another one will follow. I'll be dead after I die, and I was dead before I was born. Life is a break from death. You can't be dead all the time. Hlynur Björn Hafsteinsson, 1962–95. Might as well be the other way round. 1995–62. The only thing I know I am.

I've got light brown hair. Mom is a brunette, as all mothers should be. Dad's got gray hair. Turned gray the day after they split up. They split up four years ago. I split up with Sigrún a month later. We were together for about six months, lived together for four. My year in hair. Sigrún was 25,000, but then crashed in value, and by the last day was down to 9,000. Sigrún is the only relationship I've ever been in apart from Hrönn (15,000) in secondary school. Sigrún was OK, she just got up too early.

Reykjavík on a dark winter morning: a small town in Siberia.

Snow drifting in the glow of lampposts under a dome of darkness, enshrouding a shivering salted sea of porridge and shorelines of milk curds.

Masticated frozen mush around the darkness. The mountains—heaps of ancient debris, forsaken refuse, a junkyard from heathen times, scrap iron from the Bronze Age.

Hardened glacial diarrhea, hideous mounds of mold, encircle this transient town of cards, a camping site littered with computers doomed to disappear in the next blackout.

Two-story concrete houses, cracked walls and fractured facades. The gardens full of frozen trees and brittle branches of porcelain waiting to snap under the weight of a bird that never comes. A manless, leafless, birdless, insect-free ghost town where even the dead desperately cling to the clotheslines, lashed by contemptuous blasts and wicked winds.

Endless blizzards whipping you to the marrow, winds winding around your neck, tightening their grip by fourteen knots, biting your cheeks, flinging salt into your wounds, spraying frost into your eyes.

You fly, tumbling, over the shelterless streets, ice sheets pearled with polar sweat, deserted, toothless gums, gaping mouths pushing out their final gasp. Streets that would never be on this side of the Arctic Circle, had their length not been measured by taxi meters.

Taxis roam through the city, faint glimmers of hope in the storm, converting the cold into krónur. Their warm, shiny black dashboards are the only confirmation that this island is part of the civilized world: featherweight chunks of Japanese plastic sailing smoothly over the icy bays and creeks, like canoes, playing the sunny rhythms of LA pop on their all-night radios. Freedom and democracy safely preserved in the glove compartment.

There it is, on the corner of Snorrabraut and Miklabraut, the northernmost cab in Europe. The light on its roof is a lighthouse, marking the final outpost of the western world.

Taxi.

People only live here because they were born here. I feel like a child borne out to die.

I walk home. Stagger, I should say. The time is 874.

Home. Nothing but mommy sleep and darkness. I turn the light on in the kitchen and have some Cheerios with the morning paper. Keanu Reeves is unhappy with his life. Roseanne is having a tattoo with the name of her ex-husband removed. A woman in Arkansas has her newborn tattooed: Mom.

I glance at some college football, Iowa at Michigan State, before I slip the tape in. *A Taste for Tits.* Six giant-size bazoomas by the edge of a pool in Las Vegas, and some well-hung beefcake turns up for a visit. I can feel my ears thawing as my little man starts to freeze. But I can't be bothered to jerk him off, and drift to sleep to the sound of silicone groans and visions of all-American sex in deck chairs. I like drifting to sleep in the blue glow of porn. My dreams get more interesting that way. I've just dozed off when the phone rings. I leave it to the machine to do the talking.

"Hlynur speaking. I'm probably in right now. Please leave a message after the tone. I'm listening."

"Hlynur . . . Hlynur Björn . . . I've got to talk to you, pick up the phone . . . Hlynur, I know you're there . . . would you please talk to me . . . You . . . Hlynur . . . . will you please? . . . . asshole . . . . . . "

Hofy. I'm surprised at how well she . . . how well her voice works as a soundtrack to the film. There's an impressive blow job being performed on the screen and I get quite a kick from hearing Hofy's voice over it. He's standing to full attention now and needs very little help from me, a quick shakedown and he spurts it all out. I think of her at that moment. I dedicate this one to her. For a moment, I contemplate the crumpled toilet paper I've just dropped onto the floor. Hofy . . .

"Are you OK, Hlynur love? You're such a zombie today. Were you up late? Where did you go last night?"

Mom is sitting at the dining table, making Christmas cards, I think. She's taking night classes at the Art School. My back is turned to her, I'm sunk deep into a chair with a two-liter Coke bottle beside me, watching TV in the living room for a change. Some music videos. I keep the volume down so that I can hear the fizz in my glass. I tilt my head slightly and talk toward the commode with the framed photos. A confirmation picture of me: a spa with a psalm book (somehow they've managed to clasp my hands around the book, caught that brief moment before I jerked it into the air). Also: a confirmation picture of my sister, Elsa, all adultlike, with breasts in a white frock, like a groomless bride. And an old black and white of Dad. What's she got a picture of him up for? As if he were dead. Ah well, he's died a million deaths before. I look back at my spastic self as I answer.

"Just down at the bar, the usual."

"What bar do you go to? There are so many places now you can't keep up anymore."

I'm in no mood for talking. But I'm in no mood for TV either. (Sting.) And I've just had a sip of Coke, and I've just stubbed out a cigarette. So I say: "Yeah."

"I'm totally out of touch now, just can't keep up anymore."

I get an idea and turn, slipping my legs over the armrest.

"Yourself and Lolla go out sometimes, don't you?"

"Yes, we do in fact. She took me to the Two-and-Two the other day."

"And what? Was it just the two of you, then?"

"Yes, but she knows so many of them there. It was a gas time. They played some fun songs, you know, from the disco days. We boogied like mad."

"You and Lolla? Did you dance with Lolla?"

"You don't dance with anyone anymore, do you? I just danced with everyone and no one."

"Sorry I missed that."

"Yeah. I don't think I've danced like that since my heyday with your father. But tell us—"

"Have you heard from him?"

"Me? No, you know he doesn't call anymore. Your sister bumped into him the other day, in Kjörgardur. She said he was in great form."

"I heard he fell off the wagon."

"Really? Where did you hear that?"

She looks at me.

"Thröstur."

"Really? What a shame. I thought he was . . . And what about Sara?"

I look at the box. It's Björk (190,000). I stretch out for the remote and turn it up. My name Isobel. Married to myself. Good lyrics. Corny video. I wait a moment and then say: "I don't know."

"I'm sorry to hear that. He was slowly getting there."

"Crawling there, you mean."

"Maybe you should try talking to him."

"Why have you got a picture of him up there?"

"Of your father?"

"Yeah. So that you can pretend he's dead?"

"Why do you say that?"

I hear her putting the scissors down on the table and turn my head again. I look at her. She at me.

"People don't have pictures of other people on the wall unless there's something wrong with them, they're either newborn, confirmed, or dead."

"Don't talk like that, Hlynur love. Your father is a part of my life and we had some good times together."

"Some good binges, you mean."

"Let's not bring all that up again."

"Sometimes I just don't get you women. You're so quick to forgive and forget. What does Lolla say about all this, how does she feel about you having a picture of him here in the living room?"

"Lolla? What's she got to do with it?"

"Well, isn't she?"

"Isn't she what?"

"Nah. Just . . . Doesn't she know all about this? About him?"

"You're in quite a mood today, Hlynur dear. You're not sick, are you? Have you had something to eat? There's some shrimp salad in the fridge."

I turn back to the box.

"Yeah, I know."

There's some kind of hovercraft thing on the screen. With some wannabe rock band in wet suits.

Mom: "By the way, that Hólmfrídur girl phoned yesterday. I told her you were asleep. She wants you to phone her."

Halldór Kiljan. She's got Mom's number as well.

"Yeah."

"Isn't Hólmfrídur the daughter of Páll what's-his-name?"

I stand up and grab the Coke bottle from the floor.

"Yeah, something like that."

"Hum?"

"She's a Pálsdóttir, all right. Her dad's a dentist."

"Yes, that's it. Palli Níelsson. Lolla used to work for him in the old days."

"Huh?"

"Yeah, she worked as his assistant for a while. Always a good laugh, Palli. Isn't she a nice girl?"

"Yeah, she's all right. She's got a stud in her nose."

"Yes, I'm not surprised. Palli was always like that as well."

"Hum?"

"Her father. He was always such good fun."

"Yeah."

I swing the Coke bottle out of the room. God, I feel like shit. One of my dizzy cigarette spells. Must have another one. I float back into the living room, clinging to the bottle like a life buoy, and grab the cigarette packet on the coffee table. I barely have enough energy to grab my lighter. Seriously doubt whether I can even make it to my bedroom. Another sound from Mom and I'll be paralyzed. I'm shipwrecked out on the open carpet when she says: "By the way, there was something I was going to tell you. Lolla is going to be with us this Christmas."

She looks at me. I have to conjure up all my energy again to be able to wrench my head toward her. She waits for eye contact:

"The people who own her flat are coming home this Christmas so they asked her if she'd mind staying with us in the meantime. It'll only be for two weeks. It'll be fun to have more people around at Christmastime. That OK with you?"

"Yeah, sure. As long as she brings plenty to smoke."

"We're not having any hash here this Christmas, and that's final. We've got to try to cut down a bit."

"What does she want for Christmas?"

"Lolla? Yes, good question."

"Maybe. Maybe a picture of Dad. No, a picture of you."

"Why don't you give her a picture of yourself. She thinks you're such a laugh."

"Or undies. Do you think they still have some of those ones you bought me in Bonus?"

"But they were only men's."

"Yeah, exactly."

"Hlynur."

"Berglind."

I take refuge in my bedroom.

Katarina is Hungarian. She lives in Budapest. I ran into her on the Net. Chat room. We've been communicating for seven months now. My longest relationship to date. I look at her. A picture of her that is. She's got dark hair, kind of Sandra Bullock–ish (3,900,000), but with a smaller nose and rounder cheeks. She's cute. Edible. Juicy. Pretty. Passable. Wicked. I haven't heard from her in more than three days:

> *Hi, Hlynur!*
>
> *I am terribly sorry that I have not spoken to you for some time now. There have been examins in my school and I have been terribly buisy. But everything went well, I hope at least, and now we have vacation soon. What are you going to do for Christmas? I will go with friends to Vienna. Yes, I know the Ritz-club. It is not my type of bar. They play punk rock. Maybe you have friends who like this kind of music. Have you heard the new Oasis record? I like it very much. Hope you have fun on the weekend. I have to be home and study. The last examin is on monday. Until next time.—Kati*

I mouse back to her photograph. I look at her. She's a stare. I picture her in some Hungarian principality, in a room in an old house. Yellow walls, a window, a tree, perhaps. That's all I see. I've no imagination. I swivel around on the chair and zap over to CNN, teletext. The weather in Budapest: slightly overcast, 2 degrees. Smoke two cigarettes. Lie down. Then go back to her homepage hunting for more data: Katarina Herbzig. Born 23.07.69. Student. She's doing some kind of marketing course. Still lives with her folks. Katarina. Kati. Kati. Kati.

The phone rings. As phones are wont to do.

It's Elli. My uncle Elli. Uncle-ish. Dad's half-brother, Ellingur Adolfsson. The only ectopic pregnancy in the family. You'd wonder how he actually made it out of Granny at all. Such a weakling, poor bastard. And no one's too sure about which Adolf it was either. Elli has been a cabdriver since as far back as I can remember. And probably since as far back as he can remember too. Works for City Cabs. A loner. Always looking for someone to drive, and drives them crazy. Granny, the Queen of Alzheimer, has forgotten she ever had him, and the rest of the family feigns to suffer from the same amnesia. But he remembers them all, all right. I seem to be the only one who still puts up with him now. The last ear in the valley. And he phones. And phones. And he remembers everything. And he knows everything. Gets it all from the backseat. A wonderful diehard narrow-minded reactionary. The world squeezed into a rearview mirror. Unusually perky today:

"So what's the news, pal?"

He's obviously got some news for me.

"Listen, I picked up your old man the other night, drove him out to Breidholt to this lady friend he's got there. He's drinking again, the poor sod."

"Yeah, I know."

"And listen, he was telling me that your mother's been turned into a lesbian or something. Any truth in that?"

"Yeah, we came out of the closet the other day."

"Huh?"

"Me and Mom. We came out of the closet together."

"Yeah? Right. Because hey, you know, this thing is spreading. I even get it in the backseat of my cab now."

"What?"

"Well, you know, this homo shit. What's it like for you? Your dad's in a real state about it."

"No, it's great. The house is always full of girls now."

"Is that right, yeah? Yeah. And listen. I see you got lucky the other night. I saw you there up on Langahlíd, with a nice piece of crumpet on your arm."

"No, you must have seen somebody else."

"No, no, you're not getting out of this one, Hlynur, pal. I'd recognize that nose of yours anywhere, small as it may be. So listen, what was she like, then? Bit rough, was she?"

"Yeah, we had a bit of rough, all right."

"Wha'? Rough, right. Yeah. And listen, did I ever tell you about that Danish one I met? Birgitta. When I was still driving my Taunus. And anyway. I tell yeh, it was one of the best rides I've ever had and I tell yeh—this was behind the airport like, behind the airport like, you know—and on top of that she paid me for it. I was thinking of giving it to her for free, but the meter's the meter, and I've always been a man of principle, you know. Man of principle. That's such a basic rule in the driving business. You can't allow it to get personal. I mean, that's like a basic rule like, you know. And listen, yeah. She was a bit, she was a bit . . . different. This Danish woman. I haven't really been into foreigners much, if you get my drift, because you never know how it'll come out afterwards, but I said to myself sure it can't do me much harm if she's Danish. I mean, they used to be a part of our republic."

Elli. The last of a dying breed. They'll have him stuffed one day.

I'm on the phone. Thröstur is next. Says he's going to pop over later. I'm too numbed after Elli's twenty-year-old tales about his sordid escapades down the dirt tracks of Lavaland to say no. And what's more I'm in the middle of sending an e-mail to Kati. And what's more I need a crap.

WC. Water closet. This is Mom's closet. I lock the door. Strangely horny today. The sight of the sink is enough to give me a hard-on. This is Mom's world, even though I've got my shaving cream up here on a shelf somewhere between all these soaps, balms, bubble bath, skin lotions, shampoos, hair conditioners, hair removers, hair sprays, antiperspirants, combs, brushes, perfumes, eaux de toilette, tablets, sleeping pills—pain killers, laxatives, PMS tablets— mascara, eye shadow, makeup and creams for every hour of the day. But men? Clumsy nincompoops with facial hair: Yogi Bear in the middle of a forest of perfume flacons. All the things you need to be a woman. This whole system. I read the labels. All men's names: Karl Lagerfeld. Yves St. Laurent. Oscar de la Renta. Calvin Klein. Pierre Cardin. Vidal Sassoon (does he exist?). Parisian poofs, every single one of them. Women smell of poofs.

Women make up for men.

I find the cream. Gillette. I shave. Isn't there something rednecky about that? Isn't there something rednecky about being a man? About having to shave. Having to harvest your face every day. Rounding up your hairs in the sink. And hosing them down. Isn't there something unnatural about all this hair sprouting out of us men all the time? What kind of a deal is this anyway? Seventeen thousand blackheads germinating every day. Remnants from our ape days. OK to have hair on our skulls and down below, but there's something so Jurassic about facial hair. Every time you go to a swimming pool it's like a visit to Planet of the Apes. I never go swimming. Water bores me. Hairy men. Passé. Stone Age oafs. They're all bald in *Star Trek*, aren't they? Has mankind ceased to evolve? I shave the past off my face. Yeah. Hair is time, Timer says. Each beard hair is a year. I wash seventeen thousand years down the sink.

I comb myself, nick some of Mom's hairstyler and spray. I comb my hair up, over my receding hairline. I realize I'm saddled with an outdated kind of new-wave hairdo. It's like an old Stray Cats song glued to my skull, but it's the best I can do. Gives a slight lift to that flat-screen face of mine, with my tinted glasses and medium-range missile of a nose. Even my belly button protrudes more than my nose. My lips are so thin my mouth can barely call itself a mouth. Who'd want to kiss that slit? I'm little more than forehead, cheeks, and chin. A frame for my glasses.

I dry myself. Mommy smell from the towel. An unspeakable mommy smell. I sink my face into the terry cloth. Like mother's skin. Thick and smooth mother's skin. All of a sudden I feel like I'm inside my mother's womb. The bathroom is a womb. A terry-cloth womb. I'm inside Mom. A bra dangles from a hanger. Two concave cups before my eyes. I gape into them. I'm seeing Mom from the inside. I'm inside her. Hard-ons are strictly forbidden inside the womb. I crouch into a fetal position on the lavatory seat. Push out the umbilical cord. My reversed umbilical cord. Everything inside out. I'm inside Mom's closet. I'm inside a lesbian's womb.

The phone rings faintly in the distance: I hear it as an unborn child might hear it from the womb. It's the Man Upstairs. "It's for youhoo," the nurse yells down the groin, as the toddler scrapes his way down the tunnel. "He'll be there in a sec," she says to God, who patiently waits at the other end of the line with a cell phone in his hands, not bothered by his phone bill ticking away at the rate of kr 1,200 a minute. When the kid finally crawls out to pick up the phone, he says, "Listen, there was something I forgot to tell you, something about women. . . ."

Lolla answers the phone and knocks. The midwife.

"Hlynur! Phone call for you!"

"Who is it?"

We talk through the door, through the hymen.

"Hólmfrídur."

"Tell her I'm in the bathroom."

Good job I'm here. Inside this sanctuary. Safe. With diplomatic immunity. Unborn.

Thröstur's here. Sitting in a chair. I'm sprawled out on the bed. We're watching some Japanese sumo wrestling. Live from Osaka. Don't like having him in my room. I'd rather not have anyone in my room. Wouldn't be so bad if Marri were here as well. It's the one-to-one thing I don't like. Talking to just one person. Like having only one channel. No alternatives to turn to. At least he's brought some beer along. We sip to the sumo. It's the big man himself. Takanohana. Thröstur provides an unsolicited commentary.

"Those guys are incredible. How much do you reckon they eat? They must put away a restaurant a day, man."

I don't answer. He shifts awkwardly, but I let him stew in his own mess for a while. After a pause:

"Yeah, I mean, those guys must weigh at least three hundred kilos."

I'm still silent. He's even more uncomfortable now.

"Imagine having to sleep with one of those fat fucks. I mean, how? Do you reckon? Do you think they can do it?"

He sinks deeper with every sentence. And he obviously knows it. Then, a few beats later, he says: "Must be a nightmare."

He's actually reached the bottom now. I can almost hear the panic alarms echoing inside his head, as he tries to fight his way out of this dead end. Like listening to bubbling porridge. I give

him a look, just one side glance. He pretends to look at the screen.
I watch him as he raises the tuft of his beard. Stiff nerve ends.
Then finally he resurfaces with a gasp:

"I mean . . ." and then he spurts out the rest, "how many
rounds are there in this thing? Are there any rounds in this or, I
mean, what are the rules in this thing? Do you know?"

"No," I say, and change the channel. The European Wheelchair
Olympics. Live from Essen. Change. *Cheers*. Change. Ads. A
model (175,000) eating French yogurt. Change. John F. Kennedy.
Change. Music video. Ice Cube. I give it a try. Rap is crap. Change.
Ad. German escort agency. Change. Soccer game in Bogotá.
Change. Italian variety chat show. Let it roll for a while, but
change a split second before Þröstur comes out with "Those
Eyeties are really crazy, aren't they?" Sky News. Watch that.

"So how about it? Shall we go for a spin?" I say when the beer's
finished.

The K-bar is pretty tame tonight. Saturday night is always Friday
night II. The remake. Without the freshness of the original. Lenny
Kravitz. Everyone talking about last night. A pretty dull atmosphere, even though Keisi's behind the bar. Everyone just drinking and talking. As if they were at work. As if they were being paid
to drink those glasses. Cocktail atmosphere. Tales of the cock.

"And what? Did you go home with Hofy?"

Oh no. Þröstur wants to peer into the condom and dissect it all
under his microscope. He always tells me everything about his
homework. The little bit he gets done these days. He comes in with
an essay the day after and I sit there, nodding like a teacher, cor-
recting him now and then. I look around. Nothing to look at. A
Þorrablót feast at every table, the usual assortment of traditional
meats: oversinged sheep's heads and crushed skull jelly, ram's testicles heavily pickled in pussy juice, and putrefied shark. Reykjavík is just a melting pot of leftovers. Everyone's fucked everyone
else. This place is worse than the waiting room up at the VD
clinic. Everyone hooked to the same DNA chain. Like the family
reunion of a family that never was. Abortions under every table.

You can barely get to the can with all those tiny white embryos cluttering up the floor. Fishlike fetuses hovering at your ankles. The specters of the unborn.

Over there, there are some girls that Thröstur's been inside, and I know everything about what they're like in bed. That one gives good head, this one doesn't. This one's loose and burps, that one's tight and quiet downstairs, but screaming upstairs. That one's a real octopussy. This one stuck a finger up his ass. In fact, you get a finger up your ass the second you walk into this place. Which is fine by me. Wicked place. We sit in the corner. Hertha Berlin is at it a bit early tonight. She drifts past the table—like a seventy-kilogram lump of wobbly chewy meat, heavily marinated in alcohol—and waggles her tongue at us. It seems to be clearing up for the Cranberries. Phew. Thröstur is on the Hofy track:

"And. What was she like?"

"Why don't you just try her out for yourself?"

"Ha ha . . ."

"What about you? Where did you end up?"

He's burbling on about something, but I'm not listening. "Where did you end up?" As if Thröstur could ever end up anywhere. Where could he possibly end up? There is no end to that guy (apart from the tip of his beard). Thröstur in fifty years' time? Can't exactly see his name up in lights in Las Vegas. "Fifty Years of Thröstur." Nah. He'll just hook up with some shoe number, and they'll share a phone number, and then buy a house number. Some under-Mount-Esja kind of thing. 24 Monogamy Lane. Holy Kiljan. She walks in. Huffy Hofy on high hoofs. Glaring at me with those two eyes of hers and that third eye on her nose. I chin her a hi. She stares at my face as if it were a rotating display board, waiting for more information, waiting for the panels of my face to revolve into some new expression. But it's just me again. There's nothing behind me. My face is everything I am. Strip that away and what are you left with? A skull with two cavities and twenty teeth. A perfectly ordinary and anonymous sea urchin smiling to the world for the rest of eternity, happy forever. Hey. How come the dead are always smiling? She looks at me as if I were dead. Attention, please, calling all archaeologists, stop all that mucking about in those ancient graves and just come on down here to the K-bar. Drill into my bones and file your report; examine this glass, these deposits and foam: "This receptacle probably contained a fermented beverage of some kind. . . ." They don't think enough about the future, those archaeologists. Prevention, that's the key.

She vanishes into the bar. The K-bar is just one room but there is a pillar, a chimney in the center that comes in handy sometimes when you're trying to hide from someone. It's been a great support to me over the years. Thanks, pillar. Pillar, thanks.

Thröstur hasn't spotted her. His back is turned. Rosy and Guildy come in and sit down. They've got it sussed. Two supergays. Always together. The longest-standing relationship I know of. Rosy is the "crantsy" one, and Guildy is "stern." Some in-joke of theirs. I haven't the faintest idea of what they mean.

"Hello," they say in unison, like two gay horses. And Rosy looks a bit equine with that forelock dangling over the bridge of his nose. He's got orange hair and adds: "Hi, guys, we're not disturbing you or anything, I hope? This isn't going out live, is it?"

"Nah, just the same old repeats," I say. "Thröstur's going over last night."

Guildy sweeps the long tails of his trench coat to one side, and sits, leaning his face into the candle flickering a Christmasy light in the middle of the table—half drowned in wax, and struggling against the might of the mid-December darkness, which, outside, is filled with some strange kind of precipitation (nobody knows what it is: rain, snow, hail, seawater? Might even be sour milk for all we know), falling over these little bleary-eyed houses. Rooftops that still have the same old partings down the middle, same old curls of corrugated iron, and comb-shaped aerials. Guildy glances swiftly around and then looks at me and drops his jaw. Guildy always drops his jaw when he's about to speak. Must be a gay thing. To wait with your mouth open for the words to come out. Plenty of treble in his voice:

"Guys, have you seen the new production at the Traveling Playhouse?"

I mouth a silent no.

"No, of course not, who am I talking to? Hlynur, you never go to the theater. But this you must see. We've just come from there. An awesome show. Absolutely awesome."

"What play was it?" asks Thröstur.

"*Omelette*," says Rosy, and Guildy smiles:

"*Omelette*, yes, a ham omelette, *Hamelette*. It's such a farce. The kids did it all themselves and they did it wonderfully . . ."

Guildy continues to knit his account of the show, but I drop out, or in, I should say, into his nose. He's got a fairly massive one, with a kind of rugged face. His cheeks are a lava field. Steel-wool bristles. It seems to me that all gay men have these rugged faces. I think it's because one's always thinking about what it must be like to kiss them. To dip one's tongue into those extinct pimple craters, suck sweat out of those pores, nibble at the hairs up those nostrils, inhale that deep-voiced bad breath through those clouds of aftershave, to collide with those front equine teeth and take that coarse horse's tongue into one's mouth. Yeah. Like kissing a horse. Homos are horses. Rearing. Guildy's still rearing on about this show of theirs by the time I reemerge from his nose:

". . . it's a modern tragedy, but it's just so disgustingly funny, so abominably funny, done in that yes-we-can-see-through-all-that-now style. It's got everything. There's a touch of Gudbergur in it, a bit of Hamlet, a bit of panto, Tarantino, and even a pinch of Oedipus. . . . Yeah, it's a real mixed omelette, with just about everything thrown into the pan."

I haven't tasted this egg dish he's rambling on about (except for the pulp master, of course), but I nevertheless try to strike a facial expression that says I like omelettes. Rosy and Guildy are always going to the theater. They're hairdressers, with their own salon, but every now and then I think they also dabble in some of this theater lark. I haven't been to a theater since I was a toddler and got dragged along in handcuffs to see some tra-la-la musical at the old Idnó Theatre. Maybe I'd be willing to go to the theater if there were more than one play going on at once, if they'd give you a remote at the entrance, and you could turn the revolving stage at will.

Thröstur twiddles the tip of his goatee and asks Rosy: "What about you? What did you think of it?"

"Yeah. Yeah. It was fineokay."

"And what's it about?" Thröstur asks.

"About? It's about . . . well, it's about all of us, really. All this shit that's going on. It's got everything in it: the family, the alco, the mother, bar life. Hlynur, you should run along to see it, and take your mother with you. She'd like it, your old dear would. How's . . . how is your mom, anyway? I haven't seen her. . . . She hasn't been to the salon for ages . . . Although, yeah, we met her at the Two-and-Two the other day with Lolla. They're so dynamic, man. . . . Jesus, the energy in those women . . ."

"Oh yeah?" I interject, suddenly curious.

"Yeah. Your mother's always in such great form, Hlynur."

"Are they together or what?"

"Who? Lolla and Berglind? Ah ha ha . . ."

They laugh one of their gay laughs. Gay laughter sounds like a coughing car engine. No. Like sheep on Ecstasy.

"Hlynur, you don't expect me to tell you about the men in your mother's life, do you?"

"No, the women."

"Ooooh! . . . Guarding the closet, then, are we? You should get a job at the Vesturbaejar swimming pool. You'd look good in clogs, spraying us down with your hose. Are you trying to say that your mother's in the closet? Is that what you think?"

"I don't know. You ought to know that better than I do."

"No, no, Hlynur darling. After all, you're the one who lives in there, inside the closet with her, aren't you? What's it actually like to share a closet with your mother?"

They giggle like two masochists on morning aerobics. Like sheep on Ecstasy being shagged. The ring in Rosy's nose waggles like a lamb's tail. The tip of a tattoo can be glimpsed stretching under his collar. Swelling like a snake. Thröstur, the thrush, laughs too. The bird on the branch.

"There's nothing better than a breast in the dark," I say. They ha-ha and tee-hee and Guildy answers:

"Aaah . . . now we know why you never want to leave home. Maybe that's why she's coming out of the closet. . . ."

I try to nail him on that point and ask him: "Is she . . . ," but in the middle of his cackle he suddenly spits up what must be a deciliter of saliva—enough juice for two heavy-duty homo kisses—and accidentally extinguishes the candle. A wax-scented darkness hangs over the table. Thóra, the bartender (35,000), appears and empties the ashtray.

"Thóra, dear, you don't have any milk in your breasts, do you? We've got an undernourished baby here. . . ."

Says Guildy.

The pillar game is going quite well. She's obviously playing along. She doesn't look at me again until we're outside. A glance that turns sleet into hail. A good thing I'm wearing glasses. Icicle Works. It's basically the same group of demonstrators we had yesterday except that now we've got an extra two queens with megaphones, and the weather is even worse. There's a party at Rosy and Guildy's, and they're sifting through the crowd, selecting their guests, like a couple of casting directors recruiting extras. No, more like Siegfried and Roy selecting victims to feed to their white tiger. I'm seriously considering insulated overalls. I tell you, this is no stand-up standing out here like an arrow on a weather chart. I mean. It's raining now. Blobs. The spitting contest of the gods. No cigarette can stay alight. But Thröstur's high on E. The Puffin came to our table earlier on and gave us all freebies "just cos it's Christmas." Rosy and Guildy said they were saving theirs up for Christmas Eve. I couldn't deal with E-ing myself right now, stuck it in my breast pocket. Maybe cos I've already knocked back so many beers. Or is it something else? I'm feeling a bit d-ish. Thröstur on E is a TV on legs. He stands there like an anchorman, spurting out his intestines. News from the crotch. Live from his underpants. Looking into his eyes is like looking into the wilderness. What's he thinking of? Alone on E (the Puffin got netted away by Jökull and co.). Yeah, helps him rev up for the girls. Although he'll have serious problems revving up your man below. With all that xtc inside him. A guest from the future. An E-tard stuck on stupid. "Hello," I say. "Will the bus be long?" he says. I move away from him to a safe distance. To take a look at this. This is definitely newsworthy. Worthy of a cable to Reuters:

"Ignoring the Arctic rainstorm of almost tropical proportions, fifty hard-jamming natives partied on well into the small hours in this city of 100,000 . . ."

We walk up Laugavegur, if walking is the word. More like battling your way through a car wash. On the moon it's always still, nothing but stillness and quietness around the American flag. The gales numb my spine like an epidural, but I can still feel Hólmfríður's piercing gaze on my heels. (I can't call her Hofy right now. Cos of the wind. She needs to cling to every single letter in her name to stop herself from falling. Or maybe. Maybe I should let her fall.) I'm following Rosy, Guildy, and Thröstur, and most of the conversation is just "What?" and "Huh?" Cos of the howling gusts, Rosy's outfit, and Guildy's heels. Rosy is in some kind of captain-cum-general-cum-safari uniform. I.e. the uniform of a captain in the Russian navy, of a Southern general in the American Civil War, and of some kind of Aussie bush hunter. He sways on the pavement with loud crunching sounds from all these layers of leather, suede, canvas, and kangaroo hide. He does get ten points for actually being able to move in all that stuff, though. Three continents on his shoulders. A crunching walking war museum. I pretend I'm listening to them and stay abreast to make sure I don't slip back into Hofy's posse still following behind. Bloody hell. Worse than living under a dictatorship. One bad move and they follow you for life. This will end in an interrogation. I prepare my answers.

She pretends not to see me when her wet face skims past me through the door near Hlemmur. What's she doing here? Why is she out partying all the time? Why isn't she at home boiling some dyes for her fabrics? What was I supposed to do? Stay there, sober and wide awake, under her arm until noon? A daddy's girl with wedding bells on her brain. . . .

It's always a bit of a downer to have to step into the homes of people you know. The mild tedium you're willing to put up with when you're lounging around with them in pubs downtown becomes intolerable the moment you set foot into their headquarters. Having to crawl into the unbarred cells that some of these life-term convicts actually pay rent for. That whiff of bad breath you barely managed to dodge down at the bar is cemented to the walls at home. That glance you so skillfully averted fogs up all the windows in here. So this is where he keeps his fluffy cliché of a jacket—with those balls of snot under the collar—in this cupboard here. In there with his three brothers. This is where those filter yellow teeth are brushed, see, there's the toothbrush, more like a dish brush, and the crumpled tube of toothpaste, like a fading soul, squeezing out its final rays. And hiding somewhere, far away in the depths of this mirror, are seven hundred wanks.

As a rule I don't go to people's homes, not unless I'm desperate for an after-hours party. But Rosy and Guildy's. Well, that's different. Stepping into this place is like stepping into a theme park. There's the costume collection, the wig room, the velvet room, the record collection. Takes you deep into Detroit. Rick James spinning on the turntable. "Super Freak." A deep cocaine bass, masterly fingered, and a cool funky beat. As if they were beating three long black dicks on those drums. That licorice-black-laidback-dusty-vinyl feel. OK. This is no CD lark. We're talking LPs here. It's like Dennis Hopper's place in *Blue Velvet*. Always raises the spirits to come into this place. Gives you that lift. Puts you up on high heels. But I sit, as it happens, woozy myself onto the sofa, and soak in the atmosphere.

There are about sixteen people here, if I include Hofy. She's staying in the kitchen, feels better there. I'm monitoring Thröstur. The Christmas he's having: "Remember *Crocodile Dundee*? I'm the . . . I'm the crocodile, right? I'm not him, I'm the crocodile." I block my ears. Guildy's pouring whiskey. Rosy has tucked his kangaroo and general gear away on the shelf. Under all those continents he was actually wearing red trousers and a violet T-shirt inscribed with "To Me or Not to Me." Ha ha. I can tell Rosy is about to open himself to me, and I'm in no mood to be headphoned into the sofa so I try to look at the face of the guy sitting beside me: a moderately well-known face that's slowly fading out of the national consciousness. Used to host a TV show, presenting music videos. The kind of guy who's at his best between tracks. Can only talk at three-minute intervals and everything he says sounds like the intro to a song. Sitting opposite me, Gudrún Georgs (5,000, sales tax incl.). That blotting paper from Breidholt. And hey. There's Timer. Like some installation in the corner. Somebody must have DHLed him all the way over here. And kiloed him down into that comfortable armchair where he's showing his tattoos to two girls. The tattoo horse. They say he's got portraits of all the ZZ Top members, under his armpits and on his crotch, with real beards. And they say he shaved below when one of the band members had his beard removed. Thröstur is with another one (15,000) of those two girls that were at the bar, the one I know everything about in bed. It's the one with the finger. She's a Ferguson (red-haired). Two female friends are dancing on the rug (20,000 and 50,000). The more expensive one quite passable. My eyes move intermittently between her lips and breasts. Maybe I should have dropped that E after all. Guildy is telling the story about when he met Bryan Ferry in Amsterdam. Good story. Good music. Good view. There's a kind of Polaroid atmosphere here. One that calls for instant developments. If only Rosy would shut up. He's still trying to open himself to me:

"But I've always wanted to get back into costume design. I've done everything in hair now, everything I could do really, and I want to get out of hair now and maybe work in theater or something. . . ."

"Yeah," I say and manage to establish some eye contact with the video presenter sitting beside me. It works. He's obviously used to this from his TV work. I think it's what they call a cue. One glance and he knows he's on, he's got to say something:

"But you have actually worked in theater before, have you not?"

Good. We've slipped into the chat-show mode at last. And Rosy can finally open himself. I sneeze, as I always do when people are about to open themselves. Rosy's orange hair. I feel like patting him on the head and saying "good boy," but think it might be a bit too . . . I dunno. Guildy slips on another record and waves the sleeve at me:

"Hlynur, this is it. This is the song from the show I was talking about. The *Omelette*. Just listen. It's good. Awesomely good."

I'm not too sure about that. The crappy jangle of an Icelandic guitar and a whiny beardy voice. But I listen to the opening lines for Guildy's sake:

Hamlet lives in Reykjavík and smokes his Danish Prince
A dithering lounging indoor type, girls just make him wince.
His mother, she's a megababe, a right little beauty queen
But E. D. Pussy, his brother, is plotting some wicked scheme . . .

"Awesome, isn't it?" says Guildy.
"Yeah," I say, meaning no. "The lyrics might be a bit . . ."
"Yeah, the lyrics are pure Megas, aren't they? Here's the chorus:"

To be or not to be, that is the question
What am I going to do with my latest erection?

Ophelia's always there, on his answer-phone
But every time he picks it up, he turns into a stone.
Cos Hammy boy has had enough of all this endless strife
He doesn't want to grunt and sweat under a weary wife.

To be or not to be, that is the question
Or maybe it'll be OK if I use protection . . .

Icelandic music. Sugary cubism. I head for the john, brushing past those kr 50,000 breasts, and pass through the kitchen unscathed. Egill's Gold down the drain. But when I come back from the john my Hofy is waiting for me. My Hofy is waiting:
"Hi."
That's more than just a hi. I try to make mine sound lighter:
"Hi."
"Thanks for last night."
"Yeah, thanks for last night."
"Are you so sure about that?" she says, her eyes glistening like testicles.
"What?"
"Are you sure there's something to be thankful about for last night?"
"Y . . . Yeah. It was OK."
"OK, you say. OK for you. Come and go. Really great for you."
"I didn't actually come."

"Ha ha. Hlynur. Isn't there something you've got to say to me?"

She's cornered me in the corridor. A face passes (20,000). I look at it. It disappears into the bathroom. I reverse. We tumble into a room that, at first sight, seems to be a costume storage room, but might actually be this gay couple's bedroom. She sits on the bed, folds her arms, and crouches slightly, as if she were having stomach cramps or something. I stand. This should be the other way around, if she wants this to be an interrogation. But she's the silent one.

I say: "Something wrong?"

"Something wrong?"

"Yeah."

"Hlynur, you don't just sleep with a girl and then vanish the second she closes her eyes. What do you take me for?"

"I couldn't sleep."

"Couldn't sleep. Why couldn't you sleep?"

"I don't know. I can't sleep with girls."

"Can't sleep with girls? What do you mean?"

"Just. Maybe I can sleep with them, but I can't wake up with them."

"And why not?"

"Don't know. Something wrong with my sleeping muscles."

I'm tired of standing and sit on the bed too. The mattress wobbles. She looks at me.

"You could at least have said goodbye. Why didn't you wake me up?"

"I . . . You were so fast asleep."

"Oh, how touching. But you heard me calling you. I woke up. You walked out even after I called you. And then you don't answer the phone. Pretend not to be in. Get your mother to lie for you. You can never face up to things. Can't even face yourself. You can't face anything."

Hofy, as has already been stated, has red-streaked hair. Down to her shoulders. Her glossy taut white skin stretches nicely over her facial bones. A thick layer—not fat, just a thick layer that uniformly covers everything, precisely what I like about her, and reminds one of an egg, a soft-boiled glossy egg out of its shell, lukewarm and quivering—that curves around the cheekbones, down the cheeks, and under the jaw. She's all kind of oval-shaped, smooth and firm. You'd think that it was her skin that was holding all these pieces together and upright, not her bones, that they were just the thin crust of the cake underneath all this cream. No. A cheesecake, more like it.

I lose myself in her right cheekbone for a moment, and notice how well the skin covers it, how the skin gently stretches every time the bone moves when she speaks. I'll say that for her, she certainly knows how to use the movable parts of her skull. Even though she's hard-mouthed. And she's got a stud in her nose.

"You don't even have the guts to look me in the eye right now."

"Hum?"

"Yeah. Look into my eyes, if you can. Why are you always in those dark glasses?"

"To cut out the glare. You have such bright pure skin."

"I don't feel particularly pure right now."

"No?"

"No. Not that you'd understand that. I felt like some kind of a whore this morning. Not even that. Men normally say goodbye to whores, don't they? At least they settle their accounts before leaving. Why don't you just pay me for it?"

"I think they normally have to be paid beforehand."

"Oh yeah? So you know about it, do you? Speaking from personal experience, are you?"

"No. Seen it in the movies."

"Sure."

"Why does this have to be such a big deal? We only slept together. I mean, there's nothing between us except three shriveled condoms. I mean. It's not like we've been living together for the past seventeen years. This is just a . . . procedure."

"Procedure?"

"Yeah. An operation. Clinical."

"I think it's a little bit more than that."

"OK, so maybe a little bit. I'm not saying you have to wear rubber gloves or anything."

"Right, so for you it's like filleting fish or something."

"No, I was thinking more like a minor operation."

"And who's the patient? I'm the patient, am I? And you'd probably rather . . . rather knock me out with an anesthetic and wear rubber gloves?"

"That's what a condom is, isn't it, a rubber glove?"

"Are you saying it would be different if we didn't use a condom?"

"Then there'd be nothing between us."

"For Chrissakes, Hlynur. Don't you have any feelings? Have you ever even—"

"I wish you wouldn't say 'for Chrissakes.'"

"Oh, why not?"

"I can't stand all this Chrissakes stuff. We're not Americans."

"For Christ's sake, then."

"You could also say Halldór Kiljan, for example. I'm trying to introduce it. It's open to quite a few variations too. You can say Halldór Kiljan or just Kiljan or Halldór Laxness. Holy Kiljan is a good one too, or 'Laxness, man . . .'"

"Oh, Hlynur. You and your stupid jokes. Stop being so corny. I was talking about feelings."

"Feelings, yeah."

"Hlynur. What am I to you? How do you see me? Look at me, Hlynur. What am I to you?"

"You. You're a beautiful girl."

"And?"

"Does it have to be followed by an and?"

"A beautiful girl. Who isn't a beautiful girl?"

"There aren't that many. I mean, there are cute girls or they can be homely, womb-ly, wicked, awesome, passable . . . Ponies, eyefuls, stares . . ."

"Hlynur, please."

"Hang on, let me finish. Then there's the older ones. The very-best-of types, the Greatest Hits ladies, the double-chin cows, the bronchitis hags, the bureau-cats, the jeep creeps, the slot machines you have to put a coin into but never come, and the further-education lezzies. But a beautiful girl—"

"What are you on?"

"Disability benefit."

"I knew there was something wrong with you."

"I'm seventy-five percent disabled."

"You just can't take anything seriously."

Oh no, not that again. I try to breathe more seriously. I try to inhale the air as seriously as possible and then exhale it through my nose. A bit too hammy, I feel. Not quite convincing enough. I try something else. I try to look at her. I do my utmost to look at her as if I weren't joking. But then I raise an eyebrow and my lips start to curl. I don't know if you could call it a smile. She:

"Got a cigarette?"

"Have you started smoking?"

"Have you got a cigarette?"

"Yes."

I dig the packet out. Prince. Give her a light. Profile. Hofy. Smoke billows out of her. That nose. A straight nose straight from Páll Níelsson's production line. Well executed. And then the stud. It suddenly strikes me that it's like a safety valve on a tire. If I were to unscrew it a bit, some air might come spurting out, lower her pressure, and suck the shape out of her cheeks and breasts. She'd turn into a terribly ordinary girl, a doctor's secretary, a psychology student: a perfectly ordinary run-of-the-mill citizen down Laugavegur. I remember when I accidentally bumped into her at the bank. I barely recognized her. If she didn't wear lipstick I would never have slept with her. Women. "A beautiful girl." What's beauty? If you have to paint over it to make it worth anything? What's that? Just a con. A single tear and the whole thing's blotched. Dampens the powder. All those marriages—with all their luggage of offspring, sucklings and barbecues, jeeps and skiing gadgets, garden huts and Jacuzzis, snowmobiles, baptismal gowns and deluxe coffins—all of that—hangs on two miserable grams of powder and lipstick, dull, dull eye shadow. Bloody hell. Our Father who art remote, hallowed be thy fifty channels, give us this day just one tiny little birthmark of unblemished beauty! I'm sloshed; 75 percent disabled. Isn't that what I said? Some Rosy-scented leather hat on the bed. The gay boudoir. I fall back on my elbows. Party sound effects in the background as the storm continues to rage through the drafty windows. Hofy taps her ash into a glass on the bedside table. Shimmering light from the lampposts just like the night before. We're silent. It's a kind of heterosexual silence. Two sexes with nothing in common but some ancient custom that says they're supposed to mate. Two sexes with nothing in common but self-propagation. The plug and the socket that have to be connected so that there can be light. But these are cordless times we live in. This is all so outdated. Has humanity made no progress at all? For Chrissakes. Shouldn't I just start quoting the Bible? Is that where we've got to look for all the answers? Isn't this conversation written down in there somewhere? "You can't take anything seriously." What was the answer to that one again? All of a sudden I have a desperate craving for the remote. I clutch it in my inside pocket. My eyes skim the room, and land on the leather hat again, and I put it on for the sake of doing something. Everything but the girl. Yeah. There is a thought hidden inside this hat: it must be easier to be gay, at least they all belong to the same sex. At least they all speak the same lingo. No makeup between them. Hofy stabs out her cigarette. If she didn't wear lipstick . . .

"Why did you sleep with me?"

Spock.

Hofy turns and looks at me propped up on my elbows with Rosy's hat on my head. Must look pretty weird, I suppose. I tilt my head to allow the hat to fall off, and look up at the ceiling. Looking down at me are two fat, hand-painted, and pretty well-hung angels. Nice one, guys. It's like that chapel in St. Peter's. Michelangelo was gay. Yeah. Maybe it's all in the Bible. I look at her again.

"Why did I sleep with you?"

This is the kind of question politicians get when they—

She cuts me short:

"Yeah. Why did you sleep with me?"

"You mean the first time?"

"Yeah, for example."

"Just. Cos I felt like it."

"And why did you feel like it?"

"Cos I could."

"Exactly. Because you could. Because I came up to you when

53

we were outside and asked you if you wanted to come home for some tea. You never talk to me. Pretend you don't know me if I meet you in company . . . Hlynur. You're so lousy. You can be so lousy and base. . . . I don't get you. I just don't get you. . . . You probably just slept with me for the sake of sleeping with me, right?"

"Me?"

"Yeah, answer. Try to answer me. Why did you come home with me when I asked you?"

"Cos there was nothing else to do."

Hofy swallows this with a slightly dramatic nod and then utters two yeahs. Red and angry yeahs. She'd hit me if there were any talent for violence in her family. I think I can relax a bit now, I think we're finally pulling the plug on all of this.

"So that's where you've been hiding. Wow, something heavy going on in here, I can tell," says golden-haired Guildy as he enters like a clumsy angel. "Am I interrupting something?" He looks down at us with his hands on his hips. "God, you two make a pretty sight. Heart troubles?"

"He doesn't have a heart."

Guildy kneels, smiles.

"You don't say? Hlynur doesn't have a heart?" He puts his hand on my knee. "No, he's a bit special, our Hlynur is. Has to get by on a pacemaker. He's so sensitive, our Hlynsey is, but he's a good lad, really. But it's true, though, sometimes you just don't know whether he's dead or alive, do you? Ha ha ha. Needs a bit of a pinch sometimes, you have to know how to handle him, right?"

Guildy stretches and pinches my stomach.

"See what a cute little smile he has now. Ha ha ha. He probably needs a heart massage. And if that doesn't do the trick you'll have to try mouth-to-mouth resuscitation. Ha ha ha. And if that doesn't work you just come and talk to me. I've patched up many a relationship over the years, they don't call me Superglue for nothing."

He grabs both our knees and squeezes hard.

"Feel that? Feel it? How's that for power? Ha ha ha."

"But this is no relationship," says Hofy.

"No? But I'm trying to establish some contact between you here," says Guildy, squeezing harder and quaking all over. Then he stops and laughs:

"Hey, did you hear the one about the man who got a heart transplant? They gave him a new heart, right? And they gave him the heart of a woman. And this guy was as tough as nails, a real brute, and they gave him a woman's heart, a real sensitive woman's heart. And guess what. Guess what happened?"

"He turned gay?" I say.

"Tee-hee-hee . . . no. No, no. He didn't change at all. He was just as tough as he always was. Ha ha ha . . ."

Guildy stands up, walks over to the dressing table, and grabs a book—I think it's *Man Boy*, Boy George's autobiography—and then he adds: "No, kids, I'm afraid this is a hopeless case. Just forget about it. It'll never work. You're far too hetero for all this. Boys and girls . . . it just doesn't work. That's only for making babies, maintaining the species on this reef. Our mission is to destroy it . . . tee-hee-hee . . . No, not really. At least we boys don't have to go through all that hassle of giving birth. We just live on pure love, man, ha ha ha . . . The only thing we have in common is the condom, you use it to prevent the spreading of life, and we use it to prevent the spreading of death."

He goes out. We're both silent for a moment. Then I stand up and leave the room.

The party goes on into the small hours. I go home with Hofy.

Our little Christmas town. Decorations dangle over the streets. The whole center's been bulbed up. Everyone wrapped up and tottering about like mummified elves. Smoke out of every mouth. Everyone polluting the air with their diesel breath. One day we'll all have to give up all this breathing. These overalls are just great. I'm in mid-film. Mom sent me out to buy a tree. Gave me a kr 5,000 note. I was watching *Scent of a Woman*. Al Pacino is waiting for me at home on pause. They've closed the traffic down on Laugavegur, but it's even more difficult to walk on it now, a serious risk of crashing into someone you know:

1. Lóa: Hi. Hi. Buying presents, are you? Yeah. And what? On holiday, are you? Holiday? Yeah, Christmas holiday. Yeah. OK, I've gotta rush. Bye. Yeah, bye.

2. Reynir: Hi. Hi.

3. Thröstur and Marri: Thröstur is carrying a giant cactus. It gives Bankastraeti a kind of *Miami Vice* atmosphere. A frozen voodoo cucumber.

"That a Christmas present?" I ask.

"No, a Christmas tree."

"Are you going to have a cactus for a Christmas tree?"

"Yeah. It'll look great once the lights are on it. Like Ben Kingsley with tinsel hair."

I'm too old for this. I check out his eyes. E? No. Just a, b, c, d. I examine Marri's eyes as well. Everything seems normal there too. The usual two bulging golf balls that someone has dotted pupils on with a marker.

"Is this the new fad?" I ask.

"Just trying something different, man. We're also doing it for Thor. He's never had a Christmas like this before. It's his first Christmas in Iceland so we're trying to give him that back-home-in-the-desert feel," says Thröstur.

Thröstur and Marri live together. After Marri sexed up his mother's phone bill. Thor is their pet. Thor is a lizard. Some Arizona thing Marri smuggled into the country this autumn.

"Right, and how's he doing?"

"Fine. Getting longer . . ."

I don't actually know Thor very well. Only met him once. And have been trying to avoid their place ever since. Their entire apartment has been transformed into a sauna for him. It was 42 degrees the last time I was there.

". . . turning into a real cobra."

"Right. And where did you get this?"

"The cactus? The flea market down at Kolaport. Marri's brother-in-law has a stall down there, you know that José guy, the Mexican."

"The one who works in Mexville?"

"Yeah. He owns that place, doesn't he, Marri?"

"Yeah. Well, him and my sister."

"And where are you headed?" Thröstur asks. "Aren't you coming down to the K?"

"No. I have to buy a tree as well. And I'm in mid-film."

"What?"

"*Scent of a Woman.*"

"Yeah, good one."

"Yeah."

"Pacino, he's wicked in it."

"Yeah."

"And what's the name of that other guy again?"

"Chris O'Donnell."

"Yeah, him. And then there was some piece of skirt as well."

"Yeah, I think so, but I haven't got that far yet."

"What bit are you at?"

"They're in the hotel room in New York."

"Yeah, right. And then they go into the cave and read the poems and that. That was a great scene."

"No, that was *Dead Poets Society*. Robin Williams."

"Oh yeah."

We stand there like three old steam engines in the freezing cold. Three billowing clouds of smoke around a cactus. In the middle of Bankastraeti. A nearby tree laden with lightbulbs; like heavenly fruit. Parents dragging their elves across town. That evergreen itch in their souls. This festive spirit is killing us. Christmasturbation. Thröstur. How could he mix up those two movies? Al Pacino and Robin Williams? He wasn't even blind. The Prime Minister's offices all lit up. PM Oddsson setting the table somewhere deep inside. I leave them to it and edge my way across the square. Robin Williams follows me down Hafnarstraeti. *The Fisher King*. Such a weird thick torso. 'Member when I saw him on *Letterman*. David Letterman. I slip into the Coal Port, unnoticed. The guys told me José also has some Christmas trees. The traditional ones, I mean. I meet Dad in the entrance. By the hot-dog stand.

"Oh, hi."

His body looks sober, apart from his mouth. Which is probably why it's the only organ he chooses to express himself with.

"Hi. Buying presents?" I answer, trying not to act like a son.

"No. I was just getting some dough for the laufabread."

He raises his bag as he says this, and gulps down the last of his hot dog. There's a trace of cocktail sauce on his beard. It somehow reminds me of me. This is his dinner, I imagine. But I continue my interrogation:

"I thought Sara made her own."

"Yeah, no, this is for Mom, I'm going over there to give it to her right now. Your aunty Gútta's there. Would you like to come along? It's been a while since you popped in to see your grandmother, hasn't it?"

"No. I went to see her in the summer."

"See what I mean?"

"She's gone dotty. Forgets who you are the second she turns her head."

"Rubbish."

"Anyway, I'm in the middle of a movie. Sure I'll see her at Christmas."

"What's the news otherwise?"

"It's Christmas."

"Listen, sorry about that the other day, I was just a bit, you know, but ehm. Ehm . . ."

"What?"

"No, nothing. I'll be in touch. Send my regards."

"OK. And say hi to Sara."

"Huh? Right."

By the look of him, he hasn't seen her for three weeks.

Dad's shorter than I am. He's in a raincoat. An open raincoat. Light brown. He normally wears a tie but you never really notice it. Exudes a kind of friendly chaos. Dad supposedly runs some obscure company. Once upon a time he was doing some kind of accountancy work for others and then he started importing stationery. Difficult to pin down what kind of company it is now, or where it is, come to think of it. I looked it up in the book the other day and could only find a phone number. Company Services, Hafsteinn Magnússon, 561-4169. Maybe he works from home now. When I was a kid and people used to ask me what my dad did, I always used to answer:

He keeps his own company. That was usually enough. Sounded quite good then. Now it's "Business Consultant."

The Coal Port. The coal mine. Minors digging for gold. Coal-black plebs prospecting for a little ray of sunshine in their existences for a few krónur. A CD player going for kr 2,000. Kr 500 for a pink radio alarm clock bought in the Canaries that used to belong to a sailor called Sigthór. Accompanied him on three trips to the Barents Sea, and wakes you up in Spanish and English. I like this place. I've picked up some pretty good items for my collection in here: John Holmes in a 1976 Danish magazine, a Farrah Fawcett (300,000) poster from the same period, a rare Woody Allen alarm clock, and a Barbie acupuncture set, made in Taiwan.

I check out Parti's stand first. Parti's pretty much a permanent fixture in this place, always at the same stall, always with the same stuff. Parti with his parting hair. Parti, the man of parts. Sells putrefied shark and videos. Well, officially he sells only shark. Keeps the videos under the counter. "Wildlife documentaries," he calls them, standing there like a specter in his padded ski outfit. A downhill man in downhill gear. There's grime on his face and the snuff up his nostrils looks like mud, as if he's just been dug up and given the once-over with a duster. Pissy smelly fingers. You have to know how to approach him:

"Have you got some new ones?"

"Wildlife?"

"Yeah."

"Well, that all depends like, you know? All depends."

He splits his tapes into three categories. Horse, cow, and lamb documentaries. Horse documentaries are pure animalia. Cow documentaries are big women with big tits. Lamb documentaries are schoolgirls. I've bought two cow tapes from him. Pretty antique stuff normally, Danish super-8 footage from the heyday of porn. I ask him about the horse tapes. He says he's got one new one, watched it himself last night.

"It's an Amsterdame, quite a lady."

"What's in it?"

"Yeah, there's a male pig, a fat old bastard. And a dog, got a dog too, he joins in towards the end. The poor thing is a bit tattered, though, but the pig does a great job, a star performance," he says as he sucks the loose snuff up his nose and bends over to dig into a cardboard box under the counter. He holds out a copy: a naked tape in his paw. Five grimy fingernails clutching seventy minutes of buggery from the seventies. They just don't make movies like that anymore. Maybe because of all this animal-rights stuff. All this save-the-whale lark. You can't exploit animals like that anymore. You can't make love to an animal like that. Cos of the "psychological trauma" it can cause them. When are we going to get animal psychologists and animal counselors? I take the tape. Parti never puts them in cases and I don't know why he's handing it to me like that. To take a better look? It's just a normal black cassette with two white dented eyes and no label. I give it a sniff, just for the sake of doing something. It gives off that kinky putrid-shark stench.

"How much?"

"Three thousand five hundred."

"Don't you have anything with reindeer?"

"Reindeer? No, afraid not."

"Or turkeys? I'm looking for something Christmasy."

Parti snatches the tape back, shoves it under the counter, and turns to serve the next customer. I traipse over to José's. Marri's exotic brother-in-law. Short and sturdy. A muscle pumper from Solarium Ville. That must be Bára (12,000), I take it, Marri's sister. That same seafood look. Except more like a fish pie, maybe, baked inside that down jacket. José's wearing a baseball cap. Nice one, man. Cleveland Indians. What a couple. Iceland, Mexico. White sauce meets salsa. What'll their children be like? A weird concoction of birthmarks. And this is a colorful stall they've got here. A pocket version of Disneyland. Sombreros and Christmas lights, and those rugs they wear, bottles of sauce, and guacamole, nachos and cactuses and Christmas trees. José speaks Icelandic at Spanish speed and likes to say "no problem" a lot. Like Icelandic is no problem to him.

"Is very good to buy dis you see use it again and again just look at dis just plug in and is ready see no problem no mess don't have to hoover all the time is much better you see . . . no problem."

"How much?"

"Yeah, no problem just little four dousand five hundread grónur, OK?"

We're haggling over an artificial tree here, complete with lights and all. I'm really into this frosted contraption, but I'm not sure Mom would appreciate it. I check out the more traditional article in the corner. An Icelandic Christmas tree. But the smallest is going for 6,000 so I go for the José tree. Ask him to put it aside for me—"yeah, no problem"—while I hunt around for a present for Mom. I find a book by the entrance. *Beginners Guide to Thai Cooking*. Yeah, I've been into Thai take-out lately. Not a bad idea to get Mom cracking on it too.

I carry the tree across the center of town. It's small and neat, and utterly ridiculous. People look at me. Feel like Christ bearing his cross, carrying this thing up Laugavegur. Christ with an artificial cross. Quite appropriate for Christmas, I suppose. Doing my bit. And yeah, I'm pretty much the same age he was too. No, hang on, that was Easter, wasn't it? Yeah. When he was knocking around with the cross.

Lolla's in when I get home. She's moved in. Sleeps in Elsa's old room. Sprawled over the sofa reading the weekend paper. Socked feet up on the coffee table and a cigarette. I plant the thing in the corner and plug it in. Cool tree. Lolla puts the paper down on her stomach and looks at me, the tree, and me. Nibbles her cigarette. As if she were trying to decide which of us looks worse. Me or the tree. She seems to prefer the tree. If anything.

"What the hell is that?"

"Something to cheer us up."

"Is that supposed to be your Christmas tree?"

"Our Christmas tree, Lolla," I say as I look into her eyes, striking one of my more angelic poses. "You're family now."

"Piss off."

"What, don't you like it?"

"I mean. It's . . . it's like some fucking hairdo. Some ghastly hairdo."

"An angel's hairdo."

"Is it artificial?"

"Artificial? No, no. One hundred percent Icelandic."

"Where did you pick that up?"

"The Kolaport flea market. What d'you think? Isn't it just brilliant? I mean, with the decorations and everything. What d'you think? Seriously."

"Well, you bought it. I mean, your money not mine."

"Yeah."

We both look at the tree until she coughs, puffing out a cloud of laughter.

Me: "You don't like it, do you?"

"I'm more for the traditional ones myself."

"Oh yeah? But I got it especially for you, decided to dyke things up a bit this Christmas."

She gives me one of her don't-even-think-about-it-I'm-a-lesbian looks, stubs out her cigarette, and picks up her paper again. Some Santa on the front page. Without a hat. Arrested for butchering Rudolf and trying to sell him to restaurants. "Caught with 60 kilos of reindeer meat in his sack." Guess it's jingle bells all the way to the slammer for him. Lolla is wearing jeans. Filled with her shapely thighs. Surprisingly small feet. The tree in the corner looks a bit crushed after her putdown. But bravely flickers its lights. Like a sick old relic from Las Vegas. Weird how many books we have. I haven't opened one since I left university. Owing to some printing error on my astrological chart, I ended up in the English Department for half a semester. To be or not to be. Never really understood that phrase. Maybe those two stoned winters I had. To buy or not to buy? Is Lolla bi? Never really bought that one. Bi? With both men and women. Some kind of bridge between the sexes. What did she mean by that joke of hers the other day? "Less b than bi?" Yeah. Apparently she was in a relationship once. A non-lesbian relationship, I mean. Some sea captain somewhere, who started to drink the ocean instead of sailing it. Which is why she became an AA counselor. So is that why she became a lesbian? Out of disillusionment? "Less b than bi." She's a clever one. The hell she is. What the hell is she? Wouldn't mind peeping into her hell. And yet she looks like a one-sex-only kind of woman. Quite attractive. Just a slight thinning in her hair. And then those hips, they look androgynous, all right, broad and bisexual. Quite boyish. I'd give

her 30,000 plus an extra 20,000 for being bi. It's always difficult to
put a price on friends and family. What would Thröstur put on Mom,
for example? Rosy's T-shirt said: "To Me or Not to Me." There's
something in that. There's something more in that. Hey. Our next
step on the evolutionary ladder: lesbo-homos and homo-lesbos.
Homos who fancy lesbians and lesbians who fancy homos. As
time goes bi. Lolla looks like a little boy behind that paper.

"Where's Mom?"

"Popped out."

All of a sudden we're like brother and sister. Lolla would have
made a fine sister. Maybe better than Elsa, the square one with the
big heart. The nurse. Still, though. She's all right, really. It's just
that Magnús husband of hers. Hey. Magnús. Nag-mús. Nag mouse.
That's what he is, a nagging, nibbling mouse. All belly and mouth.
And nothing in between but the frequent passage of food. Comes out
with these indigestible sentences. Can think only with his stomach.
Some of the shit he comes out with. Guess there's more intelligence
in what comes out the other end. Magnús the nag mouse. Yeah, I
like that. Maybe there is some truth in our names after all. Hillary
Clinton (45,000). They called their daughter Chelsea (35,000).
That was original. Bristol Rovers might have been better, though.
Bristol Rovers Clinton. Peter Osgood. No. He played center-forward
for Chelsea. The header with the curls. Quite a handsome-looking
guy too. What ever happened to him? Probably managing some
classy pub in Bristol, with a Jag in the garage, and sneaking out for
quickies every lunchtime. Yeah, yeah. Wish I could find a database
on the Net with all that kind of info. Want to know it all: Like
where's Samantha Fox (600,000) at this precise moment? How
many fucks are there on average every night at the Singapore Hilton?
What ever happened to Cindy Crawford's (2,200,000) tits? What
song is being played in the lobby of the Sheraton hotel in Qatar right
now? Where and when did the first AIDS fuck take place? We need
that info. Everything's so obsolete. Everything's so incomplete.
What's Maria Schneider's (2,000,000) address? How many women
has Al Pacino had? Hey. The movie. I'd forgotten the movie. Tape's
probably melted by now. Poor Al. Frozen on the screen, blind and
all. I stand up and have reached the corner of the dining table when

I suddenly hear what sounds like a song, a Japanese electronic jangle. "Silent Night," I think. I freeze. Lolla drops her paper. Looks at me. I look at the Christmas tree. Then at Lolla again. I raise my eyebrows over the rim of my glasses. She bursts into laughter. The song plays on. Then a chirpy computer voice comes out with: "Merry Christmas, everybody!"

"For Chrissakes, man," I grumble. Normally I never say that. I'm only saying it now because it's Christmas, and I'm standing by the window in the living room. "Happy Christmas!" Some ever-grilling geek on the other side of the street has just plastered those words all over his house in neon lights. A bad case of Christmas fever, he's gone berserk and wired 70 meters of cables and bulbs to his front yard. The trees are ablaze with light: electric spring. Will people never grow up? The children's festival. Who cares? Celebrating a birth for the 1,995th time. Oh, that's original. Still, the neon makes a change. I hardly do any decorating myself. But it's the thought that counts. I just put up some dental floss, tied it between the chandelier and the curtain rails. Used dental floss, that is. Decorated with half-chewed morsels of food, pale pink beads, like minuscule bulbs. Hey, yeah, could be an idea. But. Christmas Eve and I'm standing by the living room window. It's 5 A.M. for the 1,995th time. The lamppost is still and so is the snow, like tons of beautiful cocaine neatly spread on the street. Glistening. Yeah. Beautiful. Especially if you think of the billions it's worth. I pace the room sipping a flat soda. Can't sleep. Christmas is such a difficult time. Everyone on holiday, no one working. It's so uncomfortable being around people on vacation. They lose their sense of purpose. Cooped up at home all day long. There's something so pathetic about people who aren't earning. Why should the heart bother beating if it's not even getting paid for it? A flickering candle on the screen. The tree switched off. It was driving us bananas today, this piece of junk. "Silent Night" every half hour. Funny the first five times. Good old José. He's fast asleep now, the little Mexican, topless in Bára's bed, his hairy chest like a dark jungle under the Icelandic eiderdown, his pitch-black Aztec stubble

scraping against her white fish face. Locked together like something
out of a United Nations brochure, everyone's so good tonight, the
nations of the globe making love to one another, cos it's Christmas. . . . Do people actually make love on Christmas Eve? No, probably not. I watched two tapes (Mom gave me a Woody Allen, *The
Purple Rose of Cairo*), but no blue movies, felt it wasn't appropriate—what with the virgin birth and all that. That's how much of a
co-Christmasholic I am. No wonder I can't sleep. Sleep better to the
sound of panting. Always good to know someone's manufacturing
love somewhere. Not a mouse stirring in the house. Both asleep. I
fondle a cigarette on the sofa. Get nothing out of it. Everyone's so
good on Christmas night, everyone's friends, everyone's kind, no
sound of gunfire over Bosnia, even the nicotine withdraws from the
cigarettes. The virgin birth. Now, that's original. Still works as an
original idea. Maybe that's why Christmas is still a sellout. The
1,995th production and people are still lining up for it in front of
every door, everyone beaming and delighted. And the critics too:
"Best Christmas for decades." All of a sudden I remember the birth
tape. Maybe I'll watch that. Check out some of those virgin births.
In honor of the day. I creep past the two closed bedrooms—stick my
ear to the doors, listen to the silence: yeah, they're both in their
respective rooms. I take a quick leak. Even my piss is pure, clear
as water. Damn it, why should I give in to all this outdated crap? I'm
a victim of mass hypnosis, mass narcosis. Why can't I stand up to
them and piss out my beer-polluted ammoniac in peace? Why does
humanity have to lean on me like this with all the weight of these
historical demands? To squeeze out these few immaculate drops of
holy water?

When I monk my way back into my cell it's CNN live from Bethlehem. Yeah, yeah. Laura Johnson (60,000) reporting live. But a bit
too late for that. The Three Wise Men bearing their Sonys, Olym-
puses, and Canons, an interview with Joseph, and the last photo
ever taken of the Virgin Mary (4,200,000). I slip the tape in. Live
from the Womb. Three amateur births, somewhere in Baltimore. A
bit long, that third one, but some good crying from the baby: quite
an entrance. A tiny black Gospel singer. The mothers pant and
groan in different keys. Actually, not that far from the sound of an

orgasm. Only more powerful. And totally real. I watch the rest of the tape on the fast-forward. Children bursting out, dangling from their umbilical cords, like puppets on a string, yelling their heads off in protest as the link is severed. Guess we want to hang on to that cord forever, until it lowers us into the grave. I'm no nearer sleep after witnessing these seventeen births, in spite of a tiring day. Had to wake up early to spruce up and dress before six. Mom had her leg in the oven. Leg of lamb. Haven't had wild ptarmigan since Dad's hills turned gray. Lolla got to bring a pal along. Ahmed something, from Morocco. Doesn't have anyone up here. She's really good that way, Lolla. The rehab counselor. Always taking these lame ducks under her wing. Like this long nose of a loner she picked up in some slum downtown. He works in Grund, the old folks' home. They met in rehab. He was going through rehab, that is. These foreigners are really beginning to integrate in this country if they're even starting to go into rehab. Hey. A Muslim alco? Isn't that something? Ahmed's Icelandic is practically nonexistent. All he can say is "frábært" (great), "gódur skítur" (good shit), and "hvad vilt thú drekka?" (what you wanna drink?). Maybe that's all he needs. Enough to get himself a whore. Anyway, so we had to speak English for the whole evening, which was OK—a change—except that Ahmed isn't an awful lot better at English either. Unfortunately, all of the few sentences he can string together have more or less the same meaning. So all he ever said was "aha," "yes," "very good," and "no problem" all night. I'd never actually met him before, just seen him sniffing around town. Comes across as a bit of a Simpson. But that could be the language barrier, of course. After all, there is a limit to the amount of concepts these no-problem phrases can express. The thing that surprised me the most, though, was finding out he'd been through rehab. Funny, he looks so un-alco somehow. Or maybe that's what an Arab alco looks like. Just doesn't have that haggard look. Which makes the Simpson streak even more blatant. I've noticed that: doesn't matter how stupid you are, if you've got that haggard, wasted look, you don't look so stupid somehow. Which is why it's so cool to look wasted, I guess. But anyway. It was a kind of lesbian Christmas veiled in a Muslim chador. Very refugee-friendly and we all felt like saints afterward. Opened our presents with glowing clear consciences. Still, I got the feeling Ahmed would have preferred to stay at home. I think he was bored. Might have been misguided charity on Mom and Lolla's part. His best moment was when the tree started to sing and his face lit up. Then he laughed and said, "Singing bush! Like singing bush!" which was funny the first three times, while we were still trying to work out what he was going on about (the singing bush was in some Mel Brooks movie or *iThree Amigos!* with Steve Martin and those guys), but soon became just as tiring as this cheap José joke. The worst bit was that he kept on asking me, "You like? You like singing bush? Yes?" I don't know what tongue Lolla uses to communicate with this guy; the one in her mouth, maybe. Maybe she's "bi-lingual"? I lie down. Waft in front of the blank screen. I lack the energy either to get out of bed and change the tape, or to close my eyes. I just let it snow. It's 6:30. I kill the box. Blackness. Silence. Stillness. Like it's all been erased. Like my brain's been switched off. All thoughts evaporated out of the room. I lie there like a zipped-up body bag in an LA mortuary. Can only hear my ears. As they rub against the pillow. Hey. A monk. To listen only to your ears. Look only at your eyelids and feed on your tongue. No. A man can't think in silence and darkness. No wonder humanity took such a technological leap as soon as Edison lit upon the lightbulb. More books have been published this century than all of the other centuries put together, someone said on TV the other day. No data, no thinking. No programs, no fun. "And that concludes our broadcast for tonight." That's the problem with Iceland. Always concluding its broadcasts. Some state android of a TV anchor telling you to turn your brain off and just go to bed. No wonder this society is so primitive. No continuity. No stamina. No follow-up. Always back to square one every day. Everyone doing the same thing. Everyone going to bed together. Hofy. Fast asleep in her myriad patterns, wrapped in Christmas presents from Mommy and Daddy, a soft cotton nightdress from Benetton, enveloped in her new quilt and pillows, some Sussex-designed autumn leaves shit, her stud glistening from the depths of a forest of femininity. Happy Christmas, Hofy dear. These Christmas greetings are sponsored by Laura Ashley and Benetton. Do I have a crush on her? Fuck, no. Crushes don't depend on lipstick. Or do they? Still. Always think of her when I've sunk to the bottom of the night. There she lies with her taut white breasts, topped with nipples. She came around just before six with a gift for me. What'd she do that for? Got me all shaken up. Maybe it was a good job Mom invited her in after all. Gave me time to find something to wrap into the paper for her in the bedroom (ended up giving her the Trésor perfume I nicked from Lilja Waage's). Then walked in to them, all flushed, and sat there like some psychology student, listening in silence as Mom bombarded Hofy with all sorts of inane questions about teacher training college, and let Lolla tell her what a wonderful dentist Páll Níelsson is. Wonderful dentist? My eyes darted between the stud and the beauty spot. Hofy actually quite fetching in that short black velvet dress of hers, but her stay turned out to be just as short. Lerti, her brother, was waiting outside in the car with some pinup (Bryndís, 100,000), about to head out for a Christmas grill in Gardabaer. Hofy gave me a shirt. I've had worse. Mom: "Seems like a really nice girl." Lolla, with a grin: "And her dad's a dentist, Hlynur . . ." Ahmed: "I see Lolla like, yes? He he . . ." He's quicker on the uptake than I thought. But what the hell possessed these Moroccans to come here, of all places? Is that all those poor Casablanca kids can aspire to? Coming up here to freeze their balls off in the north, and clean up the shit of decrepit, incontinent Icelanders? To work in a laundry room in Grund? But maybe it's the women. Yeah, they must be here for the women. "What you wanna drink?" Lolla said Ahmed has a son in Grindavík. A little one-year-old Arab nose stretching south toward the sea. Yeah. We could do with a bit of nose in the Icelandic face. Why do Icelanders have such small, flat noses? We who used to live in holes in the ground, but never developed mole muzzles. Maybe God did us a favor and limited our sense of smell to make life in those shitholes just a little bit more bearable. According to Guildy, we fart more than any other nation in the world. I rub my nose, as if I could get it up that way. Going too far, maybe, trying to wank your own nose? I'm astounded that I've actually mustered up the strength to finally slip a naked one into the VCR. A monkey special. In honor of the day:

Holey Night.

*   *   *

I travel to the Blue Lagoon mud baths with Ahmed and Hofy, and
he makes an instant pickup. Just as he's coming out of the showers
(where I noticed he had a much bigger nose than mine). Some girl
from Grindavík with grinding hips and a user-friendly ass with
whom he immediately disappears into the women's dressing room.
I totter around at the back in my Bonus briefs, can't face getting into
the psoriasis-infested pool, just stand there doing the goosebump
twist. Hofy comes out of the dressing room in her Christmas dress
and holding a shirt. She asks me if I want to wear it, and aren't I
cold? She adds that the Grindavík girl has just given birth, and that
Ahmed has already inseminated another two. "And what about
you?" I ask, but then someone knocks on the shop window and I
turn. It's Dad with a hot dog. He knocks again . . . I wake up.

Mom glides in and says: "Happy Christmas! It's two o'clock,
we better get going if we don't want to be late at Elsa and Magnús's."

Mom's such a softener. Like a voice-over in a detergent ad. She
has that, you know, soft voice and always talks in the same tone.
Doesn't matter what she says, always sounds pretty good. She
hardly ever loses her temper, and only on the phone, with people
she doesn't know: mechanics who've taken the car as hostage and
are demanding a ransom, or some surveyor who phones her up
for the twelfth time to ask her out for dinner. She has that warm,
matte amber voice, with a coffee aroma.—Maybe it's the Danish
element in her. Gevalia.—And it's as if her voice moved her thick
lips and not vice versa. In photographs she looks a bit like Mao.
Apart from the eyes, of course. Chairman Mao.

It's Christmas Day. Most difficult day of the year. The family
get-together.

Elsa is two years older than I am, but seems to have made the
most of those extra two years. She's got a man, a house, a car, and
children. All that social responsibility crap has built a wall
between us, and set her in a generation apart from mine. Which is
cool, I suppose. And just as well, maybe. Mom isn't the type to
dance hands-up over a new jeep or to strip at the sight of a new
leather sofa, but Elsa, the microwave mother, saves me the trouble

of having to give Mom grandchildren for Christmas. We're nothing like each other. I mean, there's nothing wrong with her. Elsa is the ideal citizen. Brings new life into the world and keeps death at bay at the Municipal Hospital. And now that Dad has irrevocably fallen off the wagon and started to dine at the flea market, and Mom is slowly but surely slipping into lesbiandom, and what with me being the way I am, Elsa's the only "healthy" individual left in the family. We trust in her. And she is to be trusted. In her solid house and well-kept garden. A terraced house, as it happens, but so well insulated that you'd wonder how even radio waves can penetrate its walls. And everything so spic and span and toothbrushed that you're always surprised to see children there. That children could even have been conceived in such a place. The kids stuck a sign on the wall: "No Smoking Area." When you slip down the corridor to go to the john, you half-expect to see a similar sign on the parents' door: "No Fucking Area." Just one look at that door and you know that the chances of the AIDS virus ever crawling over this threshold are about as great as the Japanese navy invading Iceland. I've never been able to picture my sister copulating. Not that I've ever really tried very hard, but the real challenge to the imagination is trying to visualize Magnús in any kind of physical activity at all. He's such a lazy slob you'd wonder how he finds the strength to hoist on his suspenders every morning. Maybe Elsa takes care of that. The nurse. Magnús Vidar Vagnsson. Works in the psychology business, runs an "alternative" travel agency, some New Age lark called "Inner Journey." Advises people on how to spend their holidays in a fruitful way. Stay at home. Discover the world from the comfort of your own armchair. Find inner peace. Don't add stress to stress. Yeah. He lives on holidays. He lives on other people's summer holidays. This house is built on other people's artificial problems. That's what I say. But Mom just says: "Who, Magnús? He's a psychologist."

Elsa and Magnús live out in the country. A country called Suburbia. Mom drives and Lolla has tagged along. Which might help, I suppose. The three of us are sitting in the red Subaru in silence, waiting for the heating to kick in. Christmas Day. And Christmas Eve still inside me, my stomach still full of darkness. I try to keep my eyes open to allow the daylight—if one can actually call that porn blue haze daylight—to drip into my veins. We're silent all the way up to Grafarvogur, like a hearse on its way to the graveyard up there, so close to the junkyard. Junkyard, graveyard. Same thing, really. Although the graveyard probably gets more visitors. And the garbage is all marked there. Marked with a cross. On the registry roll. Graveyard here, junkyard there. Coffins this way, garbage bags that way. Granddad to the left, the old VCR to the right. Guess the VCR must be in better shape than the old man. Souls and tapes. Tapes and souls. Kindly rewind after use. We give the graveyard a miss. Mom went yesterday, with a candle. A torch flickering on every grave. Very grave.

I always feel like a foreigner when I step into Elsa's kingdom. Maybe it's just too far away from the center of town; I even have problems with the local lingo. I'm Ahmed. I almost check my pockets for my passport as we climb the internally heated steps, half-worried that I'll be stopped at the check-in. That I might be frisked. The remote. Mom rings the bell, the door opens, and a welcoming band of three brats, led by a mongrel, comes blasting toward us, followed by Elsa.

"Oh, hiiiiiiii. Great to see you and happy Christmas! You're looking really smart, Hlynur!"

I let Mom do the interpreting.

"Yes, he got that shirt from a girlfriend, isn't it nice on him?"

"Yes, it's lovely, so what are you saying, has he finally got a girlfriend, then?"

"Yeah, right." I laugh. I'm being spoken of in the third person. I smile like a retard. Like a retard who has a new girlfriend.

"Great to see you, Hlynur dear," says Elsa, kissing me. That's the problem with one's "close" ones. They're too close.

"You're happy," I say.

"What?"

"You're looking happy."

"Happy, yeah . . . ha ha . . . Come on in."

Elsa isn't exactly Christmasy in that terraced-house uniform of hers—bet you the whole row wears that same tracksuit top, just needs some numbers on it: 22–28 Back Row, or whatever this street is called. And those three kids hanging in the doorway, scrutinizing me like little customs officials, with that dog of theirs: some fluffy Energizer thing. He sniffs around me with all the expertise of a canine junkie from narcotics.

I step on board, having removed my shoes. Looks like a full plane. A four-hour flight ahead of us. Nonsmoking. Elsa does her hostess bit, moving down the aisle with cups and cookies. Captain Magnús is reclined far back into his master of the house's chair, almost horizontal, armed with a remote and directly facing a TV set that stands like a Christmas tree in the corner, surrounded by a group of kids. TNT. Cartoon Network. Ted Turner and Jane Fonda (90,000). They're probably on their private yacht right now, celebrating their bare-breasted Christmas. Yeah. Bet they've both got gray hair below.

Ted and Jane. Dad's there, with Sara (45,000)—that could be entertaining—and Granny. Granny's a bit of a social problem. Should have croaked years ago, but somebody in the health system seems to be doing his utmost to keep her vegetating. Maybe they want her to do some stand-up at next year's Thorrablót at the rest home. I give her a kiss. She gets up for me, and her entire body starts to shake as she stretches out her hand to me. Looks like she's dancing to some hard-core techno. Yeah. Not bad, Granny. At last someone who can dance at 120 beats a minute. As I'm wobbling there with my vibrating granny, I miss Mom's greeting to Dad, but manage to catch a glimpse of his handshake with Lolla. Perfectly normal, it seems. Magnús's family occupies the entire sofa. His parents and a sister (2,000) in bright lottery outfits: three variations of Magnús's belly. Just sitting there like infants, like they've never seen anything of life, like the most daring thing they've ever done is pay a mortgage, like they've just been cloned from a DNA sample scooped out of Magnús's paunch. I shake their hands over the glass coffee table. Accidentally address the mother (2,500) as "sir." Magnús's sister's pubescent son looks strangely incongruous, looks like he's seven years older than the rest of them put together. A smooth operator, he sits on a spare chair beside them, with his arm draped over the back of the sofa: a manic-depressive terrorist, carefully guarding his family of hostages. I end up in a window seat, beside Mom and Lolla, opposite Dad, Sara, and Granny. I look for the safety belt to fasten it, but can't find it. Ah well. Besides, the only sign that seems to be on is the no-smoking sign. The sofa set is a brand-new leather monster, positioned at a rather odd angle in the room, by the wide windows, looking out into the garden. Like a shop-window display. We're sitting in a furniture shop, the twelve of us, gazing outside. It's a pretty drab still life: the white garden, the snowdrift in the barbecue corner, and the houses next door. Still, though. There's a slight flutter on one of those twigs over there. But it's not exactly what you'd call entertainment. Not captivating enough to sustain a silence.

Elsa: "So, then, what's the news?"

Mom: "Oh, same as always, you know."

Elsa: "How was it at your place yesterday?"

Mom: "We just had it really nice and cozy."

Elsa: "But, I mean, the weather. We had this dreadful wind up here."

Magnús's mother: "Yes, it was like a fully blown blizzard at our place."

Mom: "You don't say? It was so still on our side of town, barbecue weather, as Hlynur called it."

Elsa (laughs): "You don't say; is that what he said?"

Magnús (grinning): "So you were grilling yesterday, were you, Hlynur? The Christmas steak?"

Me (with an inane smile): "Yeah, yeah."

There's a sudden intermission. I feel like I've said something wrong. But hunger and insomnia are my real concerns. My stomach's like a broken-down radio stuck on search. I need coffee and cakes. Breakfast. I send a silent prayer to the coffee percolator gurgling in the kitchen and apologizing for the delay with a slight cough, like someone who has been occupying a toilet for too long. I try to keep myself awake by speculating on Sara. Yeah. She almost looks like Jane Fonda. The old wrinkled goddess. Yeah. Jane is the bottled version, Sara is the can. Sara is an ex–night queen, but now she runs the Rosenkrans Café. Dark hair and dark makeup, and a slightly haggard air—brushed under layers of makeup, or is that a sunlamp tan? I count 1,040 weekends (20 x

52) in her eyes—a glittering career stretching from the Glaumbaer Club to the Iceland Hotel ballroom—before I look away. Reckon Dad must be number 156. I heard her say in an interview once that she'd had well over a hundred. Hey. Wouldn't it be great if they all met in the swimming pool? Sara. Swimming pool. As for me. I've only slept with six. Embarrassing, really. Yeah. There's something wrong with me. Look at me. Sitting with my six in the hot pot, while Sara is surrounded by her swarm down at the deep end of the pool. And I wouldn't even want to be with my exes in the hot pot. I've never had anything over 30,000, which I'm told is the average price of a whore in Amsterdam. Ah well. Hofy was 40,000 in the beginning. "Why don't you just pay me for this?" she said. I stretch out on the sofa, both to switch to a more horizontal position and to check whether Dad has a blue rubber band with a locker key around his ankle. Too much reflection from the glass coffee table to see.

Mom: "Was your mother at your place, Hafsteinn?"

Dad: "She was, yeah, and Sara's brother."

Granny: "Huh? Where was I?"

Dad: "I was just telling her, you were at our place. You were at our place yesterday."

Granny: "Was I really? Was I there for long?"

Dad (smiling): "No, not really. We drove you home at about ten."

Granny: "Oh, that's good. I need my beauty sleep."

I picture Sara naked. No. I quickly dress her again. Her breasts need pumping. She's been driving on them for too long. Which is a drag, because I've heard about them, they were quite famous in her day. Greatest tits in town. I picture myself naked in front of her fully clothed. Reckon those earrings must be number 673. Her earlobes are beginning to show some wear and tear. "Where have all the earrings gone?" What was that song again? Elsa comes in with the coffee.

Mom: "Are those new cups?"

Elsa: "Yes, aren't they nice? We bought them in Boston this summer. Are you all right there, Lolla? Shall I get you a chair?"

Lolla: "No, no thanks, I'm fine."

Lolla sits between me and Mom. Thigh, thigh. Thigh, thigh.

Dad: "So how are things? Have you had much snow up there, Vagn?"

Vagn. That's his name, Vagn. Yeah. Magnús's dad's name is Vagn. Magnús Vagnsson.

Magnús's dad: "Yeah, probably just a little bit more than what you got down here."

Dad: "Is that right?"

Magnús's dad: "Otherwise, we've been very lucky this winter."

Dad: "Is that right, yeah?"

Magnús's dad: "Yes, and of course it's a whole new life now that I've got myself a jeep."

Dad: "Right, you bought a jeep, did you?"

Magnús's dad: "I did, yeah. Got the latest from Toyota and it's made all the difference to us."

Dad: "Yeah, big difference, is it?"

Magnús's dad: "Ah yeah, no question about it, especially when you're—"

A beeper suddenly sounds underneath all those layers of basketball sweatshirts that young kid has managed to put on, and the sofa family looks at him with terrified eyes. A message from above to proceed with the executions? The kid immediately kills the call and glances at the pager.

Magnús's sister: "Who is it?"

Kid: "Dad, I think."

Another silence. Everyone's thinking about that dad. Now everyone's picturing him holding a phone somewhere. A pay phone in the local jail, a car phone outside a closed-down Sunday café, a cell phone in a heavy-metal sound studio in Hafnafjördur . . .

Dad: "They're quite nifty, those new Japanese numbers."

Magnús's dad: "Yeah, they're pretty nifty, all right."

Nifty? You don't say. I laugh. A low-gear chuckle. Ho, hum. Coffee's too weak. Silence. We all look out into the garden. We're the furniture shop again. We watch the light as it slowly fades on the eastern horizon, witness the mountains in their final battle against the powers of darkness, a battle they're doomed to lose, heroic but doomed, about to be wiped off the map of the visible world . . .

What the hell am I saying? Where the hell do those sentences come from? Out of books. Never read again. Books are for block-heads. There are more ideas in one unsmoked cigarette than five hefty tomes of Sagas.

I look at Lolla. She looks back at me, silently mouthing if it's all right to smoke. I shake my head. Why did she come along? Volunteering for forced labor like that. She sticks out in here like a hand-rolled cigarette in a packet of Salems. I suddenly switch my gaze from Lolla to Dad. He gives me a look. A perfectly sober look. I ogle Sara again—sorry, Sara, sorry—and then glance over at the sofa. Magnús's family. Boing, boing, boing. These sort of people are best viewed in hot pots. At least then you'd only have to look at their heads and shoulders, with their fat paunches mercifully tucked away below the surface. I'm about to open my trap to ask them if they have a hot pot when Elsa appears behind me with some coffee.

Elsa: "More coffee, Hlynur?"

Me: "Yes, please."

Elsa: "You're very quiet, Hlynur. What have you got to say for yourself?"

Me: "How much is this sofa set?"

Elsa: "Hum? How much was this sofa set? God, I can't remember now. Magnús, can you remember? Why do you ask?"

Magnús: "Are you thinking of buying it, Hlynur?"

Me: "Yeah. It's a nifty sofa."

Magnús's mother: "Yes, I was just thinking that myself. What a nifty sofa it is."

Me: "Yeah. Really nifty. And really nifty to sit in. Too."

Magnús's mother: "Yes. And it's a nifty color as well."

Me: "Yeah. It's not exactly horrendous, is it?"

Magnús: "What's your offer, then?"

Me: "Well. I don't know."

Mom: "I think it might be slightly beyond your means, Hlynur dear."

Magnús: "He can pay for it in installments."

Elsa: "Magnús."

Magnús's sister: "What are you up to these days, Hlynur?"

Me: "Me?"

Magnús's sister: "Yes, you were in computers, right?"

Me: "In computers?"

Magnús's sister: "Yeah. Isn't that what you were saying, Elsa? That he was in computers."

Elsa: "Yes, or so I thought. Otherwise I never know what to say when people ask me what my brother does. What am I supposed to answer, Hlynur? What am I supposed to say you're doing?"

Me: "Nothing."

Elsa: "Nothing?"

Me: "Yeah."

Elsa: "I never know whether you're joking or not. . . ."

Everyone seems to be staring at me, but I can't seem to strike an ironic pose—was I joking?—and that word "nothing" seems to fill the air, blows up in front of me like a ginormous airbag. The leather squeaks as the family shifts uneasily on the sofa, searching for their life jackets under the seats. Elsa, the air hostess, tries to restore the calm by grabbing a pot of coffee:

"More coffee, anyone? Sara?"

Sara: "Yes, maybe just a drop."

The innocent sound of coffee being poured becomes unbearable in a silence like this, deafening. I look at the floor, searching for the lights that are supposed to lead you to the emergency exit: got to say something but Granny—Granny, the Alzheimer's champ— spurts out: "Hafsteinn, how was it at your house yesterday?"

Dad: "You were with us, Mom. It was really nice."

Granny: "Oh. So you'll collect me there, then, will you?"

Dad: "Hum?"

Granny: "What's the time? I have to go to bed early. I need my beauty sleep."

Dad: "Yes, but it's not that late yet. We've still got plenty of time."

Granny: "Right. And would you be so kind as to collect me then?"

Dad: "Yes, yes. You've got nothing to worry about."

Elsa: "Hey, here's an idea, have we shown you the video we took of the barbecue last summer? You haven't seen it, Dad, have you?"

Dad: "No, I don't think so."

Elsa orders Magnús out of his master-of-the-household chair. It's quite a sight to watch the psychologist hoisting himself up, pressing the lever on the side of the chair. It's been decided that we're going to watch this homemade video, then. But when Magnús, the cameraman, can't find the grill tape, it's decided that we're going to watch last Christmas's video instead, since apparently no one has seen it yet. Bit of a protest from the kids, who don't take too kindly to being interrupted in the middle of *Aladdin*. The TV is wheeled in front of the window, and the children bowleg toward the table to stuff their faces with the home-baked cookies, ignoring the two grannies who have secretly been competing for them with their laps. There are three of them. The youngest one is a girl, I seem to remember. But I wouldn't swear on it. Not without further inspection. But those two older ones are definitely boys. My maybe-five-year-old nephew is staring at me as if he were seriously thinking of suing me for abuse. The dog snuffles from under the table, sniffs my socks, and then sneezes away from them again. The short one laughs: "Frodi thinks your toes stink!" I try to take it as well as possible, bend over to take a cookie I don't want, and say: "I thought dogs were really into smelly toes." But you just can't shut these kids up, not unless you're holding a king-size bag of M&Ms. "He doesn't like the smelly toes of a smelly scumbag like you!" answers the nephew. The grannies shush and the mammies scold. OK, so I'm a smelly scumbag. Children never lie. I'm a stink bomb. Hlynur Björn, smelly bum bum. There's a string on the back of my neck. If someone pulls it, Sara will strip down to nothing but her bra and start to give me a blow job, and Lolla will sandwich my face between her breasts, and everything will be just fine. . . .

The tape's in, Magnús is in his chair, and it's Christmas again. Xmas, the rerun. Last year's Christmas Day videoed in this very room. Same guests, apart from Lolla. Shot from the master of the house's armchair. Some pretty shaky camerawork. He pans his family on the sofa, who are wearing the same lottery outfits. Voices can be heard offscreen:

Dad: "And how is it, Vagn? You bought a jeep, didn't you?"

Magnús's dad: "I did, yeah. Got the latest from Toyota and it's made all the difference to us."

Magnús's dad: "Ah yeah, it's a whole new life, a whole new life . . ."

I scan the sofa. Everyone smiling. I check on Mom and Lolla. They smile too, although Lolla's smile is more of a grin. Holy Kiljan. What the fuck's going on? "A whole new life?" Not exactly. I feel like Einstein having coffee with the Frankensteins. I'm Einstein drinking coffee with all the Frankensteins in the history of filmmaking. This whole crowd should be buried along with their home videos, like pharaohs with all their regalia, so that they can watch themselves again on the other side. Or maybe we're already on the other side? Who knows, maybe it would be better that way. I mean, since we have to put up with these family dos anyway, maybe we could just as well watch them on videotape. At least we wouldn't have to worry about where our next line was going to come from. Anyway, it seems to have been a bit livelier last year. The Xmas of '94 was a pretty good year, so why don't we just celebrate that one for the next ten years? Still, though, ten minutes into it and I'm already dozing off. Glance at Granny. Even she's yawning, although she should be immune to it all by now, after all those years in Alzheimerland. My head's about to drop out of my hands, but I give a start when I suddenly hear Magnús's sister's voice on the tape: "What are you up to these days, Hlynur?" I don't believe it. And there I am in another shirt muttering some bullshit about computers. And then the dog comes and sneezes at my socks . . .

I nod off.

I dream of a hot pot. I'm sitting in it with the family. We're sitting in it on the leather sofa. We're all fully dressed. I fart and the whole pot erupts into a loud whirlpool of bubbles and bobbles. Elsa asks me to do it again, she's going to make some more coffee. Mom sits beside me in a wet dress and stands up . . .

I wake up.

Lolla is standing. We're leaving. I raise myself from the dead. Nobody seems to have noticed my coma. Or what? Mom slings her bag around her shoulder. The goodbyes have started. To shorten the ritual as much as possible—the traditional fifteen minutes of shifting feet in the hallway, and the trip into the kitchen to find that salad recipe, and all that yak about how we must definitely meet again very soon—I head for the john. I have to slip between the sofa and some palmy thing and accidentally rub up against the back of Magnús's father's head. Very unfortunate, as it happens. As usual, I woke up with a hard-on, and I've just brushed it against the back of my in-law's thin-haired head. "Oh, sorry," I say. Vagn glances back at me, and for one brief moment I catch a faint glimpse of respect in those Toyota eyes of his as he answers: "That's all right, sorry about that." Maybe that's the only way to impress these guys, by sticking a stiff dick into the back of their necks.

Elsa and Magnús's john. He uses Paco Rabanne. An electric razor. Lazy bastard. I feel like shaking this hard-on off, but the sight of my sister's Tampax packet seems to drain all my blood away. Elsa Always Ultra Nice. I sit on the bowl and wait for him to droop and shrivel so that I can switch him back into pissing mode again.

The dick. Split personalities. Dangling and erect. Like the difference between a man when he's drunk and when he's sober. My man, one moment he's all puffed up, full of crazy ideas and revving to go, but the day after he's all coy and withdrawn and just lies there, deflated, on those two shriveled apricots, recalling the previous night with horror, and can do no more than piss transparent Coke.

"To piss sitting down." Some ramboid guy said to me once that that was only for old ladies. He'd obviously never heard of hard-ons. Elsa's towel hanging on the wall. I smell it. Very similar to Mom's scent, with that extra touch of Johnson's Baby. Flush. I want to steal something, but am out of ideas after three hours of non-smoking. Until I find Elsa's pills in the cupboard. If I take one away, that'll be another grandchild for Mom. A good deed? Maybe Hlynur Björn, Jr.? Yeah. And on his confirmation day I'll march up the aisle, as the good old uncle, with the pill in a cotton-padded box, having had it mounted into a beautiful necklace inscribed with some appropriate words in verse. I might even make a speech, enlighten them on the origins of this confirmation boy, with some philosophical conjectures thrown in, an ingenious comparison between half a gram of white matter and the sanctity of human life. Then I'll bestow the gift, as my confirmed nephew rushes into my arms in some ghastly suit, with a hairy upper lip and two hidden pimples on his forehead. And he'll be about to cry, "Thank you! You saved my life!" when he'll realize that's not quite appropriate enough and say: "You created me!"

I feel like God Almighty here as I press a pill out of the pack. I stick it into the breast pocket of Hofy's shirt and wash my hands, after a slight struggle with the tap.

I meet Elsa out in the hall. She laughingly asks: "What, were you talking to yourself in the bathroom?"

"No. There was a slight misunderstanding with the tap. I thought it might be one of those new high-tech things you have to talk to, and say 'water' and 'hot' to and all that."

Elsa gives off one of her hearty sister laughs. She's quite cute, really.

"There's no one like you, Hlynur."

She's quite cute, my sister is. And then she drags me back into the bathroom to show me how the taps work. I just need practice, that's all. I think they're Sony. Then she smiles and our eyes meet in the mirror of the bathroom cabinet and I freeze this frame: there we are, brother and sister. Take away the glasses and we're identical. Karen (25,000) and Richard Carpenter. The only difference between us is our gender. My face might be broader than hers, but it has the same features, except that hers are smaller and thinner, minus the lips and the eyes. Hey. Women get all the best senses. Taste and vision. All we ballbearers get is smell and hearing. Ah well. End up as old geezers with ginormous noses and ears, blood-gorged sausages, and flappy lobes, rampant with bushy undergrowth. I saw on a program once that these are the only spots where hair continues to grow, all the way into the depths of the morgue. Some people die of suffocation, they've got so much hair up their nostrils.

Our eyes meet in the mirror that conceals "The Mystery of the Missing Pill." Yeah.

When we come out again, Sara and Lolla are hand in hand. Mom's saying goodbye to Dad.

Go on, then, show us a French kiss, just for old times' sake, just for me and Elsa, I think to myself.

Elsa: "And you'll be staying with Mom over the New Year, won't you?"

Lolla: "Yeah, for a while."

Elsa: "Well, maybe you'll come over on New Year's Eve, yourself and Hlynur, since Mom is going up north."

Lolla gives me a glance. I say no, no, no with my glasses. Which is actually a very difficult thing to do. She says: "Yeah, maybe."

As Elsa kisses me that old Christmas favorite starts to reverberate from the jukebox of my mind. Sung by Eiríkur Hauksson and Halla Margrét (125,000): My Christmas gift to you this year / cannot be measured, it's so dear / for you're the very one who rules my dreams. I hit a false note.

We Subaru our way back into town. Christmas darkness is somehow more bearable. Just like holy water tastes better than normal water. Best cure for a hangover, they say. They're in the front, the female couple. And Hlynur Björn in the back, the six-year-old with the stubble.

Hlynur: "Well, then, Lolla. Are you having second thoughts about joining the family?"

Lolla: "The family?"

Hlynur: "Yeah. You're part of the family now, Lolla. Those were your initiation rites. You did quite well."

Lolla: "Oh yeah?"

Hlynur: "Yeah, Sara was forced to sing 'All Is Quiet in Bethlehem' last year. Pity the tape ran out before she did."

Mom: "'O Little Town of Bethlehem.'"

Hlynur: "Yeah, whatever. They made her sing that. 'O Little Town of Bethlehem.'"

Mom (to Lolla, but looking down Miklabraut): "It's just the way he is."

I don't quite pick up that last sentence, and lean forward to stick my head between the seats.

Hlynur: "Huh? What d'you say?"

Mom: "Nothing. I was just talking to Lolla."

Hlynur: "What's all this secretiveness about? Is there something between you two?"

Mom: "No, how do you mean? . . ."

Lolla (grinning at me): "Apart from you, that is . . . right now."

Mom: "Weren't you saying you wanted to find a shop, Hlynur? To buy some fags?"

Hlynur: "They're all closed now, aren't they?"

Once Mom gets something into her head . . . A shop she will find. We, or to be more precise, Mom, tries three shops in town before we end up out in Nes. She forces me to get those cigarettes.

It should be mentioned that there's slippery ice in front of the shop. A girl (6,000) comes toward me, like an old Prince song. She says hi. I ad-lib something until I realize it's Thorbjörg or Thor-something and I've slept with her. Those were the days, my friend. When she was 25,000 and sat on the floor at the Safari club. She was number two. Not bad, really. She blurts out some spiel about a fish-breeding course in Norway, and considering these minus 5 degrees out here, I should be freaking out, but instead I listen to her lecture with surprising patience. With one eye on Lolla in the car. Her lips are moving. All of a sudden I remember that it was this Thor-something who gave me my first blow job. My second-last blow job, as it happens. Which is why I'm being so considerate to her. When a girl's given you a blow job, you somehow have more respect for everything that comes out of her mouth. Even if it happens to be all about how she takes care of "fish eggs and stuff . . ." I even laugh about it with her.

Then some shit starts falling from the sky and we say "Merry Christmas!" and I'm suddenly sucked into a festive mood again as I march into the shop. Get my Prince from the wench behind the counter (75,000). Then hum "Purple Rain" under the hail on the way back to the car. I see Mom and Lolla are still talking until I throw myself into the backseat. Then silence. I wait for them to ask me who that girl was so that I can proudly tell them all about my first blow job, but neither of them says a word. Mom turns on the radio. Choirgirls. We sit in a chorus of silence.

*　　*　　*

Night. Back in my room. What are they feeling guilty about? There's an artificial strain in their voices when they call me in to play cards. I don't play cards. I don't read books. I don't watch serials. (Not if you have to follow them. Apart from *Star Trek* and *The X-Files*.) All that fiction stuff. Not my thing. It's reality that I want, fact, not fiction. Only read newspapers. I only watch movies to see what the actors are up to, not the characters. I don't play cards, but they won't give in.

We play Stationary, some brand-new New Age gimmick Lolla got as a Christmas present. Like Pictionary and Actionary except that you have to remain "stationary," and just stare into your opponent's eyes to coax an answer out of him. Bloody hopeless. They wipe the floor with me. There's something between them.

Mom is going up north between Christmas and New Year. To her sister Sigrún's (4,000) place in Hvammstangi. Up where the other granny lives (I won't put a price on her, if you don't mind; she's my granny, for Chrissakes), the Danish granny, that is. Still tottering around in her rest home, she's already packed all of her eighty years into photo albums and has long been ready for departure. The rest home. An air terminal for the terminally old. Everyone waiting to be beamed up to heaven. But flights are constantly being postponed. I just couldn't face dragging my ass all the way up there to guest-star in yet another family video. I did go there once, though. Well, drove through it with some pals on our way to a rock gig in Húnaver one summer holiday. Granny was so shriveled up you really had to step back and squint your eyes at her wood carving of a face to be able to make out any kind of expression. And strain your ears to understand her accent. Else, her name. The old dear's tongue had finally given up converting Danish thoughts into Icelandic words. Sigrún was OK, though; fried a lot of eggs for us and invited us to watch an old recording of the *New Year's Eve Comedy Special*. But there was such a gamey stink in the air. Dry sweat on the sofa. Like sitting under someone's armpit. Maybe people just work too much up there. We ended up sitting in the car, listening to the Clash, until she was ready with the eggs.

Just me and Lollypop at home. We take out a video. Order pizza. Smoke. Nice and cozy. Rosy and Guildy drop by. She answers for me when Hofy calls. We even go to the bar together.

"Is that your girlfriend? Her?"

"No, she's my new stepfather."

Then she vanishes into the Reykjavík party darkness and doesn't come home. I watch the box into the early hours and have zapped myself all the way down to Channel 68: amateur uphill cycling in Spain, somewhere in the Basque region. A rerun from last summer. The anchor interviews the contestants as they pass the finish line. Breathless answers. No sign of Lolla. Of all the languages I don't understand, Spanish is the least irritating. Yeah, they sure know how to cycle up a hill, those Basques. I saunter out of my room. I've turned into Mom. Waiting up for her Lolla. I peep into her room. Unruffled bedclothes, a shapeless, tattered old bag on the floor, T-shirts draped over the chair, lip balm on the table. Mott the Hoople. I feel like a thief as I pussyfoot into the room and pick up her bag. No. More like a private eye: Who is she? Who is Lolla? Her leather bag is like the sack in that old folktale about Farmer Jón, the sack that contained his soul. The contents of hers: a tattered scarf, a brush, more lip balm, a book, another small book, phone numbers and addresses, and a few snapshots stuck between the pages. Four flashes of Lolla's life. A lezzie trip to Dublin, with some Amazonian-looking women in a restaurant, Lolla wearing shades at a party, laughing Lolla hugging some Bartman (actually more of a cross between Bart and O. J. Simpson). Then Lolla and Mom, a picture taken in some kind of classroom, some kind of course atmosphere. A lezzie course in the Faroes? Both with their hands behind their backs. A slight gap between them. People always laugh in photographs nowadays. Beam at the flash. People used to be serious in the olden days. Because they knew this was the only picture that would ever be taken of them, and it was so expensive. What'll they make of us in five hundred years' time? "Yes, that's my great-great-grandfather at a party." Try finding a photograph of yourself where you're not grinning from ear to ear like some historical idiot. No matter how hard you try, it's always: "Hlynur! Give us a smile! Don't be so serious!" These are cheap

times we live in. No one's going to erect a statue of you in front of
the Parliament building with that inane grin of yours. Something
stirs. Feel a rush to my head. My heart pounds at the thought. Prick
up my ears. Pulsations. Nothing. I take a closer look at the book: a
ticket to a U2 concert in Dublin. Cool one, Lolla. And memos, written diagonally across the page in neat embroidered patterns. They
always have such steady handwriting, women:

*Talk to Berglind, get C from Nonni, 551 1320 health shop,
meeting 9 a.m., lift from Geir,* then some soy recipe, a yoga
timetable, and a list of all of Bob Marley's records. Yeah. There's
a touch of the old Rasta in Lolla.

Talk to Berglind. And that's it. Nothing more than that. Look at
me, sitting here in the dark, snooping through her soul. Yeah,
those Basques certainly know how to cycle up a hill.

I wake up alone in the house. What's happened to her? Got lucky?
And what about Mom? I'm getting jealous, on her behalf. Nobody
two-times my ma! Good job we're here to stand up for her, me and
my man. So maybe there is nothing between them after all. Nah.
Cheerios. Milk's finished. I'm filled with an inexplicable sense of
despair, standing here in front of this open fridge. Somehow feel
totally alone. Not even milk . . . I stare into the fridge. Like a mir-
rored image of myself. Cold and empty, and the lights come on only
when you open the door. Otherwise ice-cold purring darkness.
They're like that, fridges. Deceitful. Nobody ever knows how they
feel inside. They stand there, all silent, in the corner, and put up
a brave face, shining in all their splendor. But inside they're full of
cold darkness and sorrow. Oh no, no matter how often you try to
creep up on them to catch them off-guard, they're always one
step ahead of you, and the second you open that door it's all
lights and smiles. I'm a fridge. You have to be real careful when
you're moving a fridge around. Got to let it stand for a good twenty-
four hours before you even plug it into the wall. I don't like being
moved. Like that time they moved me into the country. Totally
unplugged at first. Didn't speak for days. Couldn't understand a
word. That farmer blabbing on in that animal lingo of his. Only
started to understand him once he started talking to the animals.

Cursing at them all the time. It was either the blithering hellhound or the mommyfocking cows or the devilish sheep or the sodding cat or the fucking whores (hens), except for the horses, they commanded respect. Just like bar life, really. You bad-mouth everyone but those you want to ride.

I'm heading for the shop when I suddenly realize it's Sunday. Even more depressing. Sundays are the worst. So empty. As blank as a moron's forehead. Sundays are just so passé, a remnant from the times when everyone used to work. A relic from our slavery days. As for the Sunday between Christmas and New Year's Eve . . . That's like altar wine diluted with holy water. I stroll up Skólavördustígur with that grumpy Steve Martin look, probably quite funny to watch, except no one's watching. Without a cameraman we're nothing. Nothing. In future societies we'll all have our own cameraman. Seriously. I must have my own show. I tried to once, sent in my idea, absolutely brilliant, I thought, and really low-budget: *Watching TV with Hlynur Björn*. Just me holding the remote. Zapping around. Never got an answer.

A motherless child hunting for milk. Finally find a carton in the corner shop. I say hi meaning bye to a familiar face from the K-bar. A real bye type. I can't stand people. Why is that? I just can't stand them. Not "live," at any rate.

Lolla still hasn't come home yet. I can't take it. It's one thing to want to be on your own, another to be left on your own. Abandoned. Just forget her. You can never trust a woman like her, anyway. A dark-haired she-devil with a he-devil hidden in her crotch. She's out there somewhere. Out there flaunting her bi-ness. Up in some crummy loft somewhere, high on some Mary Warner, Marleying around with a spliff in her pussy. Lolla. *Talk to Berglind*. Was there something more to that? She's trying to get me to miss her. Trying to take over my mind. OK. Out of my mind. Get out of my mind. I mouse my way on to the Net. Katarina. Beautypest. I type to her:

Hello

What comes after hello? What can you say to a Hungarian working-class girl, grinding her way through college in Trabant

City? I draw a blank. Hello . . . I stare at that hello, that word on the blue screen, what am I doing? It's like a distress signal in the middle of the ocean. It's got hell in it. Hell-O! O Hell. A raft on a blue screen. Hello and then a vast ocean of light. . . . I push that word out into the ocean, a solitary unmanned hello fading into an ocean of light, look, there it goes . . . like a granny dispatched to heaven.

I'm not quite myself somehow. Not quite me. I press the remote at random and watch, or rather allow the box to watch me. Channel 53: car ads. A white Nissan drives down a winding road and vanishes into a pine forest. A Nissan Pathfinder. I feel like a white Nissan driving down a winding road, vanishing into a pine forest. A Nissan Pathfinder. I'm a white Nissan in the forest. But no Pathfinder. I drive through the Gothic German forest to the sound of a symphony orchestra, this lease-purchase technical wonder, with all its belts and brakes, this reclining-seat-and-halogen-headrest-power-steered thing . . . and I'm almost on the point of stooping to phone Hofy. In fact, I'm halfway through dialing her number when I suddenly remember her dad's a dentist. I try Thröstur. Thor answers. Don't get much out of him. I kill the next twenty minutes snooping around the apartment. Mom seems to have forgotten to pay the rent for this part of the hallway. Oh no, I forgot. She owns this apartment. I'm so out of myself that I'm even rooting through Elsa's old record collection in the living room, which says everything. Well, actually, I do do that sometimes. There are a few tracks in here that occasionally beg to be played, and sometimes they're the only thing for it. Mainly slow tunes, really, like "Hello," for example, written and performed by Lionel Richie. I slip it on the turntable and writhe on the floor. Home Alone Dancing. Piano fingers, slow foreplay, and then the lyrics: Hello! Is it me you're looking for? several times and then the solo. A pretty awesome guitar solo. A heartrending guitar solo. It's as if the notes are being sucked back as soon as they're plucked from the strings. Or as if he were picking berries with that guitar. This solo sounds like every single organ in your body is being stirred. Great song. Realized that last year. Got it on the brain. Couldn't stand it before. Are you somewhere feeling lonely? Or is someone lovin' you? She was blind, that girl, in the video.

And a real eyeful, too. 120,000. She molded a bust of Lionel Richie in clay, with his big nose and lips. Dear old ugly Richie, where are you now? Lying in a four-poster bed in a Beverly Hills bungalow, waiting for a song that might never come. I put the song back on and pump up the volume. Sit on the sofa and light a cigarette. Hum along between drags. A blind girl. Maybe that's not such a bad idea. Probably better if she were deaf too, though. Wouldn't that be the ideal woman? Put the song back on.

I'm listening to Lionel's "Hello" for the eighteenth time in a row, slouched on the sofa with drooping eyelids, when the blind girl finally steps into the room . . . with her beauty spot, jolting me out of my Hollywood-sincerity mode and back into my Icelandic cool. I stretch toward the volume button and switch on an all-purpose smile . . . and open my eyes like a fridge full of light:

"Hi."

"Hi."

She dumps herself in an armchair and puts her feet up on the table. We both wait for her breasts to stop heaving under her blue sweater. Or I do, anyway. I look at them. Don't. Those are Mommy's breasts. Those breasts belong to her.

Lolla gasps and then asks: "How are you?"

I can't answer that. You can't answer a question like that. How are you supposed to answer a question like that? I just smile and we decide to cut the small talk. She smiles too. She tries again:

"What's the news?"

"Welcome home."

"Yeah . . . Thanks."

"Where . . . Did you go to a party?"

"Yeah. We went back to Ásdís's place and she insisted on dragging me along to Akranes, a friend of hers was having a birthday party. It was OK. What about you? What have you been doing?"

"Me? Just stayed in, listened to records and stuff."

"I see. Is this the B-side of Hlynur Björn, I wonder?"

"Must be."

"Got a fag?"

"Yeah."

We're serious again, as people are wont to be when they've got fire in their hands. There you go, Lolla dear, have a smoke. Do you good after your trip up to Akranes. Picture your breasts slowly undulating to the sway of the waves on the ferry. Hey. Cool video. Swaying breasts on a ship. Just that. The sea is flesh. Woman is an ocean. And me the aquaphobic landlubber with the water wings.

"Did you take the ferry?"

"Yeah. Have you ever been to Akranes?"

"Me? No, only been down to the pier."

"That far, huh?"

"Yeah."

"And what about Kópavogur? Ever been to Kópavogur?"

"No. Oh, hang on, yeah, I think I ended up there at a party once."

"You never go anywhere?"

"No."

"What are you really like?"

"I'm . . . perfect."

"You're a monk. You're such a monk. A monk in Mommy's monastery."

"Yeah, in a mommystery."

"There's something cute about that. You're such a kid, really."

"Yeah."

"And what's the plan? How do you see your future?"

"Don't know. In an old folks' home trying to get it up in front of a video."

"What about that girl?"

"Hofy?"

"Yeah. Haven't you got some plans with her?"

"Nah. She's too much of a dentist's assistant type, but not clinical enough."

"What's so bad about that? I used to be a dentist's assistant."

"Yeah, that's not what I mean. I mean, she's always spouting all these feelings into your face instead of just giving you a good mouthwash."

"You can't stand feelings."

"No."

"Except for Lionel Richie's . . ."

We both smile and she adds: "Put him on again. Let me hear it."

I'm not too keen on the idea, but do. "Hello" breaks out again, but sounds completely different now. What a crappy song. What a load of schmaltz. I'm sitting there like I wrote it myself. I smile inanely at Lolla, who smiles back, but not quite as inanely. My face grows hotter with each drag. Very little smoke seems to be coming out of me. Feel like I've got Lolla sitting inside me, her cigarette a glowing little beauty spot. Feel a burn inside every time she inhales. This has got to be my most pathetic moment of the year. Not many moments of it left, thank God.

I take the garbage out. Yeah. New Year's Eve. The last day of a year that's already started to rot. There's already a burnt smell in the air, even though the crackers haven't been fired yet, that singed odor. Our last day on the grill. The sky is a nicotine yellow. Moldering clouds. Sour rain, if it were raining. Stale polluted air. A stagnant lumpy gunky sea. Like everything's on the last day of its shelf life. Everything on its last legs. The streets are littered with the backlog of twelve months of disappointments, the sleeping policemen slide into irreversible comas. The cracks in the ice, our shattered hopes. The dirty old snowdrifts like moldy dreams. New Year's Eve is a condensed year, 364 days squeezed into one, vacuum packed.

I lower the bag, the year, into the bin, the coffin. Where are the garbage men today? When will those undertakers come to take these old days to their final place of rest? I'm getting sentimental here, with just a few inches to the finish line. Lyrical. Rhapsodical. Maybe cos I'm in these weird slippers I suspect Dad left behind. I even look at the tree in the garden. I stand and look at the tree in the garden. The tree stands in the garden showing its ten fingers to the heavens and, with the aid of some special effects kindly provided by the film industry, they turn into ten burnt knuckles: black sogging bony twigs, the singed skeleton of a tree. And a black cat suddenly leaps into the garden and slowly develops at my feet, like a Polaroid. Animals on New Year's Eve. What do they make of all these fireworks? Dogs have to be sedated in their beds or driven out into the country. Do they remember their last injection? An animal's sense of time. Are they on some kind of Muslim calendar? The year is much longer for them. Animal psychology, is that what it's come to? Yeah. Their species is moving up the evolutionary ladder. *Memoirs of a Dog from Húsafell,* interviews conducted by Gestur Thórlindsson. Yeah, we've all seen those documentaries with horses complaining about their traumatic foalhoods. I take a good look at this black tomcat. All of a sudden, it's like he's not a cat anymore, but a baby who fell into a fire, got singed black and lost all his fingers and toes, and most of his nose and chin, but still has the whites of his eyes. What. Yeah. A burnt smell in the air. The flames of purgatory? All that bible-babble still inside me. What's happening? No, New Year's Eve ain't for animals. This is a purely *Homo sapiens* thing. Thor isn't likely to be in a very celebratory mood tonight. Thröstur and Marri are throwing a party.

New Year's Eve is a mini apocalypse. The pocket edition of doomsday. A dress rehearsal for the real thing. Men face their final judgment and ridicule . . . on the *New Year's Eve Comedy Special.* We fire rockets into space and try to imagine that all the planets are exploding, that the whole galaxy is falling apart. Comets come whizzing toward us, blazing suns falling, suspended on parachutes, the last fireball crashes to earth and then that's it, it's all over, the end of time.

But, viewed through a telescope on Saturn, it just looks like a few beard hairs sprouting out of the earth's face in fast motion.

Saw a program about meteorites on the Discovery Channel the other day. Apparently, space is full of the things, and zillions of state budgets ago one of them even struck a beach in Mexico. A rock about the size of Reykjavík. And the earth, which was just one massive Jurassic Park at the time, got it right in the face like a pellet from a gun. The meteorite sank into the earth's cheek, but didn't pierce it, and our good old planet—which was still only a young virgin at the time, with an unviolated ozone layer—survived, but only just. The dinosaurs took a final curtain call and ran for the nearest natural science museum. (Probably just as well. Or we'd all be four-footed vegetarians with long necks and E.T. faces.) That's what they said in the program—some thin-haired cosmologist in a lab in Kansas (thin hair like a stratosphere over that bald head of his)— that space was full of meteorites that burn up in the atmosphere every day, just small ones, but that a big one could hit us any time, tomorrow or in a million years. And that could mean the big end. The only solution is to blast them off their trajectories in time, nuke the bastards. The only problem being that there aren't enough astronomers glued to their telescopes on meteorite watch. About as many as you'll find at the immigration desk at Keflavík Airport. They screened footage of what could happen, footage that was taken last year when a beaut of a meteorite walloped Jupiter and scarred its face with a black spot. They showed us some American college kids watching it in a live broadcast from Jupiter in a real party atmosphere, flinging their arms around each other, like soccer fans, when the 100-megaton meteorite whammed into the surface. Americans are twats. Assholes. Overlubricated assholes. So what if they've got the best technology and satellites . . . Just you wait and see what it feels like to get a 100-megaton suppository up your ass. Try to show some respect.

The universe is nothing but a shower of pellets out of the big-bang gun. And the earth is a ptarmigan lazily flying through the air, about to trade in its seasonal camouflage. As if that will change anything. All of a sudden I feel like I'm clinging to the edge, standing here in these treacherous slippers, on top of this slippery globe, rapidly spinning out of control as it whirls through the war zone. An old woman in a wheelchair, slowly moving through the streets of Sarajevo, from one target to the next.

I go back in. The radio: "What was the most memorable moment of the year?" I start thinking about the pill I took out of Elsa's pack. I feel bad. What was I thinking of? I find it in the side pocket of my leather jacket, a tiny white speck, a minuscule atom between my fingers. I scrutinize it. Hold it before me, like Mel Gibson in *Hamlet* holding up that skull and talking to it in his highfalutin English, saying how incredible it was to think that this used to be a really funny guy, and I feel just like him, just like Mel, with all these fancy Icelandic subtitles flickering on my chest, except it's the other way around: I'm talking to the death that precedes life, the obstacle blocking its path: a tiny white ball manufactured in a lab somewhere, 0.5 grams of uranium, designed to nuke my sister Elsa's ovaries, to protect herself from the meteorite shower of Magnús's spunk. Alas, poor Yorick, behold this speck. No bigger than the dot on an *i* of a name that'll never be. It's absurd. This is life. Our lives are worth nothing more than this forgotten pill, and yet everyone's out there trying to turn this thing into something meaningful and eternal. Divine intervention or blind chance? Wonder or blunder? Yeah. Me. Introducing in the role of God: Hlynur Björn. I clasp the pill between my fingers, holding it up to my eye, to see if I can discern a facial expression, a twitch in the mouth or a smile. Yeah. Smile now if you can, smile to your god, you pathetic little speck.

Maybe I should phone her, take the pill back to her? No, too late. Five days gone now. She's already missed a day. But she must have realized, she's always so meticulous about these things, being a nurse and all that, but still. Elsa standing in front of the bathroom cabinet on Christmas evening, ready for bed, just one thing left to do, no, hey . . . have I already taken it today? And then into bed . . . and what? Not much of a chance of the psychologist getting it up, I mean, he can barely get his body up off the chair. Nah, they must be past all that by now, like everyone else who's given up smoking. "No Fucking Area." Maybe that was their New Year's resolution last year: "Try to cut down on fucking." It's a sin to screw, it's a sin to smoke. Everything that's good is bad for you. Everything that's bad is good. All this what's good, what's bad stuff. Original sin has plagued us all the way from Adam and Eve. And Noah, the lover of all animals, somewhere in the background, about to sail off again on his umpteenth journey. Like a bouncer sifting through a line in front of a club entrance: this one . . . and this one, no, not you . . . And the second they pull out to sea, he goes straight for the minibar, long bored with the missus, having taken her on more than two thousand Mediterranean cruises, so he's started to abuse the animals instead, committing adultery with the antelopes, necking with the giraffes, who howl with divine lust across the horizon as they sway to the swing of the waves, until Noah finally loses control and shipwrecks on Mount Ararat. But she's on the Pill.

Elsa, I mean. Feel bad. And it'll come back to haunt me, I know. They'll make me baby-sit. Maybe it'll be mongoloid? Holy Lax. All of a sudden I get the feeling that somewhere out there in distant space there's a meteorite—seen through a telescope, about the size of a pill—traveling at a light speed of approximately 100 watts, slowly falling toward my head. Doomsday.

"At the stroke of midnight . . ." echoes in my mind as I go out to the shop. They play minigolf, those guys on meteorite watch, kills time. Quite apt, really. Knocking white globes into black holes. Somehow it's always better to be sent out to the shops than to have to go of one's own accord. Like being sent out into space. Yeah. Definitely some weariness in the air. A vacuum. A couple of astronauts cross my path, complete with moon boots and all. Sliding down the slippery sidewalks of Reykjavík. In slow motion. I try some moon steps. Get a blast of déjà vu. As I reach the corner of Bergthórugata and Frakkastígur, just in front of Hallgrím's Church, I get the following feeling: I've been here before, we're back to where we started last year. The earth has come full circle and, as I breathe in the air, I can feel that same old spacey fragrance in my nostrils. I'm just a small nose revolving around the sun.

Back home some unpeeled planets are boiling in the pot and Lolla is pissing about, trying to make white sauce for the first time in her life. Cold smoked lamb, Mom's legacy. Mom is of the last generation that can cook. Then it'll be a world full of Lollas with their women's rights. Can't even make a decent cup of coffee. She tries to open a jar of red cabbage, but soon gives up and hands it over to me. Women. And then they have the cheek to ask for equal pay. Yeah. Mom will take all her recipes to the grave, all that knowledge is doomed to fade, she'll just leave a cold leg of smoked lamb on the coffin lid, and meatballs in the fridge for us to "just stick in the microwave." Smoked meat will keep for a long time, but in a hundred years from now, no one will know how to make white sauce. Our only hope is that Domino's won't disappear. Or there'll be a famine in this country. I buy Coke and salsa. Icelandic food is utterly tasteless. And when the only reason you eat is to be able to smoke afterward, the cigarette always tastes better if you've lubricated your throat with a little bit of hot sauce first.

We eat alone, just the two of us. Managed to wriggle out of the Elsa do. And Ahmed has forsaken us. Didn't take him long. A week into Christmas and he's already shacked up with some girl, so he's eating with his new in-laws tonight, a respectable family of electricians up in Mosfells town who want to get some nose into their genes. They're obviously not into men with the gift of the gab, these Icelandic girls. More Muslims, less talk. It must be nice to live with a man like that. "Very good" in the mornings and "no problem" when he walks in on her at night to find her in bed with her ex-boyfriend.

We eat in the living room, watching the annual review of domestic news. I realize some stuff's been happening. Mom phones from the north and asks about the white sauce. Then talks to Lolla, and Lolla says: "Your little boy? He's been very quiet and well behaved. . . ." Lolla's mother (5,000, judging by her photo) calls. Lolla's mom lives in Denmark, went shopping there twenty years ago and never came back. I hear candlelight in her voice, as I'm about to hand the phone over to her daughter. Sounds phony somehow, like all Icelanders who've spent too much time living abroad, like a twenty-year-old reel shot by the Tourist Board, hackneyed turf-scented phrases from a faded 1974 Icelandair brochure, with a picture of the year's Miss Iceland in traditional dress on the cover. A touch of schnapps in the accent. Good morning, Vietnam. Lolla's mom also asks about the white sauce.

Elsa phones to ask about the white sauce. It seems to be improving with each phone call. She delivers a brief lecture on the New Year's hats she's bought. Dad phones to ask about a party. The old man. Pissed already? After a slight hitch I tell him about the party at Thröstur and Marri's (could be interesting if he were to bring Sara along), and tell him Thor is dying to meet him. They have a lot in common. Dad says he'll see what Sara says. See what she says.

I watch Lolla laughing at the *New Year's Eve Comedy Special*. Icelandic humor really sucks. Phone. Uncle Elli. Who else would call me in the middle of the *Comedy Special*?

"Do you think it's funny? Is that what you call comedy? Just look at it . . . are you looking at it?"

He's unusually angry. The hunchback. Yeah. Sounds like he's calling me from Notre Dame.

"Where are you?" I ask.

"I'm here on Langholtsvegur, I've got a TV here in the front seat, fuckin' hell, missed two rides because of this, I can only take three at a time, see, and then it's not even bloody funny. . . ."

"Why didn't you just get someone to tape it for you?"

"Tape it? Does this look like something that should be taped to you?"

He's better than the *Comedy Special*. I try to get more out of him:

"And how do you see the new year?"

"New year. It'll be an old year soon enough, like all the others. I mean, I don't mind them taking the piss out of politicians, but as I say, as long as it's funny, I mean, it's got to be funny, and this just isn't funny. I just don't think this is funny."

At the end of the show we look out the window to see if the year has ended yet. Me whiskey. She gin. They've started firing. I nip into the john for a quick wank. That's a good old tradition of mine, call it superstition, but I want to ring the old year out of him, clear the tube and start the new year on an empty tank. I pop my cork, shooting the last seeds of the year into the air, as good as any fireworks display. Sobers me up a bit. Lolla is out on the steps by the time I'm standing in front of the TV in the living room again. I watch the number of the year as it fades in the middle of the screen. She calls on me to come out. Slight dilemma. I prefer to follow the event on TV, more convincing somehow. I wait for the year to die. "1996" slowly emerges onto the center of the screen in a pattern of white dots, and I go out onto the steps to the deafening gong of church bells and collective hysteria. I make a point of kissing her on the mouth, in a bright red glow. Happy New Year! They should divide leap year's day and spread it over four years. Grant us some limbo time around New Year's. Twenty-four divided by four makes six. That would give us a six-hour break from time. From midnight till six in the morning. Hey, yeah.

A pause in which everyone could do what they wanted. With the meter turned off. That's the problem with time. Never stops. You've just completed 365 days of galley slavery and they're already throwing you into the next ship.

We stand there with our glasses on the steps, Lolla with a sparkler and me with a cigarette, which I later flick into the garden, the only rocket you'll see from me this year. I want to go in, I'm cold, as always, when I'm outside. Besides, Mr. Chirpy from over the way might walk over for a kiss and a chat. But Lolla wants to stick around longer to draw in the new year. A breeze yawns past: 1996 oozes out of the darkness, blowing across the city. They say nature is eternal, and pays no heed to time, but still. Maybe we've been on this planet for too long. Nature is like an old reptile that used to be wild in its youth, but gradually got tamed into being a family pet, and surrendered to the technological supremacy of humans. Even started to celebrate New Year's, although its own was ten days ago. Yeah. Maybe Thor will be wearing a hat tonight, in a prehistoric mood.

The neighbors from across (the Christmas neon set) are out in the garden, trying to finish the family pack of fireworks. Whining fireworks wrestle furiously with the branches and lights. The Lazy Bunch. And fat. No risk of them getting stuck to those rockets, I'm afraid. The only high point comes when a rocket blows up one of the lightbulbs on the tree. Lolla shrieks like a woman. What, you too, Lolla? *Apocalypse Now* over the city. A shower of six hundred suns. Baghdad at the beginning of the Gulf War. Oh no. Mr. Chirpy walks over to the steps and:

"Happy New Year! And thanks for the last one!"

"Yeah. Thanks."

"So how's the crack? Hey, I was just talking to my son there in the U.S., and he was in a real state because they haven't got it yet, it hasn't arrived, the new year, I mean, so I told him not to worry about it, and that it was on its way, on its way, ha ha, how's it going, Hlynur? Are you well? Where's your mom? Is that Elsa? No, you're not Elsa, what am I thinking . . . So what do you reckon, then? Reckon it's gonna be a good year? Well, it's a great start, isn't it? Great bloody start, great bloody start, ah, it's gonna be a good year, all right, I'm as fit as a fiddle ever since they put the pacemaker in. Hlynur, did I tell you what I said to the doctor after the operation? I asked him to make sure he put alkaline batteries in it. Ha! Ha! Get it? Alkaline?"

He's like a man stuck in a year gap, somewhere outside time. A monologue between the ship and the pier. He's coming up the steps, and I offer him a drink to stop him, and he declines. Given up the drink. Then he beckons me closer and whispers:

"Damn fine-lookin' woman you got there . . ."

And then he shoots off on his overpowered pacemaker, a battery in his heart that'll last him all the way to eternity, like that rabbit in the Energizer ad, beating its drum in the face of death: Are you well? Are you well? Are you well? He waddles down the steps and totters down the street, greeting everyone he meets, and whoever they happen to be with, as much an enigma as ever. That's what we'd all be like in limbo time.

It's a really hot New Year's Eve party at Thröstur, Marri, and Thor's. A Mexican heat wave sweeps through the apartment, and everyone's downing margaritas. The city vanishes behind the fogged-up windows. Ice-T sounds like Ice-Tea. Thröstur came to the door wearing Thor on his head like a hat. Yeah. Lolla is dancing with Ahmed in the living room. I talk to Ahmed's new woman (10,000) and she gives me the lowdown: "I've always been into hairy men like him. But this guy's hair is much rougher. Really prickles you, like, you know." Hula Hoops in a bowl on the table, and some hot dishes on the sofa: 15,000, 35,000, and 50,000. I make an exception to my never-speak-to-people-first rule and turn to José to give him a bit of a bollocking for ripping me off. "That joke of yours didn't last thirty minutes on Christmas Eve, we had to unplug it." Bára translates my obviously too-complicated Icelandic for him. José, the angelic con man, launches into a flamenco about how he didn't even know the tree could sing. I press him further until he finally breaks down with "Some peoples really like dat, no problem for dem . . ." He ends by promising to take the "dree" back. I just have to bring it down to the market. No problema. Yeah. Marri passes by with a question mark on his face. Lolla drags me into a dance. I dance my I'm-not-really-dancing dance. Lolla is in full swing, pushing me and prodding me, her beauty spot spiraling all around me. She's in top form tonight. While she's bumming a cigarette off Marri, I take the opportunity to glance over at the aforementioned 50,000 piece on the sofa, and check my pockets. Only got 1,500 on me. The beaut glances at me with an I-don't-take-credit-cards look. Rosy and Guildy in the doorway. Lolla throws her arms around them, pouring in sweat and happy new hair, and carries on dancing. "Kaya." Bob Marley. Reggae in the house. Rosy is in some rat-theme costume "because according to the Chinese calendar this is the year of the rat." Thröstur comes out of the kitchen with the lizard on his face. It's clinging to his nose, clutching his nostrils for dear life, its tail dangling over his face like a new and better goatee. Some girl (20,000) thinks it's really cute and starts talking to Thor in baby language. No sign of Dad. Hasn't seen what Sara said yet. Lolla dances alone in the living room. Some party extras in the hall. It now seems to be a rule that whenever I go to the john, Hofy's always there, waiting for me, when I get back. Like in a fairy tale: I only have to flush once and there she is. My genie. In a long dress. With curls and suburban confetti streamed around her neck. First hi of the year. And thanks for the Christmas present. I fill her in on Mom's whereabouts and dutifully answer some questions about the white sauce. Hofy's obviously been keeping an eye on us. It's the mother in her. Basically, I'm into two kinds of women: mothers and whores. The latter for sex, the former for the rest. The only problem being that there are no whores in Iceland. I've never been to a whore. Tried to once in London, but chickened out at the last minute. Halted by the sudden thought of Mom, as she appeared to me in a vision, at the end of that dark hallway in Soho, with a fried egg in the pan. And this was before AIDS. And I'd already paid and all. Probably the only guy in history who paid a whore for not fucking her. Ended up shooting my load in the intimacy of a peeping booth. Splashed onto a thin panel of British orange plastic. To all the walls I loved before . . . Thröstur once said that it was "all right" to go to a whore, but "you don't kiss." You don't kiss a whore any more than you kiss your own mother.

Something they have in common. Not that I've ever really been into any of that tongue-and-throat stuff. Kissing is strictly for girl-friends. I've had two boring girlfriends. I've always found kissing a bit of a drag, and when it's come to watching TV while you're doing it, it's time to say goodbye. There's no whore in Hofy, but she has that mommy touch. Too many drinks in this mix: first, she's a female acquaintance, then a friend, then girlfriend, then sleeping partner, then non-sleeping partner, and now family friend and Christmas-present giver. It's getting too muddled. Losing that mommy element. I want something clean and clear-cut. Love? Love like this whiskey: double, strong, and dry. I'll never fall in love. Katarina.

'Member when I came out of the video rental store on Klap-parstígur last summer and suddenly halted in the doorway with two tapes under my arm, Steve Martin and Michelle Pfeiffer (2,900,000), and there was that stillness in the air, slightly colder outside than inside, like stepping into a fridge that's been defrost-ing for seven hours, except that it was bright, summery, and it was just before closing time, the red whip marks of the midnight sun stretching across the sky, with the jail below, full of reading pris-oners, and the trees were leafing over the rooftops, birds getting laid, and the cars were well handbraked on the hill, the meters full of coins, and all the traffic wardens had been cleared off the streets, along with the rest of the boring set—handcuffed to their homes and the eleven o'clock news—and a whole library of tapes behind me, seventeen thousand days of filming in LA, and I could hear the sweet rattle of the credit-card machine as I looked down at the two tapes in my hands, and there they were, side by side, Michelle Pfeiffer and Steve Martin, like a match made in heaven: the smartest guy and the most beautiful woman in Hollywood—I even forgave her for not having breasts—and everything just seemed so right and well organized, and good weather, and well filmed, and well lit, and everyone together, on earth, in space: it was a moment of happiness. For fifteen seconds I was actually happy. On the doorstep of the video store on Klapparstígur at 23:04 in June. Some-one else in my shoes might have had a Damascus experience and gone back into the store to find God on the "Drama" shelf. But I lingered a bit, tried to prolong the moment, but it was over, it was over the second I realized it was there. Was that some kind of "love"? But love for what? That was last year. The most memorable moment of the year, apart from swiping Elsa's pill and Dad's little powwow in the Castle. Oh, there he is. That's what Joseph, Jesus' dad, would have looked like if they'd had cameras in the year 33: gray-bearded and divorced, sloshed and eternally bitter: the victim of the most famous case of "adultery" in the history of mankind, hanging out with an aging groupie, some Pussy Pilate in an old Pontiac. Sara:

"Hi and Happy New Year."

"Same to you. So you decided to come after all."

"Yeah, we were at my brother Geir's place, but your dad really wanted to see you. Great party. Really hot in here."

"Yeah. That's for Thor. He's performing naked tonight."

"Oh yeah? A striptease, then? Ha ha ha . . ."

"Lolla, this is Sara. Sara, Lolla. Of course you've met."

"Yeah, the other day, at Elsa's."

"Yeah, that was a great party, man. Did you stay there for long? Did you do anything afterwards?"

"Nah, we left straight after you did."

"Hlynur had a great time. He's such a family boy."

"Oh yeah? He's such a laugh, Hlynur. As soon as you started talking about that sofa, I thought I was gonna—"

"He's always poking fun."

"They didn't even notice."

"No, they're a bit . . . I mean, they're great people and all that, but they're just a bit, you know . . ."

"Stupid?"

"No, maybe not stupid, just a bit . . ."

"Fat?"

"No-ho . . ."

"Wonderful?"

"A bit stiff, yeah. A bit stiff. And you're a friend of Berglind's, aren't you?"

"Yes."

"And, hang on, don't you live with them now?"

"Yes. Just over the Christmas period."

"We took pity on her. We're all she's got up here in the cold and distant north."

"I see, do your parents live abroad, then?"

"Yeah. Well, Mom does."

"And your father?"

"Dad died ten years ago."

"Oh. I'm sorry."

"Nothing to be sorry about. It was a DIY job."

"Oh . . ."

"And I think you knew him . . ."

"Oh yeah? What was his name?"

"Halldór Birgisson."

"Not *the* Halldór Birgisson?"

"Yeah."

"Who used to be in Kox?"

"Yeah."

"Yeah, I knew him, all right. He was always a bag of laughs, Dóri was. He was such fun to have around."

To have around. To have inside. Sara looks from Lolla to me, and I spot the two bags under her eyes that Halldór Birgisson, the Kox bass player, left behind: more like two deep lines, tire marks on a slushy road, hidden under a thin veil of virgin snow: dry makeup. And a taxi follows those tread marks, like a train on tracks, from Sigtún, the carpeted disco, to an apartment block in Álfheimar back in 1978, with Dóri and Sara in the backseat, his bass fingers up her now-hanging-in-the-flea-market old skirt, and her throwing her head back as she laughs at one of Lolla's dad's better jokes. And then it's up to his bachelor pad for a boink, boink on the mattress. Yeah, yeah. So Lolla's dad and Sara. Who is now with Dad. Who used to be with Mom. Who . . . Hang on, I feel like I've missed and am still missing something here.

Sara's tummy, a sunbed tan under a tight black skirt, is taut and smooth, unspoiled by childbearing, but slightly wrinkled from plastic surgery, and currently busy mixing a G and T in her stomach. And Lolla's tummy stands there facing hers, hidden under that baggy blouse-tunic-sweater-smock thingamajig (difficult to say what she's wearing, really), draped over her breasts like curtains, concealing the exciting set design of her abdomen. Two tummies in my eyes; Sara's containing the fossil of a Lolla half-sister that never was, a fifteen-year-old miscarriage that precludes any half-brothers for me. (Sara has a kind of "folk hero" status and has bared her bosom to many a gossip mag. She made a few hairs curl, a few years back, when she officially admitted that she could never have children because of some botched abortion she had years ago.)

We stand there, the three of us, in the doorway and I spot a packet of cigarettes on the kitchen counter, and a lighter on the table. I make the connection and light myself a cigarette. They carry on with their half-drunken palaver, but I can't take my eyes off Sara's belly, this new unsuspected link between Lolla and me. So both our dads have been inside her. What does that make us? Fucks-in-law? Actions speak sooner than words. Hofy is talking to Ahmed. God knows how. Dad is being lectured on the eating habits of vertebrates, and stares at Rosy in his rat outfit with suspicious cop's eyes. The 50,000 beaut comes gliding toward us with an empty glass and a freeze-frame expression on her face. A carpet rolls out before her on the catwalk, leaving us no choice but to clear the doorway. Yeah, she'll make a model, all right, look at the design on that mouth—she's put a lot of work into that mouth, and she ain't about to waste it on idle chitchat. No wonder these women always make you feel so tongue-tied. The unspoken message is: "Don't make me move my lips." Her eyes haven't blinked for the past twenty minutes, they're all dried up, waiting for a camera to flash. But there are no cameras here. I look at her in the kitchen. Turn around, bright eyes. Mind you. She's got those calves. Those piano legs. She takes a nosedive down to 15,000. Feel better. Feel better about that. And I sense a bonding between Sara and Lolla.

Sara to Lolla: "But how was it, you did know your father, didn't you?"

"Oh yeah. But I was only eleven when they split up."

"And were you still in touch with him after that?"

"Yeah, I was. Of course, he was in the entertainment business, always out playing somewhere. Pop stars don't always make the best Sunday parents, always hungover. But he was fun. We got on very well."

"Yeah, he was a fun guy, Dóri was."

"Yeah. Just drank too much, ruined him."

"Yeah."

"And how did you meet him?"

"I was a good friend of Valli Stef's, who spent a lot of time with the guys from Kox at the time, and then Dóri joined the band. But I never knew he had children."

"He never mentioned it?"

"No. Do you have any brothers or sisters?"

"No. Well, Mom has two sons out in Denmark. That's where she lives."

"Yeah, that's right. Hang on, what's her name again?"

"Laufey Johannsdóttir."

Lolla becomes serious, as people often do when they mention their mother's name. She furrows her brow and raises her eyebrows, like dockyard gates opening to let out a ship. Yeah. Mothers are ships. Lolla launches a ship from her face, and Sara has that stevedore look in her eyes as she unloads the full freight of Lolla's mother's past: her eleven years with a father Sara slept with for four weeks. This is getting too complicated for me. Time for another drink. The 15,000 ass. I want it, never mind the calves. Marri with a beer. It was good to see Lolla's face when she said her mother's name. She's human. Then I picture Halldór Birgisson from Kox in a box, six feet under, the bass fingers probably having lost their touch by now, but the ten-year-old pop hairdo still miraculously preserved. Rattle my brain to remember a Kox track. Yeah: I ain't gonna stand in the rain forever / And even though you know I love you not / I'm not going to be the one who couldn't have her / So let me be your dog and tie the knot.

Somehow pop deaths are different from other deaths. Pop stars die differently. Maybe cos they've died so many times before. Maybe cos pop is so superficial. (Kox were never what you'd call underground. Apart from Halldór right now, that is.) The lid slides over the coffin as if it were a popping pot of corn. Pop, pop . . . But

I guess Halldór Birgisson got his little patch of immortality after all. And the conniving little bass plucker will continue to live on "for as long as humanity continues to throw parties." And even though you know I love you not . . . I pour myself a drink. I pour myself. And the stuff goes straight to my head, cos for some inexplicable reason I suddenly find myself saying:

"How 'bout you? What's your mom's name?"

I've suddenly got a new pickup line. "What's your mom's name?" 15,000 (who has actually shot back up to 50,000 again) looks at me like I'm her father, who's hitting on her and forgotten her mother's name. Nice one, Hlynur. Ah well. Just wait now, and keep your cool while this girl looks up her mother's name. An interminable moment as she withdraws into her nineteen-year-old head to quickly consult with her brain (aren't they cute, these females, when the steam starts puffing out of their bimboid brains) on whether she should deign this half-wit with an answer. Girls are so dumb. But it doesn't matter how dumb they are, as long as they've got that IT, they can reduce any Kasparov to a total Schwarzenegger at the blink of an eyelid. 50,000's brain is working so hard her hairdo almost topples off. Maybe she just doesn't remember her mother's name. Yeah. She finally babes it out:

"Helga. Why do you ask?"

"Just. The time had come."

"Wow, is that the time?"

"What?"

"Happy New Year!"

"Yeah. Happy New Year. You're looking good tonight. Nice look."

"Thanks."

"How much do you want for that?"

"How do you mean?"

"How much do you want for that look? The dress, the hairdo?"

"Are you hitting on me?"

"Ehm."

"Hum? Are you?"

"Ehm? No."

"Are you one of those guys who left school without a cap?"

"Cap?"

"Yeah, a graduation cap, hello?"

"No. Ehm. I went to agricultural college."

"Oh yeah? And what caps do they give out there? Some hand-knitted job?"

"I dunno. I failed."

"Surprise, surprise."

And she's off. Into the next room. With her genetically engineered calves. Yeah, man is evolving. Or women, at least. I stand by the kitchen sink. A kr 50,000 bounced check. When it comes to women, I'm like a crap defender who suddenly finds himself in front of an open goal. He always loses his bottle and kicks it into the crowd. Mind you, she had those calves. Yeah. Not erection-worthy. Ah well. Yeah. All of a sudden this kitchen layout starts to make sense to me. Yeah. Drawers and cupboards. They have their logic. A cigarette. Dad comes in, clasping his glass like a microphone:

"Well, then, what have you got to say for yourself?"

"Just hello, hello, testing one-two-three."

"Your mom up north?"

"Yeah."

"She staying long?"

"Nah. Don't think so."

"Just for the New Year?"

"Yeah."

"And how . . . ?"

Dad looks toward Lolla, while Hofy skirts around me, inquiring about the wine supply. Then the newly befriended Lolla and Sara come over. The little "family" huddles around me and, maybe cos I'm the tallest, all tongues seem to be directed at me.

Sara: "So what's your New Year's resolution, Hlynur?"

Hlynur: "Just the usual, be out of bed by noon."

Lolla: "And how about out of the house? Hey, Hlynur ventured out into the garden today."

Hofy: "You don't say?"

Lolla: "Yeah, he actually took the garbage out, the darling."

Hofy: "Is this something new, then?"

Lolla: "You obviously don't know him well enough."

Dad: "Maybe it's your good influence."

Lolla: "Yes, I think we've almost got him trained now. Then he'll be able to leave home."

Sara: "Is that the plan, then, Hlynur?"

Lolla: "Yes, do you know any single mothers who might like to take him in?"

Sara: "No . . . but I've got loads of unattached girlfriends."

Lolla: "No, not that . . . [glances at Hofy] . . . I don't think that's what he's looking for."

Dad: "Now, now, girls, let him decide these things for himself."

Sara: "Are you a friend of his?"

Hofy: "I'm not sure. You never know with Hlynur."

Lolla: "Yeah, I haven't quite figured him out myself."

Sara: "Why do you say that? I think he's such a . . ."

Lolla: "Mature person?"

Sara: "Yeah, just a bit . . . special."

Hofy: "He's a case."

Dad: "Don't let them bully you, my boy. Women never really understand men, anyway. And as soon as they do, they drop them, ha ha ha . . ."

Lolla: "We don't understand you? Is that the problem?"

Hlynur: "No. I don't understand you."

Sara: "But we're so stupid. I always think we women are so stupid, don't you agree, girls?"

Hofy: "No. I've always got the feeling we have to do the thinking for them."

Hlynur: "The thing is, you can never be yourself with a woman. You always have to be holding back."

Lolla: "Oh yeah? Now this is interesting. How do you mean?"

Hlynur: "Yeah. Like when you're desperate to fart, but you have to keep it in all the time. Clogs up the tubes."

Sara: "Clogs up the tubes! Ha ha ha . . ."

Lolla: "Oh yeah? Now I know why there's always such a stench in your place whenever I come over. Men need women to keep the stink in."

Hofy: "Exactly."

Slight pause here. I look at Sara, who gives me a tender smile. An old Bruce number blasts from the living room: "Everybody's Got a Hungry Heart." Some words of truth from 1980.

Dad: "Yeah. So that's how it is, huh?"

Hlynur: "But, Lolla, you should know all about that."

Lolla: "What?"

Hlynur: "The great divide between the sexes."

Lolla: "Oh yeah?"

Hlynur: "Yeah. You know both sides of the coin, don't you? From your own experience."

Lolla: "Because I'm a lesbian, you mean?"

Hlynur: "Er. Yeah. And b—"

Sara: "That's right, you're a lesbian! Tell me, what's it actually like? To be a lesbian. I've always wanted to be a lesbian, you know, just to know what's it like, tee-hee . . ."

Lolla: "Well, come on home, darling, and I'll show you the ropes."

Hlynur: "Can I come too?"

Dad: "Well, well . . ."

Sara: "Ha ha, you're making your father blush."

Hlynur: "Don't they have a course in these things?"

Lolla: "Yeah, you should sign up, Hlynur."

Hlynur: "But I'd have to go to gay school first, wouldn't I?"

Lolla: "Yes, probably . . . and sever your umbilical cord . . ."

Hlynur: "Oh yeah? . . ."

Somehow everything starts to sag. This is all getting too shabby with those puddles of wine on the kitchen counter, empty glasses, cigarette butts in the sink, and sticky Coke patches on the lino. Thröstur approaches, looking like a guru with that lizard dangling from his face, but actually quite normal compared with us. And Rosy and Guildy beaming with happiness and in love.

One party hour later I'm sitting on the sofa with Hofy on my arm, the arm of the sofa that is. Some manic rocker with serious DJ delusions has just muscled in on the stereo and is doing a pretty good job of ruining the atmosphere, with some rusty old U2-boat number from the last world war that sinks into an empty sea. Nothing changes on New Year's Day. Hofy is telling me about a friend of hers who's just discovered she's pregnant when Lolla comes over to say she's leaving, promised she'd pop into another party. I seize the opportunity to say, "Oh yeah, and listen," stand up (slightly wobbly on my feet in my current state), and manage to mutter myself out into the hall, without Hofy realizing that I'm leaving. Yet another escape attempt. I tell Lolla I'd like to tag along and she doesn't mind. I leather myself into my jacket, but Thröstur and some guy are fooling around on the landing. Thor has broken out of his tropical cage. He's crouched between the radiator and the wall and they're following him with their fingers. I'm hijacked into a conversation:

"Hey, what's this? Don't go. There're lots of people on the way, Reynir and that crowd."

"Yeah, I'm just going to have a look around, and I'll be back."

Lolla stumbles down the stairs and almost trips, but manages to grab the railing and sits on a step, laughing.

"Hey, Hlynur, Hlynur, ehm . . ."—that's Thröstur swaying beside me—". . . Nah, never mind, tell yah some other time . . ."

"What?"

"Nah, nothing . . . Hey, did you really mean that about what's-her-name?"

"What?"

"You know, about . . . Jesus, I'm a bit whacked right now, hey, did you give José a bollocking? Marri was going on about it, or Bára, I mean, you've always got to watch out for the small print with that guy, like with Thor, for example, have you heard the news?"

"No, what?"

"Apparently Thor is a she, the guy's a she, that girl was here, you know, the one who has that TV show with the seal, and I was showing her Thor and she says there's no dick on him. He's a female. Hey, do you think we should rebaptize him? . . . Dunno why, but something like this always happens on New Year's, I mean, just think about it, there's always something, some change on New Year's Eve. No, Beggi, he's on the other side; see, there's his tail, or hers. . . ."

Thröstur turns again and starts searching behind the radiator.

Lolla has reached the bottom of the stairs and asks if I'm coming with her. I follow her. Thröstur chases after me, mumbling that he never realized that "your dad was with Sara, man. Nice move, graybeard." We've reached the hall. Lolla says she's leaving. Steps outside. I freeze with Thröstur standing over me on the stairs. I'm trapped. The door is ajar, with the cold new year in one ear, and the same old garbage from Thröstur in the other:

"I get it, you're chasing her, aren't you? You'll only end up at some lezzie orgy, you know you've gotta watch out on New Year's Eve, there's always a spell on it, everything you do tonight will haunt you for the rest of the year."

"So you'll be running after Thor all year."

"Ha ha . . . yeah, or maybe I'll give him a sex change. Could be a new fad, to change sex on New Year's Eve . . . Maybe it's a lizard thing? Otherwise I might . . ."

I've switched off. The hall is full of shoes, untaken steps. In the corner opposite me there's a pair of brand-new high-tech sneakers, in a child's size, small, bright white with thick pads. Incredibly complex in design. 'Member the sneakers I was wearing when I was taken to the country: nothing but soles, tongues, laces and holes to stick them through. That was when things were still what they were. And are. But to see these shoes now. Somehow they just don't look like shoes anymore. Two XL marshmallow cushions. Tasty to grill, maybe? Good to know that, in the event of a famine, if the nation has to revert to eating shoes again. Those Nikes are probably a lot tastier than that pair made of sheepskin. The purpose of modern design is to make people forget what things are. That progress? Yeah, maybe. Tried on a pair like that once. "Air-padded." They give the word "gravity" and the verb "to walk" completely new meanings. One can only marvel at how these designs manage to distance us from the surface of the planet. When will they start doing the same for condoms? Just do it. I come to:

"What?"

"Hofy," says Thröstur.

"Yeah. OK. Listen, ehm."

"Yeah, listen . . . Just remember we're going out live . . . no re-editing afterwards."

"Yeah," I say.

I shut the door behind me, and am now standing on Hverfisgata. A taxi passes by, spraying snow from under its tires, but I somehow get the feeling—maybe it's the new year, maybe it's the scotch—that I'm still indoors. Reykjavík is a giant set. I run across the stage, up Barónsstígur, and—without really knowing what I'm doing—up on Laugavegur. The Loans & Trust building, Landsbank. Looking for Lolla. Lights. Lost. All of a sudden I'm surrounded by Ls. What else begins with an L? Loser. Lassie. Lesbian. Lie. Life. Leak. Lech.

Time is 03:58. Yeah, still on leap-year time. Where is she? I don't know where that party is. Burnt firecrackers and dead pinwheels. A rumpus of singing new-year-olds, howling out in Danish: "Og når de gik, så var de bom, de var alle sammen jomfru når vi kom . . ." Obviously ghosts from an old production, although the set design looks quite new. I look up and down Laugavegur. Up and down Baronsstígur.

I walk down Laugavegur in the fatness of these pursy times. "In the fatness of these pursy times"? Where did that come from? Yeah. I feel like I'm caught in some rotten ancient plot when Lolla suddenly appears from a door: "Oh hi, listen, we've got to get more drink, they've finished everything in there, isn't there something left at home?" I remember a half bottle of Campari in the kitchen cupboard. We walk past five shops—You and I, Tea and Coffee, Gold and Silver, Adam, and Eve—and turn up Frakkastígur. Lolla slips on a patch of ice on the corner of Bergthórugata, I catch her in time.

I dump myself into a chair in the living room. Lolla nips into the bathroom, comes back, and drops the needle onto the turntable: "Just one song and then we'll go." I light a cigarette. Piano notes. No. "Hello." She shrieks with laughter and breaks into a bizarre mock dance, grabbing me as she moves, hoisting me to my feet. I manage to drop my cigarette into the ashtray. She's still holding my hand and shakes it about, as if she were trying to resuscitate a corpse. I try to pretend I'm playing along with this joke, which seems to be targeted at me. This is a long song. We draw closer to each other. Closer. The blind girl and the ugly guy. She half dies in my arms during the guitar solo. Hangs on me. Her breasts pressed against my chest. Dear airbags. All my biggest organs are dancing inside me, cheek to cheek. Her dark hair under my chin. That Lolla scent. Then she throws her head back and looks at me with her swimming eyes. It must have something to do with the gravitational pull of the earth, and that what-the-hell-we're-just-ants-in-space feeling that presses me toward her mouth. We kiss a we're-not-really-kissing kiss, and then look into each other's eyes. I guess she's thinking what I'm thinking, and maybe in English too: "Maybe not the right thing to do." I always think in English in an emergency. Probably something to do with NATO and "the Cold War years," that little Pentagon that's lodged itself in all our brains. I don't know about her, but maybe I've just watched too much TV: I see the CNN logo hovering over her right shoulder and everything is somehow placed in a much broader context: that ant image is still crawling through my head, and I see the earth sluggishly squeaking on its stiff rusty axis: just another gallstone in space—and, compared with that, these fusing mouths of saliva on these bouncing carpeted floorboards in Bergthórugata are no more significant than an ant in the Amazon. And so I continue.

Maybe it's my imagination, but lesbians seem to kiss better, they put more into it, they're all part of the same sisterhood. Lolla kisses me like she kisses Mom. So I try to kiss her like Mom.

The sofa.

All of a sudden I see myself, like I'm standing on the living room floor looking at myself on the sofa: a big, heavy, clumsy horse with glasses, craning my neck over the fence for grass, ravenous, as I stiffly sink onto Lolla's body with depressingly stupid sad eyes, in slow motion—notice how my glasses and hair don't move—and there's a sparkle in my tiny teeth as I purse my lips, but it soon gets sucked into the kiss with all the rest.

My cigarette breathes its last in the ashtray on the coffee table.

I'm in a real hurry to get naked. I, for one, like to practice my lovemaking bare. The shoes always slow me down. Always get tangled in my shoelaces. Meanwhile the lady lies there with her head on a cushion, calmly waiting, while I wrestle with the knot in my laces, with my shirt half off, like an idiot, just can't remember how the darn things work. Robin Williams said on the Letterman show once that God gave us a prick and a brain, but a bloodstream that can only reach one of them at a time.

For once I say fuck the laces and bounce out of my shoes in the blink of an eye. There's just a slight pause, when I release a soft "hey" as I recognize the underpants she's wearing (an old pair of briefs of mine), and let her know by clumsily fumbling behind her back that I'd like her to take her bra off.

This is much more than your regular "oh, here we go again" screw. No, sirree. Lolla is more than just number seven on my list. We're talking basic instinct here.

Ólöf Halldórsdóttir, social security number 071057-3099, domiciled in Kárastígur 33, 101 Reykjavík, lies naked in the middle of the living room floor. The underwritten, Hlynur Björn Hafsteinsson, social security number 180262-2019, domiciled in Bergthórugata 22, 101 Reykjavík, lies naked on top of her. Using her right hand, Ólöf Halldórsdóttir steers the underwritten's fully erect organ toward her orifice. The underwritten thrusts his organ, measuring approximately 16 centimeters in length, into Miss Ólöf's vagina. In the heat of the moment, the underwritten neglected to sheathe his organ.

Lolla is a small miracle. Lolla doesn't just lie there like a woman. Lolla doesn't just lie there like a woman and allow herself to be screwed. She's totally unhinged me with that fiery lust of hers. I get a slight fright when she suddenly flies under me, shakes all over, and starts to shudder and groan like a . . . Like a foal being held down by three vets for an injection. I feel slightly nervous. She seems possessed. Or is this what being bisexual is all about? Is this "the man" in her? But men don't yell like that, we just breathe a bit louder. Compared with her, with that trance she's in, I'm just a sperm donor here. And yet this is the best sex I've ever had. Maybe sex just wasn't meant for men? I really have to keep a tight grip on her so as not to lose her. I follow her. Follow her toward the dining table. Mommy. This is your table. This is your table, Mommy. Maybe Robin Williams was wrong. Or maybe I'm just different. My brain is still working overtime. I mean, I'm still thinking. But Lolla. Her brain is just a giant erect clitoris. She's a whole. Lolla is the perfect sexual being. And no long-distance runner. She's straight into a sprint, running for the big O. A real hurdle racer, by the feel of her, contracting her pelvis with each thrust. Her breasts in my face. I recover my concentration by looking her nipples in the eye, until I suddenly realize—when I manage to free my other hand from the floor to squeeze one of her breasts—"No, these are Mom's breasts." No. Has Mom slept with her? I let go of the breast. Try to stick to areas Mom wouldn't and could never reach. I'll always be this much ahead of Mom. I'll always be 16 centimeters ahead of Mom. Oh no. No, no. What am I doing? To do or not to do? To come or not to come? That is the question. Should I carry on like nothing's wrong, and just enjoy this, or allow doubt to hop in, like a fireman leaping into my veins with his hose to quench this fiery blood? Mommy. Respect. I'm her son. And yet so far gone from her. Can there be any greater rift between a mother and son than this? My little man, like a diver under the Arctic, swimming somewhere deep below, way below, my consciousness. Can a man plunge any farther away from his own mother? And yet I'm thinking about her . . . LOLLA. Three Ls in that. Lust. Lips. L . . . No one backs out of a woman with a full hard-on. But. Mommy. "Just remember we're going out live," Thröstur said. The camera records and the camera never forgets. No retakes.

A tear in slow motion, played in reverse.

I gradually manage to forget myself. Gradually start to shudder and tremble. Gradually free my mind from thought, or coherent thought, at least. Gradually put thought on hold. Gradually turn into nothing but flesh and bone. I suddenly feel the skeleton inside me, all white and hard, my flesh wobbling on its frame like jelly. My ears vibrating on my skull. Fins in water.

A tear in slow motion, played in reverse.

All the movies of the world roll before my eyes. All tapes on fast-forward. Snowstorms and blizzards on all channels. All the toilets of the globe unite in a flush. The sky erupts into a constellation of birthmarks. And then. The silence in the navel of the explosion when she comes. The stillness in the eye of the cyclone . . . when I come. I come and, for a moment, everything brightens in a flash, a fireball lighting up the atmosphere and several continents below, before dissolving. And vanishing. What becomes of the sperm?

A tear in slow motion, played in reverse.

I'm sunk deep into the sofa. Keep myself afloat with a cigarette. New Year's Day in the windows. Yeah. The light seems slightly fresher somehow. I'm in a gown I found in the bathroom. Mom's. Last year's Coke in the glass. The annual review of foreign news on the box. Lost all its fizz.

Haven't slept. Since last year. Lolla is still in bed. My man's back in his kennel, hiding behind the gown. 9.5 centimeters. Where do those extra 6.5 centimeters come from? Blood. The extra centimeters that I wish I'd never had. My cigarette is 9.5 centimeters. Counting the filter. My lighter is 9.5 centimeters. My index finger too. Yeah. There's some kind of harmony in all this. Everything is as it should be. 1996. Couldn't have started any other way. Only 16 centimeters into the year and. No retakes. No retakes ever again. One shoot, all uncut. Filed for posterity in the Video Collection of Time. Question is, which section? Drama? Comedy? Horror? Children? No, of course, in the back room, on the porno rack. Tape number 16.978, rack number 5.048, shelf 7. "Hlynur and Lolla, 1-1-96, 45 min." Handwritten by the Man himself in a thick marker.

Lolla. The little bomb. She was incredible. No wonder Mom fell for her. Although it must be a little bit different for them. Surely not that good. Are me and Mom fucks-in-law too, then? Something uncomfortable about that. Just try to be cool about this. Nah, it was nothing. Could have happened to anyone. To ram into a family member by accident. Yeah, sure. It was great. Still, I'm a bit worried I might have cried out "Mommy" when I came. Or "Ma . . ." Hope she didn't notice. No. She was totally out of it. Only came around when I pulled out of her and collapsed at her side. "Sweet Jesus," she said. I looked at her, she looked up at the ceiling. No way of knowing what she meant by that. Unless she's religious. Then she hoisted herself up on her elbows—her breasts succumbing to the law of gravity—and smiled at me as she walked toward the john. I watched her upside down. Her buttocks glistening in a film of sweat and juices.

I was on the sofa when she came back in a T-shirt. We smoked two cigarettes in the living room. I picked up her/my underpants and asked: "What was that?" She just curled her lips. And swallowed. No. Mom couldn't have slept with her. She knows my underpants. Nah. This is no big deal.

The president of Iceland's New Year's address on TV. Vigdís Finnbogadóttir (125,000) for the last time. I'm into her, although I can't hear what she's saying. Took the sound off. She looks into my eyes. OK. I'm an Icelander. She looks into my eyes like a mom. The mother of us all. Phone. I pussyfoot over, a bit of a drag queen in this gown. Mom calling from Hvammstangi.

"Oh, is it you? I thought you'd be asleep. Happy New Year."

"Yeah. Happy New Year."

"So how was it, did you have great fun last night?"

"Yeah, it was OK, you know."

"Where did you go? To Thröstur's and those?"

"Yeah."

"And how was it?"

"Yeah, you know. Cool enough."

"And did you get on with Lolla?"

"Get it on with Lolla? Oh . . . yeah. Yeah. We got along fine. And Dad was there too. And Sara. At the party, I mean."

"Oh, right. And what kind of shape were they in?"

"Just. They. Good shape, yeah."

"Right."

"He handled himself OK."

"Oh, that's good. He's probably better when she's around."

"Yeah. And. And how was it for you?"

"Oh, it was just nice and relaxed up here. Sigrún made some lovely leg of lamb and then we went outside to shoot some fireworks, and then we popped over to your granny's. She doesn't go out anymore. We watched the *Comedy Special* with them, but Mom didn't really get any of it. It was far too complicated for her."

"Yeah."

"I thought it was a really good one. Didn't you watch it?"

"Yeah. But it wasn't as funny down here."

"Ha ha . . . Was it not?"

"No. Mind you, Lolla laughed."

"Did she, yeah? Is she there beside you? Let me have a word with her."

"I think she's asleep."

"Oh, never mind. Listen, just send my love, then. See you soon."

"Yeah."

"I'll be coming down tomorrow. Be there in the evening."

"OK."

"Bye, Hlynur love. They all send their regards."

"Yeah, bye."

"Bye."

I tiptoe across the carpet. There's a tiny stain on it. About the size of Lolla's beauty spot. Sticky dry fruit juice. I try to scratch it away, scratch the wound. How do you get sperm off a rug? Lolla comes in. "And today Lolla is wearing a light blue cotton T-shirt, designed by Christian la Crotch." She looks down at me as I moronically try to scrape the stain out of the carpet with my nail, on all fours.

"What are you doing?"

"I spilled something."

"What?"

"Nothing. A few seeds."

"Tut, tut . . ."

She's looking pale and hungover, as hungover as that T-shirt barely covering her ass, as she staggers into the kitchen, saying, "Is there any Coke left?" I say, "Yeah, it's here. On the coffee table." I feel a slight breeze, as her body brushes behind me, and I continue to scrape. "Wasn't it me who spilled them?" she asks, without looking up. Hear her filling a glass and dropping herself onto the sofa.

"What are you getting so stressed about? I can't see anything."

"No."

"Got a cigarette?"

"Yeah."

I stop scraping and stand up. Sit in the armchair that's part of

the sofa set. The sofa's natural son. Mom's a blend. Danish/Ice-
landic. Yeah. I'm 25 percent Danish and 75 percent disabled.
What does that leave me? Lolla puts her legs up on the table and
I'm scared shitless she might not be wearing underwear. Try not
to look. Or maybe I'm just scared shitless of her? I'm relieved to
catch a glimpse of a dark blue patch in her crotch.

"Who phoned? Berglind?"

"Yeah."

"And what did she say?"

"Just. Hvammstangi. Sigrún's leg was good."

"What, is that your mother's negligee you're wearing?"

"Yeah. Couldn't find anything else."

"You can be such a pervert."

"Yeah."

"Oh . . . Wow, what a hangover."

"Yeah. You were pretty . . ."

"Pretty what?"

"No, just . . . pretty."

"No. You were going to say something else."

"Pretty drunk."

"Drunk?"

"Yeah, if you're hungover now, you must have been drunk last
night."

"What is it, Hlynur? Something wrong?"

"No. No."

"And you? Are you hungover?"

"Me? Yeah."

We shut up for a few drags. Vigdís moves her lips on the screen.
A small flag droops limply on the desk beside her. I feel like it
should be at half mast. Vigdís stops talking and looks at us. Then
probably the national anthem. Deadly serious landscapes. Yeah.
Good to see those waterfalls are still in working order. Not a bad
rock video. Kind of thing. Feel Lolla staring at me, like a camera.
Feel my face adjusting to her as she focuses. Turn my head, look
into her eyes. For a brief moment we're just eyes. Two fish. Lolla's
eyes are ash gray. About the same amount of ash as on the tip of my
cigarette. I stretch toward the ashtray and tap it.

She says: "What is it?"

"What?"

"Something's up."

"Up what?"

"Yeah."

"No, no."

"Can't you say it?"

"I can't smoke and talk at the same time."

I pull a final drag out of my cigarette and stub it out. Or try to stub it out. Even though this is the 102,204th cigarette of my life, I'm still trying to learn how to stub them out. A vertical column of smoke billows from the ashtray. The cigarette butt, a half-dead fly lying on its back, still kicking one leg. Try again. Maybe I'm just too gentle. Don't have the heart to kill anything that still shows some sign of life. I give up, and look admiringly at Lolla as she stubs hers out in one swift move of the finger.

"Are you religious?"

"What?"

"Religious?"

"No. Why?"

"No, just . . . Cos you said 'sweet Jesus.'"

"When?"

"Last night. When we were finished."

"Good God, is that what I said?"

"What did you mean by that?"

"What do you mean, what did I mean?"

"No. Just. You said it like it meant something somehow."

"Jesus . . . I don't know. Is that what's been bothering you?"

"No, no."

Silence. A double silence if we count the TV. Talking to a woman is like talking to a foreigner. There's a whole different language behind each word. Women are foreigners.

"What did your mom say? Did she say anything?"

"No. Just to send her love."

The smoke is transparent and hangs over the ashtray by a thread. Its tip, a glowing amber.

O

IF SOMETHING
OTHER THAN THE SUN
WOULD COME UP
IN THE MORNING

I wake up to an earthquake in Japan. Feeling a bit shaky. Goose-bumps like five thousand dead Japanese heads under the quilt. Time: 14:32. I dreamed of Elton John. He said he digged my glasses. I wasn't wearing them. No hard-on. Won't come out to play. Maybe cos of Elton. I might be gay but my dick is not. I find my glasses on the floor. Zap down the scale.

RAI UNO. The Japanese earthquake on Italian TV. Not as serious somehow. Female Italian newscasters are far too beautiful. Beauty alters news. Look at her (300,000), that blonde in that enormous blue, impeccably designed studio. Human lives ooze out of her mouth, sliding down her neckline. Five thousand dead Japs slither down her cleavage. Not that I'd mind joining them. She looks into my eyes. I wake up. She's got a boyfriend in Rome, and I bet they're going to have it off, straight after the program, in some plush childless apartment with bubbling designer water on every table. All over the world anchorwomen are being fucked in the most professional and almost newsworthy ways, while I lie here under a quilt with my socks by my side. Yes, after a few more news items, my man starts to regain consciousness. That's the good thing about Italian news.

A sunset over the Persian Gulf. And a male Arab voice.

A symphony orchestra in Copenhagen. Or London. Who cares? I can't stand classical music. Classical music is just like an intro to a song, those few notes they play while you're waiting for the beat to kick in. The only problem being that the beat never comes. How can people listen to music without a beat?

Dutch dog-food ad.

Goal in São Paulo. Off the bar. Replay. Off the bar again.

A newsroom in Pakistan. An anchor with a spotted pink tie, bought at the starving public's expense, and a world map behind him. The countries are white on a blue background, clumsily drawn and simplified. Look like blobs of spunk. I watch the Pakistani news, mainly to see if they've included Iceland on their world map. The anchor is a ball of hair: hair all over Europe and Greenland. I wait for him to bend his head a little. Iceland isn't there. That's the deal with Iceland. Iceland is the kind of country that sometimes is there and sometimes isn't. Depending on the mood of whatever graphic artist happens to be on duty that day. Whether he can be bothered drawing in that island up there on his transparency sheet, in the sweaty offices of an advertising agency in the center of Karachi, with his fax machine still broken down and just two weeks after his girlfriend dumped him. Which is probably why the map has that spunky look. I'm not enough of a patriot to complain. It's comforting, somehow, to live on an island that doesn't appear on the map of the world. Invisible. We're not there. We're just watching, but no one can see us.

Women working out on the American channels. Trotting on their treadmills. You've got to hand it to those Yanks. Always on the go. But never actually getting anywhere. Just marking time. Losing weight to put it back on. Jog to eat. Eat to jog. Rats in cages. What's the purpose of life? Women with muscles. Like flowers on steroids. A sperm-destroying sight.

The weather forecast for South America. Looks like a sunny weekend in Uruguay.

I journey toward the bathroom. Lolla sits in the living room. "Hi." "Hi." February and Lolla is still here. She's basically moved in. Without us ever really talking about it. Some extremely vague problem she has with her apartment. Not that it bothers me. She's got the place Lolla-ized. She's on some kind of bisexual working schedule. Haven't quite figured it out yet. I piss sitting down, to be able to pick my nose. The nose has its own alpine micro-climate. Everything's so dry. Stick my index up the mountain range in my left nostril. Solidified blood. But manage to find some soft stuff in the boondocks behind it, and scoop out three good helpings. Beautiful, light brown, savory mud. Snot is always best on an empty stomach. The perfect appetizer before Cheerios and coffee.

I ask His Royal Highness, Lolla:

"Hey, have you got any snot up your nose?"

"Huh?"

"Snot. Mine's a bit hard here, and I need a bit."

"No, I'm completely dried up as well."

"Or do you have a used tampon I could make some tea with?"

"Yeah, no. I . . . Sorry, Hlynur dear."

"Ah well. Maybe Mom will have some."

"Yeah, maybe Mom will bring something back for you."

It's one of those days. I've got to jump-start myself and go down to the job center to play the unemployed. Dark sky. Coal black Pakistani hair looms over the city. I feel like a Muslim on the way to the mosque. That weekly thing. On your knees to pray for a stamp. Unemployed. The other day some surveyor asked me if I was unemployed out of necessity or just on principle. I told him it was a calling. And maybe there's some truth in that. I head straight for the confession box. The priest is a woman in her fifties (kr 750) with specs, a white blouse, and a cross around her neck.

"Hlynur Björn Hafsteinsson."

"Yes."

"Are you Hlynur?"

"Yes, kind of."

"Sorry?"

"Well, you never know, do you?"

She looks at me. Then there's a silence broken only by the sound of a distant phone as she works. She glances at the monitor. Employed by the unemployed.

"And you haven't found anything to do yet?"

"No. Well, yes. I did my mother's girlfriend."

"Hum?"

"I slept with my mother's girlfriend on New Year's Eve. Mom was up north. In Hvammstangi."

The woman looks at me again.

"But it was an accident. It won't happen again. There's no future career in it or anything like that. We were both drunk. What do you think? You reckon I should tell her about it?"

"Who?"

"Mom. Do you think I should tell my mother about it?"

"I don't know. This is really no concern of mine."

"So you've got no views on adultery within the family, then?"

"No."

"Are you married? I mean, imagine you're married, right? No, remarried, and your daughter is having it off with your new husband. How would you take it?"

"Your social security number please, Hlynur."

I walk down Laugavegur like a walking machine, with that unemployed stride. Pure clockwork. Like it's the only thing I do. Like it's what I'm paid for. A króna for each step. Roaming the streets, as Uncle Elli would say. Typical Elli.

The state pays me to exist. And I feel kind of grateful for that. I get a slight pang of conscience when I see all those people filing past me. All those people who call shifting money from one bank to another a job. All those people cashing in on cashing out. Getting paid to pay. To pay benefit.

A traffic warden stands by a car, writing out a parking ticket. I stroll past him and glance back. We're heading in the same direction. I check the meter. It's run out. A Japanese housewife number in the parking space. Call it guilt, but I find 50 krónur in my pocket and shove it into the meter. I look back. The traffic warden: a dreary-looking weirdo about my age. He sneers at me. A palpitation in my chest. A state-sponsored palpitation. I twist the dial on the meter.

I follow the warden on his round down Laugavegur. I dash into a shop and get 200 krónur's worth of coins. Head straight for the warden, walk right past him, and shove coins into three meters. I'm sticking money into the fourth, right in front of the Chess Shop, when the warden finally challenges me:

"Hey, what do you think you're doing?"

"Filling the meter. Time was up."

"This your car, then?"

"No."

"Where's your car?"

"I don't have a driving license."

"So what are you putting money into the meter for?"

"Got to think of one's fellow man."

"Wait a minute, you can't do that."

"Oh no?"

"No."

"You're saying it's illegal to fill someone else's meter?"

"It's just not done, that's all."

"Are you saying it's illegal?"

"Maybe not illegal, but it's just not done, that's all. Now I can't write out a ticket for this car, for example, and it might have been parked here illegally for the past half hour. Or those three there . . . You've just filled four empty meters."

"Are you on a percentage?"

"What?"

"Do you get a bonus for every ticket you write?"

"No."

"So aren't you happy you don't have to take out your fine book?"

"Well . . ."

"Or do you just get a kick out of fining people?"

"No. I'm just trying to do my job here."

"And you think I'm spoiling it for you?"

"Well, yes. This makes me kind of . . . redundant."

"Unemployed?"

The owner of the car, an OK-looking lady (kr 10,000) in a fur coat (kr 50,000) with a stressed-out hairdo (kr 2,500) scuttles over, 500-krónur guilt in her eyes. Veronica Pedrosa (kr 60,000) reads the news on CNN. She's full of apologies and sorrys and says she's going. I say no problem, put 50 krónur in, and twist the dial. Sixty minutes at her disposal. The woman says oh and thanks me and goodbyes me with a smile. I watch her going back into the hairdresser's. Then look at the warden. Poor bastard. I feel so pleased with myself as I'm walking away. So pleased I have to have a cigarette to feel a bit worse again. I pass Marri, who's coming out of the Mál og Menning bookstore.

"What are you up to?"

"Just buying a book."

"Book?"

"Yeah. Animal psychology. There's a chapter here on how to talk to your pet. We're a bit worried about calling Thor Thor, now that he's a she. We tried calling her Thordis for a while, but it didn't stick somehow. We tried Thóra too. I dunno. Thröstur reckons it's no big deal, but José says it's a bad omen, but he's always full of that hocus-pocus stuff. . . ."

The traffic warden has caught up with us and is taking his fine book out again. I break away from Marri, pounce on the meter, and throw in my last fifty. The warden glares at me. Profound irritation emanating from every single feature of his face, except maybe his nose.

Marri: "You got a car?"

"No, just doing my bit."

Hofy Pálsdóttir appears from around the corner like a piece of yesterday's news. A stern look on her face. Smoke puffing out of her, like something's burning inside. Cold is the female fire. We go through the traditional "Hi"s, and Marri shoves his book into the bag to make a quick exit. Suddenly uptight for some reason. Something's up. Yeah, something's up.

"Hlynur. I've got to talk to you. I've been trying to find you."

"Here I am."

"Mind if we go somewhere? I . . . I can't talk about it here."

"Oh yeah?"

"Yeah."

"Something serious?"

"Yeah."

"It's just that . . . I'm kind of pressed for time."

"I can never have a normal conversation with you."

"Now, then."

"OK. If you want. I'm pregnant."

"And if I don't want?"

"What?"

"Pregnant?"

"Yes."

"Who's the dad?"

"It can only be you."

Oklahoma City. Waco, Texas. World Trade Center. I feel my ribs caving in. Crashing into my intestines. Ambulance sirens howl from the depths of my bowels. My prick shrivels up, as if that wouldn't be too late now.

"Me? How?"

"How do you think? We did sleep together, didn't we?"

A policeman is standing beside me. I turn around. There are two policemen standing beside me. Did I say something wrong? Who designed the uniform of the Icelandic police force?

"Sorry, but you better come with us."

"Me? Why? But I wore a condom."

"Just come over here to the car with us."

Roxy Music. There's an empty white Volvo with two wheels up on the sidewalk, on the other side of the street. People are gawking. I look at Hofy like she's the one behind all this. How much does child support cost? I cross Laugavegur in that kind of arrested stride. American police cars are blue. Aren't they blue everywhere? Hofy stands on the sidewalk and watches me disappear into the backseat. That's exactly how I feel.

I mosey on home. There's something special about being able to stretch your legs after being held in custody for two hours. The streets are deserted. Dinnertime. There's something just so right about those cops, their ears, noses, chins, everything somehow 100 percent right, just cos of the uniform. Like an ugly picture in a nice frame. They all have that kind of universal look. With that smooth cops' skin. Maybe they just don't allow spotty men into the police force. Who'd listen to a cop with a zit on his face? There were two of them. Plus the head warden: "It may not be exactly illegal, but it's against the spirit of the law to put money into other people's meters like that." Holy Kiljan. "What's this spirit thing?" "The spirit of the law is what lies behind them." "And are you from the Spiritualist Department, then?" Not funny, they didn't like that. Probably why they left me sitting there for a whole hour. All alone. With the spirit of the law. It's just one of those days. In Fuck-a-Duck Ville. And Daisy pregnant. No way was it me. A snake is swallowing an ostrich's egg in my head as I shove the key into the door. Silence. But I can sense they're in the kitchen. Then Mom:

"Hi."

They're sitting at the kitchen table. Empty plates and a saturated atmosphere in the air. Lolla with a cigarette.

Mom: "Where were you?"

"At a séance."

"No, really, where?"

"Down at the police station."

"You don't say? Have you eaten anything? Here. Sit down. I'll heat something up for you. Hólmfrídur called."

"Uh-huh."

Three Lolla drags. And some kind of heavy silence, like being smothered in somebody else's embrace. A smell of sweaters. Eyeballs darting to and fro. The sound of cutlery. A knife and a fork. I feel like a spoon.

Lolla: "Hey, listen, yeah, I've got to run."

"Where are you going?" I ask.

"Got my shift."

"Uh-huh."

They say their goodbyes over my head. The things you can read into a bye. Especially a bi-bye. Handbag noises and a 7-meter-zipper sound. The door slamming. I feel so heavy I can barely eat. Can almost smell my own bad breath. Andrea Jónsdóttir (20,000) blabbing on Channel 2.

Mom: "What were you saying, were you at a séance?"

"Nah. Only joking."

I manage to shut her up from the kitchen. She sits in front of the TV. Mom watches the box in the old-fashioned way. Just watches. Andrea plays a Police track. Yeah, yeah. We are spirits in the material world. I count. They sing that line twenty-seven times. I get a Sting in my ears.

When I finally step into my room, it feels like stepping into a refuge on the highlands after battling through a blizzard. A scout told me once that you could always count on finding two things in mountain refuges in Greenland. Dry matches and a pile of porn mags. The bare necessities, eh? Which is exactly what I need right now. I slip a tape in. *LA Gang Bang.* I've been into this stuff lately. This one's a Miss Piggy (60,000) with two megatons on her chest—and a bra just for the sport of it, and panties that are only there to give her something to take off—and another two on her behind, all those buttocks need now are two nipples. She sits in a chair and rings her grandpa, who comes to collect her in a vintage Ford to drive her in search of some guys. This scene is far too long: them in the car. The grandpa proudly ogling his granddaughter's tits. As anyone else in his shoes would do, I suppose. She picks up three studs on a tennis court and goes home with them. Grandpa seems to be out of the picture by now. Waiting in the car, maybe. The only problem with porn movies is that they've got no suspense. You just know that everyone's going to take their clothes off and that eventually they'll all come. At least once. And no one dies. She sits in a chair. They stand around her. Slightly disappointed to see she's shaved. I'm not into bald pussies. But it's pretty frightening when she starts the unzipping and actually pulls those things out. Boy, can those guys be well hung. We're not just talking sausages here. We're talking meat loaves. At least it's consoling to know they can never get them fully up: 90 degrees, but at a stretch. Fat men doing push-ups. She sucks them all in turn. And laughs. No. Laughter kills it. Laughter and sex. Female laughter in porn. Takes the fizz out of it. Cuts off the hard-on. That stiff dry salami. As if they were laughing at you. Castrating you. She turns around and shoves one of them up her ass. The only problem with porn movies is that they're pretty boring. I fast-forward. Fucking in fast motion. They change into animals. A nature film. Am I getting bored with porn? Is this the beginning of impotence?

I press them all, all the buttons, I mean: fast-rewind, fast-forward, play, slow motion, pause. They ejaculate onto her face, each in turn, spunk in slow motion. Like three goals viewed in action replay. All we need now is a sports commentator. I'm doing everything I can to get the most out of this. I get nothing out of this. Three pretty boring—but nevertheless immortal—orgasms in a quaint little bungalow in LA. A knock. I'm still lying there with a full erection, in front of the blank screen, when Mom sticks her head through the door.

"I just wanted to ask you if you'd like some cocoa. I'm making some cocoa."

"Yeah. Yeah, sure."

Cocoa with Mom. In the kitchen. And nothing else to it? Yeah. Of course there is. There's something else to it. Nothing's free in this world anymore. Not even between a mother and son. Buys me off with cocoa. She mommies down my hard-on, lulls me out of my blues, nights the day out of me. She says she was looking at some old snapshots of us, the family, at Aunty Sigrún's house in Hvammstangi. A camping trip to Strandir. Me and Elsa, six and eight years old, in similar trousers in an empty fjord. Iceland is full of unused fjords. Mountains with absolutely no purpose but to be photographed. Elsa was always mucking about on the beach, with Dad, she says. I just wanted to stay in the car. To listen to the radio. But I was supposedly very funny, she said. "I remember when you said the sea was a bogeyman, and you said that someone should shoot him." Mom laughs. Childhood jokes. Was I funny or plain idiotic? Yeah. Me, the freckled blond dwarf, barely visible in a yellow Saab, sitting with a funereal air, listening to news about drowned sailors, scanning the ocean with accusing eyes. Those were the days when Alan Ball was still playing for Everton, hadn't moved to Arsenal yet. The past bores me. I can't stand the past. I even seriously doubt I was ever small. Or that wasn't me. Childhood is stupid. A fuckup you just happen to fall into that takes decades to recover from. Still, though, just for Mom's sake, and because I sense there's something on her mind, I ask:

"And what was I like?"

"As a kid?"

"Yeah."

"You. You were always wonderful. Always so calm. We never had to worry about you. You could just sit there for hours, perfectly content, but I . . . I never knew what you were thinking about. You were probably just thinking. You were a kind of philosophical type. That's what Sigrún used to call you, the 'little philosopher.' 'Where's our little philosopher?' she'd always say. Her boys were so completely different, of course, a real wild bunch, they were. You couldn't let them out of your sight for a second."

"Isn't she always asking you when I'm going to move out?"

"No, no . . . She sometimes asks if you're any nearer to getting engaged yet, but your granny says not to rush into anything foolish."

"Yeah."

"You were always such a mommy's boy."

"Oh yeah?"

"Yeah. Your father was a bit worried about you at the time, but you weren't the usual type of mommy's boy. I mean, you didn't come up for cuddles and things. You wouldn't let anyone near you. Got on your nerves if anyone tried to hug you."

"I couldn't stand it?"

"No. Lolla said it's well known in psychology. What did she say it was called again? Physiophobia or something."

"And is that some disease?"

"No, I don't think so."

"Is there no medication for it?"

"Nooo . . . ha ha ha . . . apart from the human touch, maybe."

Mom stops turning her cocoa cup on the kitchen table and rubs my upper arm and smiles. I smile inanely. She lets go.

"Lolla knows more about these things than I do, she did psychology, just ask her. . . ."

I stand up and walk to the counter. Take a cookie out of an open packet. Chocolate on both sides. Bi-cookies.

"Lolla," I say, with a full mouth, to a half-open closet.

"You get on with Lolla, don't you? You don't mind her staying here?"

"No. No, no."

"It's OK with you, then?"

"Yeah, yeah," I say, and turn toward her.

"Are you sure?"

"Yeah, yeah. So how could I be a mommy's boy if I didn't want anyone to touch me?"

"You. That was just the feeling I got."

"And what about Dad? Was he . . . ?"

"Yeah . . ."—Mom peers into her cup. Coffee cups are for reading the future, but cocoa? The past? No. Chocolate won't tell you anything. I wait for the outcome. Something serious? Is she finally going to come out with it? Something horrific. Something about Dad abusing me, some heavy-duty psychological-trauma shit. Something I've blocked out. Some nasty childhood joke.—". . . No. He was just a bit disappointed you weren't more keen to go to football matches with him and things. I think."

"Yeah, I always preferred to watch the games on TV."

"Yes," she says, sucking in her breath.

I wait a moment. I suddenly remember the clothes I'm wearing. Brown jeans and a plain blue T-shirt. I'm moving away, but I turn when she says:

"Hlynur, there's something . . ."

"Yeah?"

"There's something I've got to tell you."

"Yeah."

"There's something I've been waiting to tell you."

"Yeah."

"Something I probably should have told you a while ago."

"Yeah."

I walk to the fridge and lean on it. Feel its purring vibrations. Prepare for the crunch. She hesitates and looks at me.

"I don't know how to . . . say this, but I'm . . . I'm . . ."

This is getting far too serious. Too much aura here. I always sneeze when people start opening up to me. Must be allergic to auras. I sneeze and say:

"Excuse me."

"I've been thinking about this for such a long time . . . and I just wanted to give it to you straight . . . but it's just so difficult to say it, to you. But I . . . You might have heard something, people are always gossiping . . ."

I feel sneeze number two is about to shoot through my head. Mom doesn't seem to be able to finish this on her own. She needs help. All of a sudden I feel I have to fix this before the sneeze comes.

"You're telling me you're a lesbian," I spurt out and then sneeze. Meanwhile Mom answers. I don't hear whether she says yes or no.

"God bless you," she says.

"Thanks."

"What do you say to that?"

"What?"

"That I'm in love with Lolla."

"That you're a lesbian?"

"Y . . . eah."

"Does that mean we can never . . . ?"

She gives me a reluctant smile.

"No, I mean. If that's what you are, that's what you are. Cool."

"It is?"

"Yeah."

"You don't find it strange?"

"Maybe a bit late in the day, but . . ."

"Yeah, I know . . ."

She peers into the cup again. Does that mean she was a lesbian all along? Or is this a taste one acquires with age? Picture her peering into the same cup, twenty years old. A coffee cup. Full of future. She must have been too insecure and shy with it, or drunk it in the wrong way, so that the wrong visions appeared. Dad, Elsa, and me . . . Maybe I should just count myself lucky she didn't come out of her closet before now. Otherwise. What would I be? I might have come out of some other closet. Out of Sara's . . . No . . . The fridge turns silent. I move away from it. She stares at me and waits with her eyes—eyedrops in her eyes—for me to say something. I make something up for her.

"I mean. It's just a question of coffee or cocoa, no big deal, just as long as people know what they want."

"Well, that's good to hear."

We shut up. We shut up for a moment. I turn back to the fridge. Open it. Light. Mom rubs her face in her hands. I steal a glimpse of her, unnoticed. People rub their faces every now and then, as if they were trying to erase an old expression, as if they were trying to stop their faces from locking into a fixed mold. Yeah. Somehow she's changed. I close the fridge. My trousers pull me toward the doorway. I hover over Mom. She looks at the fridge. I'm about to say something, but all words have suddenly vanished from the Reykjavík sky. Not a snowflake in sight. I move away. The john. Sink. Mirror. Son of a dyke. Sounds like something out of an old Western. Something bad. Me too. I also try to rub that old expression off my face. Piss. I'm on my way into the bedroom when I remember I left my cigarettes on the kitchen table. I nudge a sentence into the kitchen before entering: "I've got some tapes for you two if you like, some women-with-women stuff. . . ." Mom looks up. Tears in her eyes. I can't take these mommy tears. Mommy tears I cannot take. I turn to a dry packet of cigarettes, pick it up, Mom grabs my arm. Forces me to look into her swimming eyeballs . . .

"Thank you. Thank you, Hlynur love, thank you for . . . taking it so well."

"Yeah. No problem, Mom. No problem."

"You don't know how much weight you've just taken off my shoulders."

She pulls me over and throws her arms around me. She sitting, me standing. Physiophobia. Her hair against my stomach. Reminds me of Lolla: her hair under my chin. But different. I feel like I'm up to my neck in deep emotional shit, sinking rapidly into a swamp. A female swamp. Then she lets go and looks at me:

"Sorry, but I . . ."

"OK, Mom. No problem. OK?"

"OK."

I take the packet of cigarettes into the bedroom. One of those days. These are the kind of chores you get assigned to when you're unemployed. Rescuing people from parking fines, dealing with pregnant girls around town, making sure the local police force doesn't get too bored, and edging middle-aged women out of the closet and . . . and what else? Just give me a call, whatever your problem is, I'll solve it.

I lie in my bed, like a tired old steam engine that has finally reached its destination after a long journey, sighing puffs of smoke into the air. Turn on the box. An American talk show. The subject of the debate: "I slept with my mother's girlfriend." Well, did you now? Some ghastly cheeseburger fatso sits proudly on the bench of the accused, beside his couch potato of a mother (100), and an upholstered lump of a lezzie (500), whose skull has started to sprout, but is still shaved bald. The female host (15,000) fakes interest and surprise, and looks like a mare pasted in makeup with a microphone, as she asks the son:

"And so, you didn't know that they were having a relationship?"

"Yeah, yeah, I knew."

"And that didn't stop you from sleeping with her? Why did you do it?"

"I just, you know . . . I always wanted to sleep with my mother and, you know, she was the next best thing . . ."

The audience bursts into gales of laughter and cheers. The mother smiles. The lezzie smiles. The son all cocky and proud. Americans. Have they reached the top of the evolutionary ladder? Doesn't matter what you've done, how big the problem is—it all vanishes into thin air if you can confess it on TV.

I scratch my crotch. Some stains on my trousers. Two dark stains on my fly. Mommy tears.

Dingaling. And me. One head in two shoes. Guitar solo over Mount Esja. Robert Plant. I've started to see airwaves. Robert Plant glides over Reykjavík, cars tangled in his hair, that long outdated Zeppelin hair. Twisting in their wheels. People walk by in that old-fashioned stride. As if they were just walking down Laugavegur. Sad. Maybe because the air is so still and stagnant. Stagnancy makes everything so local. People can't even spare a warm thought for Robert De Niro. Poor guy. There he is, hanging on the outside wall of the multiplex, womanless and totally available. Some Icelanders drive past in their vintage cars of the future. The telephone poles on Long Island are wooden, and have blue skies behind them. And De Niro, freshly shaven, behind the net curtains, curses down the phone, and then steps out into a cold and still American morning, into a golden Continental. What should I say to her? Yeah: (a) I was wearing a condom; (b) I didn't come; (c) there's no way I could have made you pregnant.

A February feeling on the Snorrabraut tarmac. Sad to see so few people sparing a thought for the pile of dirty old snow on the sidewalk by the state liquor store. OK. It's my turn to spend some time with it now, but I can't stay for long. The Pearl restaurant on the hill looks like it's being filled with a low instrumental version of "Careless Whisper" by George Michael. Mom took a day off today. Workers are entitled to that, part of the new labor deal. Coming out of the closet: one-day leave. Now, for the first time, they're sleeping together in broad daylight. Lolla and Mom. Make it a good one, for my sake. For good old Hlynsey boy here. Yeah. Had to do something about this Hofy case. I.e. I'm on my way over to her place. I.e. she told me to come over. I feel like I'm on my way over to pick up something I forgot. Hofy says I forgot a seed inside her. And that now that it's been planted, it's following some itinerary of its own. Started to do its own cooking, that thing scientists call life. Yeah. An egg is hatching inside Hofy's little taut stomach. No fucking way. I shoot forward, propelled by the same force that once shot me out of my father's dick.

"Ring My Bell." That song made it to the top because of its double meaning. I press the clitoris and Hofy instantly comes. To the door. Hi. The snot valve is gone: the stud out of her nose. Is she trying to mother herself up? I try not to look like a dad. Don't take my shoes off. I send my eyes in to take a quick peep at the bedroom. The scene of the crime. I'm a cop. An undercover cop checking under the covers.

Conditions at Hofy's place: calm, good visibility, a sudden outbreak of tears, tea, temperature 37 degrees.

A weeping woman. I'd have absolutely no hesitation in saying that that's number one on my things-I-cannot-stand list. Except it's even worse if it's a weeping mother-to-be. I'm allergic to people's auras. And this is a wet one. I try to keep mine dry. I'm on a raft here. Rowing toward the dry land on the sofa. While she cries into two cups in the kitchen. Then comes back in with them. Ah well. Might as well just wind this thing up, no point in beating about the bush, like a cop:

"So, according to you, conception took place on the night of the fifteenth of December?"

"Oh, Hlynur . . ."

"That's when you got pregnant?"

"Yes. It must have been then. Or the other time."

"The other time?"

"Yeah, I can't remember exactly when it was, two days later, maybe. The last time."

"Hang on a sec."

"Yeah, after that party at Rosy's and those."

"Did we go home together after that?"

"Yeah. Have you already forgotten?"

"No, no. I'm just trying to fit the pieces together here."

"What, with all your other pieces? Is that all I am to you, a piece in some kind of jigsaw of yours?"

"I . . . No, no. Two pieces, you're at least two pieces. At least that."

"Two pieces out of how many . . . five hundred?"

"Well, you can see for yourself, it's a difficult jigsaw."

"And how's it going?"

"Putting it together? I've only just started."

"Haven't you made anyone else pregnant?"

"No."

"Sure?"

"Yeah, well. Wouldn't say that. These things happen sometimes. I found some new stuff when I went to London once, an abortion lotion, well, more of a spray, really clever. It's basically a big cylinder, someone said I looked like an exterminator with that thing on my back."

She sucks air into her nose. Maybe it's just like the "water cycle." Seawater evaporating into clouds, before turning into rain over the rivers and flowing back into the sea again. In fact, I've never really bought that crazy theory, but still. I can see it now. Hofy sucks air into her nose, and that changes into a salted sea in her head, and oozes out of her eyes. And then it starts all over again. How come no one's ever tried to market tears? As an allergy antidote, for example? Thirty women crying into glasses on a conveyor belt in Eskifjördur. Hofy stands up and leaves the room. Comes back with Kleenex and says, like a snot-stuffed head that's been in the oven for thirty-five minutes and started to sizzle in its own juice:

"Would you get out of here?"

"Go?"

"Yeah. Get out of here."

"But aren't we going to talk about this?"

"Talk . . . I might as well be talking to . . ."

I spot a tattered teddy bear in one of the chairs and say: "Him?"

"Yeah. Will you just go! Get out of here! Creep!"

Yeah. Hólmfrídur Pálsdóttir is really red in the face now and snot is pouring out of her eyes. She doesn't pick her nose enough. And the old ventilation shaft is clogged. Or maybe it's just the pregnancy. Spunk plus egg equals snot, turning into a gobbet, turning into clay, turning into flesh, turning into life. Still, though. This. This pregnancy is just a pipe dream up her nose. And now it's started to leak. It'll all be over by tomorrow. She stands by the door. Speaks in a phlegmish accent. With a Kleenex under her eyes like a veiled Muslim. Yeah. Women are foreigners. I stand up and say, in as deep a voice as a man with glasses can conjure up, enunciating each syllable to be sure she understands:

"Sorry."

"Out! Just get out! Out!"

I have to pass her to get out of the room. The territorial waters surrounding auras are said to extend for one meter. Which means there's bound to be a collision at the door. The meeting of two worlds. Two auras. Mine is getting wet. Hers is drying up. I pass her, shielded by my glasses. She hurls some words at my back:

"You might think this is some kind of p . . . This might be some kind of . . . [sob sob] . . . some kind of pest to you."

The thought had crossed my mind, yeah. Saw a program on Channel 75 the other day, the Discovery Channel, about the first grams of human life. You just couldn't tell what it was at first—if you were a third party, I mean, another species—impossible to say what kind of program was going on. For the first few weeks the fetus is just a shapeless growth. Then it sprouts a tail, looking much more like a mouse in the making than a future student, doesn't get its graduation cap until later on. Wonder how many weeks she is. I turn. Wonder if there's a tail inside her. But I reckon that's probably not exactly what she wants to hear right now, and switch back into *sapiens* mode. I try to look as twentieth-century-like as I can:

"Sorry. That was just. I was just. I'm not used to dealing with stuff like this."

"Like what?"

"You know."

"Yeah. I know, and you . . . you obviously . . ."

"How far gone are you?"

Oops. That made it sound like she's got cancer. But still. Maybe you can say that the fetus is some kind of tumor that grows and grows but is benign, and gets removed with a cesarean and eventually learns how to talk. But she doesn't take it that way. Fortunately. She even manages to break out of this crazy female tantrum she's throwing and calmly says:

"Six weeks."

"And what are you going to do?"

"I'm going to have it."

"Are you sure?"

"Yeah."

"But. I mean. I. You. Ehm."

"Hlynur, this baby is due on the twenty-second of August, and I'm going to be there for it."

"Yeah. I just hope he'll be there too."

"Who?"

"The baby."

"You're *not* funny, Hlynur, OK?"

"Yeah, no. This is a serious matter."

"Yeah. It is. This is a serious matter."

"But I don't get it."

"Don't get what?"

"I mean, I was wearing a condom."

"Yeah."

"So I don't understand."

"They're not a hundred-percent safe. It can happen."

I picture the courtroom with a top lawyer in a live broadcast on Court TV. The first lawsuit against a condom manufacturer. Hafsteinsson *v.* Durex. Exhibit 1 in a cradle in front of the judge's bench. Yeah. A chance to be famous. A chance. Maybe I left the condom inside her and it sailed into her womb with its full cargo, and then the fetus will grow inside it, and pop out with a swimming cap on its head. No. I remember. The condom was on. Not a chance. I approach the next question with more caution. She's standing there with her hands behind her back, leaning against the doorway. I'm standing on a maze of a mat in the hallway. Yeah. Better not lose my bearings.

"And, ehm. Am I the only one you . . . ?"

"Yes."

"No one else?"

"No . . . Although I've a good mind to, after . . . after this . . ."

"What do you mean?"

"Just. To behave like you, as if, as if this were just some kind of a . . . lizard . . . Is that what you were hoping? Were you hoping it was someone else?"

"No, no."

"Yeah. Just say it. It would be a huge load off your mind to know that you weren't the dad, but someone else. . . ."

I just stand there on the mat with my mouth shut, but probably haven't quite managed to hide my thoughts behind my glasses. She sees through them. The tears are back again, she starts pumping them out like an old generator. If there's one thing that's outmoded it's got to be tears. Sexual desire means nothing but trouble. Copulation equals complication. Outmoded. If only it were a mouse . . . if only there were a wire sticking out of Hofy, attached to a mouse, and you could just delete it all and . . . defrag her. I stare down at the mat. No mouse. She says bye before flying into her bedroom and locking the door behind her. Wet streets in Singapore. I'm left standing in the hall. Like a clumsy piece of design, an unnecessarily complicated contraption that was designed for the sole purpose of supporting this perfectly mundane hairdo. I wait a moment. Walk ever so carefully—to be sure my hair doesn't fall off me—into the kitchen and unscrew the tap. As if it contained some secret. Glass of water. Wet Kleenex on the counter. I take out a cigarette, and am taken aback when I see how it shakes between my fingers. I want to get the hell out of here, but all of a sudden I get a flash of Lolla and Mom in my head and . . . I sit in the corner. I've painted myself into a corner. I've screwed myself into a tight corner. "In love with Lolla." More than I could say. Put the cigarette back into the pack. All the women in my life, in bed, crying in sorrow and joy. Lizards and mothers changing sex. A fetus sacrificing a tail for a nose. Suddenly I think of Elsa. The pill. An embroidered sunset hangs on the kitchen wall, with two fluttering seagulls, and the following words inscribed below it: Life is a flower, growing in your heart. Oh, Hofy. So that's what it looks like inside that head of yours. What remotest chance could there be of our cells ever merging into one? We're diametrically opposed species. Can an ass calve a cow? Hofy . . . You're in bed now, watering your life flower with your tears. I could do with some watering myself. What time is it? 18:45. Yeah. Must go down to the water hole. I leave the kitchen—a pregnant silence in the hall— and reach the doorway. I'm about to step out of the building when an externally lit face appears in the wicket of the door. Eyes flashing in the darkness. I automatically look away, but I realize (a) that he saw me and (b) that it was Páll Níelsson. In person. I swivel back to face the door. He's looking far too chirpy, with his face pressed against the glass, knocking on the window. Palli Níelsson. OK. I briskly open the door, knee him in the groin, and make a run for it. Nah.

"Hey, hiiiiii!"

"Yeah, hi . . ."

"How are you? Hlynur, right?"

Somehow Palli Níelsson is just like his name. You could juggle those thirteen letters any way you like, but always come up with the same result, that same guy standing in front of you. He's even wearing a baseball cap (P), has squinting eyes (ll) behind his glasses, a small chin (a), and a thin stroke for a mouth (i). He's wearing a plastic leather jacket, which makes a lot of unnecessary noise as he squeaks into the hallway. Bald when he takes his cap off. I see he's about a head smaller than I am (not sure which head) when he steps down from the high threshold. Maybe it's his tan, but he reminds me of Mr. Nilsson, the monkey in *Pippi Longstocking*.

He asks me if I'm leaving and I say I'm leaving and he says don't leave. He asks about his little Hofy, and is happy to hear she's having a rest, and then talks me into the living room. His tongue holding me hostage.

"And I heard the other day that you can watch TV on a computer now. But I can't see what difference it's going to make."

"No."

"I mean, I'm afraid that people will lose human contact altogether, with all this Internet stuff and things."

"Yeah."

"Not that we've got much to worry about, we dentists, I mean. There'll always be a patient in the chair, and some tooth that needs mending."

"Yeah."

"Not to mention life itself, you can't create that on a computer screen, now, can you? Ha ha . . ."

That plastic leather jacket of his squeaks with every syllable, and he doesn't seem to realize what it's doing to my eardrums. So obnoxiously chirpy in that plastic skin of his, where he's sitting in the chair, waggling his baseball cap to and fro, trying to scoop some content into this inane monologue of his, but it's just hot air, in that hat, the same hot air that fills his mouth as it gapes at the end of every sentence. Look. I feel like he's forgotten to anesthetize me. Before boring me with all this dentistry drill. A cavity in his soul. That no filling can fill. Maybe dentists have no sense of the soul and the metaphysical because their handiwork is doomed to remain in the grave forever. Six thousand years from now their fillings will still be clinging to those skulls. There have been many debates about the exact location of the soul in the human body, but I think there's a fairly unanimous consensus that it's not in our teeth. Fifty thousand smiles buried under the earth. Hey. When does the soul enter the fetus? On what week? When the tail drops off? And where does it come from? Is there a soul in sperm? Maybe those extra 6.5 centimeters . . . Maybe they're the soul? Arise, arise, my soul. Yeah. There's something in that. Hofy comes in with double eyes, with a double soul. The dentist doesn't seem to notice his daughter's swollen tear glands. Teeth, that's all they can see. No fear of him seeing mine, even when I try to smile. Hofy nestles into the other end of the sofa like a red-eyed bird, and lies there on her egg, with her legs tucked under her wings. While the baseball cap blabs on in front of us.

The dentist's jeep is white like a police car. I sit in the back, a condemned man, heading for the penitentiary to face the harshest sentence I've ever had to serve: dinner in their semidetached palace out in Suburbia Ville. That's it. I'm not sleeping with a woman again. Marinated in Hofy's tears, my appeals were quashed and ignored. Got fiancéed straight out to the car where Palli, in person, strapped me to the chair. They're both in the front, the family squad, the pigs, while the head screw waits at home, roasting her spit over the fire. The moon looms over the city mall and Tom Hanks stands behind it, on its dark side, gazing sadly out the porthole of *Apollo 13*. I lean against the window of the car. Lights on in deserted Kópavogur living rooms. Somehow difficult to imagine anyone ever turning them on. Heaps of filthy snow by the roadside, old hardened meringue, Xmas leftovers, buried under a dirty crust of February, the frozen mud on the windscreens will be thawing over the hot hood at the next traffic light. Snow tires gnawing at the asphalt. Snobville, measured in square meters of parquet, kitchen aromas of roasted pork-ette. Batteries buzzing in pacemakered hearts. A golden retriever barking in a cradle. And a full freezer. Full of life after death.

The lampposts droop their heads in commiseration as I pass.

The jeep—financed by the defrauded public—is as spanking brand new and as impeccable as a dentist's surgery: white polished enamel, anesthetized tires, reclining seats with headrests. The engine runs on schoolchildren's pain, drilling into their shrieking molars with each spin of the wheel, the sound of that CD player has had to travel down thirteen root canals to reach our ears. And the driver is in a gleeful mood, as men who extract their living from the decaying mouths of candy junkies so often are. A brain in a baseball cap.

As I walk up the garden steps, I try to picture the largest condom in the world covering the whole house, so that I won't be able to get in. The mother (30,000) is waiting with—well, of course, yes—a wonderful in-law-ish expression on her face, and sucks me into an embrace. I disappear into her, like a seed into an egg. Hofy's ma. Sigurlaug Fridriksdóttir or Didriksdóttir. The same sirloin steak as Hofy, but more well done, very well done. After seventeen trips to the Costa del Cancer. Her skin's more tanned than leather. Women are better cooks than men, but sooner cooked by life. She releases me from her embrace and I'm suddenly worried I might have made her pregnant. Hofy gets her nose from her mom. And now a picture of mine is being developed inside her darkroom. Hope the enlargement is included.

Hofy's home. The family manor. The childhood abode. A carpeted valley, overgrown with ebony and pine and oak and birch— but that's just spruce, isn't it, that table in the corner?—and driftwood and ivory and Formica but . . . this tall, thirty-three-year-old Hlynur is beginning to lose all his leaves in the middle of this evergreen forest. Yeah. The living room is crammed with all those useless artifacts that dull-witted people give to people who already have everything, including birthdays: all those pointless dainty little-knitted-Chinese-puppies-skipping-in-the-woods-with-picnic-baskets thingamajigs: statuettes on the sideboards, ornaments on the windowsills, their lifetime-achievement awards. And boy, have they achieved. This is like a stall at the Kolaport flea market in twenty years' time.

Visiting a dentist's home is pretty much like visiting his surgery, except worse: you don't get the anesthetic. Mind you:

"So what can I get you? Gin, whiskey, beer . . ."

"A whiskey, maybe."

Lerti, Hofy's bro, is sitting opposite me with his Bryndís trophy (100,000, as already mentioned). She's chewing gum. Remember that. Bryndís is a model. I recognize her from a two-year-old towel ad, the white cotton hardly covering her naked body. Pity she never advertised sponges. Mind you. A skeleton of skin. She's got the type of body that seems to have been designed to hold up two arms. A face that's only there to remind you there's a skull underneath. The question is: Are there any thoughts in there? She seems to wear all her thoughts on her skin. Pity she doesn't have more of it.

They sit with a gap between them, like in a car, and I can't see any evidence of hanky-panky between them or any tail formations when I X-ray her model womb. Maybe Lerti can't afford a pregnancy, although someone said he's got some job on the stock market or something. I try to establish some eye contact with Bryndís, just for the hell of it, but it seems to require a telephoto lens. Her eyes can only focus on Lerti's face, which is actually a full-time job in itself, because he's started to move his jaw now, to chew on his thoughts. He speaks as if he were chewing, regurgitating the same old crap:

"Like Antonio Banderas, for instance . . . I mean, he's Spanish, isn't he? I mean, you can really hear the accent . . . But it doesn't seem to be any problem for him, I mean, he's a star now, got loads of work out there in Hollywood."

They are what you'd call body people. People who are first and foremost bodies. Bryndís's designer legs. Crossed. I look at them until I get a thought from them: there's nothing remotely human about those legs, nothing to remind one of man's millennial struggles up the evolutionary ladder. Those legs were grown in a lab. Progress? All these people here are body-built. A slight overgrowth in the parents, I see. Palli's seven months pregnant in his armchair, trying to balance that G and T on his paunch. Difficult to make out the contours of Sigurlaug's body, though (I don't have the decoder to descramble that kind of tracksuit she's wearing), and she's busy performing some kind of hara-kiri in the kitchen right now, pouring her soul into a sauceboat. Hofy's the only one with a bit of soul in this place, yeah. Or was. Before she blew the hatch off that valve on her nose, and let it go, to make room for the new one growing inside her. As for me. Well, I may be no medium, but I think there's more to me than these wobbling jaws, pumping blood, and stomach juices. But where is the soul in us? Somewhere in there between our organs. Somewhere in there between our organs there's an air bubble floating around (like when you fart in a swimming pool and the air gets trapped in your trunks), and it'll stay there until the flesh drops off your bones. Then it evaporates into thin air with that ghastly smell. Which is why corpses stink so much. Remember the hospital. That summer job at the mortuary. Anyway. I have a soul. In fact, the only purpose of my body is to stop it from going up in steam. But this crowd here has had far too many steam baths. I check the remote. I've got the whole world in my right inside pocket, everything that's happening right now. The street corners of Belfast. A Greenpeace dinghy in the Pacific. Fifteen hopping cheerleaders in Texas, in a sunny football stadium holding seventy thousand people.

But of all the seventy channels I could choose from, I'm stuck on this family test card and all I can think of is: I need a piss. Somehow I'm reduced to nothing more than my bodily functions here, surrounded by all these body people, and actually hear myself saying:

"And Schwarzenegger."

"Yeah, right, exactly, Schwarzenegger . . . and, hang on, what others?"

"Others what?" says Palli Níelsson.

"Foreigners making it in Hollywood," the son continues.

"Yeah, wait a minute, who was that guy in *The Godfather*?"

"Marlon Brando?"

"No, starts with an A . . ."

"Al Pacino? No, Dad, he's one-hundred-percent American."

"No, not Al Pacino—Anthony, yeah, Anthony Quinn."

"He wasn't in *The Godfather*."

"Wasn't he?"

"No."

"Yeah, right, I'm getting mixed up, he was in *Zorba*, he's Greek, he's from Greece, I knew there was something, at least I remembered he was a foreigner. He used to be a big star here in the olden days, you know."

"Yeah? I never knew he was from Greece. Did you, Hlynur, did you know that?"

"Yeah. I mean no. He was born in Mexico. Or his mother was Mexican and his father was Irish. But he was brought up in America. Los Angeles."

"Yeah?" says the son.

"Are you sure? I'm pretty sure he was Greek, you know," says the father.

"No."

"Hey, why don't we just look it up?"

Palli Níelsson stands up and disappears into the depths of the house, searching for an eighty-year-old, but not forgotten, conception. Turn-of-the-century Mexico. A windswept plateau at night, shutters banging against the windows of a village motel, and inside, an Irish Quinn shooting his little Anthony into the darkness of a native vagina. I picture a close-up of that glistening turn-of-the-century dick, faintly reflecting the moon as it slides in and out of that moist Mexican vagina, when Hofy appears from the kitchen with a glass of water and sits down. A phony angelic look on her face. Yeah. Must be an immaculate conception. Lerti goes on:

"And anyway, it doesn't seem to matter, even though they're foreigners, I mean, obviously they all speak English, but it doesn't matter that they have a bit of an accent."

"Sure," I say in a slightly mocking voice.

"Huh?"

"Sure . . . he said sure," says Bryndís, and I've never heard her voice before. I feel Hofy's gaze. Her X-ray eyes.

"Yeah . . . hahaha, exactly. Exactly, yeah," says Lerti.

Palli returns to confirm Anthony Quinn's Mexican roots, and the housewife makes her entrance, asking everyone to sit at the table. Asks Lerti to bring in a chair from the kitchen. For me. His name is Lerti. I ponder on that as I go searching for the john, hidden in the depths of this bizarre palace. WC: Wonder Closet. Forty square meters of tiles in my eyes. No wonder these people never come out of the closet if they all look like this. I hide behind the shower curtain and wait for them all to fall asleep. Nah. I relieve myself (accidentally spill some yellow ones over the edge) and then hunt for evidence. The lady's got enough facial creams here to take her into the next millennium. They look like barbecue sauces when you think of that carbonized-steak skin of hers. I take the lipstick and write on the mirror: I fucked your daughter, fuck you all! Not. They'd all know it was me, then. I've probably been hanging out in here for far too long. Don't think much of that cream. Walk back in again.

The prisoner is fed. The earthly remains of a lamb we try to swallow before it rots.

Sigurlaug: "Healer, dear, wouldn't you like to take that off?"

"What?"

"Take it off, your jacket, wouldn't you like to take it off?"

"Yeah, maybe."

I'm a retard. I peel off my skin and slide it on to the back of the chair. Deplumed. I'm "Healer." Suddenly I remember a slit in my turtleneck, in the right shoulder, where the seam's come undone. The turtleneck is dark blue and I'm wearing a white T-shirt under it. My entire soul is assembling around that hole right now: my inner man, that tiny glow. Bright white and awkward. Farewell, Mom. Lolla. All the best. Everyone here seems to be in pretty well-sewn clothes. Supertramp. Maybe I should have taken something else off instead, my head, for example. Everyone's sitting and, praise the Lord, Bryndís is sitting beside me. And not on the hole side. Feel a bit like Inspector Derrick as I watch her taking the gum out of her mouth and resting it on the edge of her plate. Must get it. Need it in my collection. At least it would give this nightmare some sense of purpose, since I screwed up in the toilet. Too bad I didn't bring a box for it. Came unprepared. Ah well. Sigurlaug reenters, bearing the sauceboat like a chalice. Carefully holding it in both hands like a sacred relic. Her soul. I baptize my meat in it and piously pass it on. It moves around the table in a kind of ancient ritual. We humbly swallow.

"No, give the sauce back to me, Lerti darling, must keep it hot," says the housewife, placing it on top of a kind of designer candle-cum-altarpiece thingamajig. Let us pray:

"Pray, could you . . . could you pass me the mint sauce, please?"

"And what were you saying, Healer? Where do you live now?"

"Mom. Hlynur. His name is Hlynur," says Lerti.

"Yes, that's what I said, didn't I? Where do you live, Hlynur?"

"Bergthórugata."

"And it's just the two of you, isn't it?"

"No. Three of us. With Lolla. They're partners."

"In business?"

"Not exactly."

"No? Oh, what then? Some kind of project?"

"Mom." (That's Hofy speaking, the future mother of my child. Hip-hip-hurray! More Icelanders!)

"Yeah, you could say that. They've got this project going together."

"I see, some further-education thing, is it?"

"Yeah. Mainly night classes."

"I see, and what are they studying?"

"Oh. Ehm. Dykes. Dykes and other forms of irrigation in the Amazon."

"Dykes? God, they have courses for everything now, don't they?"

"Yeah."

"Sounds very technical, did you know about that, Lerti?"

"Ehm. Yeah."

"There's always a new one, isn't there?" says Sigurlaug, dipping her eyes into the sauceboat, adding, as she stands up: "I'll just get some more sauce."

Bit of a heavy silence at the table until she returns.

"So she lives with you, then, is that it?"

"Yeah. They're partners."

I'm repeating myself. I don't often do that, but it finally seems to have the desired effect. They inch their noses back, knitting their brows, until Lerti hops in, 50 percent scandalized and 50 percent joking:

"You mean they're . . . lovers?"

"Lerti, please," says the mother, clinging to the boat in her hands, but unable to utter another word. A revolutionary silence

explodes over this 700-square-meter patch of suburban carpet—
I glance back at Bryndís's gum on the edge of the plate beside
me—until Sigurlaug shifts key, and tries to drown the whole thing
in sauce:

"More sauce, anybody?"

"No thanks."

"No, couldn't, thanks."

"Yeah, no thanks."

"No, I'm absolutely stuffed."

Palli Níelsson has the last word. The dentist drilling his hole.
And everyone thinking, no one looking, everyone thinking about
that hole in my turtleneck, on my right shoulder. They all see
through me. They all see how bloody and disgusting I am inside,
under that superficial skin of mine. I'm nothing more than a blood
pudding. Raw blood pudding. Podgy, pudgy pudding. A slimy
glistening throbbing heart of blood pudding. Covered in a disease-
infested sauce. A Reykjavík werewolf in Gardabaer. Creep! Get out
of here! Creep! She shouted at me. Showed my body to the door, as
soon as she'd sucked one blood cell out of it. Maybe that's why.
She'd got what she wanted. A chip off the old block. A seed in her
tummy. Two seeds locked in an embrace. An irreversible embrace.
An ever-swelling embrace. That's about to swallow me into child
support. I've got food in two stomachs here at this table. And I've
had about as much as I can take. Suddenly I feel like hopping onto
my chair to yell my innocence like a convict on death row, to let
out a scream that will make those crystal glasses rattle in the
sideboard, and flatten the lava relief in that golden frame against
the wall:

BUT I WORE A CONDOM!!

But I never get a chance to do it. No one dares to mention the
bloody clot caught in Hofy's intestines that will presumably—presumably—do everything in its power to keep me chained to these
rococo table legs for the rest of my life. So I have to settle for silent
protest instead, and perform just one pathetic terrorist stunt: my
heart beats like a serial killer's committing his first murder as I
steal the daughter-in-law's chewing gum from her plate. Remarkably well done, if I may say so, I manage to swipe it, unnoticed,

just as the plates are being whisked off the table. Hofy looked at me twice during those two hours and thirty-seven minutes.

The bartender's got a ring through his nose. That's not Keisi. I don't think. Nah. This one's got a ring in his nose. Like a ring on a door. I knock, order a beer. A candle on every table and just about as many faces flickering in the dark. Pretty empty, the K-bar, at ten, eleven, twelve on a February Saturday night. My thirty-fourth February on this planet. I'm standing by the bar. Probably the only thing that will stand by me right now. Trying to shake off all those embraces: Mom, the "in-laws," Hofy . . . All embraces welcome. Isn't there anybody else out here who'd like to embrace me? And weep into my trousers, unzip my fly, and shed some tears . . . Yeah. I'm wearing tearstained underwear. Hugged to death. Smothered in fathomless embraces. I'm six fathoms under, just some numb bum with a beer, blowing bubbly, bobbly bubbles. No feelings. She said I had no feelings. And me with a cigarette trembling between my lips. How could I have expressed my feelings more eloquently than that? I might as well have been wearing a sandwich board with "I'M FREAKING OUT!" written all over it. But now I can relax. Smoke and drink in hand. Right, then. You just go ahead and be pregnant, then, and be lesbians with all your gagas and gobbledygook, and sauceyologists and dykeonomists. . . . Just bloat yourselves with children and grandchildren, and mother them all to death, and let the whole world feel pity for you and you for us. Onward, Christian soldiers, marching as to war. Dead men. All over town, with teeth marks on our eyeballs, trying to water them with wine. Our veins are full of blood, yours are full of tears. Tears from a sore. I asked her that: "Are you sore?" I asked her if she was sore. Of course, all women are sores. Pink, bloodred, hairy, gaping sores. Conscience does make cowards of our balls. But we'll wait until all eyelids are closed. Eyelids. How do you keep up those eyelids? Oh, sorry . . . sorry . . . What's your name? I can hardly. Everything's so goofy. There's a Goofy over there: 50,000. She smiles. I crack a smile. Smile a crack. By the bar. Suddenly realize I've been holding my cigarette right in front of my fly. Hey. Yeah. Like a dick. A Prince's dick. With a filter. I tap the ash. Ash falls off my dick. David Bowie.

Ashes to ashes. Look at her again. Did she see that? That was a cool brash move I just made, wasn't it? To tap the ash off him just like that. Oh, Goofy dear. My little ashtray. How many have you put out so far, Goofy dear? Where was I? Where was I again? Yeah, Hofy. And I said, "Are you sore?" That's probably the greatest effort I've ever made to be nice. Nice not wise. Worked far too well. And of course it had to end with her embracing me. Cried into my hole. In the T-shirt. Baby-tear-lotion. Boohoo. Hofyboo. That saintly look of hers, with her glass of water. Pregnant women, sacred cows. My ass. As if they had the right. As if they had the right to hug you all the time. She'll always have one up on me now. Boy, is this beer in a hurry to get out of the glass. Must be those bubbles. My soul. Cheers to tears. Boy, is this beer stressed out. Two sips and it's gone. Hey, look. There's Timer. Sitting alone in the corner. What's he always hanging out here for? Counting the bubbles in his glass? No. That's a cup he's got. The bartender has a ring in his nose. I grab it. Not. "How come you've got a ring in your nose? Wouldn't it be better if you had a buzzer on your nipples? I mean, isn't it sore with everyone grabbing it to get service all the time?" A song wafts through the speakers: My wonderwa-a-all. Wonder wall? The hymen? "Never mind, same again, another beer. But not so stressed this time, don't you have a calmer beer?" Robert De Niro. Rio de Ja Neiro. Things to do in Denver when you're dead. Things to do in Iceland when you're alive. Just try to die. The bartender has a ring in his nose. Makes it easier to wind him down. Yeah. Just try to die. Find my final place of rest. I stagger between the chairs. "Sorry . . ." Yeah. Santa Claus is coming to town. Lolla on the carpet. Had her on the carpet. Still got some new year in me. This year is still a bit new to me. My soul coming apart at the seams. A yesterday that won't heal. My name is Healer. Mom fondles her tits better than I do. Well, she knows what to do with them. The barman has a ring in his nose. So that they can haul him home when they close. Nah. I'm not sleeping with anyone tonight. I'll just fuck these tables and chairs over here instead. Not. Five fingers on my shoulder. It's Thröstur. Oh yeah, and my dear old Marri as well. My beloved friends. My beloved babeologists.

"What happened to you, man?"

"Just. Ohio."

"What?"

"Ohio."

"What happened to you?"

"Guys. I'm dying. Help me to die here. Give a man some dignity."

That's the problem when I'm pissed, I never lose consciousness. Always got these glasses on my nose. They are on my nose, aren't they . . . ? Yeah. I've had so much to drink here, I'm starting to see the blue light, but . . . I haven't quite finished making my funeral arrangements yet. Please, no flowers. A hundred and eighty-one centimeters are about to collapse. The lads prop me up against the corner, ease me onto the sofa. "Let him be . . . he's dying." A man only lives once, so it's good to be able to die every now and then. Every now and then. I even get to take the beer with me. To be able to make a toast on the other side. This dumb-show procession must be providing a welcome midnight diversion in the midst of this battlefield in the K-bar. "Violently Happy," I think I hear. No flowers. And yet I die like a flower. My head droops over my chest. My glasses slide. I push them back up with the back of my hand. That's the last thing. Then it's just a blank.

I'm dead.

Alcohol death. The abridged version of the real thing. Just a drill. I step out for a while. Leave a message pinned to my chest: "Gone out. Back at one o'clock. HBH." I leave my body running, like a car. There's smoke coming out of the exhaust, the dashboard lights are on, and so is the heater, but there's no one there. The brain's thinking for itself, at last, spinning on its own steam. I'd love to know what that old gray matter is thinking about right now. What he thinks about, once he's finally been freed of me. Probably just going through the standard rescue procedures, pumping out the alcohol, trying to save the last few cells from drowning.

If the body is a handbraked car, spinning on neutral, then I'm its soul running errands around town. Bye-bye, blood and skin. Bye-bye, nails and nose. Freed of my trousers, belts, and strings, I step into the darkness to take a spacewalk over the city, with a small glistening oxygen tank strapped to my shoulders, a toothless soul tiptoeing over the lampposts, somersaulting over Reykjavík in slow motion, suspended in a vacuum, with an anchor dangling over the tower of Hallgrím's Church, while radio waves scratch my back with five different drumbeats and television waves blow me apart, dissolving me into soul particles, scattering me, sprinkling me over the city. I'm in all places at once, equally, divided but one, in the same way that all the seconds ticking around the globe belong to the same time. I am me, and I am everything, and everything is me, and I'm inside Adalsteinn Gylfi Magnússon's clock, as he falls asleep on Vesturgata, with a copy of the new university syllabus on his bedside table. I'm a fly trapped between the double glazing of a bedroom window on Bergthórugata, and lie there on my back, kicking my legs in the air, watching Mom and Lolla, chatting under the covers; I'm rust on a drainpipe on number 18 Laugavegur; I'm clambering up the double chin of an Arbaer spinster who's asleep on a sofa under three flying ducks on the wall; I'm battling through my father's beard, clinging to a hair, as he shakes his head over the radio news in a taxicab on Hellis Heath, with half the Örk Hotel bar flowing through his veins; I'm hovering over the Westman Islands; I'm jammed inside a crumpled note with a Canadian phone number in the right-hand pocket of the jeans of a Romanian girl, lying on a Breidholt floor, all trampled and dirty; I'm under a row of dark seats, in a cold, empty Icelandair plane at the airport; I'm between the paint and the wall; I'm the space between the mouse and the pad and I'm stuck between Siamese molars. I am me and me am I. Me oh my. I'm everywhere and nowhere, at one with everything, the territorial waters of my soul stretch 200 miles out of my toes and fingers, and would stretch even farther . . . if I were dead for a little bit longer.

You can't be dead all the time.

I slowly return toward the body I left behind, like a car with a running engine, and feel slightly apprehensive as I approach it, in case it might have stalled or been stolen (keys in the ignition). No. It's still there. But it's been moved. Onto the sofa's right corner. Good to feel some warmth again, a tingle of life in my fingertips, but someone's rolled me up, and I'm lying there like a human prawn, with my face pressed against the wall (quite a disturbing sight, I imagine). I regain consciousness with a feeling of pain in my left cheek, and feel like I've been turned inside out—a label sticks out from the back of my neck: "Made in Iceland, 100% Cool, Wash Separately in Warm Water, Dry Tumble Low, No Dry Cleaning, No Ironing." It takes a while for me to tune in my soul to my brain's aching wavebands: nothing but a hiss on the air, and snow on the screen, then the picture suddenly comes back:

The first thought to spring to mind is that I'm on the other side. The first thought is that I've actually died. The first thought is that I'm . . . yeah, OK, maybe not in heaven, more like the other place. Visual noise. Kurt Cobain is singing, and Old Nick himself is plucking a double electric guitar. Crazy demons dancing on the tabletops, and swinging from the chandeliers. Dripping candles of ice glowing on the tables, the wax turning red as it bleeds over the edge. Gusts of snow blowing from the ashtrays, and waves of beer. A glass smashes to the ground, and I feel the flutter of skirts on my eyes, and the face of a devilishly made-up girl appears to me (16,000 in the other-side currency), half dead in a blazing red-orange haze. A shaveling of a doorman looms above me with a snake tattooed to his back, hurling some poor devil out into the cold—sparks flying off cigarette tips, everything drowned in smoke, and . . . I'm in hell. I'm in hell and it smells like teen spirit. It's obviously still a hit down here, or maybe they're just a bit behind on the old top ten, and . . . or maybe they don't have much to choose from, bored listening to Elvis, Hendrix, and Lennon all the time, and Marvin Gaye and Karen Carpenter. But I can't see the band, I can't see Kurt, hard as I try, because I want to see if he still has the gunshot wound. But at least he still sounds just as good, and the rest of the band sounds even better, if anything. Maybe that's Jimi himself on guitar, Sid Vicious on bass, and Ringo on dr . . . no, he hasn't arrived, not yet . . . Keith Moon, of course, and I check out the crowd to see who's there, maybe Lolla's dad, maybe Bugsy Malone, that friend of Guildy and Rosy's who died of AIDS three years ago, but I see . . . All I see is . . . I see Thröstur and, ashamed as I am to say it, I feel a gush of relief: another one to bite the dust, I'm not alone down here. That's one of the things that's always bugged me about death: that if there is another life, it's OK if you're at the top of the line, and they're handing out wings at the gate, and you get to rub shoulders with all the angels, but what if you don't know the doorman and can't skip the line? Chances are you'll get tired of queuing and end up going to some seedy joint below, like this one here and—yeah, I reckon anyone could get into this place—spend all your time hoofing around the bar, trying not to pierce anyone with your horns or to step on anyone's tail. That, I've got to say, is what's always bugged me the most—not to mention my worries about having to step into the next world naked, do we really have to face death with no clothes?—not knowing anyone, having to go through the whole rigmarole on your own, all alone, dead and stupid, and not sure of what language to speak down there, and so insecure about everything, like your first swimming class at school, but anyway I can see Thröstur and hey . . . Marri, too, and for some reason I feel a rush of happiness and lightness, and somehow regress to a state of mind I haven't known since I was a kid and say: "Wow, man." Thröstur spots me and leans over the table with a "heeeyyy," and then twists his mouth and contorts his face, as if someone has just plugged an electric guitar up his ass. And everyone else does the same, everyone wincing horrendously and writhing, and everything is bright and yet somehow dark, until I finally find my glasses under me, between my back and the cushion, and put them on.

Meanwhile the track has ended.

In the bathroom, a pale me in the mirror, teeth marks on my left cheek. That cranial feeling. Touch of rot. I look like a man who's been dead for an hour.

Well, how about that? Life seems to be beckoning me back. That's how I walk back into the bar, like I'm walking back to life. Isn't it wonderful, the way our arms have been hinged to our bodies? With all the space they need to swing, but, at the same time, never leaving us for a single moment. There's something just so perfect about that. Such good design. So beautiful and comfortable at the same time. I'm full of idiotic joy to be alive. I manage to sit and offer myself a cigarette, and suddenly feel Jimmy Carter inside me. There he is, behind my face, the good old gray-haired Jimmy Carter, talking about some peace proposals with peace bags under his eyes, and a wobbly double chin, peacefully quivering over the collar of his light blue shirt as he talks, and I feel a slight itch in my eyes when he blinks his drooping seventy-year-old eyelids inside my head. And it gets a bit rough when he starts to cough, maybe he's coughing because I'm smoking. He vanishes in a puff of smoke, and I feel an uncontrollable urge to shave myself: two ads crawl up my legs, for two different types of razor . . . for women, I cross my legs but it's no use, I've got women's legs and they're shaved from the inside, right up to the crotch and there's a dark hairy face in my crotch and some Arab comes out of the beard and changes into a blind Indian with sunglasses, telling a joke onstage, he's right under my chin, and . . . I don't know which is worse, to be dead or to be alive.

I somehow realize that I'm not smoking the cigarette anymore, but can't figure out what's happened to it and, partly to make sure my body's still in working order, I stand up and try to shake it off, try to shake off these Jimmy-Carter-woman's legs, but I still have a Gillette foot and a Remington leg as I stagger toward the bar like an eighty-channel old man with a Zimmer frame for a skeleton, not strong enough to sustain a collision with some dancing guru, who sends me flying over a blonde (40,000) at one of the tables, and she drops her glass and says, "Hey, fuck you, pal!" and says I have to buy her another drink, and I ask her if she shaves, and she repeats I have to buy her another drink, and I say her legs, does she shave her legs, and she repeats I have to buy her another drink, so I say OK to that, and resurrect myself again, and I just have another 75 centimeters to go to reach the bar, with two bimboid asses on special offer in view, when I open my mouth to help me take my last step, and it's suddenly filled with hair, a whole head of hair, which disappears but still leaves a mesh in my mouth, as I feel a tidal wave of dancing or falling people, and lose my balance on my Gillette foot, and grab on to something that feels like a bra, the back of one, that is, under some kind of sweater, and there's screaming, and I fall with some guy on top of me, and some couple on top of him, and I'm trapped between some chairs and something that could be a wall but is harder than a wall, and I'm below this pair on the floor, and I'm staring into the eyes of that cap lying here on the floor with me, and that rubber heel that's stepping on it, and I'm almost OK being down here with that beautiful ash snowing down on us, but nevertheless I feebly mutter, kind of between my body and myself, "Ouch."

Iceland is 103,000 square kilometers. It's generally believed that there's no shortage of space in this country. I know there are six hundred fjords out there somewhere, full of biting winds and good-for-nothing peaks, and some crazy muscle-pumping god who's arranged the godforsaken rocks along the shores. Why?—who gives a shit?—because there's not a single soul mousing about in those six hundred fjords, not a single bypassed or broken heart beating in a sleeping bag in any of those log huts, let alone plowing through those totally useless and waste-of-money drifts of Arctic cocaine in plastic jeeps, on roads that just lie there like squiggles on a map. And all that crazy big-time valley crap, way beyond the reach of television waves, and no one even looking at the stuff, let alone working this shit with a lawn mower or a microphone, and what's more, not even an animal jerking off under a rock, or a bird attempting a shit in the sky, or a tree break-dancing, just a few blind fish in the sea, finning their way through that ridiculously cold bazaar called the ocean, some inedible senile cods bubbling toward their graves, in their single-striped Adidas outfits, eternally gaping mouths, their vacant staring heads containing the only thoughts that float around this reef of a country of ours, which for all I care could just as well be an asphalted whale's back, dotted with lampposts and parking meters, with a U.S.-sponsored fountain gushing through its spout.

Iceland is a big country and yet here I am, squashed up against a radiator with the whole town on top of me, squeezing me ever tighter against this radiator, and I can feel the heat from the water, which is obviously reaching me after a day's journey from the center of the earth to warm me, and there's something about that, right now, there's something so socially comforting about that. Hot water on my cheek. At least something has warm feelings for me.

Something has warm feelings for me.

Iceland is a wind-beaten asshole and Icelanders are the lice on its edge. Clinging to the hairs. Of course, Licelanders have acclimatized themselves quite well by now, but still have to hold on for dear life when the crater starts to rumble. And all that brown lava starts to erupt.

Iceland is a big country and cold. OK. And even though Icelanders no longer have to shack up in old farm huts, and can now move about in climate-controlled pink cars, filled with the heat of Japanese summers, and lick the country's ice from the comfort of a cone, they're still recovering from thousands of years of goose-bumps, eternally cold. They force their children to sleep out of doors for the first five years of their lives to make sure the chill takes its hold. Always ready with that frozen sneer, those cold sarcastic replies. But there's earthly warmth below that crust. They're not totally heartless. There's always someone there to think of you. Even if you're paralytically drunk and sprawled over frozen vomit on the sidewalk in the middle of the night with nothing but snow in your pockets, like a frozen carcass with glasses, looking like surplus meat with grate marks on your left cheek that some yeti had tried to grill the frost out of, but then given up. Even then, there's always some girl (18,000) who'll stoop over you. Who'll talk to you. Who'll wake you up. Who'll take care of you. Even though you've been hauled outside and died again, they'll still drag you along to a party. Drag you to a party.

In the warmth of a taxi, I listen to a conversation between some kids I don't know, and the girl beside me, the girl who dragged me along, asks me if I'm OK and I just mumble, "The Welfare State. That's the Welfare State for you. We live in a Welfare State," and look out the window—if only there were a word for mumbling with your eyes—at the rows of terraced houses, thinking of all the radiators inside them, all that warmth. "I mean, it's great. It's all so great. The heating system. The welfare system. We live in a Welfare State." One of the kids in the back:

"Hey! Are you some kind of . . . euh . . . taxpayer?"

I manage to clamber out of the taxi by aping the kids' every move. Difficult to tell where this party is. But I just count myself lucky that I'm still wearing both shoes. Those are the only basics I can deal with right now. Yeah. The house reminds me of the dentist's palace in Gardabaer. Or something. Am I back in Hofy-wood? I walk straight into the kitchen. Two girls talking. Salt and pepper. (I'm in no fit state to start putting prices on them.) Salt looks at me, and says: "Hi."

"Yeah, hi. And thanks for the food. It was really good, really good . . . really good sauce," I answer.

I sink into an armchair in the living room, in my cold leather jacket and slowly warming black jeans, with pain in my cheek, and half a cigarette that I can't remember putting into my mouth but now try to remember to smoke. I feel like an elder sitting here. Feel like a patched-up geri in a patched-up cardigan. On the cover of *Rolling Stone*. Kids on the sofa and on the floor. Their dialogue belongs to a completely different movie. Everything is "batso" or "zomboid": "It's really wrecking my buzz, know what I mean?," "Totally wicked," and "Hey you, taxpayer! Got a cigarette?"

I don't answer, but dig into my inside pocket in slow motion and take out my crumpled packet of Prince. It's got melted slush in it and the cigarette I pull out is both wet and broken.

"Oh."

"You call that a cigarette?"

"That's all they give you when you're on welfare."

I felt that was reasonably witty of me, but he didn't seem to get it. The elder obviously has an older brand of humor. A girl (400,000) is suddenly standing beside my chair. I very slowly twist my head and eyes and look up at her. She looks down.

I say: "Heeey."

"What?"

"Fucking hell, you're so . . . you're so . . . you're . . . fuck, you're just so . . . ."

"What you talkin' about?"

"You're so you are."

"Yeah? And what about you? What are you, then?"

"I'm, I am, I'm so much I am, you know."

"What?"

"I AM, you FM."

"Yeah, yeah. What happened to you? What's that on your cheek?"

"What? You can see it?"

"Yeah, your cheek's all red, with, like, grate marks. You look like you fell into a toaster."

"I do? Yeah, I've been . . . branded."

"Yeah?"

"Yeah, I'm branded."

"Brain dead?"

"That's what happens to you if you have too much you man . . . too much human contact."

"Oh yeah?"

"Yeah, you're . . . you're young and . . . and four hundred thousand . . . so watch out."

"Human contact?"

"Human contact."

I'm fucking pleased with myself here, and try to take a drag before continuing, but can get no smoke out of my cigarette, and realize I've got the soggy broken one in my mouth. I take it out, and am about to say: "We live in a Welfare State. . . ." And even have my next line ready: "I've been branded by the Welfare State." But she's gone. Those kids.

I sit for another forty-five minutes, half listening to a lecture on the art of smuggling through customs at Keflavík Airport ("It's a total minefield, man") with one ear, and ten tracks with Oasis or Blur or some other Beatles clones with the other. A real hippie atmosphere. Reminds me of an old hash party. Yeah. There's someone with a joint. They're doing exactly what their parents did in their day but never told them about. I'm watching a rerun. Recycled drugs. Feel slightly depressed to see mankind is making such little progress. No, sirree. I mean, it's really "wrecking my buzz." Nobody's turning to the elder for guidance. I stand up and saunter across the carpet to ask for a taxi number. I dial it twice and both times get my own answering machine. Actually say, "Hi, it's me . . ." after the tone, then I hang up and walk down a multi-doored corridor in search of a toilet. This house could do with some signposts. I open a door. There's a naked couple on a double bed, locked in some pretty intensive missionary work. They pause to look at me. I say: "Sor . . . sorry. Don't mind me. Please continue," and walk in, close the door behind me, and lean against a chest of drawers by the door. The girl (30,000) gropes for the quilt and manages to slide it over one of her legs. The guy looks at me and then at her, half smiling a "what's this?" smile. She doesn't smile. Mr. and Ms. Average. Such mundane faces, maybe cos of the positions they're in and their nakedness. They all look the same once they're in the sack, so helplessly "human" somehow, perhaps to compensate for the beast below. And always that same white ass. A lamp glows on the bedside table.

She: "Hey . . ."

"Yeah?"

"What are you doing here?"

I choose to remain silent. But they don't.

Her again: "Would you mind getting out of here? Right now."

"Why?"

"Why? Can't you see what we're doing here?"

"What are you doing?"

She crashes her head into the pillow and gasps: "Jesus . . ."

The guy gets back to work, slowly. Yeah. He's got spunk. Maybe he understands me. Maybe he's getting a kick out of this. She must be getting a kick out of it as well, but she still tries to pull the quilt over them and he lends a hand. They get back to work under the covers, two polar bears under a blanket of snow until she starts panting again:

"Oh . . . I can't do this. He's gotta go."

I suddenly feel the Holy Spirit hovering over my head. Hlynur Björn, the angel of love, floats away from the white chest of drawers and glides toward the bed with fluttering wings and a bow in his hands, and says—perhaps not as nicely as it sounds:

"It's so beautiful to see people making love, it's what I've always wanted, I've never seen it before, just do it for me, give me your best shot . . . just for me."

She looks me in the eye and says, "Fuckin' Pervert," with a capital *P*. "Yeah," the angel replies, "OK. I know," and she glares at me, full of spite, and signals the guy to plug away. He's got an earring. That tinkles. I stand over them for a moment, and then sit on a wicker chair in the corner. It's pretty noisy. The quilt slowly slides off their bodies. This is beautiful. This is my finest hour. I sober up. They're beautiful, young, and energetic, and they seem to be doing a really good job. Up and down. The usual thing. You don't get any better than this. I realize that. The apex of human experience, the ape sex of human experience. Now that I've finally seen life, at last I can die. I think. They're not panting much. I'm at a fixed camera angle here. Can't really see anything. Apart from her small but shapely tits. I sit up a little. The chair creaks. The kid quickens the pace a bit. He's got stamina, all right. A lot of hard work. He's slipped into fourth gear. Shifted his stiff gearstick. Then declutches into first. Lies on top of her, revving her in neutral. I grab the opportunity:

"Excuse me, do you mind if I smoke?" I say.

They don't answer. Sunk into that soft mattress. I find a half-decent cigarette in my wet packet. But have some problems lighting it. Finally succeed on my tenth attempt. Had to strike that noisy lighter ten times. And I've probably been shifting around in my chair too much because the girl suddenly springs up on her elbows to chide me in a headmistress's voice:

"Look, if you're going to be here, at least sit still!"

I freeze like a mouse, in a slightly awkward position, humbled, and as stiff as a pole, trying to smoke my cigarette without making any noise in the chair. Well, I'm as stiff as a pole but he isn't. Not my friend below. Nah. He's beyond all this. There's a slight tingle in him, but not enough to make him stand. Heavenly. I'm an angel now. Flittering. Fluttering. Way above all erections, high up in the clouds with drooping wings and a soft unfledged little willy, I look down on humanity copulating. Hlynur the Bear in his lair, watching a documentary about another species, his claws clutching the remote control, but he doesn't want to change channel, and thinks in wonderment: Yeah, so that's how they do it. Porno movies. Wildlife documentaries. How do the Danes do it? Are all blacks well hung? Do Japs have small ones? How do Muslim women come? Do they come at all? How do Jews give head? Has anyone ever researched that? Comparative sexology. No books called: *The Jewish Blow-Job. Coming East and West. Fifty Years of German Fingering. Fist Fucking in Ancient Greece. Getting Wet Down Under.*

I gradually realize this is the first documentary I've seen about the Icelandic species. And I've got to say it reminds me a bit of Icelandic movies. *Children of Nature*. There's no plot in it. No angle variation whatsoever. Looks like we're in for an epic feature. Talk about dragging it out. I'm getting bored. Start to think about the remote in my inside pocket. Saw a documentary the other day about those cameramen who make wildlife movies. Some British ponytailer who dug himself into a hole for a fortnight in the hope of catching a shot of a hare shag. But he didn't even so much as get a hard-on in those two weeks. Maybe I just don't have the patience. Or maybe. Mind you, I felt a slight tingle in him when I saw some rats fucking once. In a cage. Guinea pigs. During an experiment. That was the only time I've actually felt like a pervert. The problem with animals is they've got no sense of entertainment in these games. No sense of show business in them. They just do it. No nipple nibbling. No soul kissing. No smut. Has anyone ever seen lizards fingering each other? And eagles aren't any better with their claws. Hum? Guess it would be kind of sick to see reindeer sucking each other off. Or turtles . . . No. I mean, who'd accept a blow job from a turtle? Foreplay in rats consists of fourteen rapid thrusts, all equally short as the final one, the fifteenth. Maybe the apes. If anyone it would be them—the Nobel prize winners of the animal kingdom—who might indulge in some oral sex. Mind you. That's probably what distinguishes man from animals. Remember on the farm, when we used to wank the dog. Five times a day. He was undoubtedly the numero uno sheepdog in the whole county, but after three weeks of intense abuse from us big-city boys, he'd already relinquished his post, lost all interest in sheep work and staggered around the farmyard like a wasted junkie who's been numbed to the trivial daily pleasures of life, such as chasing after dots of wool across the hill. All he could think of now was his next dose, his next shot. He had that kind of apathetic, washed-up but at the same time wanton glint in his eyes. He'd actually started to look half human. He was no longer a dog. Spotty. Think he ran away in the end and moved to Thailand. Growling through his old age, panting through the streets of Bang-cock, with AIDS up his ass and some biographer chasing after him all day. "Well, it all started out in the barn one day. . . ." Also remember when he trotted into the toilet with me and stood on his hind paws as I was about to piss and started licking me. Hey. A blow job from a dog. What am I rambling on about a dumb animal for? But of course he was no longer just a dog. He'd discovered the irresistible pleasures of being human. And there I was in the can with my twelve-year-old willy being molested by a gay dog, with my stiff, spunk-gorged, little willy trying to squeeze some sperm out of myself, the first cells that never came, it just stood there with its head in the open air, all short and swollen and red with the dog's fang marks, two hundred kilometers away from its first pussy. Yeah. Spotty was 70,000. My first sexual experience. Mind you, there was another. The first time was when the cat (100,000) licked me in the barn. He only actually did it once. And it was impossible to get him to repeat it. It had been a total misunderstanding on his part and there I was—just out of primary school with my never-shaved freckled face—already abusing a cat. I was quite lucky, really, from that point of view, to have been able to seduce him into sticking his tongue out like that, that one time. Cat tongues are pretty rough and kind of dry, and massive the way only tongues can be massive, and it was . . . Yeah, it was . . . it was a nuclear explosion, or more of a test explosion, maybe. Haven't had the same kick since. Women . . . Maybe I should have just carried on with cats. Isn't that what's behind all these "cat societies"? "Cat women" with entire harems of licking experts. Still, though, I never actually went out to screw an animal, like you hear sometimes. Farm laborers having a quickie out in the cowshed before going to bed. How did they actually do it? Standing on the milking stool? Ain't that something? Nah. I was the seduced one. I was good to the animals and they were good to me. You look back on it as a kind of initiation. A kind of school. Maybe that's why they sent all those boys into the country. Different for girls. Elsa never went into the country. Maybe Mom couldn't bear the thought. Elsa with a ram rammed between her legs. No. Yeah. It was an initiation. The first step up the evolutionary ladder. Start with a cat, then a dog, then a girl, then a woman, then . . . then a woman with a stud in her nose, then a bisexual woman, and then . . . what? Mom?

Anyway. This is a dream come true: here I sit in an unnecessarily noisy wicker chair in a pretty plush couple's bedroom somewhere in Reykjavík. Late at night and at the crack of dawn. Studying sexual intercourse.

Yeah, yeah. Haven't they come yet? Isn't he going to come? No, this is obviously an Icelandic film, all right. No sense of tempo whatsoever. I'm bored. What could possibly follow this? Here I am, watching what's supposed to be the most exciting thing a man can watch, and I'm still bored. Me, who even listened to a whole Sting song once. Me, who didn't even walk out of *Il Postino*. But at least there were more characters in that and changes of scenery. Bicycles and mountains and stuff. But here it's just two people on a bumpy ride. Up and down. According to my calculations, that was thrust number 1,970. And the guy's piston is pumping away at a steady pace. Not a sound out of them. Not a pant. Poor them. Poor me. I glance at my watch. 05:26.

"How's it going?"

I ask.

"Fucking hell."

Says she.

She suddenly slips out from under him—the condom glistens—and hops off the bed, and stands over me, naked, and I'm surprised by how exciting it is to see her so naked and angry. Her tits pulsating with rage, small and nubile.

"OK, that's it, now you're gonna get the fuck out of here, you fucking pervert! Out! Get out, you creep! What do you think this is? How 'bout some privacy around here? Out, get out of here!"

Everyone's throwing me out these days. Hofy. Those bouncers. Now her.

"Nice tattoo."

"Shut up. Get out of here. Out!"

I'm hoisting myself out of the chair when the door opens in this cozy couple's room and a young ball of blond hair appears (60,000):

"Oops!"

The door immediately closes, but Miss Naked Fury opens it again, and the ball of blond hair in the corridor turns into a face with listening eyes:

"Hey. Wanna help me get this guy out of here? This is your

house, right? He just burst in here, he's been sitting here, watching us like some kind of sexologist, like totally unbearable," says Naked Fury, and there's a sudden commotion in the bed, the guy has thrown himself behind it and is lying on the floor. Naked Fury goes on and turns to me: "I mean, what's the big idea? What the hell do you think you're doing in here? Do you think we're running some kind of a show here or something?"

"Actually, I felt you were dragging it out a bit there."

"Oh you did, huh?!"

"Yeah. You could have varied your positions a bit more."

Her breasts stiffen and her face boils as she comes at me like a blizzard. I lose my balance and lean against the wall, or a picture: I unbalance some framed thing on the wall. The blonde—she's pretty—says to her:

"Hey! Take it easy. I'll talk to him."

She steps into the room (her parents'?) in a tight blue Puma top. Small tits on her, too. Is that the new trend? Lolla got the last big tits in town? She looks pensive for a moment. It's beautiful. A babe's brain at work. Brainy babes. She looks at the bed and then says:

"What. Were you doing it on my parents' bed?"

"Not me," say I, angelically.

"Not me," parrots Naked Fury. "This pervert here was watching. What do you make of that? He was watching us."

The Puma top moves over to the bed. A shuffle of jeans can be heard. She looks in the corner, and even though I'm no surgeon I can tell her organs are contracting under that Puma top. Her soul bubble bursts into a multitude of smaller ones, and one of them pops in her mouth, bearing just one word:

"Óli? . . ."

The said Óli magically materializes out of the carpet, bare on top, but wearing jeans now (the condom still on?), and his earring no longer just tinkling but trembling. He tries to move and ruffles his hair, as if he were trying to make himself invisible. Four quaint little seconds, four juicy silences, four people (one naked) standing around a very convincing, and slightly expensive, stage set: four reasons I never go to the theater. This is the theater of life. Theater is a morgue. Where life is stretched out on a slab, and the audience is called upon to bear identification. Remember the best part was always the interval. Exactly. Like I said: life is an interval between deaths. So I do prefer life to death after all. We'll see about that when I die. Anyway. That was just a digression. Naked Fury grabs her clothes. The daughter of the house drops onto the bed, sits. Óli is looking pretty awkward and trying to breathe as if . . . as if it was some big deal for him. And me. Me who's got two women tucked away in a bed back home. I straighten the print on the wall. Just to put some order back into things.

When a man's been awake for more than seventeen hours, something changes. Makes you more human. It's a trick that's often used in peace negotiations. Keep everyone up for long enough and they'll all unite against the common enemy.

My professional responsibilities in this terraced house have been extended even further. I'm half sprawled on the double bed, with my legs dangling over the edge, beside a nineteen-year-old blond damsel in a blue Puma top. She's sitting. Just the two of us in the room, and probably in the whole house. There's a beautiful post-party stillness over everything. I'm sounding like Magnús, the shrink, here:

"And what. Had you been together for long?"

"Since this summer."

"Summer. That makes it . . . seven months."

"Yeah."

"I see. Seven divided by two is three point five; what was your grade point average at school?"

"I don't believe this. Don't believe it. Óli . . . and imagine, in Mom and Dad's bed."

"Yeah. I don't know if this will be of any consolation to you, but they were pretty bland, quite a boring show, really. . . ."

"Yeah."

She looks at the bedspread, obviously doesn't want to hear an action replay. Then she looks into my eyes, long enough to make him rise. No, I could never be a psychologist. Some curvaceous woman on the couch spouting out all her problems and me with no concentration whatsoever, except on that one thing. No, you need

a dead prick like Magnús's to do that kind of stuff. I raise myself
up on the bed to conceal my hard-on. Oh God, I'm so polite.

"And what. Were you in love with him?"

"In love?"

Oops. Stupid of me. Makes me sound ancient. I'm turning into
such a grandpa here.

"Nah. I just meant, you know."

She doesn't say anything. I say:

"Love . . . Of course, that's real silent-screen stuff."

"Huh?"

"Silent screen."

"I guess I was in love with him."

"Yeah . . . Well, he looked like a nice guy, so . . . Nice earring."

"Yeah. It's really brill. I gave it to him."

"Oh yeah? Where did you get it?"

"In Florida."

"Right. Orlando, then? Or . . ."

"No. Tampa."

"Right."

Silence.

"Tampa," I repeat, but still a long way from making it sound
like a word containing millions of Americans.

"I just don't get it. I mean, I don't get it. This is just so incredible. He was always so batso . . ."

"Yeah? He looked kind of zomboid to me."

"Óli? No, he was kind of cool."

"Right."

"With that. Slut."

"Who is she? Do you know her?"

"No. Know who she is."

"And who is she?"

"I dunno."

"She looked pretty boring. With that tattoo."

"What kind of tattoo did she have?"

"It was a kind of butterfly. Right above her . . . Didn't you
see it?"

She doesn't answer. She starts to cry. Again. Leans over me. This is the third crybaby in less than thirty hours. They'll be awarding me a diploma next. I look at this beautiful long blond hair. It's quivering. Like the quivering curtain of a drama. I place a hand on her back. A trembling hand. Maybe more for me than for her, just to be clear on that point. But still. The angel of love at work. I realize I've never willingly touched another living being—another human being, that is—before, so this is new territory for Hlynur. But I feel a bit weird with my hand on her back here and I'm almost on the point of thinking of removing it when she pounces on me, diving into my arms. Blond hair all over me. Tears on my jeans. You don't water a prick with tears. Fortunately. He shows some respect. Bows out. She sobs awhile, this little Puma flower, and I've turned into a dickless daddy here, tapping his child on the back. Until she stands up, sucking a word up her nose:

"Sorry."

"That's OK. I'm used to it."

"Yeah?"

"Yeah. I'm a real expert at handling cases like this. Human relations. Weeping women . . ."

"You're, like, special."

"Yeah?"

"What's your name?"

"Hlynur. Hlynur Björn."

"Hlynur Hlynur Björn?"

"Yeah."

"That's, like, a special name."

"Yeah. And you?"

"Ingey."

"Engey?"

"No. Iiingey."

"Yeah. That's, like, a special name too, isn't it?"

"Yeah . . ." she says, almost managing a laugh. "But what were you doing there? Were you really looking at them? Why? What were you doing?"

"Me?" I say, standing up with a sigh: "I'm a pervert."

"Right. I see."

*   *   *

I'm lying in a dark green forest under a blanket of leaves, and I hear a thud in the distance. It's the last blue in the sky. The wrong sky. This is a Russian sky that's been moved. Moved to the west. I turn my head in a rustle of foliage and look out at the clearing, through the trees. Someone's playing golf. It's Larry Hagman. Larry Hagman is playing golf out on the green. Whacking a stream of golf balls into the void. The more he whacks, the darker and darker the green gets. As if green were bleeding under its skin. The golf balls shoot into the void. And don't fall back to earth. But spin through space. Forming an entire galaxy of hard white golf balls. Larry Hagman hits the last ball through the atmosphere. It revolves around the sun. Spinning on its axis in slow motion. It's got whole oceans, continents, and forests. And I'm lying in one of them. I lie in a dark green forest. Larry Hagman is playing golf out on the clearing. He's peevishly looking for some lost balls.

I regain consciousness, this time in heaven. Does one have a hangover when one goes to heaven? Yeah. Isn't life a party and death the morning after? Hangovers in the hereafter. Soft awakening, though. Very soft. Soft pillow. Soft quilt. And soft patterns on the wall. All pink and baby blue. Poster of Cindy Crawford. Her soft cheeks, lips, breasts, and the famous spot. I'm in heaven. That is to say a girl's bedroom. Without the girl. And I don't seem to have slept with her. Typical me. Me loser, you Jane. I'm under the bedclothes. With my glasses on. All lopsided. They pulled through it all. Dear old glasses. What was I doing last night? Jacket on the floor. I stretch and check the condoms in my inner pocket to be sure. Yeah. Still got two left. I always carry condoms on me. Bit stupid, really. I'm no Casanova but I carry condoms on me. One has to. To keep life and death at bay. In the unlikely event of such an emergency I know they're there, in my inner breast pocket, where my heart is, my shield against death. About as useful to me as a bulletproof jacket is to a cop out in the wilderness of Búdardalur. I don't sleep around that much. But still. They don't seem to be all that effective. Maybe they work as a shield against death, but not against life. What kind of a kid will sprout out of a seed that had the muscle power to drill its way through a rubber wall? He'll be some kind of Jón Páll World's Strongest Man. Yeah. We'll call him Jón Páll Junior. Jón Páll Hólmfrídarson. But maybe the condom had just fallen off? I check the sell-by date. 01/98. Look at these rubbers. They're almost a year old. Old and tired in these half-chewed sachets. It was a six-pack. And still two left. I suddenly feel pathetic. I can't even work myself through one packet of condoms in a year. Yeah. There's something wrong with me. Four gone. Four times Hofy, but still I used that one from Nanna Baldurs that time. Have we done it five times? No condom with Lolla. I must use them more. Mind you, 1998. Still have enough time. Sweet little condoms. Where will you lead me? These two sachets contain two hermetically sealed adventures. Two unopened thrillers. Almost feel like opening them, but I shove them back into my pocket and grope under the covers. It would appear I'm not wearing any trousers. Apart from my Bonus briefs, that is. Thank you, Johannes, king of Bonus. My watch. Sun 02 18 15:36. So it's sun. Just need my location now. And trousers. I look out the window. Garden, house, mountains, snow, and two children in spacesuits. No sun. Hey. I know that view. I look for my trousers. I find similar trousers on the floor, by the chest of drawers. Yeah, now I remember. She . . . Engey, she said I could crash out here, in her sister's room. Her sister is obviously even skinnier than she is, if her trousers are anything to go by. I can barely fit my arms into them. Young girls, with legs like men's arms. I dive my head into her shell. There's a nice atmosphere inside this jean cave. This is the ridge her crotch has rubbed up against, on her way to school. I try to determine her age from the smell. No. Innocent urine. No scent of a woman. My head's sinking below the age of consent in here. My head submerged in jeans: special effects transforming it into a hair-free pussy, and my nose into an untouched clitoris, and my cerebral hemispheres into two ass cheeks with a crack down the middle, and the ears . . . what about the ears? Cute little hip wings: my head is a holy virgin when it resurfaces from the depths of these jeans, a cherry in my throat and an asshole in the back of my head. Yeah.

No. That's just the hangover. Typical hangover when your brain feels like an ass.

And yet my skull is so full of smelly thoughts on the green mohair mat as I bare-leg around and put my jacket on so at least I'm wearing something. I finally give up searching for my trousers and snoop around, looking for collectibles. A cute little desk. The eraser of youth. Virgin pink stationery. Unwritten pages. And always that same old corkboard: a Grafar school timetable. Hang on. I've got a domestic-science class tomorrow. And somewhere in the depths of my soul I spot a glimmer of guilt, like a coin in a dark pond, flashing from the back row of a classroom in Austurbaer College. Can one never be free of one's past? No matter how hard you try. No matter how hard you try to stub out each moment as soon as you've finished drawing all the smoke out of it. Must learn to stub out my cigarettes better. Dying for a cigarette. My packet is a sogging joke. Fuck, am I drunk if I can't even keep my cigarettes dry. A snapshot on the corkboard. Like a faint photocopy of her sister, Engey. A 64 percent reduced photocopy. What's her name? Jersey? Timetable: "Vaka Róbertsdóttir." Little Vaka with a friend on the edge of a Spanish pool. Two little canaries in swimsuits. Yeah. More like birds' breasts than women's. Americans call their girls chicks. I'm more of a breast man than leg. White meat. Yeah. What else? Two pigtail elastics. This is a pony's room. Puberty hangs in the air. Hovers in the atmosphere like an invisible gas around the lampshade that sinks lower with the passage of each month—pretty soon there'll be blood between each month—slowly filling the room. Development liquid. That will transform the flat-chested canaries into real chicks. Better get out of here before I relapse into puberty. Once was enough. I grab a memento as I'm about to leave, a mini-umbrella in "all the colors of the rainbow" with a pink handle, stick it into my inside pocket. Then glance at the photograph again. Vaka. You're heading for 100,000.

My head precedes me out of the room. Felt that would be safer somehow. Because of the eyes. Silence in the house. I bare-leg it down the corridor and slowly open the door to the parental bedroom. Engey's hair on the pillow. And. And. There's always another "and" when it comes to women. Óli, the earring, tosses beside her as I pussyfoot across the carpet. I feel the strap of my leather jacket dangling over my thigh.

"Hey. Have you seen my trousers anywhere, by any chance?"

"Er. No," says Óli.

I carry on searching anyway, until I come out with a surprisingly energetic farewell at the door:

"Goodbye, then! And thanks for last night. You were great. Might pop back sometime, if I get a chance." I smile, and have almost closed the door when I open it again to add: "Just one thing, maybe. More variation. More positions. You've got good stamina and all that, but just . . . a bit of variety, you know."

"Oh . . . yeah. OK."

Where the fuck did I take my trousers off? Check another two bedrooms. The john (take a leak). And then back to Vakaland. Even glance out the window. Yeah. Something familiar about that view. I finally end up in the kitchen over a bowl of really suspect corn-flakes. Calvin Klein cornflakes. Radio, an old song from A Flock of Seagulls. Try to make out the lyrics through the loud crunching in my jaw. And I ran, I ran so far away . . . Remember the singer's hairdo. That waterfall down his forehead. And remember myself at the Borg Hotel when it came out. I still had my trousers in those days. And good vibes. That was the volcanic Katla period. Ogled her for twenty-seven weeks in a row. Waiting for her to erupt. Long overdue. I saw her again, seven years later, at the Kringlan Mall. She was serving, her volcano long extinct by now. Even her tits were gone. Some football dwarf had sucked all the juice out of them. Seven years and the goddess of all time, the stunner of the century, had evaporated into thin air to be replaced by some lipless mannequin holding a shoebox. Holy Kiljan. Time. A man ought to be ashamed to wear a watch. Vaka, dear. Watch out. She recognized me, or did she? Katla, I mean. "Yes. This is a nice pair," she said. Nice pair. Farewell, nice pair. Katla. Even I wouldn't date you now. Need I say more? There's a shuffle at the hall door. I flap my wings, a flock of seagulls, flutter from the table with leather straps and all and slip into the corridor. Shilly-shally. I can hear an entire family shuffling outside that hall door. I glance back into the kitchen. A half-empty bowl of cornflakes and the radio still on. Hlynur Björn and the three bears. I leg it down the corridor and hear a squabble coming from the parental bedroom. Engey shouts: "But I didn't sleep with him!" I hear a call from the hall door. A woman's voice: "Hello! Anybody home!?" Sudden panic. I shoot back into Vaka's bedroom. Except it's no longer Vaka's bedroom. It's the laundry room. Fortunately, maybe. Cold concrete floor. Washing on the line. Remember on Letterman once: stupid human tricks. A guy who crawled into a washing machine. Maybe? No. American machines are bigger. I vanish into a fragrant forest of clean washing. Door.

The heart beats faster out of doors. I quickly cross the garden, passing Vaka's window, into the next yard. Some kind of dawn seems to be breaking. Very faintly. Like milk rising in coffee. Little astronauts totter around their snow-white moon. The six-year-old boy says "Hi!" from the depths of his spacesuit. "Have you come for a visit?" "No," I answer coldly and speed away, around the corner, straight into my sister, Elsa, loaded with groceries.

"Oh, hi! You here? Come on in, children! *Children's Hour* will be on soon!"

The hallway.

"Yeah, I decided to pop over for a visit."

"Yeah? Good for you."

"No! He DIDN'T WANNA come for a visit!"

Hi, little nephew.

"Don't be silly. Uncle Hlynur's come all this way, what, did you walk here?" Elsa asks, looking at my boots.

"Yeah . . . well, kind of." Kind of. What's that supposed to mean? That I went as far as Ártúnsbrekka on horseback, and covered the rest of the distance on cross-country skis? The things I come out with.

"NO. He DIDN'T WANNA come! I DON'T WAN' him here."

I take the boots off at the door. Vaka's dad's boots, I expect. I'm deeply submerged in the life of this little community now. Up to my knees in another man's life. And my head lost in the depths of his daughter's pants. I step out of the wellies: bend over to look my nephew in the eye. Head upside down. He stares at me as if my mouth were really a hairless pussy and my nose a clitoris. The cherry is back in my throat.

"Hey. Are they new trousers? Nice trousers. Nice to see you wearing a bit of color at last," Elsa says in her chirpy nurse's voice. Fuck, could I do with a cigarette. Keep my jacket on. Bad enough to be in these tight red trousers. And then there's Magnús to face. Looks like he's going to hoist himself out of his master-of-the-household chair, but I'm quick enough to plonk myself on the sofa, and he changes his mind, thank God. Slobs back into it again. He's been watching Eurosport. And can't hide the fact, even though he's turned the sound off.

The coffee darkens, turning coal black, in the windows. I realize that wasn't dawn I witnessed outside. Who can tell, on these winter days, what's a sunrise and what's a sunset? What the hell, dawn or dusk, at least I'm up.

I've been sitting here, smoking half a packet of imaginary cigarettes in my mind—and chewing my way through four chocolates from this bowl on the coffee table—when Elsa suddenly says: "Hey! And it's your birthday today! I'm so sorry, Hlynur. Why didn't you just say so? Congratulatiooons!" Those three *O*s come soaring toward me. No. Come propelling toward me like those helicopters in *Apocalypse Now* and me just some My Lai village with a straw-hut haircut there on the sofa: the birthday takes me just as much by surprise as it takes her, and once I've recovered from the onslaught of her napalm kisses, equal in number to the candles on the nonexistent cake, I sit there with my face still in flames, feeling odder by the minute. The thought that I might have walked all the way from Bergthórugata to Grafarvogur just because it was my birthday, in the hope that Elsa would bake it into some kind of event. Now I'm totally pathetic, a thirty-four-year-old loser, with year-old condoms in his pocket. Good morning, Forrest Gump. I'm the completely wrong man in the completely wrong place at the couldn't-be-wronger time. But still, it's my birthday. Spock. Spock clinging to the deck of the *Onedin*, on the crest of a breaker in the middle of the Indian Ocean. Nevertheless, I try to produce a masculine squeak, shifting in the leather of the sofa and my jacket, and scratch my scalp, wishing it were an eraser, but it's not easy in these tight red trousers. My balls, a bulge of marble.

"Hey, what's that you've got?"

Vaka's cute little umbrella is suddenly sticking out of my jacket. A bright pink handle under my chin.

"Is that a birthday present? Who gave it to you?"

I take it out and show her. "Yeah. Just a joke from . . . Lolla," I say, sounding like a counter-tenor in these eunuch trousers, and then the dainty little thing bursts open, the umbrella, I mean, just like that, and I sit there, all hungover and birthdayed, desperate for a smoke and all Gumped up, under an umbrella that's so small it would barely cover a six-month-old fetus. I'm sitting indoors with an open umbrella. Over my head: a bad omen in all the colors of the rainbow.

Well, well. So it's my birthday today. I knew there was something. My private little new year. Another ring around the aura. Yeah. Annual ring. Aura ring: ripples in the water. Somebody threw a stone in thirty-four years ago and every year it makes a new ripple, each time weaker. Until it fades.

Dental floss. I'm celebrating the occasion, my private new year, alone, in Elsa's bathroom, with a traditional fireworks display (a marble hard-on). Yeah. Katla was 90,000. Then brush my teeth with . . . Magnús's brush? Thirty-four white candles in my mouth. Remember Christmas Day in here. Look for the pack of pills. No pack. She found out. Keeps it hidden now. Told the kids off. She told the kids off for stealing the pill out of the pack. She told the kids off for wanting another brother or sister. Fifteen motorbikes riding over a bridge in Rome in slow motion. I glance into the couple's bedroom on the way back. There. There in the corner, on the other side of that wall, that's where I sat last night watching mankind making love. A birthday gift from Old Beardy upstairs. The greatest gift of all time. I don't know what's got into me, but I look up and say, "Thanks." And if it hadn't been for this wall of Icelandic cement I might have finally seen my sister and Magnús at it too.

Elsa is out of cakes but offers me a beer. Wants to toast to my birthday. That is to say, myself and Magnús share a bottle of Egill's Gull. Elsa's not having any, "And there's a reason for that. Didn't Mom tell you?"

"No."

My sister looks over at her hubby. Her hubby in his creaking leather armchair with a reclinable back. Munching chocolate. And then says with a smile:

"Well. I'm expecting."

Pregnant. Up the pole. Knocked up. With child. In the family way. Up the spout. With a bun in the oven. Yeast in the womb. In the pudding club. On the hill. In pig. With an egg in the nest. Started to hatch. With a film in development. All these words for that one thing. And yet I still don't get this "I'm expecting."

"Expecting who?" I say, like a half-wit.

"Who?" Elsa laughs. "Why, a baby, of course." And we all laugh like a beautiful family.

"You're pregnant?"

"Yes. Incredible as it may sound. This wasn't planned. Bit of a miracle, really."

"Yeah?"

"Yes. It was meant to be impossible. It was the last thing we expected."

"Oh yeah? Is . . ." I almost spit out the words "Magnús" and "sterile," but manage to catch my tongue in time. Seizing it by the throat. And then, of course, remember the pill, which is hopefully resting soundly in my private museum back home, and try to strike an innocent pose, managing to end my sentence with a sufficient degree of nonchalance, I feel. While Magnús is in mid-sip, sucking the frothy dregs of his beer into his mouth, I say:

"Was it a test-tube job or . . . ?"

"No, no . . ." Elsa laughs. "What makes you think that?"

My face looks half pregnant. I feel it reddening in a hormonal rush.

"No, I dunno. Just thought you might have got your test tubes mixed up at the hospital and accidentally sipped some."

They've got a sense of humor, Magnús and Elsa. They're OK. It's fun to see how Magnús laughs with his whole body. How the laughter runs down him, lying horizontal in that chair, like a spasm shooting down a slaughtered bull, ending in his toes, which contract in a Mexican wave under those psychologist's socks, in front of some indoor hurdle racing on Eurosport. (I feel a sudden wave of depression, as always when I see men in socks.) Then he stretches toward the candy bowl, by switching gear and turning, wheeling the chair. I reckon it's been two years now since I last saw him standing. This is followed by a discussion on artificial insemination techniques and other innovations in human reproduction. Elsa talks about a new abortion pill, and I drop out for a moment, seduced by the fantasy of secretly slipping one to Hofy. Finally, Elsa says that she was on the Pill. That's why it's a miracle. I wore a condom and she was on the Pill. We must be some kind of sacred family. All we need now is for Mom to make Lolla pregnant. I look at Magnús, horizontal in his chair. The thought that he could actually do it. You'd never think it, watching him lie there like a sedated hippopotamus. Yeah. The nurse must have had to anesthetize him first, to be able to take his sample. Lifted straight from his left testicle. Yeah. Magnús seeds . . . Hey. Hey, I think, struck by an irresistible thought. As Magnús stretches out for another piece of chocolate, my brain is struck by a minor nuclear explosion. There are three pieces of chocolate left in the bowl. Yeah. Magnús had the last three. Elsa hasn't touched them. Pregnant and on a diet? I stretch toward one of them and fiddle with the noisy wrapping as Elsa gives us the scientific lowdown on the reliability of the Pill. Then I pretend I need a leak and disappear into the john. With the piece of chocolate.

Inside my leather breast pocket, locked behind a zip, I still have the two-month-old Xmas present the Puffin gave me. An orange aspirin called Ecstasy. I'd started to look on it as a kind of Bond pill: to be swallowed in the event of being captured by the enemy, to be able to kill myself before I coughed up all my secrets. But, to be honest, it was just because I didn't have the guts to take it. I'm pathetic. With year-old condoms and a two-month-old E in my pockets. When will I start to live? Not till I start celebrating my birthday in places other than terraced-house toilets belonging to Sister Elsa and that psychobabble hubby of hers. Not till I start sleeping with some 50,000 chicks other than my mother's girlfriend. Jón Páll will be born in seven months' time. But at least I'm wearing red trousers. Yeah. There's a bit of daring living for you.

Wonder who owns them? Engey's big brother, maybe? Big brother? I suspect they really belong to her mother, Guernsey. I unwrap the chocolate, carefully, like in a movie, I'm in a movie, right now, yeah, I'm in action, this is living, the sweat confirms that, it's a little hollow chocolate hut, with a smooth base. Using a nearby Q-tip, I pierce a hole through it and implant the orange aspirin called Ecstasy. Nice job. I suck the cotton on the Q-tip as I wrap the piece of chocolate again. It looks so perfect that, at the end of the operation, I look into the mirror over the sink and say, "Björn. My name is Björn. Hlynur Björn." And even though I'm not tuxedoed, I manage to walk back into the living room in an impressively professional stride. The bowl. Two pieces of chocolate left. They've turned the TV up. *Children's Hour.* I Noddy the E-chocolate into the bowl and take the other two. Thunder and lightning between my fingers as I unwrap one of them. This cellophane is so bloody noisy. Frantically shove it into my mouth. The other glued to the palm of my hand. Manage to slip it into my jacket pocket. Magnús. My dear Magnús. Soon you will be resurrected. The umbrella lies on the table. Xtc in the bowl. It's my birthday today. Elsa is pregnant. *Children's Hour.* Some dwarfs on the screen. Magnús laughs. My little nephew turns around. Looks at me. I look at the TV. Little nephew stands up. Little nephew peeps into the bowl. Little nephew stretches out his hand. I press all the alarms in my brain, got the whole fire department on alert. They've starting hosing, sweat spurting out of my forehead. A six-year-old kid on Ecstasy. Could kill him. *Bi-ba. Bi-ba.* I suddenly leap off the sofa and snatch the piece of chocolate out of my nephew's fingers. Trying to give off a playful laugh. Six-year-old eyes, one blink. Then: "Mommy! He stole the piece of chocolate from me! Maaammy, boohoo ehhehe . . . it was for meee . . . I want the . . . eeeee . . ." What? He wants the E? "There, there . . ." says Elsa. I feign to be playing with him, hold the cellophane, dangling the poison before his eyes. The boy charges toward it in tears. "Now, now, Steini, love, just have another." That's right. Now I remember. Steini. His name is Steini. In honor of Dad. Granddad. Green-eyed little graybeard. With 4,160 whiskey bottles waiting for him out on the racing track, waiting for him to turn up in his Johnnie Walking tracksuit, to start his lifelong pub-crawling marathon, tables already set up along the track, with bartenders holding out bottles for him to grab as he passes. (Four bottles a week multiplied by twenty years = 4,160, then rehab.) Saw a program the other day. They've found the alco gene and they can now detect it in children. Preventive rehab. Pre-hab. Babies Anonymous. "No, he eee, he took the last swee . . . ee . . . et . . ." That's given me enough time to grope for the other piece of chocolate in my jacket pocket and, after performing the switch, I magically dangle it in front of him. I'm so smart. "OK. Only teasing." Steini rudely rips it out of my hands and looks at me with the eyes of an abused child: "Shitdad!" Shitdad. Not bad. Not totally inaccurate. "Now, now, Steini. That's no way to talk to your uncle." Me: "Shithead, Steini. The word is 'shithead.'" Magnús looks at me. Steini: "No! You're a shitdad!" The terror of women is nothing compared with the terror of children. Those cheeky brats. They really know how to knock you off-guard. Women and children. Best to steer clear of them. Elsa and Magnús seem to be just as terrified and defenseless. If children were ever to come to power. If children were ever allowed to rule. But in practice they do rule. Over everything. With that machine-gun weeping of theirs. Hold us all hostage. I steal a glance to see if he's got a pager. A piece of chocolate. A tampon for children's mouths. All gone. He's sitting on the floor again. I've got the E-chocolate in the palm of my left hand. A pinless hand grenade in a terraced house. To do or not to do? That is the question. Beat. Elsa stands up to go into the kitchen. The perfect opportunity: I slip the piece of chocolate back into the bowl, unnoticed. Have a sip of beer. This is like a good thriller. Another beat. Then: Magnús raises his head toward the glass of beer. From the corner of my eye I can see that he's spotted the piece of chocolate. It's like watching a *Match of the Day* video. All we need now is John Motson:

"And he leans towards the glass, no, he's heading for the bowl and . . . It's the last piece of chocolate. IT'S THE LAST PIECE! The last piece of chocolate is still in the bowl and he picks it up. HE PICKS IT UP! Nice move there, Magnús. He unwraps the piece of chocolate. But what. What's this? Yes, Elsa's back on the pitch again, straight out of the kitchen, and says: 'Oh, was there one left?'

and Magnús. MAGNÚS VIDAR VAGNSSON IS ON THE BALL, AND SAYS: 'Yeah. You want it?' AND THEN WHAT? Yes. ELSA HAFSTEINSDÓTTIR, ELSA HAFSTEINSDÓTTIR IS IN THE MIDDLE OF THE FIELD, AND SAYS: 'Yeah.' AND MAGNÚS, WELL, IS HE GOING TO HAND IT TO HER . . . ?"—The sports commentary has to take a pause here owing to a slight technical hitch, I've broken down, I . . . I . . . The glasses run down my nose. Down my perspiring nose. What can I say? Yeah:

"You . . . you know pregnant women shouldn't eat chocolate."

"Really?"

"Yeah. I saw a program about it on TV the other day. There's something in the chocolate that can damage . . . that can damage the . . . the formation of the bones, it's the egg . . . the egg white, too much egg-white formation."

"Really?" says Magnús.

"Since when have you been such an expert on pregnancies?" says Elsa, heading toward the coffee table, toward Magnús, toward the piece of chocolate.

"Yeah. That's what they said. On TV. Unless you want the baby to be some kind of Stephen Hawking."

Nice one. Nice move I just made. But . . . Magnús:

"What. Didn't he get the Nobel Prize?"

No. Elsa is here, standing over her hubby in his chair . . . no. She . . . Does she want E? There is a devilish streak in her. Or there used to be a devilish streak in her. Hiding my *Goal* mags from me, and later *Bravo*, and holding the remote outside the window. She used to smoke. I think. Went to hash parties. Until she nursed all of that out of her system and turned into a goody-goody. Maybe she wants to try some E? But the baby. I think. The baby! Pregnant on E? No. She bends over toward the piece of chocolate, Magnús looks up, and . . . I can't take any more of this.

". . . AND WHAT A MOMENT OF SUSPENSE THIS IS! THE CROWD WATCHES WITH BATED BREATH. . . . THE TENSION HAS REACHED FEVER PITCH. AND THE ENTIRE STADIUM IS LITERALLY ABOUT TO ERUPT. . . . WHAT CAN HAPPEN NEXT? Bit difficult to imagine this. But yes. Elsa Hafsteinsdóttir has just entered the penalty box. And Magnús Vidar still has the piece of chocolate. He lifts it up. And . . . Nice move, Magnús Vidar Vagnsson, about to pass the ball to Elsa Hafsteinsdóttir . . . But no. Someone's shouting from the bench. It's the United trainer. . . . No. It's Hlynur Björn Hafsteinsson. He says: 'It also increases the chances of a miscarriage.' And . . . Magnús Vidar. In a bit of a tight spot there, but ELSA HAFSTEINSDÓTTIR IS NOT OFFSIDE. NO, SHE'S NOT OFFSIDE! WILL MAGNÚS VIDAR PASS IT TO HER? NO. BUT WAIT A MINUTE. Yes. HE'S LOOKING AT ELSA. SAYS: 'Yes, is that so?' AND NO. Yes. HE TAKES IT. HE TAKES IT HIMSELF. AND WHAT A LOOOVELY SHOT, MAGNÚS VIDAR VAGNSSON! HE LITERALLY POPPED IT INTO THE NET. WELL, HOW ABOUT THAT! WHAT A STROKE! WHAT A GOAL! THIS WE HAVE GOT TO SEE AGAIN IN ACTION REPLAY."

Yours truly is badly hungover, wiped out, hasn't smoked for twelve hours, hasn't seen TV for sixty hours, hasn't seen his mom for forty-six hours, hasn't slept with anyone for 1,176 hours, and he's wearing the red trousers of some unknown anorexic mother, and her husband Róbert's undersized boots; there's a bad taste of chocolate in his mouth and some heavy shit building up in his bowels (composed mainly of Calvin Klein cornflakes mixed with Hofian housemother sauce); he's been banned from the K-bar, is eternally hated by an unknown naked woman, has broken up a beautiful young couple's relationship in Grafarvogur and irreparably subverted an innocent suburban dentist's family's concept of holy matrimony, forty-eight hours after his mom came out of the closet; he's expecting a child from a woman who hates him, has made his sister pregnant, and . . . and is slowly recovering from the most difficult moments in his life. . . .

And this is me, who'd rather just be at home in my room with the remote in my hand.

I sit in the front seat, like Stephen Hawking unplugged.

Elsa drives. A white Toyota. Elsa's driving me home from school, home to Mom. Elsa is driving me home from the playschool I've just been expelled from. I put an AIDS syringe on the teacher's chair and filled the cod-liver-oil pillbox with E-tabs. No one noticed anything. Until the day after. When I was the only one who turned up at school. Elsa came to collect me. I don't want to go home. Lolla. I'd rather spend the rest of my life here, strapped to this chair, with a nurse at the wheel. So that I wouldn't have to do anything anymore. She stops at the shops for me. Cigarettes. The beautiful white Toyota breathes healthily when I come out. And Elsa at the wheel. Elsa, dear Elsa. My sister, Elsa. What have I done? What I've just done. Me who never does anything. Elsa. I wish I were like you. I wish I were you. Good. Nursing the sick. Doing your bit. Cooking and stuff. I wish I were you. Or Magnús. Magnús. Right now Magnús is up on Mount Ulfarsfell dancing techno. With a Walkman glued to his ears, stuck on XTC, and now Magnús is on Mount Esja, dancing techno in pitch darkness. And now Magnús has come home again, and is mowing the frozen lawn. And now Magnús is inside dancing techno with the kids. Now Magnús is boogieing on into the night. Alone in the living room. Now Magnús has stuck his head in the microwave to try to cool himself down. Now Magnús is over at the neighbors', banging Vaka till the crack of dawn. Now Magnús is in jail. Now Magnús is cracking. Now Magnús doesn't just sit listening patiently to his patients anymore. Now he does all the talking. Now Magnús fondles his patients. Now Magnús has been committed. Now Magnús is in intensive care. With his Elsa on twenty-four-hour standby.

Not that. Not that it wasn't worth it, seeing him there, getting all e-static in his hubby's chair, levering himself up and down, until he finally sprang out of the chair and went to the toilet and came back all pale and rubbing his tingling fingers and all of a sudden he almost looked "alive," and went to get more beer and wouldn't sit down, just stood gawking out the window, trotting up and down, and said:

"Beautiful mountain."

"Huh?" (Elsa.)

"Beautiful mountain. We've never walked up that mountain. Ulfarsfell. Ulfarsfell." Then he swung back and glanced at the TV and came out with this really funny and loud laugh at the sight of the presenter, Ragnheidur Clausen (80,000): "She's great! She's just great!"

"Magnús?"

"Don't you think? She's great. Ragnheidur Clausen. She's just great. Where are my climbing boots, Elsa? I'm gonna walk up that mountain."

The kids look at their ecstatic dad in awe.

"Wouldn't you like to have a walk, lads?"

"But we're about to eat, Magnús."

A slightly embarrassed atmosphere ending with Magnús disappearing into a cupboard to find some climbing boots and me on the point of wanting to leave and Elsa offering to drive me home. By the time she's got her coat on, and I've stepped into the hall, Magnús is standing there with some kind of moon boots in his hands.

"What, are you going? Are you going out on a binge? Elsa and Hlynur. Great stuff. Good for you."

"Magnús. You just wait here till I get back. I'm just going to drive him home."

"I'll just take the kids with me."

"Up to Ulfarsfell? Now? It'll be dark soon."

It'll be dark soon. Elsa pulls her Toyota onto the curb of Bergthórugata, and says, "Well, then," as she shifts into neutral. "It was nice to see you. Nice of you to come."—"Yeah."—"And happy birthday again, it was a pity I didn't have anything prepared for you, not even a present."—"No problem. You're pregnant. That's a gift in itself."—"Yeah, maybe, it's been a big day for all of us, and Magnús . . . I don't know what got into him, wanting to walk up the mountains at this hour. He who never steps out of the house, unless it's to go golfing or fishing or something like that . . ."—"Yeah. He was all fidgety all of a sudden."—"Yeah . . ." Silence. I release my belt. We look each other in the eye. "Well, then. Thanks for the lift."—"Don't mention it, Hlynur dear, it was nice to see you, and send Mom all my love. . . ."—"OK. Will do."—"How are things between you otherwise?"—"Yeah, fine."—"Hey, maybe I'll pop in for a second, since I'm here."—"Does she know you're pregnant?"—"That I'm pregnant? Of course, don't you remember? I was so surprised she hadn't told you about it."—"Right. Yeah, of course. Haven't really spoken to her for a while," I say as Elsa turns off the engine and puts it in gear. I'm somehow soothed by the prospect of being reunited with my room again, and am about to open the door, am groping for the handle, yes, there it is, when, loosening her belt, she says: "Do you think she's in?" I chirpily answer: "Yeah, definitely, they're always in, so we can toast to the whole package. Three causes for celebration."—"Oh, really? Is there something else?" We look into each other's eyes, both with our hands on the handle. Me: "Yeah. Mom, too. You know."—"No. Hang on. Did she get promoted?" she asks, excited and surprised. "Yeah. You could say that. No. You know what I'm talking about."—"No. What?"—"The closet."—"What closet? No! Has she bought a new closet? Where's she going to put it? You don't exactly have much space in your place."—"Elsa. Or hasn't she told you about . . ."—"About what? No. What?"—"No, she . . . She'll tell you herself."—"No. Go on. Tell me."—"I thought you knew."— "Knew what?"—"No. Just ask her."—"Closet . . . what the . . . I never know what you're getting at. Closet . . . Mom . . ."—"As in 'out of.'"—"What?"—"Out of, you know."—"Out of? Closet? Out . . . Out of the closet?"—"Yep."—"No, Hlynur. Mom? That's a good one."—"No. This is serious."—"Yeah, yeah, sure."— "Yeah."—"I never know when you're joking or not. Isn't this some kind of joke, just like that rigmarole about pregnant women not being able to eat chocolate?"—"No. That was a joke, yeah. But this . . ."—"Huh? Was that a joke? I thought you looked so serious somehow."—"Did you think so?"—"Yeah. I obviously don't know you well enough, even though I've been your sister for thirty . . ."—"Four."—"Yes, thirty-four years. How long does it take to actually get to know you?"—"I'd say another five years. Five intensive years. That should do the trick."—"Ha ha . . . But you . . . you had such a strange look just then."—"Yeah. I dunno. Maybe it's just cos Mom . . ."—"Cos Mom came out of the closet. This has got to be one of the best ones I've heard from you."— "OK. I am *not* joking. Our mother is a lesbian."—"Are you serious?"—"Yep. It's Lolla."—"Lolla?"—"Yep. Pure love. I sensed there was something. Of course, she's been living with us since Christmas and she was always flaunting it at us before that, practically came over every night, for dinner. There was obviously some dessert being dished around that I wasn't getting a taste of."—"I don't believe it."—"Yeah."—"And what, when did you realize?"—"She told me. Herself. On Thursday night."—"And?"—"Just. Well, I practically said it for her. She found it difficult. Cried a bit . . ."—"Really? Did you say something?"—"Me? No, no. She felt I took it really well. I mean, obviously it's good, good for her, to have got it off her chest."—"Yes."—"I mean, fair play to her." Silence. Elsa stares ahead of her. Headlights in her face. A tires-on-wet-asphalt sound. Red taillights. That Sunday-evening feeling. That weariness in the lampposts, those bloated houses, and something boring about the way all the cars have been parked, and that weekend's-over feeling hanging over everything. We sit. Forgetting the doors a moment. She: "I just . . . I mean . . . this is such a bolt from the blue . . . she . . . and her . . . at her age . . . I just . . . I just don't get it . . ." She looks at me. One thought on her face. Fourteen cases on a conveyor belt being loaded onto a TWA plane at Amsterdam airport. "It's the menopause, putting men on pause," I say, trying to lighten the atmosphere a bit, but she still has that frozen look on her face. I go on: "So what? It's no big deal or anything. It's not as if she's been buried under an avalanche. Just a lesbian . . ."—"Yeah . . . I still don't understand why she didn't tell me."—"Yeah. I thought she already had." Silence. She looks out on to the street again. It's getting colder in the car. Been here long enough. Want a cigarette. Elsa in shell shock. The nurse. Might have been easier if I'd told her Mom had cancer. Maybe it's because she lives in Suburbia. People who live on the outskirts live farther from the truth. She had to drive into town to get this. I look at my red trousers. Then say: "What d'you say? Shall we go in? Getting cold out here."—"Yes. That's true. No. I think I'll head on home."—"What, weren't you going to pop in? Pop in on the couple? Step in to say hello to your new . . . stepmother?"—"No, I don't think so. Just send my regards."—"You can't face it?"—"What?"—"The fact that Mom's a lesbian."—"Yeah . . . yeah, yeah . . . I just . . . I just need a bit of time, that's all. I'm . . ."—"Going home?"—"Yes, I better rush home, besides Magnús was so . . ."—"Yeah, you better rush home before he turns gay." She looks at me. "Joke," I say, but she doesn't smile. "Elsa. What is this? It'll all work out in the end. You know. Mom will be fine again by next Christmas, there must be something we can give her. A few hormone injections and in a few weeks she'll be perfectly healthy and hetero again. Man, you should know, you're a nurse."—"Always the same old joker. Can't you take anything seriously?"—"I don't know. Women over fifty thousand, maybe."—"Fifty thousand in their IQs, you mean?"—"Yeah . . . I . . . IQs . . . And, yeah. Pregnant women too."—"I'm pregnant."—"Yeah."—"So?"—"Yeah. Sorry. I was just . . ."—"OK."—"OK. You think about it."— "Yeah."—"OK?"—"Yeah."—"We'll leave it at that, then. See you."—"Yeah. I'll call."—"OK, and thanks for the lift and everything."—"Yeah, don't mention it, and happy birthday again." —"Yeah."—"Bye."—"Bye. And send my regards to Magnús."— "Yes. And you send my love to Mom and co."—"Yeah."—"All right then."—"Yeah, bye."—"Bye."

A Japanese-designed slamming-door effect killed by Icelandic frost.

I stagger across the street and up the steps. The remote. Bon Jovi in concert in Bombay. Elsa. So much straighter than I am. Never had to face a case like this at the Municipal Hospital. Does her good. Mom. Nice one, Mom. Proud of her. Lolla. Hofy. Jón Páll. My trousers. Shoes. Vaka. Engey. Óli. The condom. Condoms. The remote. Magnús. Ulfarsfell. Elsa. The baby. The piece of chocolate. The table. The pill. The piece of chocolate. John Motson. Let's just see that in action replay. The remote. It worked. Yeah. You could see it on him. Finally a bit of psyche in the psychologist. I put the psyche back into the ologist. A new man. A psychologist with a soul. Should do his business good. Do him good. It'll be OK. Forgive me, Magnús, but . . . Life is like a box of chocolates. . . . So he'll be called after me. Hlynsson. Jón Páll Hlynsson. Or Björnsson. Which? It'll be dark soon. The remote. The umbrella. "It'll be dark soon." Something about the way she said that. It'll all work out. Lolla. I wanted to fuck her again. Not.

As I turn the key in the lock I suddenly feel that everything but the key in the lock—the door, the house, the whole world— is turning.

When I close the door everything falls into place again and I realize it feels good to be home.

The red trousers. That's all they can see when I come in: Mr. Róbert's wife's red trousers. Mom and Lolla, on their way out to the theater. And it's so good to be home, and Elsa was so straight, and they're such fun, and so full of life, and teasing me so nicely about these ghastly trousers, and like a real ass I think: I love them. My darling lesbians, on their way to the theater. Women make up. For men. Mom not quite dykey enough, I feel, in those high heels, skirt and jacket (brown), blouse (white), and lily blue Lolla blue scarf. Some sign of a sex change in the hair, though. Not as high up as it used to be. Not as . . . Lolla's gone for a cute k.d. lang–ish (27,000) look. A plain black velvet jacket and dark green khaki trousers (whatever khaki is) and a silky shirt. A red AIDS ribbon on one of her breasts. Has she got AIDS? Have I got AIDS? Feel like ravishing her ear. Allow my eyes and words to do it instead. They say bye, darling, and have fun and there's some pizza left, and then Mom stilettos out into the cold, followed by Lolla in softer flat shoes, and I look at her ass and wonder is she wearing my underpants? And Mom suddenly looks so funny: to see that fifty-year-old lady from the Imports Office, stepping out of her closet, all dolled up on her high hetero heels, on her way to the theater with her girlfriend, for all of the eyes of the town to tittle-tattle about, and all the tongues in the theater to waggle about and whisper: that's her, and there she is, and they're a couple, Sigurlaug told me, you know Sigurlaug, Palli's wife, Palli Níelsson, and Dad probably serenading Sara about it in some joint downtown, and maybe I should phone him or Elsa, and Magnús on top of Mount Ulfarsfell mooning to the city with his fat rich psycho's ass. Mind you don't fart your whole psyche out, Magnús pal.

Then they come back, briskly up the stairs—holy Kiljan, how happy Mom is—I can hear it in her voice, in both of them, and they burst in, rushing into the kitchen, both of them all over me and the cold pizza: "Sorry, darling love, but we forgot to wish you a HAPPY BIRTHDAY!" And I say: "Oh yeah? Me too!" And we embrace with a laugh like a happy little lezzie family, and I'm thinking I slept with Lolla as her green khaki crotch brushes past me, and so what? It creates a stronger bond between us, and they hop out again, going to be late for the theater, and I sit there, smeared in lipstick, looking like a polar bear with red on his cheeks, I imagine. A polar bear biting into a cold slice of Domino's with blue cheese and olives and swallowing. Hofy.

I slip a tape into the machine. And lie on my bed. *Goodfellas*, for the seventh time. Fast-forward between murders. The Beauty of Death. Fountains of blood in slow motion. It's fun to watch people die, but dead people are pretty boring. Then switch over to Discovery. A documentary on pandas. Cute black and white bamboo suckers in China. Live like hermits, each bear on his own tree, sleeping for most of the day, and only stay up between 22 and 02. They're almost extinct now because they can't be bothered to fuck anymore. I glance at my white turtleneck and black jeans on the floor, and drift asleep, on top of a tree in China.

Morality is nothing more than ink on paper. Yellowed paper. Jealousy, envy, and guilt. Diseases long defeated. TB, leprosy, syphilis, smallpox. Yeah. Mankind is moving on. "It'll be dark soon." But electricity took over long ago. I turn on the light in my bedroom. We've overcome all that old stuff now. Light and darkness. Right and wrong. Morality. Ethics. Woody Allen on the wall. All that old stuff has been swept under the Pope's skullcap, stored and long forgotten under that Polish bald patch. Karol Wojtyla. Under that little white trapdoor, he keeps and polishes the final patch of purity on earth, the non-wanking monk, with the last halo in history, but it no longer hovers in the air, it's lost its spin and dangles limply on his head, the Pope's cap, the lid on a jar of tablets long past their sell-by date: God's long-yellowed commandments that say one shouldn't screw one's mother's girlfriend, that mothers shouldn't have girlfriends in the first place, that one's sister shouldn't be on the Pill, that oneself shouldn't be wearing condoms or shooting sperm through anything other than a wedding ring, that one shouldn't be sending one's brother-in-law up to the mountaintop on Ecstasy, that Prince Charles shouldn't be cameling Camilla (2,500) but Princess Di (40,000), and that Woody Allen mustn't sleep with his wife's (60,000) foster daughter (35,000). . . .

The Pope. The Pope jerks off in Rome. Not. Absolutely not. His hard-ons are only for the glory of God. The Holy Scrotum dangles limply in the name of the Father, the Son, and the Holy Spirit, awaiting its resurrection: the Pope's rises only once a year, on Easter Sunday. But he has to start before that. Obviously takes him a bit of time. Being old and all that. He stands there with that palm branch in his hands the Sunday before and whips it about until Holy Thursday. And then there's the long Good Friday. Total despair. Doesn't look good. Still limp on Saturday. But tense nevertheless. The bishop's all on edge. Can he get him up? Yes, miracle. He rises on the third day. And for a moment St. Peter's voluptuous dome is the world's clitoris, and all God has to do is to stroke it once with his finger and everyone comes. Playboy Easter bunnies and hand-painted testicles. Sex-mad rabbits and mad rabid Catholics. The faithful gather to witness the res-erection that will deliver them from all evil, gaping up at the Vatican balcony. Then the Pope comes, but without coming: he settles for a symbolic white dove instead, a flying white sperm released to the heavenly womb, and the crowd in the square erupts, their mouths foaming with chocolate joy, breaking out of their shells, prostrating themselves before their beloved Pope, who then rings in the sex o'clock mass.

The Pope gets it up only once a year. For the rest of the year he keeps it hanging on his crotch, for all our sins, dangling limply in his Popic hair. For his little Pope doesn't hop on any women other than Mother Earth, she's the only one he'll kiss: he kisses her, on the crown of her head, on the tarmac at the airport, with his chaste lips, he prostrates himself, a moment, with his skullcap glued to his skull. The last patch of purity on earth: everything surrounding it soiled with sin and desire and lust and coughs and infidelity and orgasms and lies and drugs and AIDS and Ecstasy chocolate and contraceptives and abortions and cigarettes and glasses of whiskey and video nasties and porn and incest and live sex shows and sniffing eleven-year-old Vaka's jeans: all those things that turn life into an exciting cigarette break from the dreariness of death. We painted the barracks roof in the summer of '79 with red Kopal paint, and we all stood below covered in stains, all stood below covered in blood, when we realized we'd left out a small patch in the middle of the roof. A Holy Patch. A shining, glittering strip of corrugated roof. Humanity painted the globe red, and the bald Pope raises his head in the middle of the Red Sea, with a white cap on his skull, containing all the instructions on how life should be, not this red, but shiny, glossy, untouched, and pure.

Under that cap, God's Catholic word is safely preserved, all his views, and rules about right and wrong, the universal conscience, the eternal moral code. In a live CNN broadcast from Giants Stadium in New Jersey, he performed a mass in gale-force winds and pouring rain, in front of a crowd of eighty thousand people in raincoats, and when he walked onstage his hat blew off his head, and for a moment it looked as if all of God's commandments, all the rights and wrongs, all of Moses' heavy books were finally about to be lost to the wind, and even his altar boys and holy bodyguards could do nothing but stand there. If it hadn't been for that small clip, that tiny hairpin, that Holy Pope clip pinned to his gray hair . . .

Morality is nothing more than ink on paper. All that Catholic dogma, all that ethics lark, all that thou-shalt-not-do-that rigma-role, and not that either, and not with that lot, nor this one, nor that dyke, all those two thousand years of faith in what's right, with all the might of all the 700-ton Gothic churches in the world upon us, all this you-shouldn't-have-slept-with-Lolla crap, all of that, that entire package, hanging on to the Pope's few gray hairs by a pin, in the howling winds and lashing rain at Giants Stadium in New Jersey.

And the people rejoice. Eighty thousand soaking Americans cheer—as if they were cheering the football hero, O. J. Simpson himself, speeding across the field in his white Bronco, having just slain his Nicole (90,000), with the cops on his trail; and you can't tell if they're yelling—soaking in sin—out of joy because two thousand years of rights and wrongs are about to be annihilated by the weather and the wind, or out of the terror of seeing it all hang to his hairclip by a thread. A real cliff-hanger. And the papal hat turned inside out. And God says let there be more rain.

The people rejoice. And then go home to abort and sodomize.

I lie in bed, in my monastic cell. Yeah. Jealousy, envy, and guilt. Diseases that have long been defeated. TB, leprosy, syphilis, smallpox. Scientists have broken through the maidenhead of self-righteousness. Dragged us out of the dark cave, made the caveman see the light, chromed the Cro-Magnon. Neon in Neanderthal. No longer either light or darkness. Just a question of on or off. Nothing right or wrong. Time has turned bisexual. We live in bisexual times. Beyond right and wrong. Everything is right *and* wrong. Everything is good *and* bad. Nothing is bad. Nothing is good. Everything just is. On eighty channels. I zap down. Channel 23: cancer research in Boston. Channel 41: AIDS patient in Rotterdam. Channel 74: crime of passion in Sydney. I accidentally doze off. I dream of a meteorite about to drop on my head.

A meteorite appears. Disguised in a baseball cap with a sun-tanned surface, and the brain of a dentist for a core. I nuke it.

I sit in my bunker, late on a Sunday night, shielded from the chatter between Mom and some man in the corridor. I'm tangled on the Net, in the middle of a dialogue with Kati:

HB: I hate dentists.

KH: Well, I'm not crazy about them either.

HB: They're assholes. Who wants an asshole in his mouth?

KH: Ha ha. Good one. And they even make you pay for it.

HB: I tell you. Dentists in Iceland are as rich as pop stars.

KH: They are getting more expensive here, too.

HB: I don't get it.

KH: Well, it is a boring job.

HB: And is that why they have to get paid well?

KH: Yes. Like lawyers.

HB: Exactly. Here people have to choose between bad teeth and a vacation in Greece or good teeth and stay home.

KH: What do you do?

HB: Bad teeth and stay home.

KH: Ha ha.

The girl is laughing in her cubbyhole somewhere in Beautypest when knock, knock, knocking on heaven's door and an unbearably chirpy Palli Níelsson enters. Well, oh my . . .

"Hi there. How are you?"

"Excellent, well."

I quickly sign off to Katarina:

HB: Sorry have to go now I'll send you the disk with Ham let me know what you think. Bi.

Palli Níelsson comes in and closes the door. Uninvited.

"You remember me, don't you?"

"Yeah, didn't you release a solo album once?"

"Ehm, noo, I can't say that I have."

"You should think about it."

"You think so?"

"There's a lot of money to be made in the music business. Could be a hit. You'd have a one in ten thousand chance of selling ten thousand copies."

"Yeah," he says, sitting on my bed. Holy Laxness. He should be more careful. I might hop on him and make him pregnant, even more pregnant than he is now, with his belly on my bed. I continue:

"Just need to watch out in that business. It's rotten to the core. A thousand worms squirming in the carcass of a dead bitch. And everyone trying to break through the same asshole."

"Yeah?"

"But anyway. I'm confusing you with your daughter. She's the famous one."

"Oh yeah? Famous?"

"She's working on a solo album, isn't she? Tell her to beware of the limelight. She could be a hit today and a flop tomorrow."

"I'm sorry, but I can't really see where you're going with this."

"I'm not going anywhere. I'm just going to stay in and read."

"Oh, right. Well, then. What are you reading?"

"Words. Words, words, words."

"I see."

"No. You'll have to come closer to the screen if you want to see it."

"What. What are you reading?"

"Slander, sir. This is a whole chapter on dentists. Says here they only work two hours a day but they still make a million a month and spend the rest of the day polishing their jeeps, fishing salmon, and buying air tickets for the weekend. I think that's going a bit too far, although there must be something behind it, but I still think it's a bit much to publicize it like that. Because dentists are human beings like everyone else and they can catch cancer or crabs just as much as the next man can."

"Maybe I should pop over at a more appropriate time."

"Yeah. The later the better."

"All right, then. We'll just leave it at that, then. Maybe I'll just give you a call. Bye, then."

"Yeah, whatever. Always good to say goodbye to you. Nothing greater than saying goodbye to you, except to life, except to life."

Palli Níelsson leaves. Crawls out of the room like a half-eaten crab.

My father-in-love.

I wake up in 1442. Same old story. Drag myself out of the coffin and rub the earth out of my eyes. Shamble about like a dumb medieval monk. In my black and white robe. Cheerios in the monastery. A Carmel Lite cigarette. Except I smoke Prince. Not a thought in my head. Just a turtle around my neck and smoke out of my mouth. A slight dizzy spell. As I break out of it, I suddenly get the feeling there's nothing ahead of me but my next smoke. No more life ahead of me than a cigarette. 9.5 centimeters under my nose, 8, 7, 6, 5 . . . I dread finishing it. What'll I do when it's finished? I try to smoke it sparingly and witness it slowly smoldering toward the filter. Not a thought in my head. I count the drags. Twelve drags in each cigarette. Twelve hours. Twelve apostles. Everything so calculated. Even cigarettes, each one designed to last the length of a song. First song of the day: "Losing My Religion," R.E.M.

I'm on my last drag and am somehow filled with dread. End of broadcast. Like in the days before the remote was invented. Facing the void. How am I going to kill the day? Kill it. I put the butt in the ashtray. Watch this minute burn away in a pillar of smoke. Then it's over. Vanished. If we could burn all our days. Set time on fire. Yeah. New Year's bonfires. Put it all behind me.

If something other than the sun would come up in the morning. Maybe it's because of all the events in these past few days that this Monday feels so incredibly empty. I take the night's tape out of the machine. *The Second Coming.* They say Christ will come again. The Second Coming. The maestro has been working on that album for almost two thousand years. So it better be good. The tape is hot out of the machine. Body temperature. The only human warmth I'm entitled to these days. Yeah. I'm a monk. A monk in a porn monastery. This tape was unusually hard stuff, judging by the dreams I had last night. Nonstop all-American healthy virile fucking while Iceland was sleeping, with XXL tits and hormone-pumped hard-ons. American sperm sprayed the screen all night long like sleet in slow motion. I enshroud the tape and feel a strange sadness. The porn hangover. Everyone at it, except me. Maybe it'll happen one day. Maybe I'll be able to run out of my mother's house for love. Maybe I'll run out of motherly love. I keep the TV off. We're heading for a total still life when the phone rings. Bang on cue. Elsa. Wanting to know more about Mom—"Yeah, well, she hasn't gone back into the closet, or would you like me to check?"—and I ask about Magnús—yes, he walked up Mount Ulfarsfell with a searchlight and then watched MTV all night. Yeah. I took a pill out of their lives and gave them another one instead. A pill, from her to him.

I realize why I'm so down when I can't find my shoes. Red trousers on the floor and my own lost in the wilderness, stuffed under a radiator somewhere, with the dried tears of three women. Look up all the Róberts in Reykjavík. Only one living in Elsa's street. "Could I talk to Engey, please?" The trousers will be handed over this afternoon, at a formal ceremony at Café Solon Islandus. Along with the shoes. Until then: the crumpling in a jacket on a man's back in Buenos Aires. The pedestrian crossing that the Beatles walked over on Abbey Road. A fox farm in Lahti. Four German soap ads. Boris Becker's wife (80,000). Lolla. Tony Hillerman. Trampoline. A ceramics gallery in London.

Which reminds me. I have to play the museum curator today. Been ages since I took a look at the collection.

The museum is in the cellar. Mom has granted me the use of the premises, to show me her appreciation of the importance of the role of art and culture in contemporary society. I wool-sock my way down the cold steps with six empty packets of Prince, a multicolored umbrella, a monochrome contraceptive pill, and a munched piece of gum: the most recent additions. I haven't been conscientious enough lately. Haven't worked hard enough on my chewing-gum collection. The gum collection is the real feather in my cap. That and the cigarette packets. But still, the Prince packets stuff is probably what I'll be most remembered for. My life's work. Made in Denmark by House of Prince. I started it about two years ago. I've collected a pile of about eight hundred packets to date. It's not easy to be a working artist down here in dwarfland: we don't have any hard packs. So I've had to use my wits. And stuffed the packets with Frón biscuit crumbs. Two per pack. God help me if they stop producing those biscuits.

I tidy up the shelves a bit. The museum is split into two: category A containing stuff I bought, such as, for example, the Barbie acupuncture set and heroin kit, the Woody Allen vibrator and alarm clock, and the John Holmes magazines. And category B containing stolen goods, which I'm prouder of. There are lots of precious items here such as, for example, a helping of french fries Megas left behind at the Eldsmidjan pizza joint in '92, and "the last joint in Reykjavík" that Dylan sucked on in his Esja Hotel room as he gazed at Mount Esja across the bay, as the story goes, two sugar cubes that Björk cast aside at the Duus Hús Café that historic night she sang for François Mitterrand and Jack Lang: worth millions today. Then, the Big Secret: a friend of Mom's works at the Reykjalundur rest home and collects Halldór Laxness's Nobel-prized shaved hair in a plastic bag. I must have almost a kilo of the stuff by now.

I rearrange my *Star Trek* statues a bit, to make room for Vaka's umbrella. The pink sock from that Metallica creep in Stangarholt. Not sure about this item. Need to know the owner's name. But it still smells, I'll give him that much. Nanna Baldurs's condoms. I used one on Hofy, with excellent results, as we all know. My dream is to get some used ones into the collection. I once wrote to five Miss Icelands about it but never got an answer. I actually met one of them (110,000) at the K-bar and asked her to donate a Tampax. I hassled her so much that in the end she gave me one, but unused. Better than nothing. Then there was this guy from Arkansas on the Net who claimed he had three condoms used on Madonna (4,500,000), but he wanted $3,000 for the set.

Some people might say I just copied the idea from the museum at the Hard Rock Café, but I'd started long before they came to Iceland and my collection is much more Hard Core.

The whole of life is in here. Who would say no, in two hundred years' time, to a wishbone nibbled by Naomi Campbell (3,900,000). Or now, who wouldn't want to own a napkin containing Christ's very own snot. There's money in this. In the future people won't be hanging works of art on their walls, but life itself. Mother Teresa's (1,700) hymen.

The gum collection is getting quite impressive. I count, just to be sure. Twenty-three. I preserve them in empty Tic Tac boxes with a label on them: name, place, and moment. They look a bit like tiny brains. I've got all the female TV presenters. Perfect front-teeth marks in Eygló Manfreds's gum. If only I had her famous lips. I've sometimes felt tempted to throw it into my mouth. Next best thing to a kiss. Since I'm not destined to ever lie with her. Then I've got four pop-star pieces. But haven't got Björk's yet. Then there's the supermodel department. Although only one of them is actually super: Jara Ex (120,000). But now I can add Lerti's babe. Unfortunately Bryndís's gum bears her finger marks. And mine. I normally let them drop directly into the box. The shit I had to go through to get Lerti's babe's gum. The agony of the artist. I put it into the box. I'm thinking of calling the gum collection "The Brains of the Beautiful." Or just the "She Did Not Want to Kiss Me but I Got Her Gum" collection.

I have one of Mom's old diamond boxes and take my first piece out of it: a kidney stone I haggled out of an intern at the National Hospital in 1980 for a bottle of Johnnie Walker. I open a jar and lower the pregnancy pill onto a cushion of cotton. My masterpiece.

*　　*　　*

Living room. Four meters from the window, then three millimeters of jeans fabric, then Lolla. She looks like some far too complicated mechanism designed for smoking a cigarette. Tarantino and Uma Thurman (3,300,000) over coffee. She doesn't look up. From her papers on the coffee table. The way some people pretend they're working. So pretentious somehow. To work. Her lungs doing their job. Detecting smoke. Behind those breasts of hers. Women are behind breasts. We're in front of them. We'll never get over them.

"What are you doing?"

"Files."

"Rehab?"

"Yes."

I glance over her shoulder. Tidy reports on messy lives. Bummers set down in words. Words, words, words. People who want to put a period after every minute. And then start the next one with a capital letter. Look at my watch. 17:35:21, 22, 23, 24, 25 . . . Each second is a number. Each second is a number and somewhere someone is putting them all down on paper. Somewhere in the world some bald creep is putting all these periods down on paper. Sorry. I'll never read it. Walk to the window. Snowing. Somewhere someone's arranging all those snowflakes on a black computer screen. God's hard disk. Everything we do. Stored but not forgotten. Saved. Time's tape collection. Walk to the chair. Sit. Cigarette. Feet on the table. Want to invent something to say to get Lolla to stop this phonyness. To make her turn.

"You reckon the Pope's ever done it?"

"Huh?"

"You reckon the Pope has ever done it?"

"Sure."

"Really? You think he's done it?"

She doesn't answer. Lolla's back. The B-side. An old number-one hit on the other side. Rubbish. He's definitely never done it. I picture his bishop. I suddenly realize I've had the Pope's dick on my brain all day. Can't shake it off. The holy pole submerged in white angel hair. How does he handle his hard-ons? No. He's never come. Otherwise he wouldn't be Pope. He's never lost a seed. That's what makes him holy. They gave him a thorough checkup to make sure he was absolutely holy. And found seventy-year-old yellowed seed from his childhood days in Poland, the first batch of seeds still intact. Took good care of his, the little blond Karol did, while I was spraying mine over cats and dogs. Nah. Besides, it's a steady production. All stocked up. He's full of seventy-year-old seed. The Pope. A holy sperm keg full to the brim. Sperm. Always reminded me of shampoo. Cleanses the soul, as long as you don't spill it. Ejaculation. A tinge of death in that. The human body: 90 percent water. The Pope is 90 percent sperm. That's why he's so beautiful, with that soft white skin. Try again. Try to turn Lolla again:

"So how do you think he handles his hard-ons?"

"I don't know. Hand of God, maybe."

Lollipop. You're the best. Maradona. And Shilton couldn't save it. That shot from the "hand of God." Mexico '86. Lolla. All open and bare you were, a revelation. My Book of Revelation. Pussy juice. The only taste of religion I've ever had. To be able to sit there in that wicker chair, looking at Óli and that girl. That was a revelation. That was a religious experience. To see mankind making love. The most beautiful thing I've ever seen. Divinity incarnate. Sex. Adult videos. Altar pieces. Remember the booth in London. Alone with my man. Praying for a miracle. Praying she would step off the screen to take my Host into her mouth. Flickering images on the screen, like the bright mouth of a cave, and you like a caveman, burning with desire in the darkness, eyes glowing like a wild prehistoric cat's, and each frame a revelation, an icon, coming women, speaking in tongues, with their haloed hairdos, kneeling in front of crucified men, their mouths full of the risen flesh, of Christ, as they moan: Oh God! Oh God! Remember the booth in London. And the booth in the church in London. The confession boxes reminded me of the peeping boxes.

But still. Some part of us is against sex. Somewhere deep down—a barely audible hum—somewhere in the depths of our skull, a part of our brain is sounding church bells to warn us that sex is bad, ugly, and that one should keep one's man locked up in his cage and not let him out until he's married. And one shouldn't milk him onto orange-yellow plastic and television screens. Even on me. The Pope has some grip, even on me. I feel the weight of a heavy Catholic paw on my shoulder, a lengthy arm stretching from the depths of a long, long two-thousand-year-old dark colonnade. The Pope's hand, soft and mild, and stuffed with sperm. On my shoulder. Hey. I can at least console him with the fact that Lolla and I didn't use any contraceptives during our regretful fall into sin. The Pope is opposed to contraception. Which is understandable, I guess. Otherwise he wouldn't be here. If his parents had decided to roll in the hay just for the fun of it, and worn some scientific protection. The only thing that keeps me going is the hope of a good blow job.

"Yeah, by the way. Congratulations."

"For what?"

"The engagement. Congratulations on the engagement."

"What engagement?"

"Yours and Mom's."

Yeah. This is working. Now I've managed to sound like an even sicker case than the one she's reading about: an ex-carpenter who drank away his company and car, abused his wife and children with a hammer, and then ended up at the Amsterdam Hilton on plastic money with a six-inch Dutch suppository up his ass. She finally raises her eyes from the rehab files and looks at me. I shift gears. Calmly add:

"Congratulations on Mom."

"Right . . . So she spoke to you."

"She spoke to me. I spoke for her. I nudged her out of the closet."

"Yeah. She told me how well you took it. I think that made it much lighter for her."

"Lighter for some. Heavier for others."

"Oh? Difficult for you, you mean?"

"No. Elsa. She's heavy. With child."

"Yes. So I hear. And what . . . is she . . . ?"

"Elsa is a nurse. She's used to dealing with disorders."

"You mean being a lesbian is some kind of disease?"

Darling lesbian. You who sleep with women. Sheltered from the frightening, penetrating penises of man, pulsating with abuse and bad news. Sleep well. And with your sister. On a low bed, far from the burdens of procreation, outside the cycle of life, you play with yourselves and your soft little bodies, under the umbrella protecting you from the constant shower of sperm. There you can hide your vaginas and wombs, all stitched up and sealed against any possible pregnancy. Uninvaded Virgin Islands. Island virgins. Two cows in a field, protected from all bulls and balls, sucking on udders, ruminating with lust, with tongues on tits, slobbering, and sliding your cloven hoofs down each other's crotches and coming together. Moo. A moo for a moo, and a hoof for a hoof, and a tail for a tail. Lust for lust's sake. Breasts for breasts' sake. Love for love's sake. Unfucked fruits. Yeah. Make your love in your love-full beds, my ladies and gentlewomen. Two sheaths without a sword. While we male ale men spend the rest of our pub-crawling days fencing with our members, ejaculating into the wilderness, washing future generations off our hands. Wearing our jackets full of year-old condoms, we keep on smashing our glasses and banging our heads against the wall and the woodwork, up to our necks in debt and ineptitude, lying in gutters, with footprints on our butts, pockets full of wind and tobacco in our souls. Onward, Christian soldiers, marching as to hell . . .

"No. I mean being sterile. Well, if sterility is a disease."

"What do you mean?"

Barren woman. Cold is the blood that runs through your cave, where your ovaries pointlessly hang, like empty glasses over the bar, and not a soul in sight, candles unlit for eternity, but melting with lust. No life can ever spark in here. Here there can be no light. Nothing in and nothing out. A house that houses nothing, wrapping around a void. No heart will ever beat inside this womb. No slimy heads will come crawling out of this place. You sterile woman. Gay sister, you who sleep with a mother. Your lovemaking serving no purpose but love. Your copulation a mutual masturbation.

"I don't know."

"You don't know?"

"No."

"How can you say a thing like that?"

"It's just a . . . thing you say."

"Sterile? How can you say that to a woman? Who are you to say that?"

"No, I didn't mean it like that. I just said it because lesbians can't get pregnant . . . they don't have babies."

"And is that so awful?"

"No, no. It's just . . ."

"And who says a lesbian can't get pregnant?"

"Yeah, well, of course. You can."

"Why me more than any other? There are lots of lesbians who bring up children."

"We slept together, didn't we?"

"Yes."

"Forgotten, had you?"

"No."

"What was that, actually?"

"What was what?"

"Yeah. What was that?"

"An accident."

"Accident?"

"It was an accident."

"Any injuries?"

"Injuries?"

"Yeah. Accident. You didn't end up in the ER, did you? They didn't have to stitch up your . . ."

"I was drunk. And so were you, weren't you? Or what was it for you? Is this what's been bugging you?"

"Me? No, no. I've always wanted to cheat on my mother."

Most noble Hlynur: thirty-four years of bad luck in all the colors of the rainbow. An infant with a hairy crotch, an erection fresh from the womb, wearing a diaper to the bar, mixing whiskey and mother's milk, and sucking on cigarettes between feeds. Waking up in the pram with a hard-on raised to the navel, like a soldier saluting his origins, wetting mother's bed and abusing her love in the middle of her living room. Blinded by breasts and dumbfounded by lipsticked lips. Forever sexually retarded, on sexual benefit, shouting from the bathroom: "Mommy! I'm finished," and finished I am. Frailty, thy name is Hlynur.

"Cheat on your mother?"

"Yeah."

"I don't think she minds you sleeping with people . . ."

"Other than her?"

"Er . . . Yeah."

"But she might not be too happy to hear I slept with her girl-friend."

"Aren't you really trying to say that I two-timed your mother?"

"Or me with her."

"So it's obviously me, then. I'm all to blame. Wicked Lolla corrupted little Hlynur, led little Prince Hlynur into a trap."

"He didn't know that she came crawling from the queen's bed, warm and still smelling of her hair, naked but dressed with her kisses, her tongue moist with the juices that once eased him from the darkness into the light of day. Freshly crowned with her organs, she brought back to his mouth the taste of the womb."

"Wow."

"Yeah, wow."

"What is that, a play? Are we acting out some kind of a tragedy here? Look at you. With those shades and . . . always in that turtleneck . . . You're no hero out of a Greek tragedy, if that's what you think. With that cigarette . . . You just don't fit the part."

I stand up:

"I fucked you and now I'm fucked up."

Lolla bursts into a laugh. Then, full of sarcasm:

"You were fucked up long before I came along."

"You twin-sexed fury, you bearded clit, you who sleep with mothers and sons . . ."

"Hey, hey. Stop it. I was at the Playhouse yesterday, thank you very much."

"What play was it?"

"*The Trojan Women.*"

"Trojan women . . . What kind of a stripping trio is that?"

"It's Greek."

"Trojan women. Is that Greek humor? I've only heard of Trojan condoms."

"Ha ha. Ancient Greek. Tragedy."

"What did you go see a tragedy for? Isn't it enough to live out your own?"

"You never give up, do you?"

"You didn't give anything up."

"Fuck you!"

"No. I fucked you!"

Lolla turns away and pretends to forage through her rehab files. Yeah. So this is a tragedy, then. I try to get her to turn again. I walk to the table, press a knee against a chair and my elbows against the dining table, switch gear, and gently ask: "And what? Did you cry a lot?"

"No."

"Oh? Wasn't the tragedy tragic enough? Or was it just a tragic show?"

"There's no point in talking to you."

"You don't want to talk to me now. No more than you did then."

She looks at me.

"What do you mean? When?"

"Before it became too late. Before we did it."

"You mean you didn't see it coming? Poor little innocent angel. Little . . ."

"Mommy's boy?"

"Hlynur Björn."

"What?"

"You knew bloody well."

"No."

"You knew."

"To know is to know. A woman is a woman."

"Wow. Where do you get all these lines? What's wrong with you? You're getting weird. You're turning into a bit of a case. . . ."

"A case? Like one of your rehab cases. Are you giving me free rehab counseling? The Good Samaritan who lends her pussy out to those in need. Men or women, mothers or sons . . ."

She slaps me across the face. Makes a nice change. I was getting tired of all these female tears. I'm nevertheless surprised by how refreshing it feels. Even gives me a bit of a hard-on. Must try to get another one. She stares at me, flushing with anger.

"Sorry. You can't talk to a woman like that."

Here we go again. To a woman like that. You too, Lolla?

"Woman and not a woman. Aren't you bi? Swing both ways? Half and half? Woman and man?"

"And which half did you sleep with?"

"How do you mean?"

"As if you didn't want to sleep with me. Gawking at my tits through those ridiculous shades all the time, trailing after me to parties and sniffing around the flat after me, like a drooling lapdog, still tied to Mommy's apron strings at your age, lounging around with that ridiculous hard-on all the time . . ."

"Oh yeah? But not that ridiculous, though. I mean, it did its job, didn't it?"

She's in no mood for joking, not now, in midspeech.

". . . Inadequacy personified, as scared of all women as a bald wee mouse, break into a sweat if some Hofy so much as rings you, let alone knocks on your door. The only human communication you can handle is through a television screen, gawking at porn movies all night. . . . Hlynur. You're not seventeen anymore. You've got to try to accept that. You have to face up to it. Grow up! Get yourself a life! Try to face life! Try to . . . to live!"

I draw closer.

"And what's . . . what is life?"

"Something completely different to what you're doing . . . not TV . . . sorrow, love, happiness, tears, sweat, blood . . ."

"Everything but thinking?"

"Thinking? No, that too . . ."

"But mostly you're talking about human communication, hugging people and talking and all that, getting pissed and laid, and pregnant and stuff, those kind of adventures."

"Yeah, for example—"

"Then I haven't been doing anything for the past few days but live. And I'm getting a bit tired of it, to be honest."

"Obviously not."

"Oh no?"

"You obviously want more. Yeah. You need problems. You're a problem addict. You're the typical case of a man who is full of emptiness and does everything in his power to stir up problems. You've got to find something, some sense of purpose, some life . . .

a woman, work . . . something to do instead of trying to break the crust off old wounds all the time. Wounds that don't even exist."

"The pussy is a wound that never heals."

"Wow. And what's a prick, then? A tumor that should be amputated?"

"Maybe more of an inflammation."

"Oh yeah? Some kind of a boil, or pimple that you have to squeeze, to get the white pus to come out . . ."

"Hey. Pus in the pussy."

"Oh, Hlynur. Stop it. Go out there and try to get yourself some . . . some life . . ."

"I can't. You've already destroyed my life, the little that I had."

She laughs. She laughs now. Now she laughs. It stiffens. Laughter and a hard-on.

"Oh, poor Hlynur. You're so artificial and corny. You should see yourself now. Pooh-hoo, it's all over now for our little boy, no future because nasty Lolla fucked it all up."

"Nasty Lolla went down on the carpet. You were incredible. I've never slept with anyone that came anything close to you. Incredible."

"Really? Thanks."

"I can see why Mom came out of the closet for a hot number like you. Lolla, Lollah . . ."

My lips pull me toward her face. With an open mouth. My lips pull me. Not. She turns away. No slap across the cheek. Silence. She sits. I stand up. From the table. The dining table. I stand. By the dining table. Look for the stain in the carpet. Walk to the chair. Sit in the chair. Light myself a cigarette. Seven drags. Seven silent drags.

"What would you say is the main difference between me and Mom, in bed?"

She rubs her face in her hands and sighs. Hear her muttering her daily "Jesus." Then she stands up. Packs her files together and stands there with them in her arms, looking at me. Like a wounded animal. A cute wounded animal.

"You're sick."

"You suck."

"This is just pathetic."

"A tragedy. A pathetic tragedy."

"A pathetic performance."

"At least no one has to cry, then."

"Is it really that difficult for you?"

"No, just something to talk about."

"So that you've got something to do?"

"Yes, exactly."

"Don't you see enough problems with all that TV you watch? Maybe you should go to the theater for a change."

"There's no need to, when I've got all these Trojan . . . this Trojan horse in my own living room."

"What do you mean?"

"Well, wasn't that something everyone thought was a brilliant and incredible gift when they first saw it? Because no one knew what was inside it."

"And what was inside?"

"There was a whole army, wasn't there?"

"Yes, and I'm pre . . . and I'm pretty much the enemy?"

Something in that "pre . . ."

"No, no. Maybe more pre . . ."

"Yes? Pre what?"

"I dunno? Pretty? Precious? Pregnant?"

"Pregnant?"

"Yeah . . . Maybe."

"And what makes you say that?"

"Just, you know."

"Just, you know what?"

"Yeah . . . Well, I didn't wear a condom."

"Right. You didn't wear a condom, therefore I'm pregnant. Right."

"Maybe."

"I can't get pregnant."

"Really? Lesbians can't . . . ?"

"No. Just for some reason, I can't. I've tried for ten years . . ."

"Really? Why?"

"WHY? BECAUSE I WANT TO HAVE A CHILD!"

Here they come. The tears. Women's phony tears. That old pump—that seems to be built into all women—kicks in. With its whimpering engine. You too, Lolla? She turns back to the table and gathers her things, shuffles her files. The rehab counselor. Who can't create life. Can only change other people's lives. But can't produce a new one of her own. Predestined to be barren. That was the pre. Knew there was something. I stand up, probably out of commiseration, like in a church. The Pope's hand . . . Draw closer to her. Don't know what for. And once more I say that word, but still can't seem to hit the right note:

"Sorry."

I hobble around the table in my black jeans and white T-shirt like a penguin: my arms seem totally redundant somehow, no help from them whatsoever, I can't even stretch them out. To help. Lolla wipes her tears in the same way that she closes her pencil case. Zips up. A fox burying a bird in snow. I do feel some sympathy. But somehow there's nothing I can do. Or say. What can a black and white man do for a woman crying in Technicolor? I've had a fair bit of practice with weeping pregnant women lately, but this nullipara leaves me standing here with penguin arms. Nevertheless she's managed to gather all her things and, as she pulls the chair up to the table, she says in a straight and tear-free voice:

"That's OK. I am pregnant."

"What?"

She looks up with the hint of a smile.

"I'm pregnant."

"What? Didn't you just say you couldn't?"

"Yes. And then suddenly I could."

"Well . . ." I say, as a thought crosses my mind and she immediately sees what thought it is.

"Don't worry. It's not you."

"Oh no? Who, then?"

"A friend of mine."

"I see."

"He was helping me. We'd been trying for so long. . . . I really wanted a child. . . ."

"Who is he?"

"You don't know him, he doesn't live in town."

"Oh? Was he the guy in Akranes?"

"Yeah."

"What about Mom?"

"She knows. She knows all about it. She agreed to it. We're going to bring him up together."

"Him?"

"Yes. I've had a scan. It's a boy."

"Oh yeah? This is really. This is really something."

This is really, really something.

Well, then, my friend. Three pregnancies in three days. No, four days. The long Good Friday: Hofy. Ecstasy Sunday: Elsa. And Mother's Day Monday: Lolla. How did I manage to leave out Saturday? A monk in misery. Think I'll just keep my body home tomorrow. Done enough damage for the moment. Life. Get yourself a life, she said. Three lives should do for the moment. Lolla. You too, Lolla? Not me. The golden goose hatching her egg. Three babies, Hlynur. And me who can't stand children. Or like it's impossible to talk to them. They've got nothing to say. Haven't seen anything of life. I sit in the chair, working on a cigarette. She took her files and fetus back into her room. The golden goose. Said she was two months gone. Gone where? I wonder. Me? Could be me. Or that guy from Akranes . . . Hang on. She went to Akranes between Christmas and New Year's. Remember I farted around here on my own for two days. Then, a few days later, during the limbo period . . . Yeah. Could be me. She's just hoping it isn't. Why? For Mom's sake. "Ridiculous hard-on." Never occurred to me. Some guy out in Akranes. What kind of a dude is that? Some regional museum mascot, some kind of "incredibly nice guy" type, some papal hairy dick from the Society of Lesbians' Friends, some support-group chairman who lends his hard-ons to the cause: Dykes "R" Us, Save the Lesbians. Some guy with "incredibly nice genes." Some wild stud in jeans kept behind a fence for breeding. Not a bad occupation, really. Those Akranes men sure know how to score. Long live FC Akranes! Yeah, he scored. Some center-forward has sown a whole flower bed of seeds inside Lolla. And they'd been trying for so long. No. Fucking hell. Me, me, me. And Lolla swaying on the ferry on the way back, full of seasick sperms. Yeah, no. A fox burying a bird in the snow. Yeah. It's me for sure. Managed to fertilize three women in three days. And then she says there's no life in me. Yeah. I've just made three women pregnant. Hofy, Elsa, my sister, and . . . Mom.

Mom appears, stepping in from that mayhem called society. I abort my cigarette to show some respect. I manage to kill it quite efficiently for once. A pleasant change after all this life, this life . . .

"Hello, ah hi . . ." she lovingly chirps out, standing there in front of me for a moment.

Mom: in a bright coat, carrying two heavy plastic bags, with mascara from this morning, and the afternoon in her hair, in black nylon stockings, her toes barely visible, like ten headlightless cars in the dark.

Mom. The imports officer, the everyday hero, stands there, strong but tired, with her two plastic bags, in the twilight of her life, having walked the downtown mush, the brownish mix of sleet and dirt, stands there like a whole infrastructure: with her varicose veins, wheeling tracks around her neck, the appendix jammed with traffic, heart pumping red lights, dead policemen around her waist, ambulances wailing in her stomach, around a whole mall of intestines, the crowded colon, escalators, hallways, lobbies, passageways, corridors and tunnels, but beneath all this, behind all this, the warmth, the overcomplicated central heating system of motherly warmth. No snow can ever settle on Mom and her heart never freezes. Her soul is a sunny square, and you'll always find some parking space in those eyes.

Mom. Is a city. A whole city. My holy city. As great as a city. A city of 100,000.

And those blue mountains at her back, moors and hills, stretching all the way up north: the glimpse of an old threshold can be caught behind the hanging ends of her coat, an old threshold up north, and behind it, her people, in the kitchen of all ages, all the way from open fires to the modern stove to the microwave. There they sit, all her greatest grandmothers, in their long skirts and mid-century trousers, cutting liver sausages, putting hot dogs on a plate and peeping through the curtains of gone-by centuries, awaiting their master, their sailor, their shopkeeper, humming dinner is served and their children so sweet. Mom's childhood. On a cold floor up north . . .

Somewhere . . . somewhere in the back of my soul lies a paragraph, a long paragraph that someone has written but I can't read, but that I can somehow feel upon me, or inside me, a long paragraph, my mother's life . . . I feel the coldness of a northern floor creeping up through the soles of my feet. . . . On a floor up north . . .

The years between 1939 and 1941 came crawling over a bare stone floor on a spit of land up north, wearing woolen stockings, they moved between the stove and the drawers, and forty-two and -three! They were out on the steps and 1944 down by the harbor, the year of our independence, playing hide-and-seek with the world, the war years in Hvammstangi, peaceful by the open bay, when war was just a short little word, a word never waged in this land, and then forty-five, -six, -seven, and turn! Hopscotch, -eight, -nine, and fifty up to school and then fifty-one, fifty-two, fifty-three . . . the three hair-growing years at the boarding school at Reykir, an old black-and-white photograph of you up against some wall, smoking? With the cigarette sewed into your skirt, the newly budded breasts, a welcomed development in this uneventful fjord, and a slight breeze caressing them, Mom's breasts: this century's most sacred jewels, in a 1953-model bra, the soft and human tussocks entire churches could have been founded on, new religions, but were there just dressed in baggy, cheap sweaters bought from the cooperatives, caressed by nothing but the solitary ocean breeze, the breasts I was later to suckle, they first had to invade the thoughts of some down-haired boy, traveling all the way south in a truck, with the shadow of a beard on his jaw and a longing on his long face, a longing for Mom that filled the gap between the gearshifts, back when gears were rarely shifted, except when going uphill, down into first, and then the whole mountain road in second gear and you, a whole truckload of you, in the head of a boy in the passenger seat, who looks out and sees only you, your face in the hillside, and occasionally glances at the driver, Baldur Just a Sec, Baldur Just a Sec, with all the double chins of history shaking in unison down the long country dirt roads. Mom, you were the one who fueled all those engines, American pistons pumped in your name, you were the spark in all those Champion plugs, burning all the way south to Reykjavík, Dodge cars were dragged out of the mud for you and entire tanks of petrol were consumed for you, bit by bit they moved you south, locked in the luggage of a young man's memories, you were the one: Berglind, daughter of Saemi, the shopkeeper, the cutest face in the county, and they came to ask for soap and soda, and wanted to ask for more, if you'd come to the ball with them in Brú? (which in those days meant "Be my missus?"), but never dared, too shy, just pointed at a bottle and said "Yep" when you asked them, "Open it for you?" open it, open it, yes open it for me! And oh my, all that soda your dimples transformed into pee, up there in the north: far into the valleys the boys belched about you, dogs barked about you, doorknobs turned about you, and all doors stood open for you, until you finally chose the one that closed behind you, a bus door in Reykjavík in September at seven o'clock, when you added one more coat to the city and asked for directions like yet another innocent lass from the north, walking up Laugavegur and then standing on a wooden floor in Bergthórugata, in the house of unknown relatives, looking like something the times hadn't invented a word for yet, in that same spot where you're standing now, forty years later—as if you'd been patiently waiting all this time, waiting while all the Lollas of this country were learning to walk and read, to read that word and become that word—and then you spent a winter with Olivetti and three others in Versló College and allowed yourself to be kissed twice, strangely badly and wonderfully well, behind a wall in Vonarstraeti, and in a wood-paneled car in the mountains, over a handbrake, one summer, the confused kitchen maid who'd lost all control over her breasts' craving for a hand and those hands' craving for a breast, those road builder's hands under her blouse, a callus on silk, and suddenly discovered all her burning desires there in the middle of Arnarvatn Heath, and then later tied the knot on them in Reykjavík, tied yourself to Old Spice and love? Or just to whatever was on offer? In a taxi just before Christmas, 32 krónur the fare, followed by just as many years, or tears? As his wife—who paid for the taxi?! Mom! WHO PAID FOR THE TAXI?! Mom! Dad? Yes, he did, he leaned forward with his water-gelled hair and pulled money out of his wallet, that later-to-be-graybeard in the plastic-scented seat beside you, 32 krónur, and just as many years for you to pay off that debt, on your back, with that everlasting fear of going to bed, with the man who captured you in his shopping net on a Christmas evening in '59 and told you that you were "cute" and was wearing a tie, and nailed you on the spot, put a clot in your womb: Elsa, already swelling under your graduation cap, bearing a name from the north, our eternally cooking Danish granny's name, and then me, I came along in '62, like a complete idiot into this world, like a mindless idiot I came into this world, and was given a name without reason, and have ever since been looking for a reason to live, but still haven't found it, apart from that of smoking, the cigarette which lies here in the ashtray, the yellow filter—like gums in a grave, Granddad's gums, who once flaunted erections that were just as ridiculous as all the erections that have ever been, anywhere, past or present, hopeless and stupid, and deemed uncool by modern women, yet so incredibly necessary, just as much to them as to you: you stepped up from Grandpa's balls and stopped by Granny's womb, then sucked her breasts, and then I sucked your breasts, and now Lolla sucks your breasts and who would have thought it? Who would have guessed it back then? As the outdoor swimming pools in Reykjavík were puffing mist into the darkness and the iron fences around them were painted in yellow, and you stood there shivering by the edge in your black swimsuit, why didn't you look at the blondes back then? Or did you? Hiding all your secret longings under the showers, away from all your towel sisters, you escaped into the arms of the one and the only one who got to enjoy and caress your breasts, he who loved you out of this world and put two new ones inside you, and drove to work every morning with a scraper in his hand, scraping your kisses from the inside of his windscreen, could see nothing but you, in all the weathers of love, my dad in a Saab, my dad in a Saab, driving down Sudurlandsbraut at the beginning of February '69, until finally he had to get drunk before dinner—did he sense the Lolla waiting behind your eyes?—drunk before dinner; sprinkling Ballantine's into the smells-good meatballs, Ballantine's: the aftershave and eau de toilette of my childhood and Elsa's, she with the flu, in bed, and you, Mom, rushing to her bedside with a cup of hot milk, escaping the kitchen, escaping me and Daddy's eyes, those filling-the-whole-kitchen Daddy's eyes, that touched on the very few nerves I already had back then, my dad the alco, who now mumbles his regrets into his gray beard on top of Sara, his expiration date, he bemoans your bosom and those 675,038 kisses on doorsteps, steps and stone floors, lino floors, carpets, tiles (imported by heart-attacked salesmen now buried in the garden), in beds and in the front seat outside the liquor store every Friday afternoon for thirty years, and he bemoans those twenty-three pairs of trousers you used to wear and nobody knows what became of, for sale at the Kolaport flea market? He's scanning the stalls and clothes rails with cocktail sauce in his beard and wondering was it all for nothing? All a misunderstanding? All the hairdo years in that yellow Swedish-designed car and Saturday mornings in a tent, all those rain showers—then still wet—on the heath and the moss and the Laugarvatn lake and those house-cleaning hours to the sound of a radio named Nordmende in number 4 Stakkahlíd, to a Philips in number 18 Eskihlíd, dancing melodies played and sung, and he then absconding with Berti and Viddi to the Rödull Club, Hotel Saga, the Boathouse, and then to some party with an AVAILABLE sign flashing on his head until the crack of dawn, when he appeared with a plaster on his plastered eye, and a nose that whistled as he tried to pull off his socks—Dad's socks! Dad's socks! All of Dad's socks! WHERE ARE THEY NOW?!!—and crept into bed and said darling, with twelve happy hours gone sour in his eyes, falling into a sleep that kept you awake—that face, my dad's face, resting with its closed eyes on a pillow, the face that time was relentlessly drawing, never finished, always on and on, going over it with its pencil, perfecting it, trying to catch that expression, that Hafsteinn look, and no eraser allowed in the drawing class of time, continuing long into the night, a face on a pillow, a drawing on paper, and you watched it, you saw it evolve, witnessed the lines growing heavier with lead, under the

eyes, around the mouth, saw how it became too labored and heavy
in the end, this drawing by time, that far too patient artist, who
sometimes though manages to create beauty in a few simple
strokes, a beauty that lasts, your beauty, Mom, your Húnavatn
County tinted plain beauty, in soft yellow skin tones and mountain
blue eyes, two mountain springs of blue in an autumn-colored field,
where winter never comes and it never snows and never freezes, you
were a successful portrait from the start, so finely executed, so artis-
tically and skillfully drawn, a picture that never changed, only the
frames around it; all those hairstyles according to the demands of
fashion, weather and wind, and sometimes a veil, a scarf, a beret,
a bathing cap, and all those New Year's Eve hats! Mommy! Over
your laughter ALL THOSE NEW YEAR'S EVE HATS!! I see the
pair of you, two portraits, on a pillow, side by side, for thirty years,
a yellowish watercolor that dried up in the blink of an eye, and then
the ever heavier lead-laden drawing still being worked on—the
floor covered with pencil shavings and dandruff and cursing and
snoring, Mom and Dad . . . a spring in the woods and a stone in the
sea, Mom and Dad, two pictures, one with open eyes, the other
closed, the one keeping the other awake, you, Mom, watching
over him all this time while dawn breaks through the window, and
apartment blocks are built and painted, and the planes flying into
the airport change shape and design, and the Öskjuhlíd hill
changes color like a ptarmigan in fast forward, and the asphalt gets
wet and dries up and . . . they switched from left-hand driving to the
right, and Nixon took a leak at the Reykjavík Municipal Art
Museum, and chatted to Pat on the phone, and the rain that fell so
oddly on the corner of Miklabraut and Snorrabraut on the morning
of April 14, 1976, turned to nothing, and the paint on a fence in
Mávahlíd disappeared without mourning, disappeared into that
what where nobody knows, and the good old writer Thórbergur died,
and his suit was laid to rest, and all his silk shirts were swallowed
by chrysalises other than those that wove them, and Santa Claus
outfits lasted, and cornflakes boxes were buried by the week, and
without any fanfare, in the Gufunes Cemetery, and Linda P., later
Miss World (250,000), learned how to read, and Bo Halldórs, the
singer, took gas, often, and a sixteen-year-old Björk sang "Do You

Believe in Love?" by Huey Lewis at a country dance in Hvoll and
the song vanished into the Fljótshlíd hillside and never came
back, and everything somehow turned into nothing and nothing
turned into everything, and Mount Esja changed, ever so slightly,
just like you: Mom, as you stand here in front of me on the living
room carpet with your entire life around you, this open coat, and
carrying a quarter of a century in each of those plastic bags, ten
dark toes in black stockings, and how was it then? Was it all just
one big misunderstanding? An accidental stain? On the carpet
between your legs, Mom, a stain I made.

I say: "Sorry . . ."

"Sorry? Sorry for what?" she asks with a surprised smile.

"For me," I answer, snorting like an idiot.

"Well, then . . ." she says as she turns away, and, "Listen, there
was a huge queue in front of the meat counter at the supermarket so I just bought some frozen pizzas, even though I know you're
not crazy about them, is that OK? They only had them with peppers, ham, and mushrooms. . . ."

I watch her with nostalgic eyes. Watch her walking into the
kitchen, with peppers, ham, and mushrooms.

1

ON THE LOWEST DECK
OF NIGHT A NAKED ME

"What are you going to do?"

"Me?"

"Yeah. What do you plan on doing?"

"Tonight?"

"No. In the future."

"The future?"

"Yeah."

"I dunno. I haven't thought that far."

"Isn't there something you'd like to do . . . to become?"

"Not really."

"But I mean, you're not going to spend the rest of your life on social benefit, are you?"

"Is that not allowed?"

"Allowed? . . . Oh yeah, it's probably allowed, but I mean . . ."

"Maybe it'll be a bit of a shock when I switch over to my old-age pension."

"I don't think you'll get a pension if you've been unemployed all your life."

"I won't?"

"No. I mean, you're not paying anything into the pension fund."

"And what about all those grannies who've been nothing more than housewives all their lives?"

"They get something . . . but it's peanuts, twenty thousand a month. . . . And what if—sorry, Berglind—what if . . . Your mother won't always be around to cook for you and to allow you to live with her without paying rent."

"Is this a buildup to something? Mom? Something up? Have you got the big C? Have you got cancer?"

"Don't say that, Hlynur . . . no, no, I'm . . . There's nothing wrong with me, touch wood. . . ."

"Phew."

"But you know what I mean, Hlynur?"

"Yeah, yeah."

"And try to see it on a social level. I mean, what if everyone were on social benefit? What kind of society would that be?"

"Isn't that the way we're heading?"

"And what if they suddenly decided to do away with benefit and you didn't get a single króna from them?"

"I dunno. Maybe I'd try going into rehab for a few years and then reassess the situation."

"Ha ha. I'm serious."

"Hey. Doesn't Dad owe us some child support, Mom? Maybe I could live on that for a while."

"Child support? You were almost thirty when we divorced!"

Lolla obviously has some kind of axe to grind and interrogates me over the dining table, sitting there with her bump, which doesn't seem to be getting any smaller with time, but on the contrary continues to swell as the weeks pass. Heading for labor. Hard labor. Spring in the kitchen windows. Trees break-dancing in the garden.

"Yeah, of course. When does child support run out?"

"Sixteen. You get it until you're sixteen."

"Exactly when unemployment benefit begins. They've got it all worked out. It's a great system they've got."

"And what if you had to start paying out your own child support?"

OK. So that's what she's getting at. Spock. Suspense music in my brain.

"Me? Er. Why do you say that?"

"I mean, who knows, you could have got some girl in town pregnant."

"Oh yeah? How do you know that?"

Silence. Lolla looks at Mom. Mom looks at me. I look at Lolla. Lolla looks at me. A lot of looks.

"I went to the dentist this morning," says Lolla.

"I see," I say.

"Haven't you got something to tell us?" Lolla asks, trying to strike a casual air as she grabs her rolling papers. I watch her as she pulls the papers out of the packet and don't know what to say, if anything, when the phone rings, bang on cue, and I glance at Mom before she stands up. She seems faintly relieved to be able to leave the table, to leave this conversation, and her cigarette-rolling pregnant wife.

"Ehm. Wouldn't you like a filtered one? Isn't that better? For the baby."

"No thanks. It's OK, thanks."

Lolla got herself a transfer to some remote valley in the west after our little fracas in February and Marched there until April. Some rehab thing. There was quite a pouch on her when she came back. She rolls one. Nimbly. And licks. Like a highly developed kangaroo. I offer her a light. Mom can be heard on the phone in the other room: "Oh, my God, really?" After the first drag:

"Well, then, Hlynur."

"Lolla."

"Hofy . . ."

"What about her?"

"Palli Níelsson said she was pregnant . . . by you."

"By me?"

"Yes. Or maybe you didn't know? Is this all news to you?"

"Nah. She's just being a bit hysterical, that's all."

"HYSTERICAL?"

"Yeah."

"How can you call it hysterical if she's pregnant, and five months gone."

"But wouldn't you be able to see it on her belly? Or what? You're five months too."

"Yeah . . . you can't see it on her, you say?"

"No. Just a bubble of air."

"Men see what they want to see."

"And women get what they want to get," I say as I'm about to look at the rollup between her fingers, but she briskly pops it between her lips and my eyes are left on her belly. She interrupts her drag with an abrupt:

"What was that?"

Mom hangs up and we remain silent until she reenters the kitchen. Her watercolor face is frozen. A face that calls for a "what?" Lolla comes out with it.

"Elsa. She's had a miscarriage. . . ."

The pill. A bullet. Same size. A bullet I deserve to swallow my own pill I . . . I pierced a hole through a condom and now I've fed more life into death's gaping jaw. My very own sister, Elsa. Who else but Elsa? And . . . a spinning bullet, a spinning globe, same shape, different scale. Yeah. We live on a bullet shooting through space, same ratio, the sun a head and the earth a small bullet, except the sun said "what a waste" and told it "don't bother, you can't kill me," so the bullet was condemned to revolve around the sun, like a fly around a lightbulb. You can sometimes hear the hiss if you stand long enough, alone outside the video store in the afternoonsss. Ssssssss . . . seven million esses hissing together in unison, those are the souls, the sssssssouls being ssssucked up to "heaven," people say, but forget that it's just space they're being sucked into, with a buzz, as they pierce the vault, seven million souls a day: the earth's flapping wings, space flies buzzing around the sun, and what becomes of them, the souls marked Sammy Davis, Jr., Dean Martin, and Granddad and Jón Páll and Nicole Brown and a five-month-old unborn toddler?

We live on the same bullet, the same pellet, which once upon a time shot out of the big-bang gun and we just try to hold on, hold on for dear life, with Larry Hagman and the rest. . . . I cling to a cigarette and try to keep my head still, so the bullet spinning around it won't strike between the eyes. Mom sits, when?

". . . this morning. It was Magnús. He's with her now."

And me who was going to march up with a drumroll in the middle of the confirmation ceremony to unveil the pearled pill in a necklace for her or a ring for him. My poor little nephew or niece, you were never anything more than a molecule of blood. Ah well.

At least you'll never have to floss your teeth. How do our brains work? Roger Whittaker.

Down in the cellar, in my museum, I find the aforementioned pill and swallow it without water. As if that were some kind of suicidal act.

I'm no longer banned from the K-bar. Perhaps the takings went down. Inside the john I place an orange pill in my mouth and swallow it without water. As if that were some kind of suicidal act.

I come back in and grab a chair. Thröstur gives me that brothers-in-arms smile, as if we were soldiers in the same platoon in the back of some DC thing, high over Vietnam, perfectly outfitted with green helmets and parachutes on our backs, waiting for the hatch to be opened and to be hurled into the sky. We say nothing but exchange occasional glances. We wait. Oasis can be heard on the speakers, still trying to squeeze through the wonderwall. They're followed by Run-D.M.C. and Aerosmith with "Walk This Way." Suddenly someone grabs my throat. The fist comes with a face. That seems to belong to Lerti, Hofy's brother:

"What are you doing here?!"

Judging by his speech, he's on his seventh drink.

"I . . ."

"Why the fuck don't you just stay at home?!"

"I get no peace there. Your old man's always popping in."

He's suddenly stuck for words. I catch a glimpse of Bryndís, the beauty mogul, in the background. She grabs Lerti with a cigarette in the other hand, says:

"Lerti. Don't."

He: "You can't treat people like that!"

"I know. They're untreatable."

He tightens his grip on my polo neck and throws me and some beer glasses up against the wall. A bird pulling its last face before its neck gets wrung. Cold beer down my thigh.

"Don't try to be funny with me now!"

I get a slight splutter on my glasses. Lerti's handsome face up against mine. Like a pretty well-preserved but record-once-only tape. Haven't been this close to another face since I last kissed his sister. The final goodbye. But kissing isn't exactly what I have in mind right now. I look to the side. Thröstur looks at his brother-in-feathers with his thrush's eyes, moving his glass to the next table. Lerti finally spits some words out:

"And stay away from my sister!"

"What's that supposed to mean?"

"It means what it means! Pretend you don't know anything now but pretend to know everything about everyone . . . all the pregnancies of history except your own! Asshole! You stay away from her!"

"That should be easy enough."

"Yeah?"

"But maybe not . . ."

"Why not?"

"Absence makes the heart grow fonder."

"Don't bullshit me! Don't fucking bullshit me!"

"Nice teeth. Your dad do those?"

Those last words of mine weren't exactly easy to produce. I just about managed to squeeze them through his grip around my throat. Now he smashes my head against the wall. I just hope that E starts to kick in before he does.

"You fucking son of a dyke!"

My freedom of speech has now been blocked. He's trying to strangle me. Do murderers get to go to their victims' funerals? Doesn't the Church forgive everything? I've started to roll the documentary of my life through my skull. Scene 1: me in boots in number 4 Stakkahlíd and Mom . . . when the doorman pulls him away from me. Bryndís follows them outside.

I sink back into my seat. Adjust my lapels, look at Thröstur. He smiles. I try to smile. The K-bar nevertheless regains its cruising height and changes back into that old DC plane over Nam. The place shakes slightly as it skims the beach, ablaze with fires and bombs. Choppers hovering over chopped-up villages. A girl (45,000) on high heels is about to fall. I try to regain my E-nergy after that little shakedown we guys in the platoon like to psych ourselves up with before launching into battle.

A nightclub on a diesel cruise over Vietnam and TLC (3 x

70,000) waterfalls through the PA system: Don't go chasin' waterfalls. Please stick to the rivers and the lakes that you're used
to . . . We're suddenly thrown overboard. As we're sitting at the
table. The pain in the back of my head starts to spread and mix
with the Ecstasy. Don't go chasin' waterfalls. Please stick to the
rivers and the lakes. Bit late to say that now. Hand grenades go off
in our hearts and we allow ourselves to fall, the war buddies, over
Vietnam, as the explosives detonate through our veins. Quite a
kick from this free-fall. Beautiful landscape below us: as yet
unexploded forests, lakes, and waterfalls. I open the parachute and
hover for the next ten hours, the next twenty-four hours. I stand up
without getting on my legs. Walk on springs over to the bar and
hear myself ordering two double scotches from Keisi. He clocks
me and nods. I've finished mine by the time I get back to Thröstur
and hand it to him and say, "Alex, hey Alex, open your parachute
now," and then turn around again and grab the hair of a very
free-range chick (750,000) and say, "Is this your hair?" and then
look down at her breasts, she's got two. I count them anyway, to be
sure. Yes, affirmative. "And are these your breasts too? Do you
have a sister? I'm in a Suzi Quatro mood tonight. Have you seen
Tommy, the movie? No, you're not. You're too, you are. You're just
a pony." She swings her hair and frees herself from my arm. I say,
"750,000," following her up the stairs. Son of a dyke. Hertha
Berlin comes down. She says, "Oh, hi." I say, "Hi, oh." She says,
"Huh?" I say, "Did you ever sleep with Karl-Heinz Rumenigge?
What was Rumenigge like in bed?" She says, "Who's that?" I say,
"No, he played for Bayern. You were in Berlin." She says, "And
are you just hanging out with Thröstur?" I say, "Huh?" She says,
"And are you just hanging out with Thröstur?" But I've started to
dance. Have I started to dance? You could say that. Alex comes
over and says, "There're lots of chicks at the Moon. Let's go." I
say, "Alex." He says, "Jeff." We exit together. I drag my parachute
down Laugavegur. Alex carries his. We land on the Moon. There's
a model show going on at the Moon. E-zero gravity is even
smoother on the Moon. I plant an American flag in the lavatory
bowl. I'm Armstrong. I search for my dick to take a leak. I can't
find it. I go back out to look for it there. Some pregnant lezzie has

cut it off me and is holding it, trembling in her trembling hands, in some taxi darting up Hverfisgata. Son of a dyke. I'm Bobbitt. I read *Hobbit*. In college. I say "Tolkien" to some puffed-up fashion writer (450,000) in sunglasses. "It's pure Tolkien tonight." She says, "No. It's a cross between Elite and Donna Karan." I say, "Is she Gunnar Kvaran's daughter?" She says, "Are we a bit out of it tonight?" and laughs. I laugh. I'm a real laughing kind of guy. I watch the fashion babes pussyfooting down the catwalk. There's only one problem with fashion shows. The clothes. I feel a stiffening. I've found him again. I grope for him. But can't feel him. Cold sweat in the palms of my hands. I'm healthy. I'm Skúli, the muscle-pumping dwarf. All I need now is a sports commentator. Good job my leather jacket is strong and doesn't rip every time I take a deep breath. If only I hadn't been bobbitten. Seriously cramps my style. But I fully trust the cops to find the culprit and, after a blitz interrogation, my little fag end will be tracked down, in a flower bed by the National Library, and those geniuses at the Municipal ER will have it sewn back on in a jiffy, and then I'll be able to get him up again after three weeks of intensive physiotherapy at the Grensás clinic, and get Alex to take pictures of the whole process so that he can put it all on the Internet. The fashion show is over. All the babes are dead. I'd cry if I had any windshield cleaner left. Can't even produce enough liquid to piss. How can a man piss when someone's cut his dick off? Like a woman. Yeah. I'm a woman. No. I am not a woman. I walk up to a woman (1,500,000) and say, "How far gone are you?" She says, "I'm at university." I say, "I can't afford you." She says, "Oh, sorry." I say, "This is great. This is really great. I don't suppose you've seen my dickhead anywhere, have you?" She smiles a smile worth another 75,000 and says, "Noooo-o." It's disco time. Tony Bennett sings "Ring My Bell." In a falsetto voice. I seem to be dancing again. Son of a dyke. A fashion babe strolls over. I say, "Is that your hair?" She walks away. I sit on the smoke machine. Or I discover it's the smoke machine as white jets come spurting between my legs. Like I'm farting fog. A hell of a lot. Everyone's submerged in the stuff. But they seem to like it. Even my insides smell good. I spot Bryndís, Lerti's babe. She doesn't spot me. Alex comes over to ask

me if I've got the remote on me. I give it to him. He goes away. I
have a cigarette. Must have been that. I've smoked so much
tonight. I've smoked so much tonight. I head for the can. Put a condom on. It takes quite a while. So there he is. He was in the
johnny all along. The condom dangles loosely. I pull up my underpants. I seem to be wearing seven pairs of underpants. They've got
to start manufacturing bullet-proof condoms that even a knife
can't cut through. Bobbitt. Hobbit. Alex is in the john. He stands
over the sink. He's white. There are no blacks in our platoon. I
hope we won't get bitter when we get back from Nam. We walk out.
Maybe we should have exchanged some words in the john. Too late
now. For example, I could have said, "What do you think of the
women in this place? I've never been into yellow chicks myself.
Cos of those pussy eyes." Then, for example, he could have said,
"Exactly. That makes two of us." I walk to the bar on a small trampoline on wheels. The counter seems to be made of particularly
hard wood. Maybe to make sure you don't lean on it for too long.
There's a chick (1,750,000) beside me and I reckon she's softer
than the counter so I stroke her knuckle. She looks at me and I
decide to look back at her. She's got a nose. I had the feeling she
had a nose. Somehow that makes all the difference. Nevertheless
I look into her eyes, since I'm in the neighborhood. It's like coming home. It's like looking into my own eyes. I say, "Six Fífugrund." She says, "Huh?" I say, "Fífugrund number six, got a
better offer?" She says, "How about seven Krummahólar?" I say,
"Four Stakkahlíd, king size." She says, "Eight Rekagrandi, with a
waterbed." I say, "Wow!" She says, "*And* a hi-fi in the room." I say,
"Kids?" She says, "Sleeping over." I say, "Husband?" She says,
"No." I say, "Blow job?" She says, "For a tongue job." I say, "A
blow for a tongue." She says, "OK." I say, "Condom?" She says,
"Bien sur." I say, "Huh?" She says, "Of course." I point at her
breasts and say, "Silicone?" She says, "A bit." I say, "E?" She
glances at her watch and says, "Two hours ago." I say, "Same
here." She says, "Great." I say, "Deal!" She says, "Huh?" I say,
"Deal!" She says, "But you pay for the cab." I say, "Deal!" She
says, "Deal!" I say, "Hlynur Björn." She says, "Anna." I say,
"Anna?" She says, "Anna." I say, "Anna what?" She says, "Wanna

what?" I say, "Wanna go?" She says, "Yeah, let's go." We go out. We use the door. I flag down a cab. I take another quick look at her, to be sure, before getting into the car and see that she's barely E-worthy. In other words, she's the type of person you wouldn't look at twice if you weren't on E. And I am on E. So. And I also happen to be the type of person you wouldn't look at twice if you weren't on E. Like Adam. In spite of the wonderful selection in the garden, Adam only really started to get the hots for Eve (3,900,000) once they'd bitten that apple. So. I seem to have stumbled on her only redeeming feature, her knuckles. But. She's blond. And she's female. And she's easy. Finally one that gets straight down to it. But she's got cheeks that stretch down to her throat. You'd need a surgeon to draw a line where her cheeks end and throat begins. Maybe it'll fall into place when she gets on her back. At least her back isn't fat. The cabdriver is in the front. Which is a good start. Stepping into the cab is like stepping into a Soft Cell. One of their tracks is playing on the radio. Marc Almond; 1981. Anna says, "Rekagrandi, number eight." The cabbie says, "Rekagrandi, number eight." The pond flies past us. There's a kind of tooth glow in the air. If your mouth is closed, it's dark inside it. If you open it some light will filter through in. Hofy opens her mouth too. No. Anna. Anna opens hers too. Whether you'd call this a kiss or not is open to interpretation. I'm all amped up, with Duracell in my heart, 120 beats per minute, and shake all over like the backseat of a bus at a red light, with a jerky Volvo engine going like six hundred purring cats. That's what it's like. My tongue is numb, like it's being stuffed with numbness. I search for the silicone under her sweater. I can't find it. She looks for the silicone in my crotch. I can't feel it. The car stops in front of a red light. We stop kissing. The lights are green again. Son of a dyke. The car turns down Hringbraut. I say, "Driver." He says, "Yeah." I say, "Smooth shifting." The driver says, "Huh?" I say, "Smooth gear shifting. You drive like a king. You shift gear like a spoon in cream. Whipped cream. Such a delicate touch you've got." The cabbie looks back. He says, "Oh yeah, you think so?" He's got the type of face that suits dark hair. And, as it happens, very dark hair is what he has. "You must be good in bed," I say. He says, "You don't say?"

Anna moves in on me with her face that looks like whipped ice cream, sprinkled with fine-grain makeup, and pushes her fruit out of it, into my mouth. The fruit is a kiwi but a kiwi that hasn't been peeled. I allow her to kiss me down Hringbraut. As the driver goes around the roundabout, a centrifugal force pulls me over her body. Two tongues orbiting around a roundabout. We tilt over to my side and then over to hers as the car leaves the roundabout. I free myself from the kiss, and speak to the cabbie again. "Well, then. Nearly there now." The cabbie says, "Yeah." He turns into Rekagrandi without toppling us over. I say, "Just here will be fine." The cabbie stops the car and bends forward to look through the windshield and says, "This is Rekagrandi, number two. Wasn't it eight you wanted?" I say, "That's OK. We'll pay the whole fare." The cabbie says, "What?" I say, "How much is it?" The meter says 800 krónur. Anna gets out of the car. I pay the driver. I say, "What would you say your motto in life is?" The cabbie looks me in the eye, pausing for a moment. He's either reviewing his life in his mind or counting the change in his hand. He says, "I don't know. Never to shortchange anyone, I suppose. Yeah, that's what matters the most. Never to shortchange anyone." He gives me my change and I thank him dearly for the drive and say my farewells before opening the door and getting out of the car. This is late May. Anna vanishes into a building three doors down. The apartment block has already been built and is ready for use. It's even been painted and the lawn has been mown. There are three Annas listed on the table of contents on the door: Anna Sveinbjörnsdóttir. Anna Hlín Eiríksdóttir. Anna Nikulásdóttir. In this kind of light, it's easy to pretend that it's three o'clock in the afternoon, and that I've come here to select which Anna I'm going to be sleeping with. A titillating choice. I select Anna Sveinbjörnsdóttir. There's just one name below her name. It's Máni and some foreign name I can't pronounce. Anna opens with a key. Yeah, she's 800. I would have been willing to climb another seven floors, but the stairs don't seem to go any farther. Parquet. Holiday Inn, Utrecht. She makes a beeline for the living room and throws her jacket on the sofa. I do the same. We kiss again. There seems to be a consensus that the kissing should stop now. The kissing stops. I look around. It's difficult to describe this flat in words. The first phrase to spring to mind is "menswear department." Not sure I know what I mean by that. I say, "Have you paid your rent?" She says, "What do you mean?" I say, "Have you paid this month's rent?" She says, "Yes, why?" I say, "Just . . . good to know." She walks over to the sound system and slips on a CD. She puts the music on a bit high. She seems to have got it from the classical music department. She takes off her sweater and unbuttons her trousers. I take off my sweater and unbutton my trousers. I sit in a chair to loosen my shoelaces. She slips her hands behind her back to loosen her bra. I full-heartedly support their liberation. She gets straight down to it, I'll say that for her. But somehow her body doesn't feel totally naked, even though she's taken all her clothes off. It's that kind of skin. And she's got a little tattoo over one of her breasts. I can't quite make out what it is, but it's as small as an Adidas logo, which somehow transforms her skin into a tracksuit. Nevertheless, her hairy triangle radiates surprising power when she slips out of her panties. I get the feeling I have a pretty good hard-on. Although I have no way of confirming that. I manage to get out of my shoes, but she's so impatient she kneels on the floor and rips off my jeans. She starts to laugh when she pulls off my briefs. She gives off a loud laugh. Anna has a very loud laugh. There's my condom. But I'm more surprised by the fact that I don't have a hard-on. Son of a dyke. I'm wearing a condom. She unveils the short stump of meat, rather clumsily packed in the pink plastic. There's no sign of her laughter stopping. So I laugh as well. She says, "How long," but can say no more. She tries again a moment later. She says, "How long have you been carrying that thing around for?" "About a year," I say. She laughs even more. I say, "Oh, you mean . . . ? No. I put it on tonight, at the Moon. But it's a year old." She's on Ecstasy. There's no denying it. She can barely talk through all her laughter. She lies there on the floor, wriggling like a waterbed. Finally she says, "What? WHAT? HA HA HA!!! WHAT? WHAT'S A YEAR OLD?!!" I laugh too. But not quite as keenly. The stuff she's on must be stronger than mine. She's still laughing. She shrieks with laughter. She says, "And what? Isn't he about to grow soon?" I say, "Yeah, yeah, it'll only take him another few years to reach his full height." She says, laughing, "Well, then, we've got plenty of time." I slide off the chair over this cackling lump called Anna. I try to smother her laughter by sticking a tongue into her mouth. Laughing women are a total turnoff. Laughing women have a limping effect. I've watched enough tapes to know that much. I manage to smother some of her laughter with some pretty boring kisses. Until it bursts through her vagina below. A laughing pussy. There's nothing remotely laughable about that. I fondle this "Made in Iceland" flesh. And there's plenty of it. I see now that the tattoo over her left breast is a little heart with a bolt of lightning through it. We wrestle naked on the parquet. Through the lens of a hidden camera we must look like two beasts. A zebra wrestling with a rhinoceros. A rhinoceros lying on its back. Scientists have drugged us to observe this experiment in copulation. I try to prevent the horn from piercing me. The scientists have concealed themselves in one of the rooms of this apartment and are following our progress through a two-way mirror disguised as a framed print on the wall. The phone rings. I'm kissing her and listening to the answering machine. Her message says, "You have reached Anna . . ." Yeah, I've reached Anna all right. ". . . and Máni." No. I haven't reached him yet. Some puny voice takes over and I guess it's Máni. He says, "There's no one home at . . ." Anna can be heard in the background: ". . . the moment. At the moment." Máni says, ". . . at the moment." Anna says, "But please leave a message after the beep." Anna stops kissing, but I continue to rummage through her mouth. The machine beeps and a male voice starts to speak in a foreign language: Anna slithers under me and moves to the phone. I'm left lying on my back on the floor. This is a well-executed parquet. Professionals did this, you can tell. Anna picks up the phone and drops onto the sofa. She says, "Bon sour." My guess is it's French. She smiles as she speaks. Puts her legs up on the sofa. I stare at the gap between them. Anna laughs. I look into her eyes. She nods at me. She spreads her legs slightly. She slides her hand down to her crotch. She fondles it as she speaks. She spreads it open. She laughs. I gape into that hole. I gape into that hole. I don't know whether I want in or not. Frailty, thy name is . . . Anna laughs. She laughs at me. She laughs upstairs and downstairs. The laughing pussy. She laughs at me. She listens for a bit. I watch. Anna, I mean. She gives me a God-he's-such-a-blabbermouth look. She grins and spreads it open even more and lowers the receiver in front of it. The voice grows muffled as it vanishes inside her. "You have reached Anna." He has reached Anna. His voice now echoes inside his old cave. He's calling out for his little Máni. Doesn't he realize that Máni left here a long time ago and that he's even learned how to talk. It's a nice scene. Still, I have to say, I find it a bit much when she shoves the receiver into her pussy. I have to say that. I'm having problems stomaching it. I look down. Look up. I'm not a hard enough pervert. She is. Or do some men get a kick out of watching French voices disappear into Icelandic wombs? The Americans sent an unmanned craft into space, some years back, which is still floating out there somewhere in zero gravity. It was conceived as an earth promo. There's a tape deck inside it, constantly playing a message read by Ronald Reagan, who was president at the time. He kindly wishes his listeners a nice day and then delivers a short message from mankind. His closing words are: "We come in peace." Decrepit old Reagan really is out of this world now. I allow my eyes to wander around the flat. She talks again. Phew. I'm not a hard enough pervert. I'm not a hard enough anything. Everything I touch turns to dust. It's probably a good job I'm not working. Not even Elsa, the flawless nurse, could complete the pregnancy I'd organized for her. I notice the hall door is wide open. Open into the corridor. I forgot to close it. I was the one who should have closed it. Typical me. I can't even stub out a cigarette. I'm thinking of standing up, and of walking over to close it, when I notice a nightie on the landing. I'm lying on my back on the parquet with a rubber over my limp dick. Son of a dyke. The nightie turns out to be a woman (250,000). Well, maybe more of a girl. She looks at me. Even though I see her upside down her face looks familiar. I've often seen her at the K-bar. But I don't know her name. She can only see me. Anna, the sofa, and the phone are in the corner, out of her view. The girl in the nightie says, "Oh." I say, "Hi." She stands on the landing. I get up off the living room floor. I walk toward the door. My rubber dangles. The girl in the nightie grabs on to a railing. She says, "Is Anna in?" I say, "Yeah. She's just on the phone. Or the phone's in her. I know you, don't I?" The girl in the nightie on the landing says, "There was just so much noise. Is everything OK?" I say, "Yeah, fine, how about it? Would you like to come in for a . . . ?" She hops back a step and says, "No thanks." I grab the railing and say, "How about you and I having a little duet while Anna's on the phone? A bit of Eurythmics here on the floor." She sneers as she looks down at my rubber. She says, "Absolutely no thanks." She goes down the stairs. I follow her down the stairs. I say, "Hang on. Let me talk to you." She's reached the landing below. She says, "No thanks. Good night." She opens the door and swiftly locks herself inside. I'm left standing on the landing. I stare at the locked door. Feel a slight tingle in the rough carpet. Voices can be heard. I turn. Two cops are walking up the stairs. I say, "Good evening." They don't say anything. I go up the stairs. My rubber still dangling. One of the cops says, "Hey! You there, hold it a second." I turn, halfway across the landing. The two cops bounce up the stairs and one of them grabs my arm. "Having a party, are we?" says the other. I say, "No." The same cop says, "What are you doing bare-assed out on the landing, then?" I say, "Oh, that? Well, it's just that I came home with this girl, Anna's her name, and we were already in bed when I realized I'd left my condoms down in the car and decided to go down and get them. You know how it is. Can't be too safe these days. AIDS and all that." I seem to be doing quite well because both cops are now speechless. The other says, "You realize it's an offense to be naked in a public place." I look down at my condom and say, "But I'm not naked." The cop who spoke first says, "Yes, you're naked." I adjust my condom better with my free hand and say, "Is that better?" The two cops say, "No." I say, "Oh? Would you like to see more?" and show my willingness to take it off. "Where's the party?" say the cops. I say, "Oh? You're on your way to the party. I don't know. Are you sure you've got the right floor?" The cop says, "There have been complaints about noise in the building." I say, "Oh yeah? We must try to find it. Don't you have special equipment for this? I mean, I'd love to help you guys but I've got very little time, as I was saying." "What floor are you on?" say the cops. I say, "Me? I'm on the top." They follow me up the stairs to Anna's open door. She's still on the phone, but otherwise everything seems pretty calm. I step into the flat. They remain at the doorway. One of them says, "Were you making noise in here?" I say, "No. Like I said, we were just getting into it when . . . I had to, you know, get a . . ." The cop says, "I just want to warn you to keep the noise down. It's four o'clock." I say, "Yeah, no problem. I rarely make a sound, but I can't vouch for her. We only met tonight. First time, you know." The cop says, "I don't think you need to worry about her making much noise, considering your current state," and he glances down at my condom. I allow my eyes to travel down my body, escorted by the policemen's. The teat on the condom dangles loosely over my limp member. I look up and say, "Yeah, that's true." They withdraw with a smirk on their lips, and I close the door. Anna is still on the phone. She's changed position. She's lying on her stomach on the sofa. She looks up and gags the receiver. Anna says, "Who was it?" I say, "Two leather queens in uniform in the corridor." She says, "And did you invite them in?" I say, "No, they didn't seem to like the look of him." She smiles and continues on the phone, presumably still talking to the boy's father. I head for the john. I pull my condom off in the john. I try to rub some action into him, in compliance with Reykjavík police regulations. I was obviously right earlier on. It'll take him a few years to grow to his full size. I think of Lolla on the carpet at home. I can hear that Anna is still on the phone. I finally walk back into her with a hard-on. It's the kind of hard-on I'd be willing to put a year's warranty on. He's like a well-stuffed bird. I'm pretty chuffed with this hard-on of mine and walk toward the sofa, proud as a peacock. Anna smiles and sits up. I stand, or rather we both stand in front of her. She pokes at my man with her toes. I sit beside Anna, who is still blabbing down the phone in French. She smiles at me. I rub my hand in her crotch. She says something down the phone and then covers the mouthpiece. She says, "You be Máni. Speak in a baby voice." She laughs. She says down the phone, "Wee, wee, heel eh la." The things they call a language. She hands me the phone. There's a strong pussy smell from it. I hear the voice spurting through the receiver. The voice says, "Máni? Máni?" I say in a ridiculously squeaky voice, "Daddy. Is that daddy?" A torrent of unintelligible words blurts through the receiver. Anna laughs. There's a silence and I add in an adult voice, "But Máni is a big boy now. . . ." Anna takes the receiver back from me. She talks seriously now. Anna looks at me seriously. I adjust the glasses on the bridge of my nose. Anna says "Ciao" down the phone. She hangs up. She looks at me, says, "What did you have to do that for?" I say, "Who was he?" She says, "Gee-l." The things they call a name. I say, "And?" She doesn't say anything. I don't say anything. We sit on the sofa. A year's warranty, I said. She looks at him. She grabs him, carelessly, stretches him and releases him again. The sound of a hard prick bouncing on a stomach is heard as my hard prick bounces on my stomach. I don't know this person. It might as well be the "hand of God." This is how God handles papal erections. Shame on you! I look at Anna and say, "Fancy a bite?" Anna says, "A bite?" I say, "Yeah, a bite of me," and bounce it on my stomach again. She puts it in her mouth. It's weird how much people trust each other. Since when does a man shove his most precious possession into a stranger's mouth? Anna polishes him a bit. The doorknob. But nothing opens. There's a woman's head in my crotch, moving up and down. Nothing else to report. But maybe the girl likes it. I see a telephone directory lying beside me on the sofa. I browse through it. They could do with more names in the telephone directory. And a blow job probably isn't the best way to propagate them. I read the telephone directory for a few moments as she sucks me. I've forgotten what she was doing by the time she reappears under that hair of hers and smiles at me. She sits beside me. I cast the phone directory aside. Anna starts to jerk off. I give her a hand. Son of a dyke. That is to say I try to give her a hand. My pussy geography isn't good enough to be able to find her joy buzzer straight away. This is like blindly dipping a hand into lukewarm rice pudding and trying to find the almond with nothing but your index. Anna takes my hand, guiding me toward her almond. I feel she's about to say something, but manage to stop her by kissing her. We're both out of saliva. We give up kissing and she says, "A blow for a tongue." I get down on all fours and she spreads her legs over the sofa. I'm like a grazing sheep. That same old taste and smell. No strawberry flavor down here. I haven't a clue of what I'm doing and just let my tongue flap up and down this multiscented pulp. No way of knowing if I'm doing this right. Like trying to decipher a secret combination. You just carry on trying until you hit on the right number. There isn't a sound out of Anna. She could at least give me some feedback. It's been at least twenty minutes now and I've got a cramp in my neck. She slips her hands around it and crushes my face against her clitoris and surrounding area. I rub it with my nose and just try to imagine it's a moist handkerchief. She starts to heave to the rhythm. Gobbledyslurp. Slurpidygobble. We gradually shift into her rubbing it into my face. Anna's pussy wipes my face like a rag, like a warm, moist, old smelly rag. I'm in no mood to have my face raped. I stand up, my face glistening with juices, and stretch toward my jacket, pull out a condom and pull her onto the floor, put the rubber on and penetrate her. I hack into her on the parquet. Pork-ette. Yeah. Actually, this is just like hacking tattooed meat. Any carcass would do. Meanwhile it grows brighter. At the end of my 3,700th attempt to shoot some seed into her (100 per minute, 37 minutes) I give up and pull him out of her. I've never been one to withstand physical duress. I stand up and wander over to the window. There's a balcony door. I open it and step out onto the balcony. The city of Reykjavík stretches before me, surrounded by mountains. Behind them, the sun is emerging like a bald head out of a woman's crotch. Licking in the new day. But I feel cold and go back in. I turn on the TV. Anna is still lying on the floor. She says, "Why did you stop?" I say, "I was getting bored." I sit on the sofa and light myself a cigarette and press PLAY on the remote. I bang with the remote on my plastic-skinned erection while some titles appear on the screen. Anna asks for a cigarette. I light another one and throw it at her. It lands on one of her breasts, and then falls on the floor, and she says, "Hey," before picking it up again. I say, "What movie is this?" She says, "I can't remember. I've already seen it." She rolls over on the floor. There's some fluff on her ass. I prefer the look of her from behind. All of a sudden I want to take her from behind. I rest the cigarette in the ashtray and slip off the sofa to dust the fluff off her ass, and lie on top of her, and pop him back in after some fumbling for the right orifice. She props herself up on her elbows and watches TV while she's at it, smoking her fag. The movie is *True Lies*. Schwarzenegger at a do in Switzerland. I fuck Anna. She stretches out with her cigarette toward the ashtray on the coffee table. She can't quite reach it. She says, "Let's move a bit." I try to keep her on my skewer as we move closer to the coffee table. She stubs the cigarette out in the ashtray. I continue. She says, "I've already seen this movie. Let's go into the bed." Explosions on the screen as we move into the bedroom. I'd forgotten all about the waterbed. The clock on the bedside table reads seven-thirty. We dive into the bed. It wobbles and gurgles underneath us. I've seen that movie twice. I remember the plot. Anna wobbles to and fro on the waterbed, displaying great patience. No sign of me popping my cork. I pass the time by re-creating the visuals to go with the soundtrack from the TV. (I edit out ninety minutes here.) I'm filled with absolute emptiness when the tape runs to an end in the machine. Anna looks into my eyes. I look away. I carry on fucking her. This is now just plain boring. Just can't get rid of this hard-on. A year's warranty, I said. It's almost ten o'clock. But still I carry on fucking her. It's better than having to talk to her. The doorbell rings. I'm bored with that tattoo of hers. The doorbell rings again. Anna claws her way under me and away from the waterbed. She slips into a gown and leaves me bouncing on the ocean bed. I can hear it's her mother and little Máni. Lining up for my services. I'm wondering if Máni might be tight enough to make me come at last. Judging by his voice, he's about four years old. Máni comes in. He's dark. He says, "Hi." I say, "Hi." He walks toward the bed with an inspecting air. Anna and her mother can be heard from the living room. Máni stops when he sees the condom. He says, "What's that?" I tug at the condom and say, "That? A rubber." He says, "Rubber?" I say, "Yeah." He says, "What are you doing with it?" I say, "Making sure you don't get a brother or something . . ." Anna comes in, sees Máni and picks him up. She also picks up the quilt on the floor and throws it over me. Her mother appears at the door. The mommy (45,000) is cuter than Anna. She's had more years to make herself cuter than Anna. Anna takes Máni out and closes the door. I just lie there. On a waterbed on the west side of town. Son of a dyke. I take the quilt and condom off. I have a wank. Alone on a raft. Gently rocking. A castaway. I think of the mommy in the living room as I'm wanking myself. I see her face flickering over me. I see her strong red lipstick and ivory yellow teeth. I imagine her lipstick enveloping my dick. Wonder if the old dear wouldn't be much better at it? Better, just like her apple tart is better. I want the mommy. Billy, Don't Be a Hero. I stand up and walk in and lie down on top of the mommy as she sits there on the sofa in her skirt and jacket with a shawl.

The funeral has started by the time I finally arrive. They call this a chapel but it's really just a hospital room they've cleared the beds from to spare the national health service some cash. It's cheaper to die than to be born. No need for oxygen in the box.

Mom, Lolla, Elsa, Magnús, the boys, Dad and Sara, Vagn and Kerra, Granny, and a friend of Elsa's (60,000) whom I don't know are there. Mom glances back and looks me in the eye without changing expression. She's got that unwavering mommy look that is as unchangeable as the handwriting on the back of the window envelope on the kitchen table when I came home:

We've left. The funeral is at 2. Baptistry chapel, National Hospital. Go through the maternity ward.—BS.

The agony without the Ecstasy. I stand in the back row. They're all in front of me. Good job I wore this jacket. The coffin sits on a table in front of the altar. The things they bury these days. Unchristened, unborn. Just starting to develop a nose, and you're automatically entitled to your own funeral, coffin and cross. The coffin is no bigger than an average-size aquarium. Full of uterine waters. No. Not really. "Go through the maternity ward." To the funeral.

This chapel is an ex–patients' room. Lots of people have died here. Do people die in churches? No one dies in a church, but everyone who dies goes to a church. Uncle Elli once said, "You'll never see me in a church, not until I'm carried there." Lisa Lisa (1,900,000) and Cult Jam. She was a Catholic. The best tits always are. Blood from a chalice instead of blood from a drip. A cross instead of a cross-stitch. A prayer instead of an epidural. Where the doctors drop out, the priests take over. White coats, black habits. "The first Icelandic soul transplant is safely home again after a successful operation in Gothenburg." What was that again?

I still have that hard-on I acquired in Rekagrandi this morning. Couldn't get rid of it, not even after lying on the mom. Quite the opposite. That must have been the first time I actually did something I wanted to do. I lay on top of the woman and felt the shawl she was wearing, the fabric of her skirt, I lowered my face over her throat. There was that good smell. Another two moments like that and I can order my coffin. My Pandora's box. Full of troubles. People who die on Ecstasy end up at a rave gig in hell that goes on forever. Better watch out.

Elsa's dark-haired friend sits on the front bench. She reminds me of Chrissie Hynde (150,000) from the Pretenders. With those ridiculous skinny rock-'n'-roll thighs that she thinks everyone thinks are so sexy. A woman with an electric guitar. Give us a break. Like a man with a curler. Still, something about her. Women with hair over their eyes expect the worst. The Pretenders were a great band. The guitar player was called Honeyman-Scott. James Honeyman-Scott. Pete Farndon on bass. They ODed within twelve months of each other. Their funerals, with Chrissie Hynde in the front row, with hair over her eyes.

The priest is about 87 kilos. Holy meat. Elsa hidden under a ball of hair. Mom watches her, holds her hand. Some kind of sorrow going on. Still, all a little bit artificial. All this trauma management lark has gone a bit too far. Burying someone who was never even born. What if a man were to go into mourning for every wank he had? Fetus burials. Or did I miss the christening? Are they allowed to bury an unchristened fetus? "What was the baby's name going to be?" Hate the way everyone reeks of understanding in here. Shampooed souls. Just a lump of unboiled blood pudding in a box with slits for eyes and we're all supposed to weep over it. And I'm all to blame. Me, oh Lord God, father of all things, what should I say? "Sorry"? Maybe an erection at a funeral isn't so inappropriate after all, if one thinks of the resurrection of the flesh. I've a really stiff boner when we stand up, like a soldier standing to attention with a salute. My name is Gump. Forrest Gump.

I should go to the toilet and puke, but I'm afraid of asking where it is because it suddenly occurs to me that maybe that's where they take the box to flush it away. I long for some big breasts. Bigger than Anna's. Dad looks at me. Don't look at me. Dad. Don't. Don't look at me. I look at Sara. All of a sudden I long to dance with her, cheek to cheek, dance with her all the way into the highlands, until I've eroded all the makeup off her cheek, and walk with her until her perfume has worn off.

"Are you going to the yard?" Dad asks.

"At some stage," I answer.

"Are they going to bury it in the yard?" Sara asks.

"The new graveyard in Fossvogur," says Lolla.

Get lost, you and your bump. Who are you to meddle in our family affairs? Getting all big-headed because of this handmade pregnancy of yours. Elsa looks me in the eye. Forgive me, I think to myself. Forgive me, my sister. I am not what I am but what I have become.

I'm one step from the grave. Which is how I feel. After seventeen hours on xtc. The chemicals are slowly dissolving in my body but will never disappear. They'll always be inside me. Ah well. That's the thing with drugs. Which is why they never give you a hangover. Alcohol's another ballgame. It only hangs over you for a day. That's how these blessed drugs work. That's why cokeheads acquire that pasty look on their faces with age. That's why hash-heads get so smoky eyed. That's why smackheads have such bad breath: they've injected so many holes into their souls they've turned into sieves, and sucked in all the filth of the world, the stench of which permeates through their pores. And that's why we E-tards are such mummies. Not that I'm completely stuffed yet. That was tab number 7 or 8.

In fact, the whole family is now one step from the grave. We stand there over the open tomb, if you can call it that. They've dug up Granddad's grave. Magnús Hafsteinsson, laborer, 1909–1984. Sorry, Granddad. A slight hitch. A technical error. I look at Granny. It's like visiting time on the other side. Mom told Granny that this was Granddad's grave, and that stillborn chil-

dren are traditionally buried in their ancestors' graves. Granny
squinted at the grave and said, "Well. He can rest in peace now."
Then she turned to Mom: "Maybe yourself and Steini could drive
me home first. I have to have the coffee made before people
come." All of a sudden I can see the strange attraction of Alzheimer's. To be able to live in your own old world, where time is
a tamed horse that obeys your commands, without just galloping
on. Granny has succeeded in doing what scientists have been
dreaming of doing for centuries. She has triumphed over time.
Here she stands, a fresh and perfumed widow, still burying her
husband and her Steini and Berglind still married and no
miscarriages yet and no lesbians hovering above us like angry
birds. The year 1984 just freshly carved on the stone and me still
just a twenty-two-year-old English student, uncontaminated
by E-pills and the porn of time. I wish they'd make an
A-pill. Then we could all have Alzheimer's.

There they are. My mother, the lesbian, and my dad, the boozer.
What am I, then? The offspring of an alcoholic and a lesbian. I
study them closer. All of a sudden, they look like two birds, of different species. A boozer and a lesbian.

The BBC cameraman zooms in on the Icelandic species. David
Attenborough provides the commentary:

"The boozer is a wetland bird, and keeps himself close to rivers
and lakes. He is rather heavy and needs a good run-up to get off
the ground, but then can fly for sustained periods and has good
stamina. Several weeks may pass until he gets back on the ground.
During the intermittent periods he keeps a fairly low profile and
can be quite jumpy, particularly in the days immediately following
the landing.

"The lesbian is a relatively new species in Icelandic nature,
having only migrated here in recent years, and strictly in the
southwestern part of the country. She is believed to have come from
the Nordic countries, particularly Denmark, but also from the
British Isles. The lesbian is small but a swift and powerful bird,
easily recognized by the short feathers on her head. In this species
only one in every two females lays the eggs, while the other female
takes on the role of the male by providing shelter and food. The

only contact between the female and the male bird takes place at the moment of insemination. The male of a lesbian bird is considerably heavier than the female. In recent years we have witnessed cases of male birds who are unable to fly at all. Zoologists have been following their development very closely.

"Like the boozer and the lesbian, the hlynur is a water bird, but considerably larger and heavier, with long legs and a long neck and beak. The hlynur is also a sedentary bird who digs himself a hole in the earth—a type of cove where he spend his winters, with just one bird in each hole. He usually constructs his habitat on the outskirts of residential areas, close to city reservoirs. The hlynur is easily recognized by his white turtleneck and black feathers. He only lays one egg at a time but lays the biggest eggs in the country. The young of the hlynur is an unusually slow developer. It doesn't start flying until the end of the summer and stays close to its mother for the first three years. The male never comes near the nest or provides food. He is known for his long sittings close to human habitats, and has for that reason grown somewhat unpopular, particularly in the last years, where he has been increasing his presence by perching on the balcony railings of apartment blocks. Some of the inhabitants of these apartment blocks have linked his prolonged presence to television broadcasts, for which the hlynur has sometimes been referred to as the 'TV bird.' The hlynur is defensive by nature, but harmless."

Lolla somehow materializes by my side, as usual, with that balloon of a tumor of hers. If the hole were slightly bigger I'd shove Lolla into it too. That would solve all my problems. And even though she might be able to pull herself up again by her fingernails, the fetus wouldn't. "Had miscarriage in an open grave." Super cool. A real scoop for the tabloid reporters. Those wife-beating chroniclers of domestic violence. Chrissie Hynde behind. Yeah. She's 60,000, Elsa's friend. I'd like to kiss Chrissie in the backseat of a limo, with her all moist and sweaty after a gig. Mind you, I don't know. That rotten backstage smell. She went out with Ray Davies and Jim Kerr. They should form a band together. Fucks-in-law. There goes the fetus into the earth. Nothing returned to nothingness. Dust thou art and unto dust shalt thou return. There the box sinks into the grave.

Granny says: "Look, what a tiny coffin it is."

The unborn nephew is lowered into the grave. I want to go too. I say it, in a low voice, and to no one in particular:

"Can I go too?"

"You come with us," says Mom.

Reykjavík, 20 May 1996

Hi, Kati.

I went to my nephew's funeral yesterday. I didn't know him. I never saw him. My mother saw him. She said he didn't look too good. But still I was his godfather. He died inside my sister. He was buried before he was born. Maybe he was lucky. Everybody was very sad and I tried to be too. The weather was very good. Sunshine on sadness is kind of weird. Everything else is fine. Not much news. My mother is enjoying lesbianism and now they're pregnant. I mean her girlfriend is pregnant. I sometimes wonder how they did it. I went out last night and tried to meet some girl, even though I'd much more rather meet you. Hope you're well.—Bi.— HB.

PS. Could you describe your body? (Since I've only ever seen your face.)

I'm bedridden with a hard-on when the phone rings. The answering man:

"Hlynur Björn here. Please leave a message after the tone."

"Er . . . yeah . . . Hlynur . . . I'm not sure this message is . . . I . . . ehm . . ."

Uncle Elli.

Me: "Hello."

"Yeah, hi. I thought there was something wrong with your answering machine. What the hell are you up to now, lad?"

"Me? Nothing. Just surfing the Net."

"Yeah. Well, lad. Jesus, you might have told me. Treating me like I'm not even a member of the family. Like I'm some kind of stranger. Maybe it's the driving. Maybe you think I'm not in the family anymore because I've been driving all these years. Hum?"

"What?"

"I mean to say."

"What?"

"What's got into you, lad?"

"I . . . I didn't even know about it myself until it had started. I arrived late."

"Were you late for the funeral? You know what that means, don't you?"

"No. What?"

"That you'll be early for your own."

"What do you mean? Is that possible?"

"Oh yes, my lad. You'll get it sooner or later, sooner or later . . . ha ha ha . . . And tell me, how heavy do you reckon it was?"

"Do you mean that I'll go before? Do you mean I'll die before I die?"

"Hlynur, you remember this one, don't you?

*"To live is a lot like renting
a body for a while.
But when it comes to parting
I'll do it in a grander style."*

"I don't get rhymes."

"What do you mean you don't get rhymes?"

"Words that sound the same all mean the same thing to me."

"Rubbish, lad."

"Rhymes strip words of their meaning. Just turn them into a sound."

"Yeah, well. It might be a sound, but it creates a totally new meaning. Like, for example, when renting rhymes with parting, a totally new meaning that you don't maybe fully understand, but it's what the Danes call, or used to call, *poesi*."

"Yeah. Sounds Danish, all right."

"Yeah, Danish . . ."

248

"Yeah. Where are you?"

"On Miklabraut. At the traffic lights."

"Busy day?"

"Sweet fuck-all to do. And that's why I could easily have come. But I wasn't invited. It would have been fun to see a funeral like that, they're totally new to me. But sure, anyway. Of course, one shouldn't be encouraging that kind of nonsense. Just cos a woman's let a baby slip out, there's no point in making a drama out of it. I don't know what this country's coming to."

"They've even started to bury relationships in Holland."

"Huh? Relationships?"

"Yeah. It's such a trauma when people break up, see? So they have a ceremony to help people get over it. Rings are buried in the earth, in special 'separation graveyards,' and then people can go there to lay flowers on their buried troubles."

"Yeah? What the fuck. Well, that hasn't come here yet—I'm glad to say—and I know this country pretty well, get a cross-section of it in my backseat every day. Did you get a chance to peek at it?"

"The fetus? No. I missed the removal. Mom says it had eyes and all."

"Jesus, yeah. A face and all?"

"Yeah. Looked just like Magnús."

"Oh yeah? And what do you think it weighed?"

"A five-month fetus? About a kilo."

"A kilo, yeah."

"Yeah. Just a chunk of raw meat."

"Yeah. But a relative nonetheless."

Not to brag, but: the day after—headline on the back page of the evening paper:

MOTHER IN NAKED LOVER ORDEAL

An elderly woman was left severely shaken when her daughter's lover suddenly appeared naked from a bedroom and threw himself upon her. The woman, 56, was visiting her daughter's west-side apartment at around midday last Sunday when the attacker struck as the pair sat chatting on a sofa. The 30-year-old man, who appeared to be under the influence of drugs, "behaved disgustingly" and refused to leave when asked. The police were called, but the man had disappeared by the time they arrived at the scene, leaving the woman shaken but unhurt. Her four-year-old grandson witnessed the incident.

The woman's daughter, 25, said that she had met the man in a club on Saturday night. "I had no idea he was a pervert," she said tearfully. "I don't know if Mom will ever fully recover from this. We shall definitely be pressing charges." A police spokesman refused to comment on the attack.—ME

I call up the evening paper and ask for ME, introducing myself as "the naked lover here," and ask them whether they wouldn't like to have a picture of me. But she doesn't sound too hot on the idea. I offer her an exclusive. On the cover of the weekend supplement. With a caption: "It's what I've always wanted to do." She hangs up. The media are like kids. If you dangle the news in front of their noses, they don't want it, but if you hide it under a table in a room, they come running back to you with it, all stupid and delighted. I'm pathetic. I can't even achieve my fifteen minutes of fame by appearing naked.

Timer lives in the K-bar. Timer's got it sussed. A cool dude. Timer drinks rum and tea. "It's been scientifically proven that rum can't give you a hangover." I don't know if Timer has ever actually given himself the time to get a hangover. Apart from his stroll down to the K-bar. He's always drunk, but sober at the same time. He's reached that karma you can only reach if you've been on a binge for seven years straight. Can't even get tipsy anymore. Not even from those sixteen double teacups he gets through from one till one. That Keisi's told me about.

On top of the rum, Timer's deep into some kind of spiritual enlightenment New Age thing. Some kind of mental cultivation thing and manual healing or magic. Some people call him the Wiz. Always coming out with these profound statements, forever quoting

"Waldorf," some guru from the Himalayas kind of thing. Timer meets him regularly, drops out from the table, back onto the chair, and just stares out the window, holding the straw in his teacup. When his eyelids start to flutter like butterflies, it's a signal that he's flying back home. Then it stops when he lands again. "Well, guys. I was on the mountain. The message is: Let the candles burn. Let the candles burn," he might say. Actually, he's a version of Magnús, my brother-in-law, in reverse. Talks of "outer peace" and "wheeling." Not "healing." "You can wheel yourself. I'm wheeled. You need wheeling," he'd say and wouldn't laugh. He only laughs on his own, when he sits alone by the window table on a chair he had upholstered especially for himself, the best chair in the K-bar. He blows his top if he finds some pony sitting on it when he comes back from the john. Which isn't very often. He's got some kind of a Buddha bladder which he claims would get him across the Sahara Desert. Not that I've ever heard of anyone having to piss much in the desert. Anyway. Then he laughs with all his kilos, a really weird laugh. There's a bizarre squeak in him that seems to bear no relation to his voice, and his belly quivers. He squeaks like an old fridge in the back of some touring rock band bus on an Icelandic dirt road.

Timer is a "Bodyist," which is some kind of a more physical version of Buddhism. Heavy with wisdom: 146 kilos and 90 grams of it, to be exact. "Ten grams under the Seventh Zen." Today, anyway. Because it's Keisi's day off. "There's too much water in this tea what's-her-name made."

No way of knowing if that's just his sense of humor. Or a tumor.

The Wiz can give you a weather forecast by looking at the bubbles rising in your beer, predict after-hour parties from shoe marks on the bar floor, and read smoke signals, i.e., cigarettes. He can tell if you're HIV-positive, according to the direction Winston smoke blows out of you, and whether his journalist friends are going to be paid tomorrow or never. Timer. A total freak. With no hair. He shaved it all off.

"Why do you shave your head?" some expert asks him during his daily press conference at his table.

"It's not just the head," says Timer, or whispers, rather. He speaks with his so-called inner voice, and because he's so fat, it has problems breaking through. He speaks in truncated sentences and each period is punctuated by a puff through his nose. As if he were trying to demonstrate how deep he's had to dive to retrieve each word. Or had to sniff several tons of charlie to achieve this level of wisdom.

"It's not just the head. But my arms too. Legs. Know why Indians have no body hair? It's their sensitivity. Sensitivity. A thousand things on you will keep a thousand things from you."

"And is that why you shave?"

"Waldorf says," says Timer with drooping eyelids, dropping back into his chair with joined hands, as always when he quotes the guru, maybe to establish contact, "hair is time.

"Hair is time," he repeats, striking a meaningful pose, as if this were some kind of American truth.

Yeah. Yeah, yeah.

"Time. What do you mean?" someone asks.

"Time doesn't pass for me. I pass for time. Outer peace, you know."

"But the beard, why have you got a long beard, then?" Thröstur, his fellow beard, asks with understandable interest. And good point. Timer is completely shaven except for his long beard. Which is probably why everything he comes out with sounds so muttered.

"Roots. It's roots."

We're stuck here in the early Bronze Age. A B.C. atmosphere. "Let the candles burn." And he's got some kind of stud in his ear. A real rock. Socrates' fat son. Sipping on tea.

We've stopped trying to ask questions. We just sit there, humbly awaiting further enlightenment. He sips another sip. He tilts his shaved brain toward the straw. He's about to impart some words of wisdom.

"This isn't a beard," he says, blowing out his nose. "The roots of knowledge are visible to the eye. The truth is shown in reverse. What you see is what I say. As Debbie Harry said. To me. Let the flower grow inside you. But water it from the outside."

He doesn't laugh. We don't laugh. It's all just one big megamix.

Straight from the blender. A hodgepodge from Buddha to Blondie. The history of the human soul condensed into 147 kilos ("the Seventh Zen": 7 x 3 x 7). Timer is a case. A shaven-headed sumo champion with a ZZ Top beard. A top man.

His real name is Thorgrímur, Thröstur told me. Thorgrímur turned into Timer during his study years in the States. Or when he was "interning" with the Indians in the Nevada desert. Although some say he spent all his time vegetating in Vegas's twenty-four-hour bars, living in some Headache Hotel for two years. He did, however, manage to graduate from some tattoo university. He sometimes shows off his graduation piece at parties. A pretty well-executed picture on his shaved chest commemorating his meeting with Debbie Harry (95,000) at some party in LA. Which is where he got the wondrous or ludicrous idea of becoming a Bodyist and follower of Waldorf, who Keisi says is nothing more than a salad. Which is why he's such a nut, I guess. Remember he described it all at a party:

"I was standing there by the pool. I'd just met Debbie. And then looked out into the pool. And I saw this limo in the water. Or the water was like a white limo. And that's when I realized. Not just because Waldorf always appears in a white limo. It was also obviously a sign. That made all the puzzle fall into place. It's all on the outside. That's when I found the outer peace. The outer peace. That the master talks about. Of course it's all so obvious. You can never reach inner peace. I mean, thought is weather. Don't fight the impossible. Go for the possible. All you can do is polish your car. Polish your car."

And your bald head. I'll say this for him. Timer is always balanced. Or always equally unbalanced. When he speaks, or the whisper speaks through him. But especially when he doesn't speak at all. No way of fathoming what he's on about. This limo pool of his is way too deep for me. Timer says he's the same age as Sid Vicious. But he's dead now.

It's a hellishly bright Thursday evening in 101 with nothing going on but clouds. Still, I've got that certain itch. I stick my head out. My head, the tomato, can't even concentrate on the remote anymore.

It's nothing o'clock and the shop doors gape like mouths, like the mouths on those chubby women sitting behind the counter who raise their heads from the soft-porn mags as you pass. I walk down Klapparstígur. A screeching gang of sprightly kids comes running round the corner and one of them shouts at me: "Motherfucker!" Well, how about that? No more than ten years old and already fluent in dirty LA street-speak. Still, you've got to hand it to them. Motherfucker. Not incorrect. Some tourists are gondoliering up Laugavegur and everything's rather dull. The air is certifiably stagnant and the city center is devoid of all life, apart from the Waldorf Witness at the K-bar: a hundred-odd kilos of mind power in the corner.

Spring evenings can be great in Reykjavík when everyone's at home watching TV and only the hard-core drinkers are in the bar. I like that.

The place is empty but Timer sits in his chair, immersed in some manual ritual. The table is covered in gutted cigarettes and peeled filters. Rum and straws pushed to one side. I don't disturb, walk to the counter. "Two beers."—"Two?"—"Yeah, I'm alone tonight." I stand by the bar and drink them both intermittently. Watch Timer peeling the paper off the filters. Hate to see people working. I disturb.

There are twenty or thirty naked filter tips on the table. Some pretty nimble fingers Timer's got. The sumo champ's in a sewing mood.

"What's this? Some anti-smoking protest?" I ask.

He exhales through his nose. I take a sip. Feel uneasy. Look out. A woman (7,000) in a coat. A Nissan jeep. Timer finishes stripping the yellow paper off the filter tip. He then takes a piece of the wadding between his fingers and dangles it solemnly in front of my face. Whispers through his beard:

"What's this?"

"Er. A filter."

He remains silent. I try harder:

"Winston. A Winston filter."

"This is Icelandic ingenuity. Industry. Exports. Income."

"Yeah."

"Look. We import cigarettes. Those assholes won't allow us to grow our own tobacco in Hveragerdi. So what do we do? How many pets are there in America?"

"I don't know. Lots."

"Hlynur. That's your name, Hlynur, right? Yeah. Just think about it. Millions. There are millions of those fucking little creeps. Cats. Hamsters. Guinea pigs. You name it. And how many of them are female? Huh? How many bitches are there out there?"

"Ehm. Half of them, maybe."

"Exactly. So work it out. We're talking about a market that could be worth billions. We're talking about megavegas marketing here."

"From filters?"

"Look. Just add a short white thread here. I've got my mother working on that," Timer whispers, pointing at the hairy white filter, "and what have we got?"

I'm stuck on a psychiatric quiz show. The program host peers into my eyes. He continues without the hint of a smile:

"Tampons for cats and other small animals."

Timer is a top man. And he doesn't want to be disturbed. I linger, though, and keep my mouth shut at the table, with my two beers, while he continues to strip the filters. I head for the can and notice I'm slightly jarred when I see myself yanking up my trousers in the mirror and, for a brief moment, actually believe this is the hottest action in town right now. Me yanking myself up. What's become of me? Timer's buddy? He's gone through a whole pack of Winstons by the time I sit down again.

"What about the cigarettes?" I ask. "What would you do with those?"

He livens up a moment and casually says:

"Domestic market. Prerolled joints."

"What, a joint venture?" I say with a slight titter. He stares back impassively. He's running this show. His beard wobbles as he continues:

"Do you know why Marlboro cigarettes have white filters in America and yellow ones in Europe?"

"Ehm. No."

"So that Keith Richards can tell which continent he's in."

I've got myself another two beers. Bubbles popping up to heaven. Timer says he's managed to keep the wolf from the door by taking on some "special assignments," which are obviously connected to magic, despite what he says. He's a freelance wizard.

"It's not magic. The Indians can talk to their friends at a distance of seven miles. Just by knocking on their chests. But there's no guarantee they can contact each other if the distance is any greater than that. It's a question of sensitivity."

"What, like a beeper?"

"It comes natural to them. People on this island keep on gadgeting themselves up. But that's the whole point, you don't need it. It's all here," he says, exhaling through his nose again and pointing at his chest. And I'm not sure whether he means his beard or what's behind it. "See. I just have to lean back to establish contact with Dorfy. I go up to the mountaintop three times a day. I mean, don't get me wrong. I need equipment for some of the bigger stuff."

Timer is talking about minor heart operations, acute detox on his friends before weddings and funerals, and "temporary reincarnations." He tells me how he helped some childless friends of his to have a child. A major operation:

"It took us . . . Yeah . . . Altogether it took forty-eight hours. I had to stay with them for two nights. It took me a long time to recover after that. But it also made me two hundred thousand krónur. Net. For a fertility operation like that you've got to have. You've got to have a generator. You've got to have a trampoline. Although it doesn't have to be that big. Just a mini-size. And you need milk. You need lots of milk. . . ."

I interrupt him with a sudden idea I have.

"And abortions. Can you do abortions?"

"Abortions?"

"Yeah."

"Yeah, sure. It's been a while since I've done one. But it shouldn't be too much of a problem. You need one?"

"Y . . . Yeah."

"How many months is she?"

I glance at my watch: 23 May.

"She's five months gone."

"Five months. OK."

"What do you charge for it?"

"Shouldn't cost that much. Mind you, five months. I charge extra for each month after the first three. Let's say twenty thousand."

"Twenty thousand?"

"Yeah. But I'll give you a five-thousand discount. Because it's you. The standard price is fifteen. The same as what they charge up at the clinic. Except my method is painless. Who's the lucky one?"

"Huh?"

"Who's the lucky girl?"

"She's a friend of my . . . a friend of mine."

"Yeah. We have to move fast, sometime over the next few days. We'll do it at my place. Just bring her over straight after the weekend."

"Yeah . . . no . . . she . . . she doesn't want to, you see."

"I see. You're talking about a transmission."

"A transmission?"

"Yeah. It has to be done over the phone."

"The phone?"

"Yeah. You have to get me access to the woman. Better to do it at night. Don't worry. Only takes about two hours. Just a long local call. But if that's the case, I'll have to charge you thirty for it."

"Thirty thousand?"

"Yeah. Transmission costs."

"Transmission costs?"

"Yeah. We're talking about a transmission here. That means more work. More equipment."

"How would you do it, then?"

"Hang on."

Timer tilts himself back on his chair and joins those chubby hands of his over his beard. His tattoo shimmers under his T-shirt sleeve. He stares out the window for what must be seven minutes. Faint tremors under the layers of fat. A crowd has entered the bar. I watch them watch us. Timer's eyelids are fluttering butterflies when I look back at him again. Then:

"He sends his regards. The message is: Leave the beer be. Leave the beer be."

Leave the beer be. I'm only halfway through it. Holy Kiljan. I'm talking to a cream pudding. A dangerous cream pudding. Crime pudding. Still, Bad Company was a great band.

"What do you mean?"

"Look. Don't worry. I know what I mean when I mean it."

"But I mean. Is it sure this thing works? I won't pay unless it works."

"Half before the birth, and the rest when it's over."

"The birth? Isn't this supposed to be an abortion?"

"Yeah, sure. It just might take some time to work, that's all."

I've managed to avoid seeing Lolla for almost a week now. She's got her working shifts and I've got my sleeping shifts between them. My sleeping shifts. Sounds pathetic. Makes me sound like I'm some decrepit toothless Chinese refugee with bad breath and a shabby beard, roaming the streets of Reykjavík, dragging a rickety old hot-dog stand. I can't stand Lolla anymore. Not now that she's started with this homebrew-in-her-tummy lark, waddling about with her conspiracy against me and Mom: the bump that'll bump us all apart. Our joint little boy. Then Lolla'll be Mom and Mom'll be Dad and I his big brother but also his dad but still both his father's and granny's son and his mother's ex-lover. What will that make him? A bisexual brat? Grandchild and child of the child begotten from the mother of the child of the mother. Motherly he will appear, full of brotherly love, and speak to himself in a fatherly way. No, no. FC Akranes! I beg you, dearest center-forward, to score a goal and play me offside in the womb. Dearest son. I beg you. Come crawling out of Lolla's crotch with Adidas stripes on your arms, football boots on your feet, and "FC Akranes" written on your back. Remember the Akranes men, playing for Iceland, Teitur Thordarson and Matthias Hallgrímsson, who scored a fluke goal against East Germany back in Halle in '73 or '74. We were lucky bastards. Icelanders were good for nothing for a thousand years. From the days of Grettir the Great to the moment when Jón

Páll become the World's Strongest Man. A thousand-year-old infe-
riority complex. Always the outsider. Outside the world. The bar.

I can't remember why I'm standing out here in my shoes, alone
in a five-man line in front of the K-bar. The summer light over the
city is as white and as dreary as Iggy Pop's face on a hangover.
Farther down the street, some jerks are swinging their hair. Midnight Oil. I could see Mount Esja if I leaned my head back.
Which I do. I got into Esja when I heard that Dylan had spent a
whole night staring at it through the window of his hotel suite,
with another white mountain on the windowsill in front of him.
You often need something like that. Maybe we should pay more
attention to Esja. Maybe there are some hit songs hidden in it.
Some hidden tracks of snow. A seagull is scooping air under its
wings high over the rooftops. I suddenly get a close-up of him in
my eye. Dirty flapping wings piercing my ears. My inner man is
probably a cameraman.

I mouth a cigarette. The mother of the girl in front of me
(70,000) used to work at the Carnaby Street store and then got a job
as a tour promoter. Remember her breasts from the TV ads. Wow,
man. Man City. Man Utd. Man, I remember when the only thing that
mattered were the English football results. Wolves beat Swindon.
'Member when the only porn you could see in Iceland was a
breast-cancer ad. Maybe my upbringing is to blame. Twenty years
of TV-less boredom. Black and white chess games on the screen.
And all that Cleo Laine (45,000) crap. The only country in the
world where the TV actually shut down for a day every week.
Every Thursday. It will always remain an indelible blank spot in my
brain. A vacuum that can never be filled. Women aren't as loose as
we are. Maybe cos they get pregnant. They don't take in just anybody. Mind you, the Single Mothers of Iceland. If the girl in front of
me were to turn and say, "Do you want to come home for a screw?"
I'd flag down the next car. If I were to tap her on the shoulder and
say, "Excuse me, but would you mind if I came home with you for
a screw right now?" she'd say, "Oh, go wank yourself." And I'd say,
"Right now?" Women get some time to think. Their brains don't
dart down to their crotches every forty seconds, which means
they've got the whole day to focus their minds on nobler thoughts,

to speculate about things like life after death and death after life and other philosophical questions like that. Them. Soaring gulls. Us. Pissing bulls. Chained to the stall. In the cowshed of desire. Ruminating over sex after death. Women aren't plagued by all these sexual fantasies, their minds are freed from the clutch of the crotch. So how come they don't use their brains, then? What do they think about? Their bosses, babies, and budgets. Mother, house-mother, phone mother. Yeah. And their looks. Why are women always fussing over their external looks when all we want to do is get inside? Women are an endless self-promo. Check me out! Come pick me up. The magnetic power of lipstick. Makeup to fake-up beauty. Our Father who art remote, hallowed be thy fifty channels, give us this day just one tiny little birthmark of unfaked beauty. Yeah. Women. We think about them. They think about whether we're thinking about them or not.

I tap the girl in front of me on the shoulder. She turns. She is blond (35,000) with blue around her eyes. About twenty-five winters. Reckon she's had about seventeen men. Women are second-hand cars. What's your mileage? I feel like sucking the snot out of her. But don't, just say:

"Ehm. Are you wearing a belt?"

"Yes," she says.

"Can I see it?" I say.

She lifts her sweater. Her navel glitters. Brown skin. Blue moon. I saw you standing alone.

"Is it well fastened, can I see?" I ask, sliding my hand over her stomach and behind her belt. I manage to feel hair with the tips of my fingers before she yanks it out of her trousers and says, "Hey!"

"Hey, Jude, don't take it bad," I say.

Me at the bar. Dr. Hook and the Medicine Show. I'm waiting to be served. Bottles on the shelves like a class photograph. "Mother in Naked Lover Ordeal." Something so basic about that. Sheep in naked fox shock. There's some pretty sozzled Hugo standing by my side. Conversing with some Nobel laureates on the other side of me. Seems they're talking about the drummer in R.E.M.

"I thought he'd had a car accident."

"No, no, it was a tumor. A brain tumor."

"Hang on, what was his name again? Bill something?"

"Yeah, it was, wasn't it?"

"What a nightmare, man, a brain tumor, and they had to postpone the whole tour. I saw them in Gothenburg a few years ago. Great concert. Great. I mean mega-great."

"Yeah. R.E.M. The thing is, they just get better and better."

"Like good wine."

"Yeah, exactly, like good wine."

I just have to take a closer look at these geniuses. Like good wine. It's not every day that you get to hear something as ingenious as that. I turn my head like the revolving cab of a crane. They're younger. They're in coats. One of them wears glasses. Their faces somehow bear all the signs of the bullets that have been drilling through their skulls for the past two weeks, through the backs of their necks toward their foreheads: any second now they'll come popping out between their eyes and drop into their glasses. They're so deadly boring that even a bullet gives up halfway through their brains. They continue.

"And what does it mean, R.E.M.? I've often wondered about that. Do you know what it means?"

"I'm not too sure, but I heard someone say once that it was Real English Men."

"Real English Men?"

"Yeah."

"But they're Americans, aren't they?"

"Yeah, actually they are. From Athens, Georgia, or that's where the band was formed, but most of them are from California, I seem to remember. It must have been just some name they found."

"Yeah. Of course they were heavily influenced by the English New Wave. At the time."

"Yeah, right. Television and Wire and bands like that. Patti Smith, too . . ."

"Yeah. But she was American, wasn't she?"

"Patti? Yeah, actually, she was American. Or I think so."

"Born in Chicago on New Year's Eve," I interject, "1946." They look at me. Study me. I continue:

"And Television too, since we're on the subject. They were awesome. Tom Verlaine . . ."

"Oh yeah? They were American?"

"Yeah. They were one of the CBGB bands."

"Oh yeah?" say two pairs of brain-dead eyes.

"CBGB, the club in New York."

"Yeah?"

"R.E.M. stands for rapid eye movement. The dreaming state."

"Right. Yeah."

"And, ehm. Do you know anything about the drummer's brain tumor?"

"Yeah. It's quite common among drummers in rock bands. They've been stuck on the same beat for twenty years, so it's no wonder their brains give in. I'll have a beer. Tuborg."

"And what? Can't he play anymore? Fuck, that'd be a terrible blow for the band, man, if he couldn't play anymore."

"Yeah, yeah. William Thomas Berry. They say he'll recover, but then they'll have to find a new beat," I say.

Bachman-Turner Overdrive. I turn away and prepare my next line—look, it's her, focus on your beer, that's the girl whose pubic hair I touched with my fingertips, her name could be Soap, have a sip, Billy Crystal, she's ignoring me, Soap McCoy, and Timer in his usual place, the abortion, long time since I've seen Hofy, she closes her eyes when she makes love, the pregnant fool, remember her cowpat pillow cases, this one here (75,000) isn't bad, she presents the lottery on TV now, Petur Ormslev was a good midfielder, his dad was a sax player, which is significant, I guess—as I travel all the way over to Thröstur and Marri's table. Numb faces.

"What's up?"

"Haven't you heard about Hertha?"

"Hertha Berlin?"

"Yeah. She's in intensive care. Got beaten up last weekend. In town," says Thröstur. "She's hanging on by a thread."

Short silence. I look at Marri. He slept with her once. By the look on his face, he's trying to decide whether he should be sad or not. He slept with someone who is now in intensive care. Yeah. Sorrow would be appropriate. Hanging on by a thread. It's such a zero-gravity moment. Right now Hertha Berlin is levitating over a white hospital bed and the question is whether she'll fly up and out into space or fall back into the present. I break the silence:

"Hey. Did you read the news in the paper? 'Mother in Naked Lover Ordeal'?"

I'm surprised by how chirpy I sound.

"'Mother in Naked Lover Ordeal,'" Marri parrots. Typical Marri. Marri is the type of guy who needs dope to be able to be himself.

"Yeah. And what if it had been the other way around? 'Lover in Naked Mother Ordeal,'" says Thröstur.

"You mean something like, 'Hofy freaks out'?" I say.

Thröstur exhales a strange laugh, Marri laughs unconvincingly and looks at him. Obviously some in-joke between them. Starsky and Hutch. But I'm tired of keeping all this baby stuff under wraps and say:

"OK. She's pregnant."

They drain their glasses, but Thröstur manages to utter some words as he swallows:

"So you've heard?"

"Yeah."

"Did she tell you?"

"Yeah."

"Really? She never told me," says Thröstur.

"Oh yeah? Why should she have told you?" I ask.

"Nah, just . . . Yeah, maybe it's understandable. I mean, you were together for a bit, weren't you?"

"Yeah. We had a miniseries."

"Right. But it's all over now."

"Yeah, good riddance. It was never anything."

"No, I mean the pregnancy. She's not pregnant anymore."

"Oh yeah?" I say. This is really something.

"Yeah. Didn't you know?" says Thröstur, pulling on the nerve ends protruding from his chin.

"No. It was never noticeable on her anyway but, I mean. They're always coming up with something new, aren't they? So did she have an abortion?"

"I guess so. I dunno. What are you having? Same again?"

Thröstur answers, standing up and pointing at my almost empty glass. I shake my head and watch him move to the bar. Timer is there. And the usual collection of babes. The one-hundredth episode of Babewatch. But things are a bit crowded tonight due to some pop-star guys at that table over there. Blur or Oasis. Surrounded by bushes of pubic hair. But still, I've got a girl's ass staring into my eyes. Bursting jeans. Why are they in such great demand? Asses. What are they but two cheeks of fat? Two handfuls of flesh. Two kilos of wheat. That one day will be scattered in the wind. Still, though. I'd stoop to anything for an ass like that. The sun rises between the buttocks and sets between the breasts. So be it. Few things are as beautiful as the wobble of a comfortably fat woman's ass taken from behind, quivering gently to the beat of copulation, like jelly shimmering on a plate. Watched in slow motion.

Half-baked flesh slithering out of the womb. Stillborn or aborted. Drops as thick as blood pudding dripping into the earth. Refuse. Flopped lives. Aborted creations. Or probably some superhero who got too cocky and wanted to pop out too soon, one more or one less? How many Einsteins ended up in the gas chamber? How many Kasparovs were annihilated yesterday? Answer: two. I was the godfather of one of them and the father of the other. Funeral today and garbage day tomorrow. The triplets dream finally quashed. Wolves beat Swindon. Now I can only count on Lolla. She will deliver.

After hours. Thirty people outside the K-bar on a bright mid-June night, plus me behind the building pissing yellow into another man's green garden. Stick a cigarette into my mouth before wandering back to the group, as if it were a necessary filter for human interaction. The Human League. I'm seized by a sudden urge to impregnate all the girls standing on the street. Just a question of where to begin. Marri holds a beer bottle up to a pretty face (60,000). As if that were the right way to go about it. Some kind of a bum over there. He's wearing a padlocked chain around his neck. Case closed. I push my glasses back. And honky-tonk. Hofy. The unpregnant girl.

"Long time no see. Had your baby?"

"No."

"You wouldn't notice."

"No."

"Did you leave your bump at home? Is it portable or something?"

"Yeah. You could say that."

"Abortion?"

"Yeah."

"Without even telling me."

"Should I have?"

"Or asked your dad to. He comes over for a chat sometimes."

"He says you're a psycho."

"Oh yeah? I . . . I thought the mouth was his field. Not the brain. Since when can dentists diagnose mental illnesses?"

"You don't need a dentist to see that."

"That what you think, then? That I'm a psycho?"

"Well, you're pretty deranged, all right."

"Yeah. And is that why you aborted, then? To get that demented fetus out of the way?"

"Exactly."

The red highlights in her hair have fled to my face. A fairly angry silence. I throw my half-smoked cigarette onto the street. It had started to tremble too much. I stub it out with my foot, thoroughly. Then try to add, in a calm voice:

"Still, you could have told me."

"I just have, haven't I?"

"Yeah, right, when it's all over and done. It might've been nice to let the daddy know before you threw his baby into the garbage can. He might have wanted to take the garbage can out himself. Show some respect."

"The garbage can?"

"Yeah. What else would they do with it? Flush it down the drain?"

"What's this all of a sudden? I thought you said you wanted the exterminator to take care of this. So what are you being bitter about? You're not the one who had to go through this."

"Well, it's been a bit of a burden for me."

"Burden for you?"

"Yeah."

"What kind of burden?"

"Well, a psychological burden. And financial one, too. I've been working like crazy to save up for the child support."

"Yeah, sure. You working? Doing what? Jesus Christ, you and your humor."

"And you and your tumor."

She turns away and vanishes into the crowd. I follow her. Elbow through the mob. This is the first time I've ever followed anyone to be able to talk to them. Not my style. But she deserves to be hassled. A bat chasing a frog in slow motion:

"Hey. Hofy. Why did you never tell me about this?"

"You mean you would have opposed it?"

"The abortion of our child, you mean?"

"There's no need to put it like that."

"This is so . . . I don't know. I might have wanted to think it over."

"If it makes you feel any better, it wasn't even your baby."

"Oh no?"

"No."

"What do you mean, not my baby?"

All right! I've had nothing but her womb on my brain for the past six months and almost developed a tumor from thinking about it and now she says it wasn't even my child. Is she a total puddinghead or what?

"Well, who is . . . who was the lucky man, then?"

"Does it matter?"

"Yeah. Who is it?"

"Who? Are you jealous? Are you telling me you're jealous?"

A grin breaks out on that face called Hofy. She's slightly tanned. As if there were some kind of spring in that. I feel like applying for an abortion for her. But it's probably too late now. In the Soviet Union applications used to take so long to go through the system that the kids were often seven years old before the parents finally got the go-ahead.

"Jealous? And how did you manage to switch the baby's father before you went to have it aborted? Is that the new thing? Can they do it by remote control now?"

"I only thought it was you in the beginning."

"Oh yeah . . ." I say, suddenly striking a lightbulb in my head. Feel a tingle in the tip of my chin. New Year's Eve. Hearing him say, "Did you really mean that about what's-her-name?"

"Was it Thröstur? It's Thröstur?" I ask.

She isn't swift enough to say no. Lies take longer to travel, have to take a slight detour through the brain on their way to the mouth.

I walk past the prison on Skólavördustígur. I've almost passed it when I turn on my heels, walk to the gate, and ring the bell. No answer. I ring again. The intercom. A male voice: "Yes?" I answer: "Do you have any vacancies?" The voice on the intercom is deep, as if it were speaking from the lowest chambers of hell: "Afraid not. Not at the moment." Me: "Any chance of a spare cell in the near future?" No answer. I ring again. No answer.

I continue up Skólavördustígur. Deserted and hellishly bright. Pass Kornelius, the watchmaker's. If only we'd all been watchmakers. I feel like shouting it out from the rooftops: "YEAH I TOLD YOU I WAS WEARING A CONDOM!" But I don't. It's not my style. If we could all be watchmakers. The Art Supply Store. If I could sing and dance, I'd break into a number right now, to a chorus of: "She threw it all away." But I just settle for a cigarette instead. Cigarette number fifty-two today. Thröstur and Hofy. Happy Mondays, Ruby Tuesday. The tower of Hallgrím's Church draws nearer. A car drives by, transforming me into a normal pedestrian again, and I turn into "Oh, him," and lose my concentration for a moment, if one can use such a word. A part of me always disappears when people look at me. I should start carrying a gun. I meet my reflection in a glass. Realize I'm holding a glass in my hand. Have a sip. Could be gin. OK, then. Here's a song:

I gave her all my compliments
she threw it all away.
Then I went and bought her a drink

she threw it all away.
And then we went home and did it and she got pregnant and I
  thought I was gonna be a dad and stuff but
she threw it all away.

I break into a song-and-dance routine. Not. On the corner by the Granary (or there's a new store there now) I pass a couple crossing over Skólavördustígur. I call after them: "Where are you off to?" The girl (15,000) looks at me and calls back with a smile, "We're going home for a screw!" They laugh. Laughing skulls. I'm left standing there with my glass and swallow the dregs. It's empty now.

Some light blue knitting stuff is on the coffee table in the living room when I come in and plonk myself on the sofa and light a cigarette. So Thröstur fucked Hofy. And she who was supposed to be in love with me. That's why we're always gawking at women's crotches: to try and understand them. Women are lottery prizes. You think you've won the whole lot. Then you find out you've got to share the winnings with five others. I pick the knitting stuff off the table. A half-finished sweater. Size 0–6 months. I try it on. It gets stuck halfway down my forehead. Thröstur and Hofy. Maybe it's just as well she did away with all the evidence. What a dangerous cocktail that would have been. A Hofy with a goatee. I'm not drunk enough to die on this sofa and stumble about. I turn the doorknob in ultra slow motion and open their door. There they are, sound asleep in the twilight. Two women in a double bed. My mother and the mother of my child. I stroll into the bedroom, over to the window, and glance outside. June. Flowers. New flowers in the garden. They're both asleep, Mom's arm seems to be draped over Lolla. My bi-mom in her beddy-bi-byes. Two women in bed and one of them pregnant. And me standing over them, by the headrest with a light blue half-knit baby sweater stuck on my head. The sleeves dangling like blue limp horns. Father and son. I suddenly realize I look like the druid of a totally bizarre sect. I raise my hand. I bless them. The blessed creatures. In the name of the father, and the son . . . Two women in a bed and one of them pregnant. That's the future. Mommy I and Mommy II. Women will take care of the whole thing with their sperm-bank cards and we'll become redundant, total freaks, with our dangling long-obsolete tools beating in the wind. Our majestic organs as anachronistic as a crank handle from a Model-T Ford. We thin-feathered, castrated males have been relegated to balcony railings, where we perch for eternity with nothing to do but gawk in through the windows at the TV screens during broadcasting hours. When the children are born: "Oh, dear, was it a boy? Never mind." I want to crawl up to them. If we could all be watchmakers.

Mom wakes me up in the morning as I lie in Alexanderplatz in Berlin: a bum under an old yellow rug and Hrönn, good old Hrönn, under a similar rug beside me. We're lying on the pavement outside a supermarket. I'd just fallen asleep there, having spent the whole cold night hovering around Bono as he dropped in free-fall over Berlin. Bono was casually dressed, no shades, in a dark woolen coat and fell quite nicely, sang the lyrics perfectly, and only faltered once when he looked at me with a smile. Due to the speed of the fall, I didn't quite catch the song, but there could be no doubt that they were filming a video for a new U2 song. Every now and then he slowed down to perform a long somersault and sing upside down. Finally I gave up following him and lay under a rug on Alexanderplatz. Hrönn smiled at me and was exactly the way she was when we were at college. At the end of the song, Bono slowly floated down to me and perched lightly on my chest. Wearing socks. When Mom wakes me up on the sofa in the living room, I've still got the half-knit sweater on my head.

Mom offers me a trip to Amsterdam. To get rid of me? With Rosy and Guildy. A gay escapade to Amsterdam. Some fourteen-condom package deal from the local travel agent. "Why don't you go along with them? It would do you some good." Lolla's bump is bumping me out of the country. She's seven months gone now. Rosy buys perfume on the plane. We drink it as we fly over the Westman Islands because that's where Rosy is from and it's their feast day, and that's where they first met, through their respective girlfriends. "God, this is good," says Guildy, adding in a quiet aside to me, "Rosy's farts will be smelling pretty good tonight." We laugh like two gays and a straight. I'm in the window seat. The flight attendants are all well over 70,000, even counting the duty-free. I glance at the paper. The new president is being sworn in. Ólafur Ragnar Grímsson. All of a sudden I get the feeling I'll be just like him in twenty years' time. I don't mean I'll be president, but I'll have a face like his. His glasses are quite similar and my old Stray Cats hairdo could well develop into that pillar of democracy he's wearing on his skull. Rosy has an aisle seat and watches everyone going to the WC. He's wearing his bomber jacket, and has green hair these days. No more ring in his nose. Guildy sits between us. The tattoo on his arm seems to have shrunk. Losing weight. He tells me the story about the time he met Bryan Ferry in Amsterdam. Same as the last time he told it. We're well oiled by the time we touch down in Holland. Rosy and Guildy are suspiciously at home in Schipol Airport. Cab it to the hotel. Hotel Rosencrantz & Guildenstern. The coin slowly begins to drop. To me or not to me? The building is a cozy little place about as narrow as the footboard of my bed, and overlooks a broad canal. The boys kiss the helmsman in reception and I browse through the *Gay Guide to Europe*. A special edition on the Belgian sauna-bar scene. My room number is 23, which is a good omen, because Kati came into the world on the same number in July 1969. Rosy wallpaper and a bed that's been fucked to shreds. Bring out the gimp. I sink into the mattress and zap across the fifty-seven channels. Two educational videos about AIDS and the rest is all one big condomless and well-lubricated orgy. This is obviously a very gay hotel. Is Mom trying to gay me up? Of course it would solve everything. If I were to come home with green hair, a ring in my nose, and a face very red from the scratching of a three-day-old Dutch beard. I do manage to find some heterosexual copulation on Channel 52, however, so I stick to that. They look like an outfit of women's libbers at a Vaseline convention. Rosy and Guildy are back in a flash and haul me to the bar. The whole neighborhood seems to be ruled by some Gay Majority. Bare shoulders at the bar. Hefty torsos bulging through short-sleeved T-shirts. A cat's cradle of eye contact. Yeah. It's so much easier to be gay. Get to score every night. The waiter is a black blond, and quite chirpy in spite of the tear tattooed under one of his eyes. They talk to him: "No, we quit the hair business, Rosy is working on a short film and I'm working on a script," and then they say something about him, and how great he looks with blond hair.

We're talking Amsterdam and the foreign smell that permeates the streets, accumulated layers of stagnant air, and it's great to inhale a little bit of darkness after a whole summer of midnight sun. We walk with gaping mouths, in a jet-lagged daze, wading through the ocean of people, checking out the colors. White, black, and yellow.

The air is sweaty and clammy, and I feel like I've stepped into a fat woman's armpit when we turn into the red-light district, where, with a bit of cash, you can step into a real one if you want. There they are, unshaven, splayed in the windows, and we decelerate and take slower drags on our cigarettes, even though I'm sweating like a monk in this mugginess. Still, I'm not about to betray my leather jacket. I'm not going to switch jerseys just because I'm playing away from home. There's a great atmosphere here in the red-light district, where the lights blink XXX in unison with the eyes underneath them: sixteen broads on offer in about as many meters, and the video stores welcome you with a selection of seven thousand types of copulation and everything so user-friendly and well organized like in a library, catering for all tastes: big tits, small tits, no tits, duplex, triplex, quadruplex, channel 1, channel 2, Siamese twins, grannies, mammies, daughters, pregnant chicks, shaven, hermaphrodites, wanks, excretions, golden showers, blow jobs, and then dog flicks, hidden but available behind the curtains, can't help thinking of Parti, this is Parti's Paradise, and suddenly it all feels like Christmas again, merry XXXmas, yeah, wicked place, and a chlorine sperm-killer smell wafts out of the beautiful sex shops, where the stalls have tiled floors and men can wank in peace and quiet, each with his own and in his own way, and the cowshed is mopped at the end of each milking and the farmers smile in the doorways as the cans and tills are filled to the brim, and the red curtains flutter to and fro, and out on the streets handsome dark-brown boys are offering you good shit, and on the corner a brown sugar daddy will sell you a day for a night, whispering like a paperboy on acid: "LSD, Ecstasy . . . LSD, Ecstasy . . ." while the customers shift restlessly on the sidewalk, with their hands in their pockets, stroking their dicks like greyhounds before the start of a race, as they wait for the article of their choice, the one with the tits, the Portuguese one with the tits, and the hookers stand all maternal in the doorways or sit, fat and skimpily dressed, in the windows, with all their baked goods on display, well-kneaded dough, an epiphany that makes you realize, "There's my life, hanging on those two straps stretching around her back," and one smiles at you in such a way with her black Mozambican eyes and gratifyingly white teeth that you can't help but smile back, although you feel like crying and falling on your knees and proposing to her here and now.

The whores are exhausted after a long day in bed. Just one more and that's it for the night, they say to each other, as they swap Marlboro Lights, chatting to each other with a smirk, in a language that's as incomprehensible as the orgasms they've produced today. Foamy guttural sounds. Dutch is such a deep-throat lingo.

Amsterdames are mostly around or over the twenty-thousand mark, but only cost five thousand, definitely a bargain. And even though I'm no guilder mine, I should be able to afford one, but I can't make up my mind. Rosy and Guildy are raring to treat me to three hot Pointer Sisters (3 x 40,000), some coal black package deal. But somehow I don't feel up to any hanky-panky tonight, just enjoying the outdoor life here, wallowing in the bosom of nature.

We drink some Jack up in the room.

"Have you never been with a black bird?" Rosy asks.

"No," I answer dryly.

"We've got to do something about that. That'll be our mission on this trip, to get him to a black bird."

"Yeah, he can't be a real man until he's tried that," says Guildy, taking a sip.

"But isn't it all just the same Miss Pinky?" I say, a little bit too proud of my witty remark.

They sit/lie on the bed. Rosy is in his socks, watching noisy copulations on a TV that's chained to a gibbet high up on the wall, and seems to have dropped out. I'm sitting in an armchair under the box.

"Yeah, yeah, it's all pink on the inside," says Guildy, downing a white pill from a bottle on the bedside table.

"And how does it work? I mean . . ."

"Have you never been to a whore?" says Guildy, taking another sip to swallow the pill. I presume it's something health-enhancing since he isn't passing them around.

"No."

"And don't you want to?"

"I don't know."

"Personally, I prefer to pay for a fuck. It's more clean-cut that way. Take the money and come."

"And what about AIDS and all that? Isn't it . . . ?"

"Yeah, sure. But there's protection. There's always protection. If you don't, you might as well be dipping it into death's mouth."

Says Guildy. Rosy is in a *Rainbow Warrior* T-shirt. He takes his eyes off the screen for a moment to give Guildy a side glance when he's finished talking, his eyes sliding down to his crotch, and then looks back at the screen again. We let our eyes wander round the bedroom. Mine land on the chest of drawers and it feels weird to think there's darkness in those drawers. I take a swig. We take a swig. The bottle's finished. Better traipse back to my room. Still, I have a cigarette.

"Maybe I should just forget about it. You never know with those condoms," I say, thinking of Hofy and striking a match. "Why should you pay someone to kill you?"

They've never heard that one before and both stare at me. Rosy looks at Guildy. Guildy points his index finger at his chest, and nods with a voiceless "Let me know."

"Are you?" I let out in a puff of smoke.

Guildy opens his mouth, as usual, and then the words come out of him, like sounds through an open window, coming from afar, out of a deep dark night:

"Yeah. I'm positive."

The window is half open and a boat can be heard on the canal. Otherwise we could be back in Iceland. In a weird hotel on Baldursgata. I make an exception and look Guildy in the eye, then Rosy, then look at the wall above them. The wallpaper is full of roses. Stone Roses.

I say: "No."

"Yes," says Guildy.

I feel all my hairs standing on end in protest. No, no! No one I know has ever died. Just a few lost fetuses and Dad's multiple deaths. So this is a new one for me. And maybe cos he's still alive. I don't know how to respond, try taking another sip but it tastes of water, ice cubes breathing their last, I try smoking, but only add to the ash I haven't tipped yet. The cigarette is half smoked and turned gray and haggard, as if it had suddenly aged. So Guildy is in the waiting room.

"But how?"

"It was here, just around the corner."

"And what about you?" I ask Rosy.

"I'm clear, as you can see. Why else do you think I've got green hair?"

"Is that what it means?"

"Yep. It means good fuck."

Guildy looks at him.

Me: "And red?"

"Suicidal fuck. Yellow is a casino fuck."

"No."

"Oh no? You don't know how sophisticated this all is, all these rings in the nose and ears, tattoos, they're all a code for something."

"What does a ring in the ear mean?"

"Depends on how many there are, three in the right ear, for example, means you can do it three times in a row, three in the left means you're into threesomes, one in the eyebrow means you like to watch, in the lips that you love to give head, and so on."

I look at Guildy. He's got two rings in his left ear. Rosy has got two on either side.

"And in the nose?"

"That's a sniffer," says Guildy, and then to Rosy, "Show him."

"I'm not sure I can do it right now," says the green-haired one in his Greenpeace T-shirt as he leans over the edge of his bed, pressing his ass against Guildy's nose. They stay there still for a moment and somehow it's beautiful to see what a close and solid couple they are. Guildy with his big nose. Will this be the last of it? His last breath, last bye? Or will he be able to smell the afterlife? No. Guildy. A throwaway soul in a secondhand body. Like the rest of us.

"Isn't it coming yet?" Guildy finally asks.

"Yes," Rosy gasps.

A sound finally oozes out between his back pockets, but a fairly faint one, like the air squeezed out of an empty chocolate-milk carton. Guildy analyzes the smell:

"Yeah. That's Calvin Klein."

We all burst out laughing and I'm thinking he's in the waiting room. His number is up. I stop laughing when I look up at the gibbet, and see some awesome fucking flickering on the screen.

Rosy sets off on a costume hunt in some flea market, has to find some cool yellow dungarees for his short film. I get some time off and prowl back into my wicked neighborhood, walk past thirteen windows three times, with Guildy on my brain. The Pointer Sisters are a real threesome, all right, and remember me. Hi me all up. "Come on, honey!" I ogle the three of them for three seconds as my third leg springs to attention—to hump them or dump them?—but I can't stop thinking of the sixteen Arabs who've shagged them since I was pondering them last night and chicken out of the district with a mixture of relief and pain. That's the problem with whores, those flirtatious smiles are nothing to go by. Hopeless to trust them. All just a question of money. I have a beer and allow my feet to lead me around town, stumble on a Net café.

I log on to my chat room. Luckily, Katarina is on line:

KH: How are you?

How am I? I'm fine.

HB: I'm fine. How are you?

KH: I'm fine. How is Amsterdam?

How is Amsterdam?

HB: I'm not feeling too good.

KH: So are you coming to Budapest?

She's a bit too happy to be alive for my taste.

HB: I don't know.

KH: Actually, I'm leaving tomorrow. I am going to Zurich and then to Paris.

That's my girl, always the same old wanderlust. I could catch up with her in Paris. Paris. This chat perks me up a bit, although somehow I feel even more unemployed so far away from Iceland and am starting to miss my TV a bit too much. I zombie out of the Net café and move my jeans around town, look for the Van Gogh Museum Lolla said was so brilliant, but it's closed by the time I get to the steps. According to the guidebook, he was a totally hopeless loser, couldn't even get his pictures shown at the local mall, and never got a woman without paying for her, even though he cut off his ear for one of them. Which probably wasn't such a smart move. And now it takes fifteen minutes of fame to walk around his monument. The most famous Dutchman ever. It consoles me. I picture my memorial museum back home in a hundred years' time, some futuristic Pompipoo structure, a super-modern fortress. The Hlynur Björn Museum. My Prince packet pyramid in the lobby seven meters high surrounded by old American dames wearing New Age helmets and crystal earrings, wowing their way into the museum in wheelchairs. Some form of immortality. Talk to me then, Lolla. When all your descendants have, in the name of the real father, got cushy jobs at the museum or built lucrative livelihoods on the memory of good old Grandpa. What will Guildy leave behind, other than seven thousand haircuts in graves all over town? Maybe this film script he's working on. People don't really start to live until death comes knocking on their door. When will I start to live? And me, who has always known that I won't just be dead when I die, but that I was also dead before I was born. Life is but a flash in the dark. A blinding flash, with no time to strike an appropriate pose or control what's going on. Hey. Yeah. A blinding flash, and that's why I wear these shades. Just one flash . . . and everyone tries to look really chirpy, all red-eyed with that perennial yes-isn't-it-fun-down-here look. And me, who refuses to smile in photographs. People don't start to live until death knocks on the door. And now he's waiting for Guildy in his limo downstairs. He's given him fifteen minutes to get ready. Will they be his fifteen minutes of fame? Andy. Still living on overtime in his Warhole. He had silver hair. What did that mean? Immortal fuck? Green hair. All that bullshit Rosy came out with yesterday. Mind you, Van Gogh had suicidal red hair. And shot himself like Kurt Cobain in a cornfield. "Do you know what was the last thing that went through Kurt Cobain's head before he died?" Thröstur said. "A bullet." Ha ha. The problem with star suicides is that they always forget to record them. I buy a plastic ear in a joke shop and have it wrapped in gift paper. Through the window of a TV store Carl Lewis can be seen cycling through the air, his 8 meters and 50 centimeters in slow motion at the Olympics in Atlanta. Fame is a flash in slow motion. There's a smell of sauerkraut on every corner here. At the train station I change my notes into a ticket to Paris and feel a bit ridiculous holding it in my hand. Somehow I'm just not myself when I start doing things like this on my own. But it was her suggestion. I haven't looked forward to something this much since Dad promised to move out from us. Things are beginning to look up for Hlynur Björn as he ants out of the station. Some armless colleague stands by a hat by the escalator, I give him the rest of my condoms. It's time for Kati now. And love. But I feel a tinge of guilt up the stairs, what with him being handless and that . . . but figure the ladies will surely give him a hand. Yeah, he'll find some use for those condoms yet. None of my good deeds ever work out. Some drops begin to fall as I step out onto the square, as if they'd been waiting for me. The houses in Amsterdam look like old Icelandic farmhouses on cocaine. Those drops are pretty massive and I keep my mouth closed for safety, just in case of AIDS.

A Thai restaurant and the waiter, a thin-haired cloud of molecules, speaks English. Drooping palms, tigers on the carpet, and a water-fall video on the wall.

"We are three," says Guildy.

"Yes. Smoking section or nonsmoking?"

"Where's the gay section?" I ask, and the Thai man allows his mustache to grow a moment before pulling on it with a smile.

Guildy has to eat well. Orders two main courses. Dieting against death. Rosy gives him the rest of his ice cream. Guildy has to talk.

"It's like waking up from a party with a hangover you just can't shake off. It's like being sentenced to eternal crapulence. It's like having to carry all your fucks around. It's like being pregnant with death. Some wise guy once said that life is nothing but a journey from one dick to another. How did it go again? Yeah. There are two dicks in your life: the one that makes you and the one that breaks you. It would have been different if it had happened with Rosy. Then I would have felt I was carrying him around inside me. Then I could have said I'm dying from love. I love this guy."

They sit facing each other at the table and look into each other's eyes. Rosy puts a hand on Guildy's shoulder. Guildy looks at me again:

"I've never loved another person as much as him. But that other guy . . ."

"Who was it?" I ask.

"Just death himself with a hard-on. No. There's no point in thinking like that. I pity him, really."

"But how. How was it?"

"How was it? Unforgettable. Totally unforgettable," says Guildy, glancing at Rosy, then at me. "I will never forget it. I will always regret it."

Oh yeah. A faint grin on Rosy's face. A faint grin on Guildy's. A faint grin on mine. We all take two sips before I continue:

"And. Have you seen him since?"

"Yeah. Last year. The last time we were here. He sent me a poem. Quite sweet, really."

The waiter approaches to pour red wine into their glasses and I notice Rosy staring at the waterfall pouring relentlessly on the screen on the wall, as if it were immortality itself.

"Would you like another beer?" the waiter asks with a smile, in his slanted accent.

"Yeah."

"Why don't you just have some red wine with us?" Guildy asks.

"No. Light wine just makes me heavy."

"This is really light, have a taste," he says, earnestly handing me his glass. I take it and raise it to my lips, but freeze at the last moment, and suddenly look at Guildy. He knows what I'm thinking:

"It's OK, you know."

"Sure?"

"Yeah. I could stick my tongue down your mouth and you'd still be safe."

I'm not too sure about that. But I feel I have to show some solidarity to my sick friend and take a sip of Guildy's HIV-positive blood. Tastes good. Forgive me for everything, Elsa and Mom, thank you for a pleasant childhood, I shouldn't have given that beggar my condoms, Katarina, I think as I swallow. That's it, then. It's all over.

"Yes, OK, I'll have some of his bl . . . no, some of this," I say to the waiter.

We toast to the scientists. They're bound to find an antidote.

"Otherwise I'll just have to go ahead of you, and wait for you on the other side," says Guildy.

We go to some karaoke place afterward and Rosy gives us an old Sylvester number in his falsetto voice: You make me feel, m-i-ighty real. He's a wicked dancer and steals the show. Two yellow-haired blokes come up to our table afterward.

Guildy gives us a slower number: It's my party and I'll cry if I want to. You would cry too if it happened to you . . . But he's got dry eyes when he comes back to the table. Although green-hair's eyes are looking a bit glossier.

Back at the hotel I go to bed feeling a bit stressed or something and try to have a wank but can't quite get it up—my first wank on foreign soil in five years, or maybe it's because Kati is smiling at me from the blank TV screen. A Hungarian sweater draped over her shoulders. I guess love cramps his style.

I dream of Mom.

Paris is just another one of those homo cities. Gay Paris. But even more ornate. And there's the same dubbing problem here, except that French is even more ludicrous than Dutch. Reminds me of Máni. Wee, heel eh la. Gare de l'Est. What the hell is that supposed to mean? They couldn't even call an exit an exit, but had to call it a "sortie." I step onto a sunny pavement, and for seven or eight minutes I'm totally out of it. I realize I'm alone. No Rosy. No Guildy. I didn't recognize any of the faces on the train, but at least knew we all shared the same destination. I'm alone and have nothing with me but a telephone number. Which is everything. Rikki, don't lose that number.

I'm slightly relieved to see a McDonald's, at least something I'm familiar with, and after spending fifteen minutes in a sex shop I start to feel on top of things again. Somehow you always feel more secure with a hard-on. And even though they don't speak my lingo here, there's something comforting about being in a place where nobody understands you. Back home everybody thinks they understand you but here there's no danger of such a misunderstanding. The pay phone rejects three types of coins and doesn't take a Visa card. I waste two kilowatts of energy working out that there are no corner shops in France and you can buy phone cards only in bars. That is to say bars that also sell cigarettes. And you can't buy a phone card with a credit card. I try to forget about all that for the moment and spend the rest of the day touristing around Paris: check out some famous cash machines. I'm totally lost—I wish the people of Mururoa would conduct some nuclear tests here and clear away some of these buildings so that I might be able to find my way around—and by the time I've finally got some dough in my pocket the tabac bar is closed. But there's bound to be another one open just a bit farther down in the opposite direction. A difficult country. There are chairs on the pavement and most people are still on their coffee breaks even though it's dinnertime. Parisian girls don't wear panty hose. "Owner of a Lonely Heart" by Yes is playing in an open bar. Symbolic? The sidewalks are mercifully narrow and, every now and then, I come across some high-value properties, everything from half a million to one point two, which is the highest yours truly has ever seen, although they're still far from Pamela's price of 4.7. These French women are hot commodities on heels, although they're a bit too petite for my taste. There seems to be a real shortage of breasts in Paris. Just a load of frog-legged birds with tits that barely amount to two mouthfuls. But they look great in clothes. Those French scented candles.

I take the Métro. Into the blue. Into the blue darkness. An old Chinese woman (3,500) sits opposite me. She's got that disheveled look, with ruffled black hair and a phony leather bag on her lap. Her drab baggy dress stretches to her knees and her short legs dangle loosely over the floor. Old Reebok shoes. And one of her thumbs has a broken nail, a splinter of which protrudes over a grayish brown dress. A Chinese woman. I watch her. Whizzing through the world. Her eyes slanting further as she gathers speed, with a weary air and thick, desiccated lips. Who is she? Where is she going? An old Chinese woman. I'm her.

I'm an old Chinese woman.

I'm an old Chinese woman rushing into the blue, the splinter of her nail scratching the air as she moves. Yeah. My life is like a scratch in the air. That ends at the next station.

Following some senseless impulse, I also hop out. I follow the Chinese woman up some religious escalator and I watch her vanish into the multitude. I come to my senses and find a chair on the sidewalk. By some miracle I manage to order a beer. It takes just one drink to shake off the Chinese woman and to rediscover my old self again. And another three, plus four phone calls to contact the Hungarian woman. Her voice is even chirpier than I feared. "A real peach," Mom would say. I suddenly have an accidental vision of them together at the wedding. She wants to meet me in some bar tonight at ten. Holy Kiljan. I desperately need a crash course in human seduction. But instead I just sit out here, sweating on the boulevard in my leather jacket, guzzling beer. Some scented candles at the next table. Some guys puffing cigarettes. Big deal. What a noisy city. Roaring cars, like coffins on wheels, and an endless fashion show on the sidewalk. I check out some of the asses. Some without undies. My razor is in Amsterdam and soon my toothbrush will be in Budapest. Yours truly is turning into a real globetrotter. A flower vendor appears, some Venezuelan mechanic with a beaming smile, and I decide to buy a rose for Katarina, but he doesn't come to my table. Fuck. I'll just have to be me. Pathetic as I am . . .

Pathetic as I am. Le Père Tranquille—everyone does their best to direct me to the bar bearing that unpronounceable name. I do, however, encounter some obstacles on the narrow streets on the way, have to clamber my way around twenty-six pairs of sizable breasts, protruding, half naked, from the doorways. The sex industry doesn't seem to be quite as developed here as it is in Amsterdam, but the whores are considerably prettier and more distinguished, not as whorish somehow, some of them even look respectful enough to run for president back home. I'm relieved for the French nation to see all these big breasts and head for my Net date with renewed optimism. I give the sex shops a miss out of fear that I might bump into Kati as I'm coming out of one of them. "Oh, so you're one of those, are you?" she'd say in Hungarian. Women pretend sex doesn't exist, except for those ninety seconds their orgasms last for. Which might be understandable because they can't even see their equipment without performing an incredible contortion act in front of the mirror. But we men have to walk around with those heavy keys jangling in our pockets all day long. Women against porn. My ass. Holy Hofy was quick enough to shove Thröstur's pecker inside her. Remember I saw it at the swimming pool once. Nothing to write home about. Still, I try not to allow Thröstur's dick to stand in my way as I tackle this multi-colored herd in the pedestrian mall. This is no time to think about him, now that I'm on my way to meet my Hungarian princess.

I've been through the desert on a horse with no name.

I'm ten minutes late by the time I step into the bar and all my blood seems to have rushed home to its heart, which is wildly pounding, but the rest of my body is paralyzed—a peanut in my crotch. I'm struggling to remember my name as I fumble with my glasses there in the middle of the room. The place is kind of filter yellow. Small round tables with lights in red lampshades and white polka dots, very "smoochy," Hofy would say.

A head of dark hair shoots up. And hi! She's smaller than I thought. Kati. But still she strikes 6.2 on my gut's Richter scale when she smiles straight into my eyes. I have to stoop slightly when she wants to kiss me, and like a stupid twat I quickly purse my lips, waiting for her to kiss them. But she pecks me two Hungarian kisses on both cheeks.

"So you're Leaner?"

Word up. Slightly disappointed to see her two friends, male and female, sitting at the table. I greet them before I get a chance to check out the breasts that have been hanging on the other side of the screen and ocean for a whole year. It's difficult to gauge their volume, she's wearing a baggy blue T-shirt with a narrow handbag strap stretching between them like a safety belt. I don't know whether this is hot or cold sweat sliding down my neck and my first cigarette shakes like a seat in a bus. As she explains the reasons for my presence on this planet to her peers I try to chill out a little bit, while I wait for the first figures to come in. She's 50,000. No. She's 60,000. Hungarian is like a language played backward. They take back everything they say. Her buddies are a real drag, total drips. Some chess champion with Elvis Costello glasses and a swimming queen (3,500) with shoulder pads under her skin. A perfect match, though. Still, I feel strangely well listening to them blabbering on in that Lego language of theirs, and stub out my cigarette to be able to start another one that won't shake quite as much, more of a slight tremor, more like a vibrator than a seat on a bus. It's a whole Joy Division trying to work out how Katarina Herbzig gets her lips to get around those words. Her lips remind me of the lips of that French actress who was in *Betty Blue* and make you forget what lips are for.

"Have you been to Paris before?"

"Huh?" I grunt.

"Have you been to Paris before?"

"No."

"How do you like it?"

"I like it. Now."

She's got dark hair. She's got smooth hair. She's got shoulder-length hair. She's got brown eyes. She's got a straight nose. She's got brushed teeth. She's got no cosmetics on her face. She's got dimples. She's a real peach. She's giggly. She's somehow very healthy and normal, but still with a nicely subversive streak. She smokes a Salem cigarette that she plucks out of the air. She's got a few freckles under her eyes and on her nose like specks of chocolate sprinkled on cappuccino froth. She's cute. She's more beautiful than cute. She's a dark-haired sun. She's 60,000, 70,000, 80,000, 90,000 . . . We're talking about a lifelong installment plan here. She's priceless.

I'm in love, I think to myself. I'm freed from the slavery of sex. All the whores in the world can go piss in a bowl. For all I care. I feel a rush of endorphins shooting into my bloodstream from my brain. My hangover's gone and I could cry through my nipples. I could squeeze a smile out of my ribs. Mamma mia. She touches me with her fingertips. She touches the back of my hand with her fingertips. As they blab on. Her touching me touches me. I suffer a minor stroke. Her voice waters me like a withered plant. If I were to buy shares in her laughter I could live on the interest for the rest of my life. Mom, you were so good to me when we lived in Hlidar. When her lips part to reveal her teeth, everything turns white for me and I sink to the bottom of the old municipal swimming pool. I was born in 1962 and it's such a shame. Shame that I spent all those years hanging from the lampposts back home. I want to go home to have a hot shower and a haircut, and then go on a self-healing course, before meeting her again, alone. Hlynur wants Herbzig.

She tells me about her journey. Katarina is the type of girl who takes trains as easily as drags from a cigarette. Nothing is a problem to her. Her life is like a stream. Follows its course effortlessly, all transparent and crystal clear. And me with my dam. My damned dam. I can feel my shoulders are about to yield here in this bar in Paris, there are two megatons of sour dirty water pressing against my back, I can feel the dam is about to burst. The stream and the dam on a date. She senses the pressure:

"You look different than what I had imagined."

"Yes?"

"Yes. You look like an iceman. An iceman from Iceland," she says, and laughs like the love of my life. "So different from what you write to me. You have everything inside. When I look at you I could never see that you make me laugh. I always like what you write. Some people are like that. You are an inside person. I like that."

"Yes?"

"Yes."

"Well, I stay inside a lot."

She laughs. Hofy would have asked, "What do you mean?" I feel like I've really made it overseas. Picture the headlines: "Provoked Laughter in Parisian Bar." This is all moving in the right direction.

There are empty cappuccino cups on the table. The waiter appears with a Oui? on his face. Looms over us impatiently as we fall under the spell of his masterful mustache. The espresso machine burps darkness into the cups in the background and outside the Man Upstairs is pouring night into the heavens. My face is reflected in the window and we're surrounded by smoking magpies, sunburned Camels and Winston-puffing au-pair types, I'm not even price-tagging them anymore, even though there's some Holmenkollen kitten (80,000) sitting at the next table. The waiter is changing into Moses on the Mount, awaiting our commandments. I feel like a beer but I point at Kati's cup and she orders for me "on café, silver plates." I'll lay out my life for her on a silver plate.

"Nemi works for a computer company in Budapest," my peach tells me. Nemi.

"Oh yes?" My brain is chockablock with love and can only produce a yes. Smile like a twit. Nemi asks me in a strong accent:

"How do you do?"

"I'm fine," I answer and they all laugh. He persists:

"No, I mean work. How do you work?"

I try to define my occupation as glamorously as possible.

"I'm my own company."

Throws the Hungarians a bit, then Nemi with his Costello glasses:

"Hum? What kind of company?"

"Computers and collection."

The swimming queen's name is Julia:

"I hear you have a woman president in Iceland?"

"Yes. We have one president for the women and one for the men."

"What about the gays?" Katarina teasingly asks and I want to ask her to marry me, but laugh instead. The others don't laugh. From this moment onward we're together. A loud Yes! resounds in the depths of my soul.

"And there are no trees in Island?" the chess player asks. Island Records. Remember my sister, Elsa. The first LP she bought. I'm on an Island. The Kinks. OK. I'm from "Island."

"No, no. We have some trees, but it's true, it is hard to see them. They're not together. Icelandic trees are not very sociable."

A light introduction to the homeland. I'm doing quite well and head for the toilets and see a phone there, and am going to ring Mom to ask her to book a wedding reception room, but the phone doesn't take cards and I hose the hole in the floor. Yeah. This is a primitive country. The beer comes in stupid little glasses (oon demee). No Prince. No cocktail sauce. No ketchup on your chips. No corner shops. No video rental stores. No tits. No men's toilets. Just for the homos. Hommes, they call it. And not even a toilet. Just a hole. And then they pretend to be really with it with their nuclear tests. Nevertheless I try to give them some development aid by hosing down the French skidmarks around the hole. With compliments from "Island." If sweet Kati weren't sitting out there I'd just puke all over this town. All those artsy-fartsy decorations and that chichi crap you see on every railing, can't even find a simple honest doorframe in this 600-million-door city, a mega-budget film set for those mustachioed noses in size 39 shoes sipping on red wine, which seems to be the national occupation around here. France. The greatest flop in the history of cinema. They haven't even managed to produce one half-decent band. At least the Germans had Kraftwerk. Deepardew in Hollywood. My ass. No wonder Cantona fled this country. But they've got the climate, I'll say that for them. The streets are room temperature and you can wear a short-sleeved T-shirt if you're in a queer enough mood for it. I add a black leather jacket, a white turtleneck, and Icelandic presidential glasses with dimmers to this hopeless ocean of T-shirts. We saunter out and my girl is wearing a short skirt and untitled low-heel canvas shoes: there's a boy in those legs of hers and her sweet little bag dangles over one of her buttocks and I wouldn't mind doing the same. My eyes flutter away from her ankles on butterfly wings as we walk toward something magnificent, and she is remarkably light on her feet, considering she's up to her knees in my love. "Where are we heading?" I ask rather dramatically, as if I were asking her what direction my life was taking. I read some answers on some passing T-shirts: "University of Illinois"—"Yokohama Yachting Club"—"Doubter's Choice, The Biggest Menu in America, 6014 Riverside Drive, Hamlet, Nebraska"—"Aarhus Children's Theater Festival '96"— as they parley on in Hungarian. Some big-time fountain is spurting in the next square, surrounded by a roar of skateboards. We rest on some stone thing with a McDonald's logo in view and I slip yet another cigarette into my mouth. Only one left. I accidentally end up sitting beside Julia and suffer fifteen minutes of questions about tree cultivation in Iceland. "But they are planting. They are planting," I say like a boring tourist brochure and watch some transvestite from Nowherekistan mimicking Michael Jackson in front of twenty-seven people. "Beat It" beating out of his tweeter-blown ghetto blaster. And two totally unnecessary lives holding hands in front of us. All these people who are total unknowns and are doomed to remain so. The Hlynur Björn Museum. I pity these foreigners. They don't speak Icelandic and they have to squat to shit into a hole. Don't even have lesbian mothers. I must say, this swimming queen is getting a bit flirtatious. She's asking me for my address.

"It's Hlynur Björn Hafsteinsson, Bergthórugata 8b, Reykjavík, Iceland."

"Is there no postal code?"

"Oh yes. It's one-o-one Reykjavík," I say, and looking at the last drag on my Marlboro with a yellow filter I think of Timer and start to feel homesick.

I'm about 200 kilos heavy by the time Katarina finally stands up and I get a chance to see her from the point of view of the child we'll have together and who'll be called Jörgen, strange as it may seem. She looks into my eyes, that is if she can see them through my shades, and I haven't a clue what she's thinking.

And I haven't a clue what she's thinking. We walk and she tells me about her dad, who works in the tax something, and her mom, who used to be an actress, and her sister, who is slightly handicapped, and she fills me in on the most recent models of Hungarian wheelchairs, and I tell her about Dad, who works in an accounts something, and Mom, who used to be the hottest thing in Húnathing, and my sister, who has a handicapped husband, and fill her in on the miscarriage, but leave out all the Lolla lesbian bit. Then we talk about Björk for two hundred meters. And now we've reached the hotel they're staying in and they come toward us and the four of us stand there under the luminous sign and I want to rip the fender off the car beside us right there and tell her pals to get the hell into their hotel rooms and play their fucking water chess, but I don't do that, instead I just say, "Yes," when she says, "It was nice to see you," and "Me?" when she says, "Where are you staying?" and "OH OH" as she kisses both my cheeks and "Bye-bye" as she vanishes into the hotel with her fucking half-wit friends. She stretches my feelings through the open glass door and when she disappears from view they snap back on my face like a pair of suspenders, with stereophonic pain. I look up at the sign. Hôtel des Hommes. Ouch.

The time in Homo City is 00:23 and the houses on this street are from the same year. Shutters down on all the stores. I listen to the squeaking of my leather jacket. And obey. Wake me up before you go go. The sidewalks are lined with those short brown posts. I kick a few. I just wasn't prepared for that. I wasn't prepared for anything. Dead man walking. Faint female groans can be heard through a window on some top floor, pre-orgasmic groans. I stop to listen and take out the last cigarette in the pack, smoke my last cigarette on this globe. Then we'll just have to see if there's life on other planets. Smoke me up before I go go. Just another eleven drags and it'll all be over. The only question is how. Facing technical problems here in the depths of this Parisian night. The only thing I can think of is to crawl under this Citroën and give the exhaust a blow job and wait like that until dawn. Nah. Here comes a pedestrian—some Turkish Buddha—and I stall him and ask:

"Excuse me, but could you kill me?"

He doesn't understand. Just pricks up his eyes, instead of his ears.

"Execute. Could you execute me?" I reiterate.

"Execuse?" he says in a deep voice.

I grab his thick hands and am about to put them around my throat when there's a sudden hostility from him and he shoves me aside. I drop onto the hood of a car. He yells some alibaba at me and punches me in the stomach, sending me rolling between the cars and I say, "Yes! That's it! More! Kill me!" He kicks me just for the hell of it, my shins and knees, and pontificates in some obscure language. I remain silently still. Then he waddles off.

I lie motionless on the street between the cars, under the ever louder sound of copulation on the top floor. And realize I'm not quite ready to leave yet. It was a misunderstanding. The panting pulls me up from my wannabe grave. A strange sensation takes hold of me as I listen to these sounds. So these limp-dick winos can actually do it. Remember Óli and that girl, naked in the double bed in Gra- farvogur. I wipe the dribble off the side of my mouth. A slight ache in my stomach and knees. Those massive Turkish fists.

I stumble to my feet, clutch my stomach, bend over the car hood, cough. She's not going to come, that one on the fourth floor. That wailing woman. All of a sudden I remember the ear I bought in Amsterdam and realize I'll never see her again and she's leaving tomorrow, and, and.

I ask for Herbzig in reception. No phones in the rooms. He tells me to just go on up. Room number 18. My birthday '62. Well, well. The Aquarian comes limping up the stairs. It would be easier for me to kill myself than knock on this door. A Hungarian voice within. "It's me," I say, and mean it. Her nose sticking out of the doorway. That nose that I . . . "Can I talk to you alone?" "OK, wait." She's in a knee-length white nightshirt when she closes the door behind her. We stand in the awkward narrow corridor with its bloodred carpet and pissy yellow wallpaper. "I wanted to give you this," I say, handing her the parcel. She smiles tenderly and turns serious as she loosens the string from the wrapping paper, which is slightly crumpled after the train journey and a long day in the big city. It's a man's ear in skin-colored plastic, about the right weight too. There is obvious wonderment under that hair that she sweeps off her forehead with a movement and expression that I could watch over and over again on videotape. She blows the last two meshes of her hair off the side of her nose and then looks at the ear again in the palm of her hand and starts to giggle. Sandra Bul- lock interviewed on Sky. I give a faint smile and she turns serious again as she looks up at me. Her eyeballs are two galaxies. There, somewhere on a lonely planet, lies my life.

I tell her about Van Gogh, quietly purring.

We're sitting on the soft-carpeted stairs, she above—in a cozy pose with her nightshirt over her knees, and her hands over them, and her toes all huddled together, there are ten of them, my top-ten list, and two centimeters from the knee kicked by the Turk, footprints on my trousers—when all of a sudden I just don't care whether I'll live another fifteen minutes and say, as if I were uttering my last words, "I love you," except that at the last moment they change into:

"I like you."

But she understands. Leaves fall on her face and her eyes grow a thin film, like two beautifully oil-colored puddles of water on a street after a gentle frost. She stiffens and stares down at her knees. Her face vanishes into her hair. A few gulps here. A hotel silence. A crinkle from my leather jacket. Her face has lost one dimple when she looks up at me and says, with hair on her cheek:

"I am sorry."

She repeats herself after two pregnant minutes:

"I am sorry."

Then: "I like you, too, but . . ." I wait, but nothing comes after the but. I say, "What?" She says, "I, well, I, I have a boyfriend." It turns out the chess player is her boyfriend. Spock. And Mom. Spock and Mom together at a wedding on Krypton. This is followed by a lowdown on her previous relationships, warm words about me and many thanks for my e-mails. In between: silences loaded with a lot of deep breaths. The Icelandic ones being 50 percent deeper. Then Nemi's voice sounds behind the door and she says, "I have to go now." "Yes." But she says, "Wait!" as she springs up like the accelerated image of a white cotton flower in a Discovery Channel documentary. I sit there with all my teeth. She comes back and I stand up, feel the pain in my stomach again. She hands me a tube of toothpaste with a smile. "The only thing from Hungary I have for you." She's a genius. "Great. You're so . . . you're . . . Thank you." We laugh like siblings. Then she becomes serious and droops her eyelids, half closing her eyes. There is a certain distance between her eyelashes and the corners of her eyes. A whole life's journey. Domed eyelids, like the earth's surface. Life's journey. And I try to approach these globes in my space capsule, like some *Apollo 13*: it's no easy feat to approach her atmosphere from an angle of 8 degrees, one bad maneuver and they'll burn up before establishing contact with her. Tom Hanks.

"Goodbye," she says, stressing the "good." It's a goodbye. I just say, "Yeah." She kisses me on the mouth and it's a softener softer than anything to be found on this planet, or even in outer space, for that matter. Captain Kirk having a massage on Krypton. My last words leak out of my mouth like honey:

"How do you say 'yes' in Hungarian?"

"*Igen.*"

She says it with a sudden smile, as I watch her move down the corridor. Two heavy bronze church bells echo deep inside me when I feel how her loose breasts gently sway in front of her. She turns the handle and her head, smiles, and then closes the door behind her. The door closes with a double muffled sound. Like two cracking vertebrae.

It's 2:30 and I'm out on the street, with nothing but my life and a half-squeezed tube of Hungarian toothpaste in my hands. Odol Magyar Fogkrem. Pharmacies in Paris all have a blinking green cross. Can't figure out these opening hours, but I need something. Fogkrem? Fog cream? Hungary was always yellow on the map of Europe in our atlas. There was a touch of yellow to her English accent. The woman on the top floor come and gone. I walk toward another life. I guess my knee hurts. Guildy has AIDS. Good for him. At least he knows which way he's heading. I want to die from something that should be good for you, like love or vitamins. So it was Nemi. At least I came close. A goal chance. But I was offside. A Benz with a taxi light echoes down the street. The lights are out in all the windows. Don't understand how people can be content to sleep in this dump all their lives. Lots of sideburns here in Paris. Which is understandable. Nothing else to do. *Apollo 13.* They came back to the earth safe and sound. But never made it to the moon. I never made it to the moon.

There it is.

I should have said it. I couldn't say it. I've never said it. "I love you"—still, doesn't sound quite as crass in English as it does in Icelandic. Maybe it wouldn't have made any difference. It's all over. I've got nothing ahead of me. *Igen*. I wander. That was it. Only darkness. Everything is black. And so is she. She (15,000) stands on the street corner with a B-52 on her head, and her teeth light up like a sign in the night when she says seven words that I don't understand but know what they mean. Fat in a tight dress. Her eyes have that bloodshot dopish glaze. Her high heels resonate down the street as I traipse after her. Following my teacher to the headmaster's office. I'm limp-dicking behind her, down a narrow corridor. I limp-dick up a narrow staircase. Her ass leads a life of its own, has its own personality, maybe even soul. Third floor. The room is a cabin with brown-carpeted floors, walls and ceiling. An airless pussy lined in fur. Many a good man has come here, and then gone. She turns her back to me and takes a sip out of a plastic bottle. Or they do, I should say. She and her ass. She unzips herself at the back. Everything is brown here except for the toilet, which stands beside an ancient mattress dating back to the days of the French Revolution. Everything else is brown. Her skin, the carpet, the mattress. Yeah, it's more like walking into an asshole. The ass is incredible. I must say. You could read a Bible on it. Six thousand krónur for that alone. Which means that she's only 9,000 herself, and she turns, with her beehive hair and stark naked, although she's still wearing her bra and shoes. She points at my clothes. Yes, that's true. I'm still wearing them. I guess I have to take them off. I sense her grin as I climb out of my trousers. She's crouched over a toilet or bee-day thing, sprinkling herself, as I continue to undress. The cabin brightens slightly by the time I've undressed and even more when she holds out her empty palm to me. I bend over my trousers to look for some notes to put in it. About five thousand Icelandic krónur. So I'm making a profit of ten. She puts the note away and sits on the mattress. She's incredibly nimble at slipping a pink condom on to my limp dick. Particularly considering that her green nails are seven centimeters long. She gets down to work. It's about as exciting as watching her blow up a pink balloon. Her hairdo feels strangely hard when I touch it to free myself from her. She looks up with lips as big as a doughnut. Hugh Grant. I pull the condom off and lie on the bed. She looks at me and the little white she has in her eyes glitters, surprised, but then sluggishly bends over me with all her reels of skin. One of her breasts slips out of her bra and squeezes against my glasses for a moment like an airbag on a windscreen in an accident. I feel her nails scratching me around my capital area as she tries to get him up. I detect three abusive substances in her eyes. I close my eyes and concentrate on her ass—and, as it happens, Hofy's tits, Lolla on the carpet—until I get a full hard-on.

Tonight he's as long as her name: K a t a r i n a.

She offers me access to her rear tunnel but I've never traveled that way before and have had enough of this darkness for the moment so I stick to the regular route.

The night is black but pink on the inside. She doesn't care that I took off the condom. So. This is like sticking him into a breeding lab for AIDS. Which is the whole point. Out of the pussy wert thou begotten and into the pussy shalt thou return. This is like fucking Helmut Kohl, she's so fat. She gasps, "Hugh." I grunt, "Grant." Earrings of plastic gold. This is like finally meeting your childhood love. Finally, finally. We're good together. Black bread, white bread.

On the pink bottom of the night a hard-on me, and somewhere high up in the heavens above me, on the white sands of the moon, there's the shadow of an American flag. From the pussy to the moon. From the pussy to the moon mankind flew on NASA wings and now I'm on my way back. Into a black hole. Into a black woman's hole.

The problem with whores is that, even though you pay for it, you have to do all the work yourself. They could give you a little bit more service. I come pretty promptly and lie on top of her. She wriggles a bit underneath me but I keep him stuck inside her to make absolutely sure I catch AIDS. Between the pussy and the moon. My ass. She tries to wriggle again but I cling to her with all my might. This is turning into a wrestle. But she's strong and I finally fall off this mountain of black flesh. Between a hooker and a hard wall. A slight turbulence on the mattress as she stumbles to her feet. I think I hear her leaving the room.

On the lowest deck of night a naked me, nestling into a fetal position, feeling very HIV-positive with goosebumps and glasses and dope juice on my dick in a dark cell lined with sperm and the porthole has vanished out of sight, pink and wet. The ship is pulling out of the harbor. MS *Night*. Sailing around the earth, crossing all oceans and continents every twenty-four hours. From now on I'm a passenger of the night and think of how Mom will take care of me when I start shedding all those kilos and the doctors will hook me up to a drip. In the dark pocket of a leather jacket on the floor lies concealed the only light in my life, crammed into a tube.

I'm lying up against the carpeted wall and out of my ears you can hear the faint old sound of a recording from the fifties: good old Haukur Morthens, singing his Capri Katarina: Katarina, Katarina, Katarina is my girl. I doze off.

To be woken up by cursing green nails.

I add two weeks to my face.

Lolla is still working on her bubble. Eight months gone now. The number-one bubble in town. This one is no phantom. Looks like this thing inside her is actually going to have a face. But what amazes me the most is how her skin can still hold it. She still goes to work, too, and bounces over to some prenatal do every day. The Akranes stud comes for a visit, does his daddy bit around Lolla while Mom makes some coffee. Everyone is being so understanding. I sacrifice almost an entire episode of *Star Trek* to come into the living room. His name is Stebbi Stef. Stefán Stefánsson I guess must be his full name. I was expecting some dark-haired center-forward but this sperm donor turns out to be a semen blond. A real Norwegian kind of guy. He's slightly taller than I am, by about three centimeters, which probably made all the difference inside Lolla's tunnel. We greet each other like true fucks-in-law. Eyeing each other under the belt.

"Hlynur, Berglind's son," says Lolla tenderly.

"Nice to meet you," says the sperm donor from Akranes.

"Hi."

He's wearing those berg-in-socks sandals. Newly washed pre-washed jeans and a light sports jacket; incredible. I reckon he's about thirty, counting the jacket. Stebbi Stef is far too nice for my taste. But kindergarten teachers would probably call him hand-some. He could act in a Viking movie, as long as he didn't have to open his mouth, or he could run one of those trendy horse-rental services, although he looks more like the type of guy who likes to be ridden than a rider. Equine thighs when he sits down. A healthy country face straight out of an Icewool brochure and he's sand-blasted his brain with a hair dryer. He obviously has nothing to say. But Lolla seems to think otherwise:

"So what have you got to say for yourself?"

He says something, but it's difficult to say what. His hair some-how seems more interesting than the rest of him put together. But he doesn't have a country accent, sounds more Norwegian. It turns out that he studied there. Landscape gardening. Exactly. Exactly the type of guy who has absolutely no purpose in society but who can be good to have around. To turn to. If we ever need spare blood or organs. He has nothing to give but seed. The perfect sperm donor. A sly stroke of genius on Lolla's part. The crafty witch. She chose one with a blank screen to make sure her offspring got all her soft-ware. They muse on possible names for him. Lolla likes Halldór, in memory of her father. Mr. Stud doesn't seem to have any opinions on the matter. I keep my trap shut and just look at her bump and then at his crotch. I can't picture any connection between those two. At least, nothing like the connection between me and Mom. Mom presses the liberal pedal down to the max and gives Stud Steven-son a far too generous smile:

"And of course you know you'll always be welcome here," she says, pouring more coffee into his cup.

"Yes, thank you very much," he answers with a demure smile, and pours himself some milk. It rises in the cup like cold sperm in boiling blood. All of a sudden my mouth opens:

"So have you been doing this for long, then?"

"This?" he says.

"Have you done it before?"

Lolla looks daggers at me over the coffee table and I quickly try to shield myself with an innocent idiotic smile. The Midnight Cowboy freezes in mid-sip, puts his cup down, and adjusts his sports jacket with a humorless smile:

"You mean . . . You mean if I have any children? No, this is my first."

"You're not thinking of making a career of this, then?" I persist.

"Nooo, I think that'll do for the moment, one is enough," he says, and laughs as if no one had ever said that before.

"You're very interested in all this all of a sudden, Hlynur," says Lolla, pregnant with subtext.

"Yeah."

"Perhaps you'd like to ask him how he did it?"

General laughter.

"You should try it sometime. It's great fun," she bloody well adds. More laughter.

"It's not that. It's not that I haven't tried," I say with Mom's eyes on me.

"And nothing happened?" Lolla continues.

"Well. Of course there's no way of knowing how many women one has inseminated around town."

"Really? Is that true?" Mom asks in all innocence. I'm silent for a moment before turning back to the Akranes gigolo:

"No. I was just thinking about Mom, if she wanted to get pregnant again, would you be willing to—"

"Are you out of your mind? You must be joking," Mom snaps, bursting into a giggle.

"No. You might have another one in you yet," I say.

"Hlynur is a really funny guy," Lolla explains to the studman, who sits staring at me like a landscape gardener.

"No, no. I was just wondering what it's like to be a sperm donor," I say when Mom has stopped laughing and Lolla has stopped smirking. It's difficult to gauge whether Mr. Stud has fully grasped the meaning of my last sentence.

"Sperm donor . . ." Lolla intones.

"Yeah. Or what else are they called? Inseminators? Or . . ." I stop myself from saying pussy plumbers. A pregnant silence hits the room. We sit there like a bizarre family, the three of us like a bunch of albinos that have become so degenerate that they can no longer propagate themselves, like the three last dinosaurs chatting to the kindhearted scientist, Stud Stevenson, who has come to save their species from extinction.

"It's obviously a great job," I continue, trying to lighten the atmosphere in the living room.

"Yes. Well, of course you're unemployed, Hlynur. Might be something for you," says Lolla.

"Yeah. A real dream job."—I look at the donor—"What do you get . . . ?"—I look away from him—"What do they pay for something like that?"—Doesn't go down too well—"Do you people have some kind of association or something?"—A very heavy silence—"I mean, like a trade union? Or is it more of a freelance kind of thing?"

End of my speech. Hardly worth mentioning the response I get. Mr. Stud coughs. Lolla stares at the coffeepot. I pour myself some coffee.

Mom: "And how is it? Are there many landscaped gardens up in Akranes?"

I can't make up my mind. I can't make up my mind whether I've been hoping that Lolla will screw up on this pregnancy because he's the father or I am. I don't know which would have been worse. I hate him. Mr. Stud. Yeah. I hope he isn't the father. I hope he isn't the father just as much as I hope I'm not the father. I hope that. Yeah. Or what? Maybe it's no big deal to have a child with your own mother. But still. No. He's a gelding. Yeah. His sperm stiffens like wax. He waters his seedless flower in the showers of the Akranes swimming pool. They had tried and tried. But there's no point in pondering over that now. It's all over and done with. Or what? Is Timer a real wacko or a real wizard? They say he managed to detox the Puffin.

I'm standing in the National Bank of Iceland in Bankastræti. I've been standing here for a quarter of an hour. I think. Saw Lolla coming down Laugavegur. Couldn't look her in the face. After what I did. After what happened. There are people here cashing in and cashing out. I threw the little I had into Lolla's bank. No withdrawals allowed. "Not to shortchange anyone," the cabbie said. I walk out, and back in again. The security guard is there with his keys. He's about to lock up. I should get him to lock me into a safe. Lodge myself in. The guard asks if I've concluded my business. He escorts me to the door. On the steps I don't know whether I should venture home or walk into the sea. I walk up to the K-bar. I comfort myself with the hope that I might have picked up AIDS on my Paris trip. "It might take a short while to work," Timer said. The problem with AIDS as a suicide method is that it takes such a long time to work. Now I have to wait three months, just to get it confirmed. All that red tape. Just like this "abortion." It takes time to work. In fact, this isn't exactly suicide, more like an overdue abortion. Death is just a long-overdue abortion. Incredibly overdue abortion. In a hundred years' time everybody here on Laugavegur will have been sent off. There will be a whole new crowd walking down this street. Someone darts past me as if that was life. Suddenly worry about the possible wording of my death notice on the radio:

Our beloved son, father, brother, brother-in-law, and fuck-in-law, Hlynur Björn Hafsteinsson, passed away at the National Hospital on March the third. The date of the funeral will be announced later.—Berglind Saemundsdóttir, Lolla Halldórsdóttir, Halldór Stefánsson, Hafsteinn Magnússon, Elsa Hafsteinsdóttir and Magnús Vidar Vagnsson and children.

Magnús Vidar Vagnsson . . . Preposterous to think of him coming anywhere near my death. I forget the senile grannies. Else Helsinore or Helsingör and Thurídur . . . Can't remember Granny's patronymic.

How does one die?

"It takes a life to die," Guildy said.

I walk into the bar. Australian hens fly off the screen. I sit beside Timer. He's more remote than usual. Under some kind of spell. I ask him if it would be possible to halt the procedure. His cigarette wobbles.

"No need to. It's gone through."

"No. I mean. To stop it."

"Stop it?"

"Yeah."

"Impossible. The point of no return will not return."

Homer Simpson. I return to Timer the leather hocus-pocus thing he gave me and then go into the restroom and puke into the toilet. I don't know why I'm puking. Haven't eaten since. Since. I'm puking my soul out. Two tears ooze out from under my glasses. Tears and puking. That's how I feel. Elsa, Hofy. Now Lolla. Climax Blues Band. I dry myself with toilet paper and manage to slip out of the bar unnoticed. But at least I don't have to pay until "it happens." Just hope I'm not around when it does. That I've been wiped away by AIDS by then. Nah. It's all a load of bullshit. I've never been an accomplice to so much crap in all my life. That wasn't me. Or what's become of me? I'm not exactly saving very pleasant memories these days. It's been two days now since.

Thröstur gave me some E and then came F, G, and H: My First Glimpse of Hell.

The memories come flooding back to me. The abortion over the phone. . . .

On my ninetieth minute on xtc I shoot over to his table and say, "OK, now or never," and he says, "Yeah, yeah." We arrange to meet at his place at 4 A.M., but first I've got to go home to Bergthórugata and "set up the access." They're fast asleep when I bubble into their room with soda in my soul, and set the phone under the bed, place the receiver on the floor, facing upward, straight toward the bump, following his instructions to the letter, and then put down this magic gadget Timer gave me, a small weathered-leather box said to contain the gall bladder or kidney stone of some ninety-something-year-old Indian who was buried in a sunbeaten desert in the state of Arizona many moons ago. Then I snake out from under the bed again and dash down to Grettisgata, where Timer lives in a red room with a motorbike hanging on the ceiling. Getting to see his place is one of the extra bonuses of this deal and I give myself time to take in the atmosphere by scanning the objects on the wall.

Waldorf is a bit like Timer himself, only thinner. A deluxe bald monk in a white suit, he gives us a poster smile through his ZZ Top beard from the backseat of a white limousine. He is wearing violet glasses and a ring as he waves a blessing out the window. About sixty-four years old. Away from the poster: in the corner there's a Lincoln Continental grille with a fender on the floor. In front of it a can of car polish, some rags, and a row of candles. An altar. Let the candles burn. Or. All you can do is polish your car. Polish your car.

I ask him about the motorbike in the air, hanging in seventeen parts.

"It's a Kawasaki."

"No, I mean, how come it's all dismantled and hanging in the air?"

"The motorbike is speed."

"Right."

"How fast do you think it can go?"

"A bike like that? I dunno. Three hundred."

"Three hundred kilometers per hour. Speed. It's hanging in the air. Dismantled. Outer peace."

He says, pottering around a shelf. He's a head smaller than I am and two thighs wider. His trousers droop over his bulging ass, looking strangely incongruous in this immaculately polished studio flat.

"You're agitated. You need to Zen out before we start. Want some charlie?" he says, brandishing a small plastic bag in his hand. I don't mention the E I've taken but he's already worked that one out. Yeah. He knows what he's doing, I think to myself, sitting on the leather sofa. He sits in something similar. A glass table between us. Everything is so plush and spic and span here, everything from his sparkling bald head to the designer kettle on the kitchen counter. At least, I presume that's a kettle. We snort some charlie. It makes my blood pump even faster, but he was probably right, I'm calmer somehow. This is like driving a car at 100 kph and then going up to 150. You somehow get pinned to your seat and everything becomes strangely still. A very high-velocity stillness. The motorbike assembles above my head and starts to expand with a terrifying noise, wheels spinning in the air. We sit there for twenty minutes, listening to that. Although I get the feeling Timer has fallen asleep in the chair opposite me. Then:

"How far gone did you say she was?"

"Seven months. Or seven months and two weeks."

"Yeah. It could be tough. Could be tough."

He blows through his charlie nostrils. Then picks up a cordless phone. And asks me as he's holding it: "And you put the phone under the bed? With the receiver facing upwards?"

"Yeah."

He dials a number, but I don't think it's Mom's and I'm about to interrupt him when he says down the phone: "Timer . . . Yeah . . . Are you ready, then? . . . Later . . . Before five."

He hangs up, stands up with difficulty, and draws the heavy black curtains over the window. It's a bit dark. I drop out for a moment. The motorbike decelerates over our heads. I can't see properly with all this noise. Take my glasses off. Put them back on. My cigarette has vanished. By the time I spot it again Timer is sitting in front of me with seven beers. I think. The white froth is like a glow in this darkness.

He asks: "You know that guy with the goatee beard, don't you?"

"Thröstur? Yeah?"

"What kind of a guy is he?"

"He never lets a friendship come in the way of a good fuck."

"Yeah, figures. What's her number?"

I give him Mom's number. He dials. Listens. Looks at me with weary, accusing eyes.

"The line's busy."

"No, that's impossible. They're both asleep."

"They?"

"Yeah. Mom and Lolla . . ."

"Mom? Your mom? Is it your mom?"

"Yeah. Well."

"And Lolla?"

"No, she's . . . She's staying with her, you see."

"I see."

"Maybe you dialed the wrong number. Try again."

I say. He tries again. Busy again. I don't understand. But he understands. You can rely on Timer. Although I have some doubts when he says:

"There's a problem. The phone's off the hook. It's been a while since I did this. You've got to hurry back up there. Wait for me to phone."

I'm pretty fast getting back up there, thanks to some help from charlie, but the key and the lock are obviously not on the same stuff I'm on. A slight hitch that slows me down. I look up at the morning sky. I know I don't know what I'm doing: an abortion on Mom's girl-friend performed by Dr. Strangelove down a telephone line, but sometimes a man has to take the bull by the horns, especially when his whole life is at stake. I say to someone way up there over Mom's roof. Not.

I crawl under Mom's bed like some fetus hunter, place the receiver on the hook, and crawl back out, holding the phone. Abba. The phone rings in the middle of the floor. I pick it up as swiftly as I can. But Mom springs up on her bed. As I say hello to Timer she says "What?" to me.

The situation is as follows:

Mom sits in bed and stares at me, all confused, in the pale twi-light as I lie in my black leather jacket halfway across the floor, talk-ing down the phone at five-thirty in the morning. High on charlie and xtc and newly converted to the limousine fold. Not my most cherished moment. She hears me say:

"You phoned a bit too soon."

"Hlynur," she says, with a phone number in her eyes. A shrink's phone number. Duvet sounds from Lolla in the background.

"Hang on a sec," I mutter to Timer, switching my voice to dam-age-control mode, as I say to Mom: "Wrong number. You left the phone in here."

"Where were you? Were you just coming in?"

"Yeah."

"What time is it?"

"The wrong time."

"Why don't you just go to bed?"

"Yeah."

I apologize my way out of the room with the phone and shut myself off. I've shut myself off. Blown my last chance. I explain the situation to Timer.

"I see."

The silence that ensues is a bit uncomfortable, considering that this phone call was supposed to cause a fetus to eject. I hold the receiver at a safe distance in case my brain ejects instead. Timer's whispers resound through the black plastic like a very long distance call from hell. The devil with a sore throat:

"There is one thing we could do. Do you have any equipment?"

Equipment? Forceps?

"What kind of equipment?"

"A hi-fi."

"A stereo? Yeah."

How does a stereo come into this? This abortion lark is getting to be a little bit too far-fetched for me.

"Couldn't we just do it tomorrow?"

"Tomorrow? No, no. I've already invoked the Organist. It's Operation Desert Storm now. This is the point of no return."

"The Organist?"

"You'll see."

I end up turning the speakers in my room toward the couple's bedroom and taping the receiver to a mike I have and connecting that to the amplifier. "Have it on full volume," Timer said. I wait there for some sound to come out. Some totally bizarre Indian whine. Piteously faint. Obviously some magic incantation. I stoop over the taped microphone and receiver and say, "OK, I can hear you," slightly taken aback by the full blast of my voice through the speakers.

"If anything this will work even better," he says. "Bang and Olufsen never lets you down."

I'm back down in the darkness of Grettisgata. Slightly out of breath. But still I'm not quite as wheezy as Timer, who is still sitting in his chair, really busy poking a needle into the beer glasses. Bursting all the bubbles. Has to get all the froth out of the beer. Has to be totally flat. According to Waldorf's instructions. I thought this was meant to be a purely Indian operation, not something conducted from a white limousine. But I've stopped bothering about all that now. As long as it works. This abortion was brought to you by Bang

& Olufsen. Danish technology, never lets you down. Maybe we could sell them this idea for an ad. "Abortive sound." The cordless phone lies on the glass table over a cassette player from the Middle Ages marked Sony. The Indian drone sounds a bit louder here. I take a seat. The motorbike is hanging in seventeen pieces again and my blood circulation has decelerated down to a legal 90 kph.

I notice Timer is now topless. Although I can't really make out the cartoon strip tattooed to his chest, which is reputed to be the best tattoo in town. I remember him showing it at Guildy and Rosy's party. ZZ Top under his armpits with real beards and the third one shaven in the crotch. So they say. But I can't confirm that, any more than I can confirm the Blondie tattoo on his chest. Both because of the darkness and the length of his beard, and because his flab is quaking all over from the exertion of bursting all the bubbles in the beer glasses. Timer. What a freak. Light a cigarette instead of saying something. He gasps. This is obviously quite taxing for me. Then the doorbell.

Timer looks different now as he stares me in the eye and says, "The Organist. Let him in." His eyes glowing like two cigarettes.

The Organist is a lanky weed. His teeth are on a level with my eyes. His teeth being the only thing that you can see. When you look at him. His front teeth are the same size as the nails on the black whore. Except not green. Yellow. Tangled in the bushes of his beard. He is wearing a leather jacket similar to mine and weeds into the hall without saying anything, with a crumpled plastic bag. He says hi to Timer and Timer looks up and then at the bag, and says:

"From today?"

"This morning. Twenty hours ago," the Organist answers, carrying the bag over to a flashy new cooker, upon which I realize some water has been boiling in a pot. He empties the contents into the pot with a plonk and a splash. I sit back on the sofa and light another cigarette. The Organist somehow looks familiar.

"You got time?" Timer asks, continuing to poke at the beer.

"Yeah, a bit. I can take care of this. Have you got anything to go with this?" says the Organist.

"There's some Tabasco in the cupboard above the sink."

"And potatoes. Should I throw some potatoes in?"

"Are you hungry?" Timer asks, looking at me.

"Me? Yeah, sure," I answer. Breakfast seems to be included.

"Potatoes, so," he says to the weed by the cooker.

Timer is pouring in beer sweat by the time he plonks himself back into his chair. He gasps. Glows all over. Pearls of outer peace. I'm recovering a bit now, thanks mainly to the prospect of food. Like when you wake up in a fucking expensive hotel and have slept pretty badly for 17,000 krónur's worth and suddenly realize that breakfast is included in the price. I'm actually really getting into this abortion mood (whatever that is) when Timer wipes the sweat off his brow, looks around, and reaches out for a small plastic bag. He hands it to me, and then, as if he were asking me to pass him the butter, casually says:

"Go to the toilet and wank yourself. Backwards."

This I was not expecting. I didn't expect to have to do any work myself, considering all the money I'm paying for this. Reminds me of the whore. All work and no play. The bag is like a charlie bag, but empty.

"Backwards?"

"Yeah. Do it the opposite way to what you're used to."

I have the same problem I always have when I'm on E. It takes time. And having to do it backwards doesn't make it any easier. Especially when the Organist knocks on the door, shouting, "How's it going?" (Timer can be heard in the background droning some Bodyist chant.) Nor is it any easier when I remember that I'm paying through the nose for this. Thirty thousand. It's got to be the most expensive wank of the decade. There is an autographed Polaroid of Timer and Blondie in sunshine over the toilet. I'm feeling kind of limp—the foreskin isn't into all this reverse driving—when I come out of the WC with a hot blend in the bag. Timer instructs me to hand my yield over to the Organist. Which I do and sit down. Timer is still sitting with the glasses. Twelve wet needles on the table. The beer is perfectly flat. Leave the beer be. Timer holds the cordless phone and sticks the twelve beer-dripping needles in as many holes on the mouthpiece as he starts to perform another Indian voodoo ritual. The Organist is still in the kitchen. Busy cooking.

As Timer sticks the last needle into the receiver, the phone rings. Like an acupunctured cat.

"Didn't you dial the number?" I ask, and realize as I say it that, yeah, I answered, on the floor in Mom's bedroom, and add, "I mean, did you hang up?"

Timer doesn't listen to me now any more than he listened to me earlier on today. He answers the phone, speaks through the needles: "Hello? . . . Yes. . . . No. . . . I'm on the other line. . . . Call you later. . . . OK."

Telephonic abortions. What next? After that absurd rigmarole Timer tries to sound like a real pro by gravely asking me: "Did you set it on loudness?"

"Yeah."

"Good," he says, and then in a slightly louder voice: "Food."

The Organist comes in with a steaming plate and puts it on the table in front of me. Three potatoes, a splash of Tabasco, and then some short, unusual boiled-sausage kind of thing, white.

"Eat," says Timer.

I fork it down. The sausage is unusually hard and not exactly the tastiest in town. A fibrous gobbet. Naked lunch. They watch me eating this. The Organist stands over me.

"What is this?" I very understandably ask.

"Have some beer," says Timer, pushing a glass toward me with his nails, as if he had hooks instead of fingers.

I somehow feel scared.

"Can I drink it? Aren't we supposed to leave it be?"

"No, no. It's the bubbles. That's what matters. You've got to burst them with the needle. The bubbles. The vacuum. It's going through now. Down the telephone line."

"Uh-huh," I mutter with a full mouth.

"It's like a balloon. How do you burst a balloon?"

"With a needle?" I say, quite proud of my answer, insignificant as it may be.

"With air. You put a hole in it. And it opens up to the air. It sucks in negative air. Negative air. That sucks it empty. It's the same principle here. Where do the bubbles come from in beer?"

"I dunno. From the bottom?"

"See?"

I don't see. I see I haven't the faintest idea of what he's talking about. I swallow some beer with my food and they swallow some beer. We're silent. There's something weird going on in my stomach but I am, nevertheless, beginning to feel quite OK with these guys. My heart beats. A bongo beat. I try some amicable dialogue:

"The Organist. Why are you called the Organist?"

He just stands there like a tall pillar of organs. Says no more than Frankenstein's monster ever says in the presence of his master.

Timer: "Organ. Organize. The Organist. Get it? Finished?"

I've almost finished eating. The Organist bends over the glass table in a long curve and takes the plate. I'm feeling slightly nauseous.

"Breathe into the phone."

I belch into the phone, over twelve needles.

"OK," says Timer, dropping back into his seat and slipping into a trance with the phone in his hands. He gradually starts to vibrate and shakes like jelly for about seventeen minutes. Obviously a very important conversation with Dorfy. I look at the Organist. He must be some kind of organ expert. An organ delivery boy. I see. But still. He's got something missing. Maybe he's given some of his organs away. Yeah. That's it. My stomach is feeling even rougher and I stand up, stagger around the room.

The Organist suddenly turns to me and says: "My name is Hafthór."

"Yeah?"

There's a sudden change in cabin pressure in here. My ears are all clogged up. I peep into the pot on the cooker. There are little beads all over it, reminiscent of the beads you get when you wank in the bath. There's a terrible stench from the plastic bag the Organist brought with him, lying half open on the kitchen counter. The spunk bag is empty and slavering down the side. Hang on, I think to myself as Timer comes down from the mountain and snaps out of his trance into a ghastly tooth-grinding chant. He gags the mouthpiece and says:

"The message is: Let the void devoid. Let the void devoid."

Then his inner voice gushes through him with some Indian incantation, bizarrely high-pitched, as he compresses all the pins into the receiver with his thumb. Then he slouches back into his chair. The phone buried in his beard. Beat. I'm about to say right then, Are we done? But he stops before I can form an *r*, whispering:

"Sssh. Don't disturb me. The void."

Turmoil is mounting in my stomach. I've eaten some demon. Or the devil himself. Hafthór, the Organist, is still standing there. Just stands there. I'm stuffed, but am I stuck in a movie or what? David Cronenberg. Hafthór. All of a sudden I remember I worked with him once up at the National Hospital. When I worked as a trolley pusher at the mortuary. But then. Then the Organist changes into one giant organ before my eyes. Difficult to say which organ, exactly. Ouch, my ears are even more clogged up now, like someone's stuck some needles through them, six on each side. I feel puke brewing in my stomach. I throw myself back into the can again lock myself in and lunge over the toilet bowl and puke out half-chewed ligaments drop my glasses in their wake if that can be called a wake there are no seagulls fibrous wank beads the soul the puke is that thick I reach out for them cough saliva if only saliva if only now saliva flush me down please do flush me down with all this (a) grab toilet paper (b) dry myself (c) cough again (d) dry my glasses (e) I'm on it (f) fetus flushed down too (g) God almighty what am I what have I turned into look in the mirror white as a white as a sausage yeah the fucking sausage fucking Timer I'll kill you kill the door first charge into the living room and yell what the fuck . . .

The Organist holds me back and gags me. Be my guest. Timer stares at me blankly. I splutter some words into the palm of this organ's hand. I struggle, but find no strength. Timer gives a sign. The organ releases me. I slide onto the floor and say, half whimpering:

"What the hell did you give me to eat? A prick?"

Although I'm still a transatlantic flight away from my senses, I'm lucid enough to realize that this is the first time I see a grin hovering on this demon's lips.

"A prick?" He mutters.

He starts to quiver. "A prick? Ha ha . . ." His body quivers. As it would if he were trying to jerk off his rusty old inch. I hear but can't see: two ho-hos from the Organist somewhere about sixty thousand feet above me. Timer finally manages to titter down:

"No, no. It's just a plain umbilical cord."

I walk out of the K-bar with the taste of puke in my mouth and tears on my glasses. There are some drops in the air. Far more respectable drops. Tears are so artificial. Only designed as an alarm to show you when you're starting to pity yourself. Tears are reins. Reins on your inner horse: that old mare of self-pity you're riding. Discovery. They found a horse in Tibet. Some unknown breed. There's always something. I can't face going home. I roam about town. Reykjavík in the afternoon. ZZ Top. Timer. Excuse me. Mamma. Chat Channel. And. Now I don't hear from Kati anymore. Now she's just lying somewhere with the silent Nemi inside her. But maybe she thinks of me. Maybe she nibbles the ear. Van Gogh's plastic ear. "He sent me a poem," Guildy said. Maybe I should try to poetize myself out of this? I've written one poem:

Life is leaking
Like spunk out of a pussy.

I am not what I am but what I shouldn't have become. Me who always thought I was so . . . Yeah. They called me honey. The whores in Amsterdam. Hlynur the Bear lapping up honey from a beehive. It darkens slightly. The white disappears from the sky's eye. Like milk poured in coffee in reverse. I feel . . . I feel my way down Laugavegur. Some sleepwalking zombies. The cars are OK. It's the people who've broken down. Timer. A face is just movable skin on a skull. I'm roaming about town. A stand-up loner aimlessly roaming the streets and yet not. This roam of mine is forming a screensaving ellipse on a black computer screen somewhere. I saunter around town to kill time: so that its face won't burn into the screen. Mom is my son's father. Spock. And God. How does God dress? Yeah. He wears a white short-sleeved T-shirt. He's good. He

pours milk over the Cheerios in his satellite dish. *Wayne's World.*
MTV. *Melrose Place.* Vaka. Now I'm just waiting for her to reach the
age of consent. Kittens swimming in aquariums. Models moving on
private yachts. Karen Blixen. *Cliffhanger.* Clinton. Clash and Bill
Bradley, Caucasus, "Creep." And Brutus. Brand New Heavies.
Beavis. And Butt-head. And Billy Ocean sailing across and Bonnie, his wife. Bacharach, Bach, and Jim Carrey sharpening a pencil in a bank under Cameron Diaz's (3,900,000) breasts in *The
Mask.* Yeah. Remember your brain. Don't forget it's there. Geena
Davis (900,000) in Lapland. With her boyfriend and big-time
lips. The biggest they've ever seen around there. Yeah. Remember
everything. They made her drink reindeer blood at some Lapland
do. She has purpose. Her life is not without purpose. Me. I'm just
some pathetic me in the middle of some gigantic Yellowstone
thing. I'm not even on camera. So what am I worrying about, then?
What am I but an ant in the Amazon? Under a rotting leaf. While
the rest of the globe is trotting away. There's always the world.
We've always got the world to lean on. Feel better when you do. To
be on all channels simultaneously. Everything else is just too old-
fashioned and local. Loco. A courtroom in Brescia and snowing outside, a wire in the reporter's ear and the pleats in that lawyer's robe.
Don't forget them. THE PLEATS IN THAT LAWYER'S ROBE IN
BRESCIA. I remember them. The pleats in all the robes of the
world. Make sure you take it all in. You have to take care of it all.
Shoe numbers in the Arab world. Sword fencing in Poznan. Ele-
mentary schools in Taiwan. Take That. *Two Much.* Starring Antonio
Banderas and Billie Jean and Bowie, Bethlehem, *Baywatch,* Sheila
E (120,000) and Sergei Bubka, Bubbles, Koons and Queen and
Martin & Charlie Sheen and David Lean pushing daisies, Moon
Zappa (500,000) and sixteen sixteen-year-olds in Sarajevo
(320,000) and one of them (20,000) has leukemia and the airport
is snowed in, closed, some peacekeeping corpses, blue helmets and
red crosses, and yet another model from Akureyri (300,000) with
eyebrows in Tokyo. Try to face life, Lolla said. This omelette called
life. I should put my harm into it, my ham into it, make omelette
hamelette for Hamlet in Hornywood. I'm Hamletterman in Hollywood with one-liners from outer space and punchlines from hell

joking my way to the bar a real boogeyman and order a double tam-
bourine man and toast to the poisoned lakes of Mývatn, Manitoba,
and. Madness. *One Step Beyond.* And back again. I see. I see land.
I am from I.C.E.-land. I see E. And oversee everything. OK. I take
care of everything. I bear it all on my shoulders. Even the latest
teenage zit in Oakland. Sprouting out on a forehead under a quilt
in San Leandro. Me there. Nursing. Sucking all the white pus out
of the world. I'm alone. I'm everything. Except me. I'm a hundred
and one. Then I feel better. To be on all channels simultaneously
and the blue light of porno glowing in my unconscious, below it all.
Look at this crowd.

Backpacking around with their shitty lives on their shoulders.
And never sparing a thought for the world, only for themselves.
Some Hugo through the open window of a BMW shaking his chin
to the radioactive beat of his radio. A man coming toward me. He
walks as if man had never walked on the moon. A fatso Ferguson
(17,000) lipsticking her way into a fashion boutique. I look her ass
in the eye and get a longing to rape her. If I don't get AIDS I'll turn
into a serial killer. The first in Iceland. A sure way to get on the
front pages of the evening paper. Except I'd insist on not having my
face scrambled in the picture. But then of course I'd have to move
out of home. Our garden isn't big enough for a mass grave. Mom,
you've got to forgive me. I was acting under the influence. I was out
of my skull. As if that were any excuse. But I really don't think it's
working. Abortion over the phone. Am I going bananas? But there
was something demonic in his eyes.

My life is just a screensaving ellipse on a black screen. While
death is on its coffee break.

I've reached Hlemmur Square. A face comes out of a shop and
says hi. A face is just a skull with moving lips. Movable skin on a
skull. I realize after ten words that it's Marri. With his bulging eyes.
He's chirpy.

"How was it abroad?"

"I made it back home."

"Yeah. Long time no see. You should show your face more
often."

"Show my face? To you?"

"Yeah."

"I just have. I've just shown it to you."

I take that as my cue to step into the shop, since Marri has just stepped out of it. The floor is littered with social crumbs and two pieces of gum being chewed behind the counter (15,000 and 65,000). I address the pricier one, but it's the cheaper one that answers. Some fat old bag with torpedo tits under her T-shirt.

"Er . . . Prince."

"Polo chocolate?"

"No. Cigarettes."

"Sooorry. We're out."

"What d'you mean?"

"We're out of Prince cigarettes at the moment."

I lean over the counter and lower my voice.

"Listen. You better give me a packet of Prince on the double or I'll come back here to rape you tomorrow morning."

"Oh yeah? Well, I look forward to that. What time can I expect you at?"

"Early. You'll wake up all right when I stick him into you."

"Right you are. See you, then."

My face is ablaze as I fumble toward the video section, full of eyes on my back. That didn't come out too good. I don't come out too good. Videos. *To Die For.* A slight craving to marry Nicole Kidman (250,000). Wouldn't that solve it all? Swipe her from Tom Cruise. Timer would help me. He'd voodoo some nice little helicopter accident for him. I see a pay phone and one of my ears calls out your mom is on the phone, Hlynur. I pick up the receiver, dial her work number. "The switchboard is open between nine and four on weekdays." Hofy. I was connected to a switchboard. I hang up. I stand and look out the window. See Lolla when I first saw her. She slowly walked into the living room, in her socks, and immediately reminded me of that very quiet guitar solo at the beginning of Harrison's "My Sweet Lord." There was something. Already, then. I wait for the song to finish. Ring again. Home. Mom answers:

"Hello."

"It's me."

"Oh, hi, darling. Where are you?"

"I am. I was. It was me."

"What? You what?"

"I was . . . I was calling you."

"Yes, did you call me at work? I went home early today. Myself and Lolla went shopping. We've got a changing table now, so we'll soon have all we need."

"A changing table?"

"Yes. We just bought one. You should see it. Looks great. Aren't you coming home?"

"Yeah."

"And what? Was there something special?"

"No."

"Are you sure? You sound a bit strange."

"No, no."

"OK, then. I've got the dinner to think of. Won't you be home before eight?"

"Yeah."

A green T-shirt with glasses sees me to the door of the shop. The owner. I expect.

I walk home. My self. Pity. Very Hlynur Björn.

I wake up one Friday morning at 17:30 with such a hangover that my gums no longer seem to fit. I've been gnashing my teeth in bars for so many weeks that my bite has changed. I stagger to the can with a mouth like the inside of an Ahmed's underpants. I'm getting more like Timer. I've even started to neglect my remote. I've even got my allotted place at the K-bar now, and a straw in my glass. Another four weeks and I'll be on a drip. Sat with Timer for seven hours last night. He was blabbing on about *Space Odyssey* all the time. Stanley Kubrick.

"He fucked up when he got the ape to throw the bone into the air and it changes into a spaceship. He should have just picked it up and allowed it to turn into a mobile phone. That would have been better."

Then ended up at some lonely-guys convention in a house

behind Laugavegur listening to Milli Vanilli. I've sunk pretty low. I even conked out on cocaine. But hardly surprising. I dozed off when some stonewashed sports expert started to expound his theory on Icelandic handball: the Icelandic handball team lost its fighting spirit after we beat the Brits in the Cod War. Then woke up on the sofa with the master of the house licking one of my ears. With steam-boiled eyes. It's really dangerous to go to after-hours parties at this time of the year. The loony bin is closed for the summer. But anyway. This last detail epitomized everything I've always felt about Milli Vanilli. Girl you know it's true . . . I shoved a CD into his mouth. Massive Attack.

If it hadn't been for shit like that I would never have said yes to Mom when she asked—probably just for the hell of it—if I'd like to come out to the summer house in Munadarnes. But I'm not exactly leaping with excitement, sitting here in the backseat, as we drive past Hvalfjördur, which I haven't seen since '89, I seem to remember, when we went to that rock gig in Húnaver, myself, Thröstur, and Marri, and gobbled down Aunty Sigrún's fried eggs in Hvammstangi. I immediately start to miss the billboards. Those mountains are so irritatingly still. No way of zapping over to something else. The grass is doing the Mexican wave. And some chia pets grazing on the pastures. Mom beeps at two of them. Lolla is wearing a belt over her airbag.

"Ehm. Does it have a hot pot?" I ask.

Of course it does. I shudder at the thought of having to get into massage broth in my Bonus briefs. I glance at some country farm shacks. And then a short movie about the making of haystacks. "Wow. Do they make cheese that big now?" No. Mom lectures me on the newest technology in haystacking. All wrapped automatically in plastic now. Mechanized bale handling. We could do with some English translations of our place-names on the signs for the tourists. I give it a try. Esja. Mount Easy. Vallá. Hardly River. Dalsmynni. Mouthwash. Kidafell. The Kid That Fell. Ingunnarstadir. Ingunn's Place. Saurbær. Shit Farm. Geldingaá. Castration River. Nónhöfdi. Noonhead. Krumshólar. Crummy Hills. Haugar. Garbage Hills. Laugaland. Pool Country. Baula. Mount Cowspeak. Stadarstadur. The Place to Be. Ok. OK. Munadarnes. Laziness.

A conversation in the country store:

Mom: "What do you think, Hlynur? Wouldn't you like chicken too?"

Hlynur: "As a rule I don't eat sleepless meat."

Lolla (laughs): "Sleepless meat? What's that?"

Hlynur (smugly): "Yeah. You know how they're produced. They're kept indoors all their lives, gurgling around a shed under a permanent neon sun, maybe six thousand of them in the same room and all of them with that same tic in their heads, like in a crazy techno dance, it's like a six-week rave festival for the poor bastards, without the lights ever being turned off. And then we're supposed to eat them. It's like eating pure insomnia. It was on TV the other day."

Lolla (when she's finished laughing): "Since when have you given a toss for the protection of animals?"

Hlynur: "It's the animals I want protection from."

Mom: "OK, then, we'll just buy some grill meat."

The summer house is in a kind of summer-house area. Surrounded by shrubs, like pubic hair on the naked landscape. And kind of well-made rocks. I carry the grill meat into the house. Grill meat. What animal did that come from? Slight relief to see a TV in the corner. But a big disappointment when I turn it on. It's better off. Because it's quite a good-looking TV. So to speak. Then I get called out to the hot pot, Iceland's answer to jury duty. Forgot my swimming gear. If one can use such a term for something one has never had. Step outside in my Bonus briefs. I have to get into this pot pretty fast because of that piss-yellow patch on my crotch.

"That's OK, Hlynur. You'd hardly notice you're in your underpants, you're so white, ha ha . . ."

"But he's not fat, I'll say that much."

"It's the smoking."

They comment, as if I were autistic.

Hot pot. Smoking pot. Which reminds me. We haven't had a joint since Lolla got knocked up. Not good to get stoned when you've got a stone in your stomach. Mom is in a swimsuit. Phew. Lolla is in a bikini. Maybe it's the pregnancy, but I choose to focus on Mom's breasts. I watch them with the soft-lens effect of my steamed-up glasses and feel a tinge of satisfaction to be sitting in the same warm water that is now gently caressing my mother's cleavage. Lolla lets herself float, with her bump protruding in the middle of the pot. Inside it: Halldór Stefánsson. Good day to you, sir! All of a sudden I feel a touch of nostalgia for Hofy's bump. It's quite foolish not to want to have children, really. "What kind of society would that be?" Maybe all you need is a change of attitude. Just need the right ads on TV and in the papers, some good slogans: "Children. Investments on legs." I glance beyond the veranda, check out this chaotic nature lark. Plenty of work for good old Mr. Stud, the landscape toy-boy. But it's not bad, really. Except the clouds could be a bit higher in the sky. For the sake of the mountains, I mean. No sound of mooing from Mount Cowspeak, except for the birds fluttering about giving some avant-garde recital.

"Oh, this is just wonderful," Mom groans.

"Yeah. Good lighting, too. Ehm. What's that sound?" I ask.

"Sound? Isn't it the stream?"

"Could we turn it down a bit?"

We linger there until the skin on our fingers starts to wither. My hangover slowly dissolves into plain thirst. Mom makes us an Irish coffee when we get back into the hut. We talk about Mr. Stud. If it'll be OK. Lolla says he lives alone. Poor bugger. "He has to learn how to promote himself," I say. "In what field?" they ask. "In the sperm industry," I answer. They're hot with Icelandic water and Irish coffee and laughingly speculate about his future in the field. "He performed very well," Lolla titters. "Yeah, he's got a career ahead of him. He could become really in," I say. "And out," Lolla adds.

Then they fall asleep and I sit alone in the twilight provided by a candle and the late summer night, feeling somehow very human. In this inhuman setting. A criminal silence. I stare out at the gray night for a while. The poor suckers who had to crawl around this dump for all those blackout centuries when the only entertainment on offer was watching the moss grow in the lava field. Back in the days when volcanic eruptions were considered kind of bad. Me and Icelandic nature. Charles and Di. I've traveled too far beyond the pale of television waves. My remote has a range of 10 meters but

we're talking about 100 kilometers here. Still, I brought it along.
Just in case. I turn on the TV. A test card: the most popular show on
Channel 1. A docudrama that says everything about the intellectual
life of this country of ours. Holy Catholic Kiljan. I've started to
watch the knotholes on the walls. Not that they've got much entertainment value. I invent a new adjective. "Summerhoused." I'm
feeling so incredibly "summerhoused." It's so bad I've almost
started to read *The Guns of Navarone,* by some Steve McQueen. I
play with the idea of driving down to the bar in Borgarnes. For a sip
of civilization.

It's two o'clock by the time I work myself through the darkness
of the night down the side road. I'm going out to check out the
nightlife. Get pissed and chase women. Nah. I follow the white
stripe but occasionally grope through the bushes on the side of the
road, searching for females. Didn't have the guts to take the car. Icelandic nightlife. Friday night and here I am dancing with a guide-
post in the middle of Borgarfjördur. Yes! I brought my old yellow
Walkman along for the trip: the only survival kit I have, apart from
a brand-new pack of extra-strong country condoms, just in case.
There's a shitty little streak of light in the bottom right-hand corner of the sky. Prodigy playing on Radio-X. Thumb out. I miss two
cars as I'm thumbing and try sticking up the middle finger instead.
It works. A white Jap number with two halogen blonds, male and
female.

"Any chance of a ride to Borgarnes?"

The halogen couple smiles. I probably said it too loud. I pull the
Smashing Pumpkins off my ears. The female answers. I give her a
straight 40,000 even though I haven't had a chance to see her
nether regions yet.

"Any chance of a ride to Borgarnes?"

"Borgarnes? That's in the opposite direction, you know."

"Oh? Yeah. Where are you heading?"

"Up to Hredavatn Lodge."

"Yeah. Perfect. Can you give me a ride?"

"Yeah, sure."

"Outstanding."

They're what you'd call soft-rock types. Eric Clapton plucks my ass. They're both dressed in dazzling white and pretty posh but a bit rugged at the same time. Very hairy. A vibrator kind of couple. Bonnie Tyler (40,000) and Michael Bolton. Get the feeling there's more gray matter in the headrests than there is in their heads. After several kilometers I check out their IQs:

"Ehm. Are you two together?"

"Us? Yeah," she answers. "Why do you ask?"

"Just. Wondering."

OK. She gave the right answer. She could be a promo-queen in a supermarket during the day and a stripper at the local hotel in the evenings. They suit each other. They'll make a good couple. They'll put the vibrator back up on the shelf and have lots of children, glaring blond children. The halogenes will pay off. Yeah, yeah. They're good for Iceland. I mean, even though their children won't necessarily turn out to be Björks or anything. Bonnie hands me a Kahlúa bottle from the front seat. All right! We arrive as I'm handing her the bottle back.

Hredavatn Lodge. The last bar in the valley. There are seven people inside plus us and John Lennon. Free as a bird from the grave. Although he's the liveliest. Talk about quiet. The halogen couple is helloed over to a table of five. Then there are two male Dutch cyclists with a map between them. Looking for Ecstasy. I wobble over to the bar and order a beer from Miss Bifröst '96. She's 60,000. I hit on her.

"Hey, didn't you go to Bifröst College?"

"Yeah!" she answers, in a chirpy co-op college voice. "Were you there too?"

"Me? No."

"Are you a friend of Gauri's, maybe?"

"Gauri?"

"Yeah, Gauri B. and those guys."

"No."

"Oh," she blushes, "I . . . thought . . . yeah . . . ha ha."

She gets all embarrassed and I get even more embarrassed and I unwittingly blow her away in a cloud of cigarette smoke, and then make a point of moving toward a table with my beer as slowly as possible in the hope of getting a "Grab a seat!" from the halogen couple. But that doesn't happen. And to think I thought they were my friends.

I sit alone for several beers. Bonnie glances at me twice. I smile the first time. I get drunk in a rather boring way. Still, better than being in the summer house. At least there are a few decent-priced properties knocking about. Miss Bifröst behind the bar. Sorry. My attempts at seduction pathetic enough to make my victim blush. I've got about as much sex appeal as an orangutan. Anna phoned the other day, said her mom was going to charge me with sexual assault. Ruby Tuesday, Sheffield Wednesday. I prepare my case for the defense. Have so many problems reaching out to people . . . Trying to reach out to people . . . My quest for honesty in human communication. Just trying to be true to my instincts. My pure and selfless love for the whole of humanity . . . Hey. Two country lasses have just walked in (25,000 apiece) and are standing at the bar. Pissed as newts. One of them gives me the eye. The other has bags under hers. A goal in life at last. Until three o'clock, at least. I undress and dress her several times. With my eyes, that is. She seems to be enjoying it and finally responds, comes over and sits down.

"Hi. Mind if I sit? What are you wearing those shades for?"

"Cos the music is so boring in here."

"Don't you like the Beatles? I've never heard that one before. Who do you like?"

"I'm a Bonnie Tyler fan."

"Ha ha ha, Bonnie Tyler, ha ha ha. Hey, I like you, you're a bag of laughs, you are."

We've got a slight problem here. She's dead. From drink. And I think it would be disrespectful of me to carry on fucking her. There seems to be a long delay in my ejaculation. But that's not the main issue right now. The tent collapsed on top of us the moment she passed out. I can feel the cold wet orange canvas on my ass. Like being stuck between a pair of testicles and a swimsuit. The two country lasses obviously didn't pitch their tent properly. This one's name is Hanna. I'm still inside her. These pelvic thrusts are more of an attempt at resuscitation than the joys of sex. It's like fucking inside a womb. Can't really say I would recommend it. Quite impossible. I slip out of her, and then slip the rubber off me and yank my trousers back on with remarkable agility. The only question now is what to do with the body. I conduct a brief search for her panties without success. Her jeans, then—I must say it's quite a heroic feat to be able to hoist them all the way back to above her knees, particularly considering the piles of cellulite I have to tackle on the way, no small obstacle for a man who has problems putting on his own clothes every morning, let alone dressing a flabby-thighed corpse in a collapsed tent in the middle of soaking wet Borgarfjördur at five-thirty in the morning. I give up at about six centimeters above the knee. Enshroud her in an open sleeping bag. She's wearing a downy parka and a sweater underneath. I lift it and look at her breasts. Something I hadn't done yet. They're loose, and bigger than I'd imagined. I fondle them as I ponder on my next move. Dead breasts. Feel a bit different. A bit more like food products somehow. I pack them back into her body and wrap her so that she won't be cold. Hanna dear. You were number nine. Yeah. Lolla was number seven. Anna number eight. Already three this year! I should send out a press release: "Hlynur Björn Hafsteins-son's female conquests up this year. A twofold increase on the amount of women he scored with last year." I'd leave out the whore. Not sure Mom would like to read about me pecking her in the papers.

I spend at least two whole minutes trying to resurrect the tent and the pillar. Once not a scout, never a scout. Then it's the final farewell to Hanna. I don't think I've ever parted from a woman as gracefully as this. Although it's got to be said she is dead. A gift from the gods. Just died a moment too soon. I slip the condom into the pocket of her down parka as a kind of memento. With kindest regards from Hlynur Björn.

I crawl out of the tent like a totally new breed of butterfly, genetically engineered by scientists, squirming out of its plastic saf-fron pupa shell. A butterfly with glasses and an old Stray Cats hairdo, two legs but no wings. A Franken-butterfly. A slight disap-pointment for the scientists, I expect.

The dawn is a yawn. White, wet fog. Not exactly what you'd call rain, more of a spray. I wipe my glasses on my polo neck and look about. No other tents. What happened to her friend, then? "Went to the toilet," Hanna said. Never to be seen again. Yeah. Those toilets they've got in Hredavatn Lodge are really dodgy. I've heard about lots of people who went to them and never came back, I think to myself as I reach out for a cigarette. Hanna is lying inside that collapsed tent that looks like a grave mound from the early days of the Settlement. Is this a sign? No. My AIDS-infested sperm is still in its place and my cold condom in her pocket.

I saunter back to the lodge. Not. Slight technical hitch. The lodge has been beamed up to space. Yeah, there was something weird about the toilets in that place. And the road has been engulfed under a coat of lava. I grab my survival kit, put on my Walkman. Radio-X, my station, has vanished into the mist with the rest. All I can get is our good old national channel. It's the weather. As if there weren't enough weather around here as it is. I try to walk back to the tent. Hanna, dear. Snore away while you can. Everything is drowned in a mist. There's obviously some kind of program going on. Candid camera? The Man Upstairs having fun with the remote control. He's thrown me into a pretty boring episode of *Rescue 911*. Hasn't lost his sense of humor. I don't believe this. I'm lost. Stranded in an ancient hardened giant lava field. Iceland is like an old man who died from the cold. Frozen lava goosebumps on his back and me clambering over them like a louse in a leather jacket. A lousy blind louse I am. And the Old Man Upstairs pumps even more mist into the air with his smoke machines. We're talking heavy-duty fog here. OK. Let's face it, I'm totally lost. I try to set shorter and more realistic goals for myself. At least I manage to dig a cigarette out of my pocket. OK. What would Tarantino do in my shoes? Yeah. He'd allow the cigarette to show him the way. The smoke blows to the left. I follow it.

Nick Cave. I drop my ass onto a rock in some kind of a cave that reminds me of a bar that used to be on Tryggvagata, except that the stools were slightly more comfortable. The cushions weren't this cold. Kate Moss (190,000). I blink behind the condensation on my glasses. We're talking 1303 here. I've been lost for eight hours.

Seven hours since I stopped complaining about the goosebumps.
Now I'm just plain freezing. Lost in the wild. A savage. I haven't
stumbled on anything remotely connected to my former life, apart
from an old box of Smarties that had faded to black and white.
There was one left. As hard as a tooth. Not much else on the
menu. Although I'm pretty full after those seven crowberries.
There's nothing but a mossy silence ahead of me. I guess. I've got
some ancient ELO track blasting through my ears. "Turn to Stone."
On Channel 2. This wouldn't be so bad if I could get Radio-X and
if they sold cigarettes in this grotto. That and the cold. Slightly disappointed to hear no mention of me on the lunchtime news. Maybe
they're just glad to see the back of me. Maybe they're not up yet.
I get the feeling I'm crying, but it's only raindrops on my glasses.

That's it, then. I'm a caveman with a yellow Walkman. In a black
leather jacket, white turtleneck, black jeans, and Doc Martens. A
belt with a boomerang buckle. The house keys in my pocket, plus
a Zippo, 700 krónur, a Blaupunkt remote, a Visa card, and two condoms. A Casio digital watch. Basically all you need to pine away the
winter here in Lavaland, and I'm a lot better off than that old folk
hero Eyvind of the Mountains, who survived in the highlands for
more than thirty years but who probably didn't have a Visa card or
a remote to control his sheep.

I pull the radio off my ears and lie down on a mattress of moss.
I gaze at the white drizzle and black lava fields. A bird cries out in
the distance. Another vanishes into the fog like a black arrow flashing across a computer screen. I try to cry a bit. But nothing comes.
I'm out of tears. The last tear in the valley has run into the sea. My
hard life is over now. Time for you to bear this torch of tears, my son.
Well, I be darned if I don't see something white stepping out of the
fog. Hey. No. Better off getting myself beamed up to heaven than
vegetating here like some hallucinating hillbilly. Yeah, that's it. I'll
just lie here until something happens, wait here until someone
appears, a scout or God or a smiling skeleton with a scythe to give
me a hand.

The fastest thing to grow in this lava field is my beard. I'm a tiny
warm spot on a spy-satellite photo. If I had a pen I'd stretch out for

my crumpled packet of Prince, iron it out, and write on it: *Mom. Forgive me but I suddenly felt like a beer. If it's possible to miss someone when you're dead then I will.—Yours, Hlynur. P.S. I'm the dad. (Sorry.)* and then slip it into my inside pocket. The raven could pluck my eyes out, but never find my note to Mom. Nah. I would have crossed out the P.S. I would have wanted to say a proper goodbye to Katarina before leaving. *Igen.* My main worry right now, however, is that when they find me they might think I was listening to Channel 2.

A bleat pierces my ears. I wake up after a short slumber that, for all I know, might have lasted hundreds of years. I feel like an outcast who has miraculously survived in the wilderness and is celebrating his thirty-fourth year in the cave. Mist on my glasses. This appears to be a lamb (25,000) that's popped in to see me and bleats so virulently into the haze. The light drizzle has suddenly turned into a downpour. The fog still in its place, plus rain falling at an angle of 45 degrees. A shower of oblique slashes just like the ones on those weather maps on TV. The cold has really got a full grip on me now, gnaws my bones. My teeth chatter in accompaniment to the bleating. I rise from my Kate Moss–wet ass and establish some brief eye contact with the blonde. 1345 and the seven crowberries have now formed a single file in my colon. But things don't look quite as bleak now that I've got some company. Two motherless wimps. Maybe I should bleat out "Mamma" too. But after the seventieth baa, I'm beginning to get a bit tired of this lamb. Animals are more fun served on a plate. I put on my Walkman but the batteries are flat. So, there can be no musical numbers at this one-man open-air festival apart from this lonesome lambada song and, yeah, the pretty pathetic percussion performed by my teeth and the faint howl of a synthesizer in my stomach.

I rip up a patch of moss and hurl it at the lamb. It throws her for a moment but she carries on bleating, like an amateur on stage who is being booed but carries on singing regardless. Reminds me of Hofy. I poke its ass. The lamb scuttles out of the cave but then comes back. And bleats. I bleat back.

And ponder on ways of turning this wearisome musical number

into food. Yeah. I lasso my boomerang belt around its furry neck and strangle it to death, then scorch its cheeks with my Zippo and rasp a slice off with my Visa card, scoop the eyes out with my house keys, bite the tongue out of it, rip its gut open with a piece of lava stone and squeeze the entrails into the condoms, two blood puddings to be saved for Christmas.

No matter how hard I pull the belt it just bleats more. The lamb. I give up and almost let it slip from my hands. My glasses twist on my forehead. I feel the comforting heat of rage rising in my body and try to prolong the struggle, grope for the remote and try to shove it into its gob. The volume control works, but I still can't quite manage to turn the lamb off with this ingenious ploy. A lot of slaver. Lots of slaver. In the end I just slide the belt from its neck to its head, sling it twice around its gob, and pull as hard as I can. That kills most of the bleating, which now sounds like a feeble muffled cry of despair coming from the bottom shelf of a freezer.

"B . . . b . . . b . . ."

I cling awkwardly to the animal and slowly feel its heat, pull it over me, and hug it tight. The lamb breathes into my face, slavering all over me, and shifting into a cheek-to-cheek position, we half lie there for a few moments like perfect lovers. I feel the heartbeat that will be boiled in the autumn and suddenly whisper into its bizarre ear:

"I love you."

It warmly coos back at me "B . . . b . . . b . . ." and reciprocates my feelings with an equally warm discharge over my crotch. I spring to my feet and the lamb flees, staggering out into the rain and lava field and vanishing into the soup like a date gone wrong.

"No. Don't go," I say.

Then realize. The belt. I follow. Out of the cave. Into the pouring rain.

I went out to check out the nightlife and now life is checking out on me. Nevertheless I do what I can. I run. I run to keep the cold out of my bones. I flee the cold, and just want to drag my rags and bones to the nearest town, or car, or shelter, or anything that will give me a pause. Pause. Please, I beg you. I run as fast as the rain falls. Soaking wet on my way to my grave. Nothing but lava behind me. And death on my tracks, in wet underpants too. I hear the squelch of its boots. Birds cackling on cushions of moss. This is freaky. Yeah, this is freaky. That's the word that fills my mouth. "Freaky." The only thing that can help me, my only defense, "freaky." My lungs have gone haywire. Fate's got me by the balls. The Man Upstairs is checkmating me with all his might and weather. I give in. Mom. Lolla. Timer. Thröstur. Marri. All the video rental stores of Reykjavík. I ask you, do I really deserve this? Hanna. She must be awake by now, dry and hungover, and Anna. Forgive me for that incident with your mom she'll get over it I was out of it. But this is too harsh a sentence. Outlawed. I run. I run across the rough, weatherbeaten lava. At least I'm trying. I'm. There's a pizza joint in New York. Yeah. That's it. There is a puny little pizza place in Manhattan and there are yellow cars beeping outside and a couple at a table and the waiters are from Egypt and Ecuador and blacks who come in with golden teeth and steaming fresh pizzas under Roman noses in the corner and white tiles and the smell of dough from the oven and the till and on the other side of the counter an old baked radio blurting out a song by Roxette the peroxide girl (65,000) running through the streets of Stockholm singing "It Must Have Been Love" and the sulking black couple slurping Coke she (125,000) cheated on him with long pink nails. There are long pink nails. THERE ARE LONG PINK NAILS SOMEWHERE IN NEW YORK AND THE EGYPTIAN SMILES. THE EGYPTIAN SMILES. The Egyptian smiles. I gnash. I gnash my teeth. I gnash lava. I give up. I give up running. I walk. I don't know if I'm cold or what. The weather blows through me. I am the weather. I'm an instrument God plays. I'm a wind harp, my ribs . . . I stop, I listen. I gape up at the heavens. He's playing me now, as if he were blowing air over the spout of an empty bottle.

I launch a faint cry up into the thick fog.

OK. This is my last hope. That I should have had to go through something like this: try to remember the Our Father. It's there somewhere. Lodged in my brain. I try to remember it. Only remember:

"Our Father, who art in heaven, your will be done . . ."

But maybe not right now.

Walk on. It works. Bloody hell, it works. Our Father immediately reveals a barbed-wire fence to me. He's cut through the fog with a fence. Our Father who hath a sense of humor. A fence brings hope. After twelve hours of wilderness it's like stumbling across Las Vegas. Human workmanship. I follow the fence. Some bushes beyond it. Get a slight scratch from the barbed wire. Farmers. You're all right, really. I follow the fence with chattering teeth. Drops pelting my forehead. I can't stop the rain. Tina Turner (3,600,000). I follow the fence for another fifty poles and try to remember more of the Our Father, the last line could lead me to some asphalt. "Your Kingdom come." Yeah. Your Kingdom come. Your well-fenced Kingdom. Yeah. Another fence appears, running perpendicular to this one. I take it, climb over it, battle through cold bushes up to my waist until I stumble upon a bright yellow and blue deflated beachball lying on the grass—the first sign of civilization—and then a sandpit, and then a patio, a summer house locked I try to break a window with my fist but my name is Hlynur Björn a blue plastic hot pot I lift the lid and dip my hand into the hot water into the Welfare State I collapse more than climb into the pot with a splash and lie there until my teeth stop chattering.

It's 1944 by the time I'm standing, as soaked as a man can be, but reasonably warm in spite of the icy rain, on the National A1 road and thank God for the favor and raise my shriveled thumb to two approaching lights. By the time seven cars have whizzed past as many thumbs I lie down on the fairly cold tarmac in a sort of fetal position and am resigned to the idea of passing over to the other side with a Bridgestone pattern pressed over my back and skid marks on my brain, when a guy in a short-sleeved T-shirt drags me out of the beam of his headlights into the backseat of a white Nissan. "Sweet Home Alabama." On the radio.

Halldór was born via cesarean. He was received like a Caesar. On the third day he rose from Lolla's womb at the National Hospital and started to yell his head off, with a magnificent scrotum, although he obviously needed another four weeks to form a face. The birth had gone well, however, and Lolla was allowed to come home before the weekend. I took some paternity leave and lay in bed until Monday. Got away with slight pneumonia. Soon got over it, though, and could start smoking again after four days. Started on Salem Lights and then switched over to Salem, Prince Lights, and finally Prince. Mom extended her summer vacation and was at home making cocoa for me between trips up to the maternity ward and bought me a new remote to replace the one still lying at the bottom of that cave in Lavaland, a relic that's bound to puzzle future archaeologists. I sometimes think of the lamb who stole my belt. Just hope it's managing without me.

The premature creature moved in with us in mid-September and didn't take long to complete the compulsory nine months to qualify as an Icelandic citizen. He was pretty lucky with his social security number: 010996-1999. Halldór Stefánsson. But he's so obviously a Hlynsson. On my first day up, I secretly checked out the cradle and studied those brand-new birthmarks. That really clinched it for me. Although he'd organized them slightly differently. And didn't go for the Lolla beauty spot. Which he must have been offered at some stage. My boy's a true original. The birthmarks of my ejaculation. Hey. Yeah. I seem to have done a good job. In fact, I was almost on the point of being arrested for child abuse when Lolla came out of the can and I was holding the Pampers-bottomed baby in my arms, studying his toes, but I managed to tip him swiftly back into his cradle before she came in. It's too early to say whether he's going to inherit my nose, but at least he doesn't have those ridiculous small toes of mine. He's got nails on all of them. Yeah. Mankind is making progress.

I took it a bit easy on my first packets of cigarettes after my ordeal and stayed in. Lolla had to go back into hospital for a short while and Mom needed me to go out to the shops and stuff. It was pretty freaky to be left alone, me and Mom, just the two of us with our son, but then we got a baby-sitter, a dreamy-haired darling called Linda Vilhjálmsdóttir or Linda Babe Vilhjálmsdóttir. She's eighteen and 100,000 and she'll be guiding the boy around the apartment for a while. I've started saving up, have even started to

cut down on the K-bar. Partly because of the bubbles in the beer.
They really piss me off now.

Today is some day in October '96. The light in the windows is white
and dull, like mold, like it's been stored away in a fridge. The fridge
of summer. Autumn has fallen and the leaves have all turned filter
yellow. They're still hanging on in there, though, while the trees are
trying to get their act together. Like the rest of us. The Man
Upstairs has obviously got the fan working again and is about to
blow winter back our way.

I'm sitting calmly in front of the computer in my bedroom. I'm on
the Net. Talking to a girl called Judy. She's my most recent screen-
saver, the only one to answer my ad:

> Dirty-something blond and lonely unemployed male living with his
> mother, her girlfriend, and their son, who might be HIV-positive
> and likes staying inside watching X-rated movies and satellite
> TV, blind masturbating, and patient bar hanging, is looking for a
> long-term heterosexual relationship on the Net. P.S. You have to be
> single with serious breasts.—lonebear@this.is

She said it was really "honest and so original." Judy could be
around 25,000. She lives in Hoboken in the state of New Jersey in
the U.S. Mom knocks on the door. I turn. She opens and says with
a smile:

"It's ready for you."

"Yeah. Thanks."

I say bye to Judy and turn the computer off. Sit for a while. With
everything switched off. Nothing in the room somehow. Just me
and some heartbeat. Me in a nutshell.

I come out of my room. Lolla is holding little Halldór. Halldór
is crying a bit. She paces the dining room. Trying to soothe little
Halldór. Mom is in the bathroom. I go into the bathroom. She
hands me a towel and asks if the water is the right temperature.
I dip my thumb into the bathtub and say: "Yeah. Fine."

Mom says: "Don't be too long. We might have to change him
soon."

Mom walks out and I close the door. I turn on the radio on the shelf. It's a phone-in. Some guy is complaining that lots of cars didn't stop for him when his car broke down out in the country. I switch over to Radio-X. There's a song by Oasis or Blur. I brush my teeth. I've recently started to brush my teeth four times a day. But I try to use as little toothpaste as possible. Odol Magyar. The next thing I do is go to the toilet. I make a small nest out of the toilet paper before laying my eggs: I shit three turds. An appetizer, a main course, and a dessert. I wipe my ass in five rubs, look at my yield, and then flush it away. I take the rest of my clothes off and get into the bathtub. The water is at mommy temperature. Comes up to my neck. Like a transparent turtleneck. Then this: I think of Judy. Judy Osborne. She's blonde with glasses and works for a record company in New York. Her nose is really close to her mouth or her mouth is a little bit too high up on her chin. She's met both Kenny G and Joey Santiago, who was in the Pixies. It's weird to think about the distance that separates those two names. Musically speaking, I mean. *Doolittle* was a wicked album. Judy says Santiago is from the Philippines. Which surprised me a bit. I wasn't prepared for that. But that's what she says. She's met him so she ought to know. She works for Elektra. Will Halldór become a bass player just like his granddad? It would be great if I could be a pop-star dad. The next generation of Icelanders will all be world famous. The whole lot of them. Mom is much better to me since he got born. Or since I caught pneumonia. That is to say, even better. My glasses are getting too misty so I take them off. Radio-X is plugging a concert at the Moon tonight. I realize I haven't set foot in the place since I met Anna there. She called again the other day and said she'd spoken to Dad. I find that hard to believe, since Dad has been in rehab for three weeks. He's in rehab with Lolla. Or he's supposed to be, but Lolla hasn't been able to go back to work yet, what with the new little one. I remember Lolla told me once that she'd slept with one of her patients. I thought it was funny and remember asking her if that was part of the therapy. I saw a picture of Sara in the paper the other day. She was directing some beauty contest at the Örk hotel. Thröstur said she's going out with some young actor. Some George Michael lookalike. Sara can make a gay man swing straight. I hope that doesn't mean my father is gay. Thröstur came over the other day. The goatee was gone. And so was Marri. He went to Mexico. He lives with his sister and is going to study pet psychology. Remember he spoke about it. Water refreshes the memory. What would Magnús say about that? Pet psychology. Will Marri come back with all his diplomas then and sue me for abusing a lamb? Wasn't I good to it, after all? I told it I loved it. What was that? That was the first and only time I've ever said that. And now they have slaughtered the only love I had. Hofy has started college now. Now she can float through the glassy stream of teacher training college with all her fantastic garlands. And Magnús and Elsa have embarked on yet another journey in search of their inner selves. Who, this time, are apparently to be found on a beach in the Algarve. Water refreshes the mind. Revives those memories you thought you'd drowned for good. They come simmering to the surface. They bubble up to the brink of your consciousness like farts. I fart. Yeah. Incredible how I've managed to synchronize my body with my mind over the years. I only have to think of farting and I fart. To think of whistling and I whistle. To think of Lolla and I get lollaed up. Lolla is still a bit weak. She has to go back up to the hospital. If I think of dying then. Yeah. Haven't quite mastered that one yet. Hertha Berlin obviously came pretty close to it. Yeah. Thröstur told me she got beaten up in town. I fart again. Each memory with its own smell. This one stems back to when I was eighteen and worked as a trolley pusher at the National Hospital mortuary and there was always that same smell from the newly departed and I developed the theory that the soul was an air bubble stuck in our insides that pops during the postmortem. I fart again. I.e., I release a part of my soul into the atmosphere. Yeah. That's how we go. Not with a bang but with a fart.

The bathroom door opens and Lolla sticks her head in. That's what she does. Just like that.

She says: "Aren't you nearly finished yet?"

"Yeah."

I step out of the bathroom, wrapped in a towel and clutching my bundle of clothes like an Icelandic horse, holding last year's winter coat all wrapped up in a canvas bag, about to put it back on because winter is almost here. Winter is almost here. I'm all hot and steam-boiled. I saunter over to the corner of the living room and say: "I'm finished."

I'm slightly startled to see them together on the sofa. Mom is holding Halldór and a part of the breast that he is suckling is visible. Lolla sits on the edge of the sofa, watching her little melon-haired boy. She turns her head and smiles at me. But somehow it's not a smile. It's been thirty-three years since I last saw that breast. My old bar has opened again. Mom looks me up and down:

"You're putting on weight."

"Yeah," I confess.

"I think he looks better that way," says Lolla.

"Yes, he does, doesn't he? He's a whole new man now that he's stopped hanging around in those bars all the time. Aren't you, Hlynur? Don't you feel better, at home with your mom?" Mom teasingly asks.

"Yeah, maybe. Especially now that you've opened a bar here as well."

"What do you mean?"

"You're breastfeeding?"

"Yes. We're giving it a try," says Lolla, with a flush of blood to her face.

"Is there still milk in them?"

"Oh yes. My love," says Mom, staring proudly at her breast.

"You didn't think there was any milk in them?" Lolla asks.

"No, no. I just thought it was past the sell-by date."

They laugh and so do I, I laugh down at the carpet, with my Hungarian brushed teeth, notice the stain. A stain in the carpet, toes in the cradle.

They're still laughing when I walk into my room. I close the door and remove the towel. Stand naked between the computer, the bed, and the TV. I slide my eyes over my body. There's a bump growing between us. I stand there for a moment but he doesn't stand. He's somehow all steam-boiled. Baby Björn.

PRICE LIST

(In 2002, $1 equaled approximately Ikr 87)

Couch potato mother	kr	100
Hertha Berlin	kr	150
Lezzie	kr	500
Woman at job center	kr	750
Anna	kr	800
Hofy's friend #1	kr	1,490
Hofy's friend #2	kr	1,690
Mother Teresa	kr	1,700
Magnús's sister	kr	2,000
Camilla Parker-Bowles	kr	2,500
Magnús's mother	kr	2,500
Chinese woman	kr	3,500
Hungarian swimming queen	kr	3,500
Woman at the Castle	kr	3,500
Aunty Sigrún	kr	4,000
Lolla's mom	kr	5,000
Gudrún Georgs	kr	5,000
Ass on a black whore in Paris	kr	6,000
Thor-something	kr	6,000
Queen of tarts	kr	7,000
Woman in coat	kr	7,000
Mrs. Ahmed	kr	10,000
OK-looking woman	kr	10,000
Fag hag	kr	10,000

Bára	kr 12,000
Piece of gum #1	kr 15,000
Black whore in Paris	kr 15,000
Girl on Skólavördustígur	kr 15,000
Talk-show host	kr 15,000
Lóa	kr 15,000
Chick on tabletop #1	kr 15,000
The one with the finger	kr 15,000
Hot dish on sofa	kr 15,000
Hrönn in school	kr 15,000
Devilishly made-up girl	kr 16,000
Fatso Ferguson	kr 17,000
Stooping girl	kr 18,000
Passing face at a party	kr 20,000
Face at a party	kr 20,000
Girl	kr 20,000
Andrea Jónsdóttir	kr 20,000
Indian singer	kr 20,000
Girl in Sarajevo with leukemia	kr 20,000
Chick on tabletop #2	kr 25,000
Judy Osborne	kr 25,000
Lamb in a cave	kr 25,000
Pony	kr 25,000
Dóra	kr 25,000
Karen Carpenter	kr 25,000
Sigrún (ex)	kr 25,000
k.d. lang	kr 27,000
Naked Fury	kr 30,000
Sigurlaug	kr 30,000
Magga Saem	kr 30,000
Girl in queue at K-bar	kr 35,000
"Soap McCoy"	kr 35,000
Woody Allen's girlfriend	kr 35,000
Thóra	kr 35,000
Hot dish on sofa #2	kr 35,000
Chelsea Clinton	kr 35,000
"Bonnie Tyler"	kr 40,000

Bonnie Tyler	kr 40,000
Blonde at table	kr 40,000
Hofy	kr 40,000
Princess Di	kr 40,000
Nanna Baldurs	kr 45,000
Sara	kr 45,000
Girl on high heels	kr 45,000
Cleo Laine	kr 45,000
Anna's mom	kr 45,000
Hillary Clinton	kr 45,000
Two country lasses	kr 50,000
Hot dish on sofa #3	kr 50,000
Breasts at a party	kr 50,000
Lolla	kr 50,000
Goofy	kr 50,000
Miss Bifröst '96	kr 60,000
Pretty face	kr 60,000
Elsa's dark-haired friend	kr 60,000
Mia Farrow	kr 60,000
Engey	kr 60,000
Katarina	kr 60,000
Veronica Pedrosa	kr 60,000
Wicked bird	kr 60,000
Laura Johnson	kr 60,000
Miss Piggy in porn movie	kr 60,000
Piece of gum #2	kr 65,000
Roxette singer	kr 65,000
Air hostesses	kr 70,000
Mother of girl in K-bar queue	kr 70,000
Spotty	kr 70,000
Lotto woman	kr 75,000
Wench behind a counter	kr 75,000
Eygló Manfreds	kr 75,000
Holmenkollen kitten	kr 80,000
Boris Becker's wife	kr 80,000
Lilja Waage	kr 80,000
Ragnheidur Clausen	kr 80,000

Jane Fonda	kr	90,000
Nicole Brown	kr	90,000
Katla '83	kr	90,000
Debbie Harry	kr	95,000
Linda Babe Vilhjálmsdóttir	kr	100,000
Vaka	kr	100,000
Cat in the barn	kr	100,000
Bryndís	kr	100,000
Miss Iceland	kr	110,000
"Pointer Sisters"	kr	120,000
Jara Ex	kr	120,000
Blind girl	kr	120,000
Sheila E	kr	120,000
Black girl with pink nails	kr	125,000
Halla Margrét	kr	125,000
Vigdís Finnbogadóttir	kr	125,000
Chrissie Hynde	kr	150,000
Chick in a French yogurt ad	kr	175,000
Kate Moss	kr	190,000
Björk	kr	190,000
Jerry Hall	kr	200,000
TLC	kr	210,000
Jagger's Christmas Eve	kr	240,000
Linda P. (Icelandic Miss World '88)	kr	250,000
Nightie on the landing	kr	250,000
Nicole Kidman	kr	250,000
Italian anchor lady	kr	300,000
Farrah Fawcett	kr	300,000
Model from Akureyri	kr	300,000
Sixteen girls in Sarajevo	kr	320,000
Girl at Grafarvogur party	kr	400,000
Fashion writer	kr	450,000
Moon Zappa	kr	500,000
Samantha Fox	kr	600,000
Free-range chick	kr	750,000
Geena Davis	kr	900,000
Woman at the Moon	kr	1,500,000

Anna at the Moon	kr 1,750,000
Lisa Lisa	kr 1,900,000
Maria Schneider	kr 2,000,000
Cindy Crawford	kr 2,200,000
Michelle Pfeiffer	kr 2,900,000
Anna Nicole Smith	kr 2,900,000
Uma Thurman	kr 3,300,000
Janet Jackson	kr 3,500,000
Tina Turner	kr 3,600,000
Sandra Bullock	kr 3,900,000
Cameron Diaz	kr 3,900,000
Eve	kr 3,900,000
Naomi Campbell	kr 3,900,000
Virgin Mary	kr 4,200,000
Madonna	kr 4,500,000
Pamela Anderson	kr 4,700,000

SPECIAL THANKS TO:

Árni Óskarsson
Cary Leibowitz
Charlotta M. Hjaltadóttir
Daníel Thorkell Magnússon
Gudmundur Andri Thorsson
Gunnar Helgason
Gunnar Smári Egilsson
Grímur Hjartarson
Haraldur Jónsson
Hrafn Jökulsson
Hrefna Halldórsdóttir
Húbert Nói
Hveragerdisbær
Jón Sæmundur Audarson
Joe Allen
Kjarnorka
Kristófer Svavarsson
Lisette Merenciana
Magnea Hrönn Örvarsdóttir
Icelandic embassy staff in Washington
Hungarian embassy staff in Stockholm